Norway Wasn't Too Small

Praise for Irene Berman's
'We Are Going to Pick Potatoes': Norway and the Holocaust, the Untold Story

This 'untold story' about what happened to Norwegian Jews during the Holocaust deserves to be told—and now it is.
— Elie Wiesel, Nobel Laureate

Irene [Levin] Berman tells an important and— for most Americans— unknown story about the destiny of the Norwegian Jews during WW II. Being herself a Holocaust survivor, her style is emotionally very strong, though factual and sober. This comprehensive, moving and heart-rending book, with a welcome underlying optimism in spite of traumatic experiences, deserves a wide circle of readers in the U.S.A, far beyond those of Norwegian descent.
— Arnfinn Moland, director, Norway's Resistance Museum

The story of the effort and extent to which the Nazi war machine would reach out in order to annihilate even the most remote Jewish family. The story of indifference and courage, of despair and hope, of silence and action. A very Jewish and very human story which should be told and listened to.
— Michael Melchior, Chief Rabbi of Norway, Former Cabinet Minister of Israel

Irene Levin Berman has written a powerful, deeply moving book about a people, a place, and a time unfamiliar to many Americans. It is a story that should be widely known and remembered by all.
— Edward P. Gallagher, President, The American-Scandinavian Foundation

Unexpectedly precious.
— Benjamin Ivry; Foreword Reviews, June 2010

It wasn't until 2005 that Irene Levin Berman forced herself to examine what it meant to her to be a Holocaust survivor. Even after so many years, she strongly identified as a Jew and a Norwegian, as well as a United States citizen, but not having been in a ghetto or camp, she didn't feel 'worthy' of the label 'survivor.' In 'We Are Going To Pick Potatoes': Norway and The Holocaust, The Untold Story, she describes what happened to the Jews of Norway during the Holocaust, focusing mainly on her particular family; this is as much an autobiography as an account of flight and resettlement in hospitable Sweden. A child of four when she was told 'We are going to pick potatoes,' she and her family embarked on a dangerous journey through the woods in Norway to neutral Sweden, just missing the Gestapo roundup of November 26th for the purpose of mass arrests. It was 1942, and the

Norwegian Jews who remained in Norway did not realize the danger they were in . . . .Although this is primarily an account of the fate of the author's extended family during the Holocaust, it is nevertheless an important addition to the library of survivor testimony since not much is known about Norwegian Jews during this period.
— Jewish Book World

Norway Wasn't Too Small

A Fact-Based Novel about Darkness and Survival

Irene Levin Berman

Hamilton Books

An Imprint of
Rowman & Littlefield
Lanham • Boulder • New York • Toronto • Plymouth, UK

Copyright © 2016 by Hamilton Books
4501 Forbes Boulevard, Suite 200, Lanham, Maryland 20706
Hamilton Books Acquisitions Department (301) 459-3366

Unit A, Whitacre Mews, 26-34 Stannary Street,
London SE11 4AB, United Kingdom

Library of Congress Control Number: 2016935450
ISBN: 978-0-7618-6771-5 (pbk : alk. paper)—ISBN: 978-0-7618-6772-2 (electronic)

∞™ The paper used in this publication meets the minimum requirements of American
National Standard for Information Sciences Permanence of Paper for Printed Library
Materials, ANSI/NISO Z39.48-1992.

This book is dedicated in memory of my friend, Ingunn Hekneby Bassock,
whose sentiments and tolerance
always touched me with positive thoughts.

Contents

Preface

An introduction is normally the first thing to present when writing a book, and in this case it is even more vital to explain the significance of the title as it contains an important message.

Seven years ago, I was contacted by a local professor inviting me to participate in an anthology of independent stories. Each contributor was to be a Holocaust survivor, presently living in the United States. The professor expressed excitement at connecting with a Norwegian Jew in view of the limited number of people with the experience and willingness to tell this story.

I was born in Norway just before the war and escaped with my parents and brother to Sweden in 1942. Despite my young age at the time, I had retained some significant memories and recalled a number of astonishing stories from when I was older, told by friends and relatives through the years portraying the destiny of the 2000 Norwegian Jews. I was flattered to be asked to participate and readily accepted the request.

A couple of weeks later I submitted a detailed description about my immediate family, starting with the German invasion in 1940 and moving on to 1942. At that time, the Gestapo's intense and ghastly quest had peaked in Norway. It became obvious to most of the Jews that the specific plan was to separate the Jews from the "regular" Norwegians. After the war had come to an end it became evident that 787 persons, approximately 38% of the congregation, had been deported and annihilated. Some were killed instantly upon their arrival and others after being forced to exhaust their physical strength and health in the camps, rendering them ready for the gas chambers. When the liberation finally came in 1945, only 28 men prisoners and no women survived.

Shortly after the invitation to tell my story, a woman called and introduced herself as the publisher's representative. Her overture consisted of describing the extraordinary response and large number of submissions they had collected. Many survivors had expressed their willingness to reveal their personal stories, making it necessary to limit what chapters were to be included and which weren't. Most of the participants came from large cities in middle Europe.

With a rapid voice and explanation, she justified her opinion of why my story would not be included. As I listened carefully, I realized her reasoning about not publishing my story was based on a logic, which differed 180 degrees from mine. The initial interest as expressed by the professor had been focused on the uniqueness of Norway and the Holocaust, an unknown extensive country tragedy. However, this story's importance seemed to melt away as quickly as she could speak. Then came her main reason. She had learned from my chapter that Norway only had 2000 Jews at the time of the mass arrest and deportation. She continued explaining that such a small number was minimal and therefore she didn't see the necessity of including that particular country in the book.

I made a last desperate attempt to reiterate the high ratio of Norwegian Jews that were annihilated, equal only to Holland at 38%, constituting the highest percentage in Europe. Wasn't that vital proof that Hitler planned to exterminate every single Jew in Europe, regardless of the size of the congregation? She ignored me and hung up.

It took me the rest of the evening and the following night to accept her decision. By the next morning, I had become an activist. It was up to me now to relate the story of the Holocaust in my country of birth to anyone who wanted to listen!

I made good on that promise and my memoir was first published in Norwegian and subsequently translated into English, *"We Are Going to Pick Potatoes": Norway and the Holocaust, the Untold Story*. Even though I live in the US, I made every effort to make Norway and the Holocaust better known. In addition, I immersed myself in research by interviewing members of the previous generation in Norway who would recount the dramatic and tragic events that took place during the occupation. My parents had decided to keep this horror away from their children. I now realize this was standard behavior, not only in Norway, but also in most of Europe where the Gestapo had victimized millions of people. Fortunately, the first book was well received throughout the United States, with a wonderful endorsement from the best-known Holocaust survivor in the world, Dr. Elie Wiesel.

There is a specific mission now for my writing a fictional Holocaust story from Norway. The story of the two separate, yet related families, present the concept of darkness versus survival. These three words will speak for themselves as the reader gets into the story. The historical part of the narrative is based on reality and is intended to complement the fiction. It is written in a manner to attract and educate teenagers as well as their parents and older relatives.

We are getting increasingly closer to a time when fewer Holocaust survivors still live to stand up and bear witness to the horror experienced by millions of people and families, just like their own. It behooves the next generation to make it compulsory for everyone, Jews or non-Jews, to learn about the massacre that took place among humans, so that it doesn't disappear into closed historical tales as time goes by.

My hope is that this fictional story, written by a formerly small Norwegian child, who succeeded in surviving, through no effort of her own but that of her parents, will educate others. My mission is for the history of the Holocaust to persevere through schools, colleges, book clubs, and other educational resources. Let us remember our responsibility to the six million who died. May we allow them to live on in our thoughts, keeping their legacy and memories alive for many future generations.

A number of wonderful friends have held my hand night and day as I immersed myself into the world that caught on fire more than 75 years ago. When I offered the story of the Norwegian Jews to my American Friends, I was surprised at the audience, which opened their arms and allowed me to share my memories with them. Their support and enthusiasm made it impossible not to continue writing about this topic. I will always feel enormous gratitude to all of you.

First, Gerry Bamman, thank you very much for all your expertise and literary guidance. Second, many years of gratitude to my childhood friend Jack Fink who has been my supporter and part of my life and memories of Norway

Next, I want to include a few friends who have helped me on this unknown journey of fiction, which was unfamiliar to me. There were days when I doubted my own ability to create action, which was mostly fictitious, but felt real. Three women held my hand throughout day and night. I want to mention Rebecca Makkai and Karin Arentzen Stahl without whose support, skills and willingness to share their talents with an amateur in this field, would have left me lost. Finally, there is Joanne Kurnik who has stood by my side and kept me moving forward for more than thirty-five years. How lucky was I the day that we met! Peggy Shapiro and Sally Richter, my close friends, allowed me to talk, think and fantasize, telling me to keep going forward towards my goal. I often wonder where they found the patience to hear me talk about Norway, my family and the various Holocaust incidents and co-incidents nonstop. Thank you for putting up with me. And last, but not least, my most sincere thank you to my talented and energetic friend Laurel Hoskins who never turns me down when I need help, with pictures, ideas, designs and many other incredible helpful suggestions.

I want to say Thank You to my grandchildren who developed an interest in Norway and the Holocaust as a function of our conversations about my childhood. We have also talked about the legacy of relatives from the older generation who would have loved my grandchildren just as much as I love them today. These six wonderful kids have unknowingly compensated for the early loss of my parents by allowing me to talk about the family in Norway so often. I want to thank my three daughters and husbands and congratulate them for having raised such incredible children.

Martin and Leif Arild, you are both always with me on my journeys, no matter where I try to discover old history.

Irene Levin Berman

Chapter One

War Comes to Norway

OSLO, APRIL 9, 1940

Rebekka didn't finish her breakfast. Ordinarily her mother, Sarah Davidson, and Ruth, the housekeeper, would urge her to eat, but they were distracted. Sitting by the radio they were trying to find out what had taken place so far in Oslo, as well as the rest of the country. Rebekka heard words like war, invasion and Germany.

She walked over to the living room window, opening it carefully. A number of voices could be heard. A female voice called, "No, Torstein, please come back. I don't want to be alone! What if we are bombed?" A man walked away on the sidewalk with rapid steps. That had to be Torstein, Rebekka thought.

The radio was at full blast next door, and a second voice was heard crying, "We are at war, we are at war! What are we going to do? Steinar, did you keep the gun you used in the military? You may need it, you know." A man answered he would take care of her, not to worry.

Rebekka left the apartment without saying goodbye. She just stopped briefly and announced that she was leaving. Her mother had already given her instructions. "Go straight to school and check if the teachers are outside waiting for you, telling you if classes will meet. If not, return home immediately."

Although Rebekka assumed her close friend Kari would be waiting for her at the corner as usual, she was relieved to see her. It seemed as if her world had changed. The scary news, which had become known overnight, was difficult to comprehend. The tension which was omnipresent was hard to ignore. Neither of the two girls spoke. Kari's green eyes didn't sparkle as they did normally. Frankly, she looked a little frightened, with her hair hanging straight down. It gave the impression that she hadn't even combed it. Come to think of it, Kari's shirt appeared to be inside out. In addition, she must have been cold, because she was shaking, despite her heavily-lined red winter jacket.

How unusual, Rebekka thought, I have never seen her in such disarray.

"My parents gave me strict instructions on what I could and couldn't do," was all Kari said. Her friend nodded, indicating she had been given the same orders.

Rebekka had just turned fourteen one month earlier, and had been taught to be independent. Her goal that moment was to see what was going on at school.

A tall girl, she was on occasion referred to as slightly reserved. "Shy," her relatives whispered to each other when she sometimes was less than friendly. Introverted might be a better term. She had a head full of bright red curls that bounced around as she moved. The curls had been a subject of annoyance when younger, making her feel physically different from her mostly blond-haired, blue-eyed contemporaries. This feeling had gradually subsided. This accommodation, or so it felt, had been replaced by defiance, whenever some brave person had the nerve to comment on her hair color. Early on, she had been told by her parents that nature had played a genetic "trick" on her. This meant she had inherited her mother's evident and strong genes for red hair. However, both her parents had dark brown hair.

Rebekka possessed an exceptional talent, being able to draw anything she saw or recalled. It was rare for her to do without her sketchbook. "Her security blanket," her father jokingly called it.

The two friends walked slowly and quietly towards the school, both reluctant to bring up the news. There wasn't much to discuss, at least not yet. Both were apprehensive and confused about the implication of their country being at war.

The surrounding streets were relatively busy, especially when serious looking soldiers showed up with intermittent heavy footsteps. Most of the military cluster walked on the street, although next to the sidewalk. The random people on the sidewalk appeared to hug the wall of the buildings, attempting to stay as far away as possible from the newly-appeared German soldiers.

A face would occasionally appear in a window. People looking out, probably wondering if they were safer inside or out? Mothers wondering if there would be enough food to feed their families for the next few days, and whom they should contact for more information. Many fathers had probably left early to find out what was going on at their place of business volunteering to help. But what kind of help? Radios had emitted basic facts about the events of the early morning hours, but no practical communication had been provided. The still, quiet streets were eerie and intimidating. It felt like time had stopped, at least momentarily.

When the school building came into view, the issue of whether to remain or leave became superfluous. The decision had been made for them. Throngs of soldiers were waiting inside the schoolyard with their rucksacks. Harsh orders were being barked in German through loudspeakers. Guards placed at each of the school's three gates attempted to communicate with curt, strict voices in their native language to the waiting youngsters. The approaching students didn't understand them, but it was clear the school was closed.

In the very front were two armed soldiers. Even though the uniformed strangers spoke only German, it was evident from their gestures that there would be no classes that day. A number of other neighborhood inhabitants were waiting on the street, uncertain what to do.

Rebekka automatically grabbed Kari's hand, feeling almost petrified at finding herself in the middle of this unexpected scene.

"Kari, do you understand this? This is our school, and what are these people doing? Do they have permission? You know how strict the headmaster is. And where are our teachers?"

Remaining motionless for a few minutes, they began to grasp the reality. The school had been appropriated as lodging for the recently-arrived enemy. It seemed unreal nevertheless, and for a second or so Rebekka wondered if she closed her eyes hard and opened them again, would the situation revert to normal? She tried, but there was no change.

Carefully they withdrew from the area, looking around carefully to be certain they had missed nothing.

At home everything was unchanged. Mor and Ruth were still in the same position, close to the radio, worried they might neglect significant news, although nothing had come through. For a moment Rebekka stared at Mor. Sarah seemed totally engrossed in the comments that emanated from the black box. Some voices had a reassuring tone, telling citizens to stay calm, while others had a hard time hiding their concern.

Mor's left hand held on to the pendant around her neck. Family members would often tease her by calling it her signature necklace, since she never took it off. It was a small watch that her father, Rebekka's grandfather, had bought as a gift on his last trip to Czechoslovakia before the unrest spread throughout Europe. Sarah had always loved this unusual pendant, but would only wear it on special occasions. However, when her father passed away just two months before the invasion, she pulled it out of her jewelry box, held it in her hand and declared, "This is the last gift he gave me, and he knew how much I loved it. Sometimes he would ask me why I didn't wear it more often. I was afraid to lose or break it. Now that my father is gone, I want to wear it all the time, in his memory."

Rebekka wondered skeptically if the necklace had the power to protect them, especially now that they might need fortification.

Her father, Martin Davidson, had left early that morning, presumably to see how the news had affected his store in the downtown area, or so he said.

"Stay calm and don't leave the house unless necessary. I will be in touch if I hear anything to the contrary."

Rebekka had no idea what really happened and no one seemed interested in explaining it to her. With her sketchbook in hand she started to draw the intimidating scene at the school entrance. She also focused on other details, as if afraid to let the experience evaporate. A voice inside her urged her to commit this terrifying day to the thirsty, receptive white paper. It felt strangely comforting.

Within a few minutes, a rough outline emerged. Taxis, buses and private cars were moving up and down the paper depicting the relatively large street, which had led her to school for years. Pedestrians were walking on either side, all with serious faces. Rebekka's primary goal, however, was to highlight the only synagogue in Oslo, located on a small cross street up the hill to the right. This house of worship appeared to be peaceful and undisturbed, and no disruption or damage had taken place.

When she was satisfied her memories of the morning had been preserved in her sketchbook, Rebekka quickly put it away in a safe place. Her relatives were constantly asking for permission to look at her drawings, but the requests were normally turned down. She felt deeply protective of her sketches and considered her books an extension of her personal thoughts. They were there for her, and not for others—until she decided to share them, if that day ever came.

As the afternoon passed, the atmosphere inside the house as well as in Oslo in general changed. Rebekka found herself more fearful when alarming reports were heard on the radio and telephone as local rumors went rampant. There were reports of shootings and soldiers were marching up and down Oslo's main streets; just a stone's throw away from the royal castle. The king himself had gone into safe hiding, anticipating more aggressive and serious action.

Obviously the school would be closed for a while, her mother said, and Rebekka would have to remain at home until further notice. She still hadn't heard details about the invasion or what it actually meant, and this was beginning to annoy her. She thought of Frank, her cousin. They were close in age, Frank being about one and a half years older. She had expected him to show up as usual when something important took place. She knew he had a tendency to exaggerate, but at this moment, she really wanted his opinion. She was at loose ends, not knowing what was in store for the next few days, with no one to speak to. The adults seemed to stop communicating as soon as she came near them.

Frank's mother, Tante Charlotte, had just arrived, talking about how quickly the rumors were spreading. She had heard that Oslo would be the target of a major bombing attack within the next couple of days! Thousands of families were making emergency plans to leave the city. Rebekka was watching Mor's face to see her reaction, but the two women left the room.

Do they consider me too young to deal with reality? she thought to herself, slightly annoyed. About an hour later the doorbell rang, louder than usual, and she ran to open it. Facing her was Frank who was supporting Tante Marie, a close friend of both Frank's and Rebekka's mothers.

Marie had come to Norway from Berlin a few years earlier. Her husband had been hit and brutally killed by a large truck driven by two angry Gestapo men who justified their killing by claiming that Jews were incapable of learning traffic rules. It took her a long time to get past this horrible experience. Then her father and mother passed away during her mourning. She was deeply depressed. Her brother had already left Berlin for Oslo early on as soon as he had become aware of the deteriorating climate for Jews. He had encouraged her to move to small idyllic Norway, which he insisted Hitler wouldn't bother going after and where she surely would find a safe haven. Despite being reluctant and skeptical, she had accepted his invitation a couple of years later.

The two sisters were appalled when they saw Marie hanging on to Frank's arm.

"Today's invasion must have had an enormous effect on her, arousing all the painful memories of only a few years earlier," Charlotte expressed as she helped the poor woman inside. Marie looked pale and sounded slightly incoherent. With some difficulty she was able to explain that she had become dizzy when the news of the attack reached her early in the morning. She found it hard to listen, unable to relax, and became increasingly more agitated. In the middle of the afternoon she felt the necessity to contact someone she knew and trusted. She decided to seek shelter with her friend Charlotte who lived only a few blocks away with her husband and Frank, her son. Unfortunately the friend had already left to see her sister, Sarah.

When Frank had opened the door to his family's apartment, there was Marie, talking incessantly, and he found it hard to understand her. He felt that her reaction might possibly be out of control as she seemed excessively agitated. Not knowing what to do, he decided to bring her along to his aunt's house where he was headed.

Charlotte and Sarah immediately tried to help the poor woman. They wrapped a blanket around her, attempting to distract her with a cup of coffee. That didn't help. Next they gave her a glass of scotch hoping the alcohol might have a soothing effect. Luckily this calmed her down enough to confirm the source of the severe hysteria, clearly triggered by the unexpected situation in Oslo. Within a few minutes, she had regained her composure. But this didn't stop her from speaking, or rather pleading.

"Please. Charlotte and Sarah, please listen. This is not only a simple political attack on Norway aimed at capturing England. That may be the strategic plan of these evil murderers. However, a simultaneous goal is to carry out Der Fuhrer's dream which consists of annihilating all Jews in Europe. He won't stop until he has succeeded. Norway's Jewish population is very small compared to most European countries, and this will be a little showcase of Herr Hitler's plans. Please alert all your relatives and friends. Tell them to get out of this country to a neutral place where they can hide or perhaps make plans to reach the United States." Once she had finished this vital message, she closed her eyes and fell asleep on the sofa.

The two sisters stood immobile looking at each other. Eventually they adjusted the blanket, turned off the light and left her alone to get some rest.

Rebekka watched the entire episode at a distance, praising Frank for his quick thinking, as she moved closer. He was not known for practical decision-making, but this certainly was an exception. Had she underestimated him? Normally he was known to be inquisitive, actually nosy, although his parents defended him calling him overly curious. He tended to make everything his business. Sometimes Rebekka found it irritating, but other times it was helpful. They were more like brother and sister, rather than cousins. Besides, in addition to his bringing Tante Marie, this time she was especially glad he had come, as she was feeling increasingly abandoned by the adults. Perhaps he had some information to share with her, she thought, as she sat down next to him. Tante Marie's warning about the future scared her, and she wanted to hear Frank's reaction. Was there any reality in Marie's prediction? Or was this only an exaggerated consequence of her own tragic experience?

"The poor woman. Do you have any idea what she is talking about or is this just projection? What is going on? I can't get an answer from anyone. What's wrong with them? How serious is this war, and what is going to happen to us? Did your parents share any of this with you?" Rebekka heard her own voice speaking much faster than normally. Frank seemed preoccupied which was unusual. Her eyes fell on his right hand where the old scar was still visible. She didn't know where else to look. The scar dated back to when he was four and had fallen on a sharp knife. Whenever she was uncomfortable with something Frank would say, she automatically turned her eyes in that direction.

To her surprise, Frank still didn't respond and remained deep in thought. Normally he would be the first to engage in conversation if something unusual took place. In addition, didn't he appear a little nervous?

Had he been told by his parents not to talk too much to her either, she wondered? Rebekka was starting to feel even more concerned. Or, she thought reluctantly, was he scared as well?

He signaled quietly for Rebekka to follow him into the empty kitchen. He sat down, pointing for her to do the same. She still looked at his hand. Once he was certain they were alone, he spoke in a whisper. He looked around the room, checking to see if anyone was listening. He kept his eyes on the door in case someone entered.

"Well, I have overheard my parents talking at night when they think I am sleeping. It's all about us, many are saying; you know, the Jews. Marie may be right. You didn't know that? Hitler and the Gestapo are trying to eliminate us. The issue isn't about how bad the war will be, or how long, but what will happen to the Norwegian Jews." His voice was somber. He certainly sounded like he was sharing a major secret with her.

Now that the unexpected assault on the country had taken place, she felt as if her entire world had become unsteady. Not just for her, but her entire family. But was their situation really different from the other Norwegians? Who was right? Was this something Frank had made up based on Marie's reaction? Suddenly she felt guilty. What a horrible way to think about one's cousin.

She was confused. She really couldn't see any connection between the war and their religion. She had heard some vague comments about Germany trying to occupy England. What exactly was Frank talking about? She got up and walked away, feeling slightly annoyed. Why did he always have to get dramatic and jump to conclusions?

She couldn't stop thinking about it. What was the reason? Or perhaps it was a combination of both? She felt even more confused. And what was the reason why the adults avoided speaking to her?

She heard Frank's words, but found them equally hard to understand. There were so few Jews in Norway, and more than half lived in Oslo. How could this be an issue? How did he know? Had someone told him or was it his own conclusion? She was getting irritated.

She decided to ask Far directly. There was no way he would refuse to answer her questions if she asked.

But when Far returned at the end of the day, she couldn't even get near him. He ensconced himself in the dining room with the door shut. He was surrounded by visitors who showed up as soon as he walked in the door. Had they been waiting outside, she wondered?

The first batch consisted of a handful of men Far's age, a few of whom wore Norwegian uniforms. She wondered why they were there and what they needed to discuss with him. Later in the evening another small batch of secretive young men joined them, staying for a short while, before taking off into the increasing darkness. They were younger than the first crowd who had met with Far earlier.

Far and his brother, Leonard, must be leaders of the group, she thought. Did the first group consist of the men who figured out what to do now that they had been invaded, and were the younger, strong men the resistance people who were ready to carry out the orders?

Had they come to take orders from Uncle Leonard, who appeared almost every night lately, even before the invasion had taken place? He was soft-spoken and calm, almost shy, but when he spoke, they listened. He had been an outspoken and strong antagonist of Nazi Germany for many years, actively involved in liberal political issues, even when he attended medical school.

More often than not, his fiancé would accompany him—a beautiful woman by the name of Synnoeve. It was quite clear they belonged together. Seated next to each other, they seemed to communicate as one person. Uncle would start a sentence, which she frequently would complete. She never took her eyes off him. Rebekka couldn't stop looking at her. She had never seen a more beautiful woman. She was exceptionally tall and thin. Her eyes were dark blue. Rebekka had been told that she had been an athlete as a teenager, with the reputation of being a good skier, and had been a gymnastics instructor in her hometown. When she moved to Oslo, she started working at a center for rehabilitation of young children with handicaps. Where did *she* belong? Among the Jews or among the "regular" Norwegians?

Rebekka had heard that Leonard was even more involved in the political situation than her father. He spent most of his free time meeting with several groups of resistance people. The dialogue was marked by intensity and passion, which these young men would show in any conversation that touched on Norway, freedom and possible invasion. Sometimes, however, there would be terrifying rumors referring to anti-Semitism in the capital, indicating that someone had set fire to a store owned by a Jew or tried to attack the owner. 2000 Jews had settled in Norway during the past 100 years since the law forbidding Jews from entering was repealed, and the term anti-Semitism was practically new to her ears. She had never really understood what it meant.

"Let's not forget that we have a wonderful gathering of young, strong men who love their country as much as we do. We have only seen the beginning of their strength and courage," Leonard had said out loud last week. "Whether this is going to be enough remains to be seen."

Now it had happened. The invasion was here. She felt uncomfortable. She wanted to feel angry and irritated, but instead deep inside there was a new and unusual sensation of fear, which she tried very hard to ignore.

A sudden awareness had just come upon her. This was not a "maybe situation." This was the beginning of a real war.

Chapter Two

Who Is Hitler?

AALESUND, APRIL 9, 1940

"Mother, have you seen my grey sweater?" A voice sounded through the apartment, followed by Harald, a fifteen year old boy. "I'm in a hurry, have soccer practice and . . . What is wrong?"

His mother, Leyla Rosenberg, was standing in the kitchen, leaning against the sink. She looked somber, although it was clear that she was trying very hard to hide her feelings. An introverted person by nature, she preferred to listen rather than speak. She was also the shortest of her three sisters, who made it a habit of making decisions for her whenever they had a chance. The only outstanding trait she had inherited was her mother's thick, jet-black hair and dark eyes. None of her sisters had the same coloring and for the most part had plain dull, dark brown hair. However, her four brothers had grown up with the same black mane of curly hair accompanied by dark eyes that made girls and young women look twice. Leyla had always been a "giver" rather than a "taker." Her siblings felt she was a carbon copy of her mother, who was known to be helpful and generous. At this moment Leyla was quiet as usual, but for other reasons. She was scared and nervous, and not yet able to talk about it.

Her reply to Harald was short and detached, "It's in the living room on the piano bench, just where you left it last night. Finish getting dressed. We need to speak to you."

His father, Isak, was sitting at the breakfast table, focusing on firm, serious statements emerging from the radio. His facial expression reflected surprise, rather than concern. His father remained immobile when Harald entered the room, implying he was lost in thought. Harald turned to his mother, wondering what had caused the two of them to appear so preoccupied.

"Norway was attacked by Germany early this morning," she said, turning towards him. "Our country is at war, and it has even reached us this far from the capital." Despite the moderate size of the town of Aalesund, it was known as the fishing center of Norway. Located between Bergen to the West and Trondheim to the North, this area was known for its great beauty and active commerce.

Harald felt as if she was speaking a foreign language. He heard the words, but the meaning sounded almost absurd. Leyla lowered her voice and continued in a more gentle manner. "There will be no soccer practice this morning and no classes. A radio broadcast instructed all students in the upper classes to go directly to their schools, pick up the contents of their desks and bring everything home until further notice."

Harald looked around, suddenly aware that his older sister was nowhere to be seen. "Ingrid has left already. She got a ride with Margarete and her father. Take your bike. Please hurry up," his mother continued.

Harald quickly glanced at his father, expecting him to share a few remarks with him. However, Isak didn't even look up. The news of an invasion and all the related problems, had been the topic at several dinners lately, as well as a common subject whenever his parents' friends came to visit. Most of the adults were concerned and even pessimistic, but Harald's father refused to accept the potential danger. He would talk about the strength of Norway, the decency of the people, and how you should ignore the "bad apples" that always existed, even among the good ones. And now, while facing the invasion, his father seemed to be unwilling to express serious concern. Harald wasn't sure whether this was a sign of a very strong man, or one who was unrealistic. He wondered what his Uncle Leonard would have to say. Like several of his mother's siblings, Leonard lived in Oslo. He was unmarried, Leyla's youngest brother, and the most outspoken critic of Germany's desire to expand its power in Europe. They believed in a pure race, the Germans said, in this case the Aryans. Everyone else, such as Jews, was despicable and didn't deserve to live. Harald stood quietly for a few seconds in front of his father before he reluctantly decided to follow his mother's instructions.

Far suddenly got up to make a telephone call in the next room. He spoke in a gentle, subdued voice. Harald was unable to hear the conversation except for the name of Hitler, which he had heard previously. After a few minutes, his father reappeared dressed in his regular daytime attire—a pair of pants, a shirt with a tie and jacket. As most of the first and second generation Jews in Norway, he owned a retail store. This was easy to arrange and made it possible for the owner to work hard. He had chosen to open a store in town where he sold shoes, textiles, boots and winter equipment.

Originally from Sweden, the family had moved to Norway when he was a child. Only a few years ago, he had become a Norwegian citizen, as he felt a strong loyalty to the country which he had made his own by choice. He felt at home, and had established a good business while raising a family.

Harald ran down the stairs of the building feeling unsettled. He had emptied his backpack to make room for the books that were left at school, and now he put it over his shoulders and jumped on his bike. Part of him felt a strange type of excitement, as if he were about to learn and experience something he had only heard about in school or read in the newspapers. "The real thing," he thought. It was like reading a new book where you were tempted to look at the last page to see how it ended. One of his favorite subjects was history, and he often tried to identify with the main historical figures for fun. On occasion, he would try to figure out what motivated the "bad guys" and how they even felt justified, making certain he absorbed every aspect of the story. Of course, today he realized his feelings were different. There was another dimension of the news that made him anxious. There was only one word for that feeling, he told himself. It was called fear. At fifteen, he had learned to try to conceal the appearance of fear, but at times, it was hard. And today was definitely one of those moments.

As he rode his bike through the streets, he found it difficult to stop thinking about his mother's matter-of-fact announcement. He tried to stay calm as he maneuvered over the rough, sometime bumpy, cobblestone streets. He passed by a couple of relatively new buildings that had been reconstructed after the fire in Aalesund in 1904. They were beginning to look less new. He crested the hill and was able to see the city below and beyond that, the fjord. He pictured German war ships sailing into the Oslo harbor. For a moment, he had chills.

Harald looked for signs of enemy soldiers, but there were none. After all, this city was many hours northwest of Oslo. He found himself looking at the people walking on the sidewalks.

Did they know? Had they heard? Were they worried? He passed the police station, but there were no signs of anything unusual. It looked the way it always looked. He did notice there were a few police cars on the street, which was not a common sight. He also saw a few local police officers. Why were they there? Was this a symbolic gesture from the city to make the people feel secure?

During the remaining few minutes of biking through the streets he studied people's faces. Everyone seemed to be in a hurry. Were they too preoccupied with the news on the radio and in a hurry to get their routine errands completed so they could get home to listen to further broadcasts?

A few people, mostly men, had gathered on the sidewalks, or on the street corners, deep in animated conversation. He recognized some of the local shop owners—the shoemaker, the pharmacist, even the dentist whose office was in the building on the right side of the street. Harald remembered when he was in first grade and had been able to read Dr. Johannesen's name on the entrance door for the first time. Was this gathering of the local merchants related to the morning's surprise, or did they always congregate on the corner? The stores were open, but everything seemed quiet. Was he more sensitive today, or were people actually behaving differently?

Finally, he reached the school, leaving his bike in the shed made available for the students. He locked it and entered the school, and then he felt a little awkward. Would anyone really try to steal his bike on the same day their country had been invaded, he asked himself. Annoyed at his own reaction, he questioned himself. Was it impossible for him to have one single thought in his head today that wasn't related to the attack?

However, contrary to the almost stagnant atmosphere in the streets, there was nothing quiet about the climate in the school building. The closest description would be chaos. The students were running up and down the five flights of stairs. Some were carrying backpacks, and some were not. Everyone was talking, either to themselves or to one another. The noise was overwhelming.

Before he started to climb the stairs to his homeroom, he looked around for his sister, Ingrid. Although two years older she attended the same school but in a higher grade. She was nowhere to be seen. Before he reached his corridor, he stopped on the second floor, where her classroom was located. The door to her classroom was closed. He lingered outside for a minute or so, not quite sure what to do. He suddenly had a strong need to see her in person. It felt strange that he hadn't even had a chance to exchange a glance or a single sentence with her since the significant news. Finally, he slowly walked away, reassuring himself that Ingrid was probably with one of her many girlfriends, or on her way home. He recalled that she had left the house quite a bit earlier than he had.

After having reached his classroom on the third floor, he was greeted by an unfamiliar guard at the entrance to the room, requesting his name and then crossing it off a list he was holding. To Harald's relief his classroom teacher was standing by his desk at the front of the room. He kept repeating the same statement over and over, "Please clear your desk of all your belongings. No, I don't know when school will open again. As soon as I am informed, you will be informed. Please leave quietly and be aware of each other's safety. May I suggest you use this unexpected time away from school to read your school books on your own to prepare for when we return."

The teacher, Mr. Toralf Welhaven, was one of his favorites. His age was hard to tell, but Harald guessed that he was somewhere between 35 and 50. Harald always found it hard to estimate teachers' ages. When they were teaching and speaking to the class, he sometimes found it difficult to imagine them as regular fun-loving people. Did they like to ski, or did they always bury their heads in history books or chemistry experiments? Did they play with their kids, help their spouses prepare dinner or run errands? It was hard to envision.

Mr. Welhaven taught history and English, both of which were among Harald's favorite subjects. During the past few months, the history classes were naturally focused on the political situation in the world, trying to learn the geographical names and locations of the places in question. He also encouraged them to try to understand how previous years and earlier centuries of experiences might affect the various decisions made by the present heads of states. Harald loved his classes. Mr. Welhaven strove to make the students take the initiative and concentrate on seeing beyond the individual event, trying to figure out how the present situations had evolved.

Today of course, the atmosphere was slightly different. Mr. Welhaven had a strained look on his face, exchanging a few words with all the students who came up to him. He answered questions as best he could, while giving short orders to move on. Many of the students appeared anxious and asked various questions like when will we receive our history test grades? What about the school play next week? Will it take place? Do you think the enemy will bomb Aalesund?

Harald emptied his desk and stuffed everything into his backpack. How had he managed to accumulate so many things, he wondered. Once he was able to close the lid of the now empty desk, he looked around the classroom.

A crowd was congregating in a corner of the classroom where their giggles and laughter could be heard across the room. They sounded silly, giving the impression they were celebrating an unexpected school vacation, each one throwing out ideas on how they were going to spend the next few days. Harald chose to ignore them and looked for some of his friends. His buddy since kindergarten, Kristian Fredrik Hauge, appeared at his side. Kristian Fredrik had the distinction of being the tallest boy in the class. His parents were friends of Harald's and they had spent much time together. In addition, KF, as they called him, was a top student who often inspired Harald to work a little harder than he really felt like doing. Despite KF's height, he had a childish face, and tended to blush every time a girl from the class approached him. This happened quite often. He claimed it was his brain and help with homework that enticed them when his friends teased him about his popularity. Harald and KF immediately started speaking about the news, asking the same questions as everyone else. They also chose to ignore the rowdy crowd in the corner.

Little by little, the room began to empty, and the two friends started walking towards the door. Out of nowhere a series of unusually long sirens were heard, in even intervals, one after the other. Then a small break, and the signals started again, in the same sequence. It seemed to come from outside. Sirens? No. Loudspeakers with messages? No, the signals were louder and penetrating. Broadcast from a radio, which no one had noticed across the room, proclaiming, "Go into cover if you are outside; go into cover if you are outside. Take shelter, take shelter." The radio was silent for a minute, then repeated, and then stopped. Harald stared at KF, and as if by telepathy, both of them exclaimed, "This is an air raid warning," looking at each other, hoping that the others would know what to do.

The remaining students became quiet and turned towards Mr. Welhaven, who spoke in a calm and clear voice. "You may remember that we discussed this briefly a few weeks ago in class. The main purpose of this message is to alert people of the need to seek shelter for protection in the unusual event that a bomb is dropped. There is nothing to be worried about. You can either stay here until it passes or, if you want, you can go down to the cellar of the school building which is supposed to be safe. However, once you make a decision, you need to stay in one place until you hear the 'all-clear' signal." His voice was just as unruffled as ordinarily, and it was clear he had a calming effect on the students. But Harald who had been studying his face, did notice that suddenly the popular teacher's forehead was perspiring.

As soon as Welhaven finished speaking, the all-clear signal was sounded. A combination of cheers and sighs of relief spread across the room and the students began to circulate once more.

A part of the group that had huddled in the corner moved slowly in Harald's direction and stopped right in front of him. He was not particularly friendly with any of these students, who were a rather rowdy batch with frequent disciplinary problems. Harald remained still, facing three boys leading the pack, wondering what they wanted.

The leader, a rather tall, husky boy from the outskirts of Aalesund moved closer to him and said in a loud voice, "There you go, you damn Jew. We have you and your people to thank for this dangerous situation. This Hitler guy is right; the Jews are the cause of all the problems in the world, both in Aalesund and other places in Norway. You should never have been allowed into our country, my father says. Now see what you've started."

Harald remained motionless, temporarily speechless, just staring at the tall body leaning in on him. The rest of the bunch who had watched the incident, perceived Harald's reaction as passivity, and inched in a little closer.

KF and a couple of Harald's other friends were about to respond to this cruel and menacing cluster of young boys, expressing inappropriate and cruel statements. They expected Harald to be angry, but his firm and confident response made it clear that he wanted to deal with this verbal attack on his own.

For a few seconds that seemed like an eternity, Harald had an unexpected and sudden flashback. When he was ten years old, he had participated in a violin quartet with three other boys, a year older than he. During a break in the rehearsal, their music teacher had suggested they might want to take a break and buy ice cream from one of the stores down the street. As they were about to leave, one of the three, the oldest and tallest, had turned to him and said, "You can't come. You are not Norwegian."

Harald felt as if he were back in the entryway to the music studio, surrounded by the young bullies who had caused him to burst into tears—not from being insulted, but because he didn't understand what the older boy meant, and he was afraid to ask. He had been so confused and upset that he never told anyone, not even his parents. He participated in the recital, did well, but he never saw the boys again.

Harald thought he had managed to obliterate this memory, but at this moment it had come back. His body loosened and he was able to move. He took one step towards the tormentor. Having no idea where this unexpected courage came from, he declared in a calm, yet loud voice, "It's rather clear you have absolutely no knowledge about the international political situation, geography or what exactly is happening throughout Europe at this time. The German invasion is due to that country trying to protect itself from being invaded by England and is hoping to capture Norway in order to prevent this action from taking place. Let us wait and see how our Norwegian brave soldiers deal with this challenge. I am optimistic."

Then he turned around and walked away from the group without another word. Despite the turbulent exchange and the general situation, the newly-found calm remained with him. Kristian Fredrik and another good friend moved along with him as guards, one who was very tall and the other, a soccer star, who was quite muscular.

The bullies lingered quietly for a short while before they dispersed and left the classroom.

As Harald and his friends left, they were stopped by a senior staff member whose task was to supervise new teachers—he extended his hand to Harald. He was wearing the standard grey threadbare lab coat. His facial expression displayed serious concern, in addition to dark shadows under his eyes. "Harald, you are dignified and well informed. Let's hope that your predictions are accurate. God bless you."

Chapter Three

Are We Running Away?

OSLO, APRIL 11–12, 1940

As expected the next day Rebekka was once again instructed to stay inside the house. She was bored and restless. One thing she had picked up very quickly was to avoid asking too many questions of anyone. First of all, it was unlikely there would be any answers, and secondly it seemed to make people uncomfortable. The day passed slowly, as she drifted from room to room, feeling ignored by the adults.

In the afternoon, noticing that Rebekka seemed a bit edgy, Ruth suggested a short walk to the park near their house at St. Hans Haugen, where they had gone for years. The large park had a small duck pond, and the joke was that the ducks inhabiting this pond were the best fed ducks in Norway, because of the amount of bread they were given by the neighborhood visitors.

On the way home, Ruth, pushing Rebekka's two-year-old sister, Miriam, in the stroller, was unusually quiet. When Rebekka carefully asked her if she had heard from her boyfriend, Ruth's response was evasive; it was evident to Rebekka that Ruth was concerned. There were stories circulating about young men who had already become victims of fatal encounters between Norwegians and German soldiers.

A stop at the fish store forced them to join an unusually long line of people. Rebekka looked around. It seemed like any other day, except that everyone wore a serious expression. The sales people dressed in their white aprons and small headpieces, usually friendly and outgoing, also seemed subdued and, yes, wary. Sales were brisk, and she noticed that many people were buying larger quantities than usual.

Did they know something she didn't? Were they afraid of not being able to buy food tomorrow? The now familiar strange sensation made a return appearance in her stomach. Was this what people called anxiety? When their turn finally came, she noticed that Ruth bought dinner for one day only.

The constant flow of friends and relatives to the house continued. Even Frank appeared for a few minutes, but he was still not in the mood to talk. Most of the time he chose to hang around the men who were deep in conversation. She watched him listening intently, like he was trying to discover some undisclosed information. His expression was serious and he didn't speak for a change. She also noticed that he was biting his nails when he thought no one was watching. Eventually he was standing by himself, and she was able to approach him. They spoke for a few minutes, which apparently made him relax a little. She avoided speaking about the war. She still hadn't been able to speak with Far. She didn't know what else to ask Frank, but felt it was safe to mention his schoolwork which most of the time set him off on a long tirade.

In the early part of the evening an unfamiliar sound erupted out of nowhere. Rebekka found it almost impossible to recognize the source of the unusual, penetrating sound. Everyone ran to the window, and for a few seconds two or three planes cruising over their neighborhood could be seen on the horizon. She learned very quickly that this was her first exposure to an air raid, which she, until now, had only heard and read about. She felt panic stricken as she ran to find her parents. Far seemed concerned, yet his voice displayed his regular tranquil tone which went a long way to help her calm down. "It's probably just an alert, a warning, for the citizens to get used to the message," he said, as he looked out the window, only to find that the planes had disappeared. Rebekka stayed close to him, the safest sanctuary she could think of at that moment. Eight to ten minutes later the next alarm sounded, but it was different. Her father told her this was an "all clear" signal. She wanted to ask him how he knew, but something told her this was the wrong time to bring it up.

There were no more alarms. Later that evening Far announced that he and Mor had some news to share with her. Their serious faces reflected that it was important. Far took a deep breath.

"Please don't be worried. What we are about to tell you is only a precaution issued to families with children. There is a possibility, although unlikely that the crazy Germans will try to bomb Oslo, and naturally, that may turn out to be dangerous. I'm sure your friend Kari's parents will react the same way. For that reason, we have decided to leave the capital for a while. Tomorrow we are heading for the mountains in Valdres. You can bring some of your most comfortable clothing, some of your schoolbooks and anything else that will make you feel relaxed. We are all going."

Rebekka was unprepared for this news. "We are all leaving just like that? Where will we stay and what are we going to do? What about Frank? Is he going as well?"

She had always thought of Frank as part of her immediate family.

Mor looked relieved now that her oldest daughter was aware of their plans.

"Frank and his parents are joining us. We are staying at a large farm, owned and run by a very nice man who served in the military with your father. You will have a chance to ride horses and learn how to milk cows. Frank's family will be staying at a cabin just a few miles from the farm. We will all be together."

Rebekka stared at her mother. She hesitated for a second before she burst out loud: "Mor, did you really think I would feel better about what's happening because I might learn how to milk cows? What about my school and friends? What about all the unanswered questions? How about the danger for the country and the specific risk for the Norwegian Jews?"

Rebekka felt a little nervous that Mor would get angry, but she didn't answer at all. She just stood there and looked at Rebekka. It seemed Mor had run out of words. Rebekka had never brought up the issue of the Jews before. Rebekka felt a little taken aback at her own comment. Her question remained unanswered.

She changed the topic and asked, "How long will we stay there?"

"We don't know. We'll have to see." Far got up and walked away while Mor and Ruth started clearing the dishes.

Despite the late hour Rebekka grabbed a jacket from a hook in the entryway. She ran down the stairs, headed towards Kari's house to see if she had returned from the visit to her relatives. It was hard to keep the tears away. She felt a need to speak to a person who would understand how terribly unfair this was. She ran across the street, totally forgetting to look out for cars or buses. She stormed up four flights of stairs to Kari's apartment. She was still out of breath when Kari's mother opened the door, asking her what was wrong. "Please may I speak with Kari?" she whispered. The mother paused for a second, but didn't ask any questions, and invited her in. She called for her daughter, who appeared quickly. Rebekka could tell that she had been crying as well. One look was all she needed to realize that her friend was in the same emotional predicament as she was.

Kari spoke faster than usual. "We are leaving tomorrow. My parents are afraid Oslo is going to be bombed, and we have to go far up north to live with some old relatives. They don't know for how long or what we are going to do there. We will miss Constitution Day and my birthday and . . . "

Rebekka heard herself repeating Far's words, in an attempt to calm her friend. "It's a safeguard; it's because they love us. We will be fine. We can write to each other."

The two friends spoke for a few more moments and said goodbye, but not until they decided to exchange several books to take along. Kari was coming over in the morning to pick a selection of books from Rebekka's bookshelf.

Rebekka instantly felt better and less concerned as she walked back across the street to her house.

However, as soon as she was inside her apartment, the air raid alarm blasted again. The sound that had frightened her earlier that day, for some strange reason, felt a little easier to tolerate. Am I getting used to being at war? she thought. Her parents didn't think it was necessary to seek shelter that day, without explaining why, and Rebekka found herself waiting for the sound of the "all clear", which came only a few minutes later.

Well, she thought to herself, most probably there will be no air raid signals at the place where we're going.

The next morning, on Wednesday, April 11, two days after the invasion, they left Oslo. Far's car could hold all five of them, with their suitcases crammed into the back. Miriam was given a different toy to play with every time she started to get fidgety, and Ruth sang songs to her. Rebekka sat in the back seat staring out the window behind Far, holding on to her own private possession—her precious sketchbook. Her parents remained quiet for the most part.

When they reached the main road out of Oslo, it became clear that their decision was not unique. Car after car filled with children were headed out of town. A number of families had obviously decided to take precautions, bringing their children out of the capital as instructed by the radio , protecting them against the unknown potential danger.

The seemingly long, strenuous trip, which in reality only lasted about three hours, ended at an area called Fagernes, located at the top of a big mountain.

Rebekka looking at the panoramic view from the mountain when they had stopped the car was in awe. "I feel I can reach all the way into the sky from here," she exclaimed.

The main building was large and white, with a red barn right behind. Large pines and oak trees surrounded the main property, and down the hill were acres and acres of fields already planted for the spring harvest. As they emptied out of the car, the first sounds to reach them were from the cows, the sheep and other animals. Miriam was immobile, for once, holding on to Ruth, while Rebekka stared at the panorama of nature surrounding the farm, never having seen a sight like this before.

Their hostess and host, a sister and brother in their early forties, greeted them cordially, yet displayed a touch of formality combined with their warmth. The two men shook hands and patted each other on the back. They had become good friends as young men while in the military service, but had only met once or twice during the twenty years that had passed. Far knew about guns and rules and military life, and had befriended soldiers from a variety of other places. Rebekka found it fascinating that Far had retained his close friendship with this man from a totally different background.

The host, also the owner of the farm, shook hands with every one while stating repeatedly how glad he was that they had chosen to come to stay with them. His sister had never met the Davidson family before and greeted Rebekka's mother with a small curtsy. This was perhaps a residual gesture from her childhood when formality was more common, which indicated that she considered the arrival of the Oslo people an honor. Rebekka had to hide a smile, remembering how Mor had tried to teach her to curtsy when she was a little girl.

Mor immediately introduced herself with her first name insisting, "If we are going to share your home and your hospitality, we need to address each other by our first names. We are so grateful that you have opened your home to us."

Rebekka overheard this conversation, studying the hostess, who gave her given name as well. She had never seen anyone with such a kind and cherubic face and expression. The woman's hair was parted in the middle, and tied in the back with a silver comb. Her forehead was unusually high, without a single wrinkle. Her skin was tanned, probably from having spent much time in the fields. It was her eyes that fascinated Rebekka. They were dark blue and radiated kindness. Rebekka immediately felt at home.

After inviting them in to the spacious, immense living room, dining room and kitchen, they showed the Davidsons the two rooms that were available to them—one for the parents and one for Ruth and the children.

A meal of open-faced sandwiches was waiting for the guests and it tasted wonderful. When asked if they wanted to see the animals, they all left immediately, and that's how Rebekka was introduced to farm life in the mountainous area away from Oslo, her home for the next few months.

Little by little, they settled into a routine. Rebekka was enrolled in the local school for a few hours every day. She felt left out. The kids spoke with a local accent, which made her feel like a stranger. They dressed differently and seemed unfriendly. The classes were small, with two grade levels in each room in the white and beige wooden building. It felt like a big box, Rebekka thought, with nothing but desks and windows. The boys stared at her, making her think they were snickering behind her back, most probably because of her red hair, she guessed. Some of the girls seemed friendly, but she couldn't help feeling as if she were on display. She wondered if some of their curiosity was because she was Jewish. Had they ever seen a Jew before? Of course it wasn't announced out loud in the classroom; however, she heard one of the girls whisper something to the girl next to her, and heard the friend respond "I thought all Jews had black hair. Her hair is not black!"

Rebekka ignored it. She was given books to catch up with the others, but the curriculum was different and it was hard to follow. She tried to explain this to Mor, but all she heard back was, "It's probably because you are from the city, and they find you intimidating."

Intimidating, Rebekka thought, I haven't even spoken to them. I am sure they find me snooty because they have been told we're only going to stay here for a few weeks.

She felt that it would be easier to keep to herself. The teacher, a mature woman, was referred to only as Ms. Veumsen. She wore her hair in a long, brown braid at the back of her head. She came across as serious and strict. She would stand by her desk and keep an eye on everyone, and heaven help the poor child who would whisper one word to someone else, or look in the direction of the windows, rather than at her. For the most part, Ms. Veumsen appeared to be ignoring Rebekka.

Each day was opened with the standard Lutheran daily prayer and a hymn, attended by all the students in the common room in the basement, which could hold 75 kids, covering all six grades. This didn't bother Rebekka, having been used to this at school in Oslo. There she had made a habit of being quiet when the text included words like Christ and Jesus. Like most Jewish children, she was excused from religious classes at school, and attended religious school at the synagogue in Oslo. But here in Fagernes she was expected to attend all classes, and that was fine with her. The less fuss and attention paid to her, the better.

On the third day, the teacher brought up the topic of May 17, the Norwegian day of independence, also called Constitution Day. It was the most exciting day of the year for children and adults alike. Rebekka missed Kari terribly, the one friend with whom she could share thoughts and feelings. This would be the first May 17th without Kari since they were little girls.

Rebekka remembered growing up seeing red, white and blue flags flooding the entire city of Oslo. The schoolchildren would parade through the main streets of all the major cities, carrying flags and singing patriotic anthems. Music could be heard all day. Rebekka felt tears in her eyes at the memory, and it was hard to stop them. Many children would wear their "new" outfits on that day. A number of women would wear national costumes, which might have been in the family for several generations, provided they still fit! The men for the most part wore a suit or blazer but always with a dress shirt and tie. There was an implied agreement that this very special formal celebration would take place in the early part of the day, just before noon. She wondered what would happen this year.

Would the kids and adults be allowed to continue to celebrate the 17th under the circumstances? To her great surprise, the students at the school, as well as the serious Ms. Veumsen, began to exhibit some enthusiasm. The teacher put their minds at ease with an unusual lightness in her voice and a smile, yes, a real smile, which was enough to make the students pay attention. The school committee had met with the principal, she said, and decided that the celebration would indeed go forward, despite the unexpected and disquieting situation in the country. The official celebration was to be limited to the children's parade through the center of town with a band and an orchestra. However, there were no funds. The teacher therefore encouraged the students to create their own posters and invitations.

Ms. Veumsen unexpectedly turned to Rebekka, who had been sitting by quietly, thinking about how much fun she had experienced last year in Oslo. The teacher called her name. "I have been told you are an accomplished artist. Would you be willing to help us design a drawing of the flag of Norway which we can copy and use as a base for our fliers?"

The entire class turned around and stared at Rebekka, as if discovering her for the first time. Her cheeks were burning. She felt trapped and didn't know how to answer. Designing posters and signs! For a moment she contemplated walking out, running away. But of course she didn't.

Eventually she was able to answer in a half whisper, "I guess I could try." The teacher continued to smile and said, "Good, thank you. Please give it some thought and let's discuss this in a little more detail."

Rebekka consented, feeling that she couldn't say no. In addition this might give her a chance to get involved in a specific project and perhaps make some new friends. At least that's what her mother said.

That afternoon, as most days, the Davidsons joined Frank and his parents at the nearby cabin where they were staying. Frank, who normally would make a point of informing Rebekka of any new events or information that he had acquired, appeared subdued. He sat quietly, isolated, in a corner of the sitting room. The fire burned in the fireplace, but he seemed deep in thought. The warmth from the fire was just enough to make her relax. She pulled her feet up on the sofa and tried to start a conversation, but got no response. It dawned on Rebekka that something else bothered her cousin this time. Perhaps his interest in the men's conversation was not based on trying to act "adult" and show off, which he was known for doing, but possibly this time he was genuinely interested and, yes, even worried.

She got off the sofa and approached Frank, asking him how he was doing, implying that she shared his annoyance about having to leave Oslo.

"How do you like being a 'mountain dweller'? Have you gotten used to the lack of inside bathroom facilities?" she said, and pointed to the outdoor toilet, some 20 meters away, which was the norm in most vacation homes at that time. However, even this silly comment didn't generate a smile or the usual sarcastic comment. Frank looked distracted.

Frank's expression was one of sadness mixed with agitation making her wonder if he was testing her. For a second she felt almost embarrassed to talk to him, despite the closeness developed over the years. What was he trying to convey? Was he reluctant to communicate with her? Deep inside she felt he was holding something back. Finally, he spoke. "Let's go for a short walk. I just can't talk here. I can't stand the way everyone stops speaking the moment we come near them. What in the world do they think we are interested in? Missing May 17th or watching the cows being milked?" Rebekka felt a little uncomfortable. She had actually just thought about May 17th. But she also understood what he meant. It was hard to be suspended somewhere between childhood and adulthood. She got up and joined him, and together they went outside.

"Rebekka, every night I hear my mother crying and my parents whispering. I try to listen but I can't always hear. My father has, no, had, a first cousin in Berlin, who was shot on the street this year. He died, lying in the gutter in front of all the soldiers. Why? All he did was refuse to get down on the ground to pick up some dog poop that one of the soldiers had stepped in. The soldier responded immediately by raising his gun, killing him and calling out, 'You damn Jew; this is for not listening to me!'"

"These stories are being told more and more frequently. Hitler's brutes are deliberately torturing and killing Jews everywhere. And more and more Jews are being arrested for no reason at all, except for being Jews! They are being sent to camps all over Germany and Poland.

And now they are here in our country, which used to be so far away from Germany that most people never heard of us. That's how insignificant and unimportant Norway has been until now. Our country is a pawn in a political game increasing day by day."

The young boy was in a frenzy as he spoke. "There is no logic, there is no sense, and it's pure hatred, hatred of Jews. When will it reach Norway? My father heard someone mention that we, the Jews in Norway, will soon be made to have a letter J for Jew stamped in our legitimation card. What are we? Animals that cannot speak for ourselves? This may be the beginning."

Beginning of what, Rebekka thought, but didn't dare to interrupt him.

It was impossible to stop staring at her cousin, while she was also overwhelmed by the image of the victims. She couldn't speak. She had never heard Frank express himself that violently before. Where was the secure, chatty and sometimes gossipy voice that she was used to, the one who she on occasion chose to ignore? The intensity of his remarks scared her. The image of the poor man lying in the gutter kept reappearing in her mind, even though she tried desperately to erase it. Without even noticing, she started to shiver.

"What is going on here," a voice resonated over her shoulder, "and what is wrong, Rebekka?" She noticed Frank's face turning red, looking at the ground. The firm voice startled her as well, as Rebekka immediately tried to avoid Far's penetrating glance. How long had he been standing there?

Far put his arm gently around her shoulders. "You are shaking. I think it's best if the two of you let me in on this conversation, which seems to have upset you."

Frank nodded faintly but remained quiet. The expression on his face confirmed the topic, making it unnecessary to even answer the question.

Far continued, "Let's walk a little farther and see if spring finally has arrived in this area. It comes slightly later up here than in Oslo. It's still light although it's cold." He started moving slowly and the two youngsters followed him in silence. "I am not surprised that these thoughts are on your mind, Frank, as they are with most of us. The stories coming out of Eastern Europe are scary and incredible. However, at a time like this it's essential we remain calm and realistic."

"We are not in Berlin; we are in a small country far away, which is inhabited by very few Jews. We are hoping that the attack on Norwegian Jews will not be worth the effort, military planning and expense for the Third Reich. I can assure you that your parents, their friends and many, many resistance fighters in this country are watching the situation closely. Your Uncle Leonard, Rebekka, is in touch with a number of these units and will keep us informed about matters as they unfold. If you two promise to try not to worry, I'll promise to keep you abreast if the situation changes, no matter what. Your job now is to try to adapt to this new situation we are facing for a brief time, which is primarily for your safety and hopefully will make it easier for the adults as well. To be honest, I think that you two should wait another six or seven years until you start planning how to overturn Germany. For the time being let us, the 'older' generation, do our job first. When the time comes that you are in charge, I want to sit in a rocking chair and play with my grandchildren!"

Far's words made Rebekka feel a bit more calm. Far must have felt the change in the atmosphere because he continued in a very neutral voice, "Mor told me that you've been asked to design a May 17th poster at school. This is very exciting. Have you started? Do you have any drafts to show me?"

They started walking toward the cabin where the rest of the family was waiting. Miriam ran towards Frank, which she always did. Frank's parents, Ruth and Mor were sitting at a round table on the lawn, drinking something they called coffee which was a mixture of chicory, grain and sometimes barley and peas. The sun was relatively bright for late April, the sky was blue. How could anything bad possibly be happening in a world as beautiful as this? Rebekka thought, not allowing an answer.

Nevertheless, the calm was short-lived. That evening after dinner, Far made an announcement. It shocked her, although in retrospect she should have seen it coming. "I have decided to join the military unit here in this area when they start their defense. They need men. I feel that it's my duty. I trained with several of the farmers in the area when I was in the service. If they can leave their farms to defend the country, why shouldn't I? I'll be leaving tomorrow."

Rebekka stared at him, in shock. Far, going to fight as a soldier? At war? Defending Norway against the invaders? Would he have a gun? Does he know how to use a gun? Would he shoot someone, if necessary? She found it impossible to express these thoughts, and the only thing that she managed to say was, "Do you have a uniform?"

The new soldier-to-be answered quickly that he didn't. He would be given a jacket to match the other men, but intended to wear his own every-day green knickers. There was nothing more to say. The next morning he kissed his family goodbye, smiled and left, transported in the back of a large, green truck.

Rebekka waved to him, watching his knickers and greenish three-quarter length windbreaker, as he became smaller and smaller and eventually disappeared down the road. Everything seemed green to her.

Somehow the days passed. Rebekka reluctantly completed a poster, which was copied and hung in appropriate places around the village. She found it hard to make up text that wouldn't provoke rage and hostility. She ended up drawing a traditional large, red, white and blue flag in the top left-hand corner, with the year 1940 next to it. A larger drawing showed children holding flags blowing in the wind. The text read ***Happy Birthday to Norway! Today is our Special Day***—It sounded a little bland, she thought, but worried that if it was too enthusiastic, it might not pass the censor of the local Nazis.

First she had to get the text past the teacher—the ultimate judge of whether the poster was "appropriate" or not. Fortunately Miss Veumsen seemed pleased with the outcome. Consequently it was to be used wherever people wanted to display it. It would hang in places where it would be readily noticed, but restricted from the most common places. To avoid a potential confrontation with some of the soldiers who now were beginning to be quite visible in the Fagernes area, someone suggested not hanging the posters until dawn on the 17th. This would minimize the opportunities of critical spies and Nazis. Luck was on their side. As if by miracle, very early on the 17th, the posters appeared in windows and entrance doors of local stores and a number of other sites that would support a white poster decorated in red, white and blue. No one asked how they had gotten there. Their day, May 17th, finally had arrived.

In school, a few admiring kids approached her shyly, asking whether she was "the Oslo girl who could draw." Little by little Rebekka began to feel more comfortable, especially when she met other kids whose fathers had volunteered as soldiers as well.

It was impossible not to feel the excitement in town. Having been ordered not to raise their extra-large Norwegian flags, as was normally the custom, the locals tried to remain discreet. Smaller flags were seen on lawns, on cars and in store windows. The students gathered at the town green, getting ready for the traditional parade, each one carrying a flag. A band appeared and started playing marching songs. Relatives, friends and neighbors lined up along the street, welcoming the musicians. Cheers and roaring greetings could be heard as the singing and music emanated from the procession of smiling youngsters waving their flags.

A few German soldiers could be seen behind the exhilarated crowd, watching the excitement. Most of the people tried to avoid looking at them, but there was tension in the air. Would the children be told to leave? Nothing happened. Gradually the number of men in uniforms increased. Some appeared to enjoy the music and smiled. Some of them had a quizzical expression on their faces, wondering what was going on, and where did they, the invaders, fit in?

Rebekka left the school crowd; she felt a sudden need to be with her family. She walked over to Ruth who had Miriam in her stroller. Rebekka bent over to Ruth's ear and expressed her amazement that the locals had been able to carry out this celebration without interference by the Gestapo.

Ruth didn't seem to enjoy the festivities. Unlike most of the other spectators, her face didn't exhibit joy or pride in the moment. Her face was expressionless, tears ran down her cheeks. She looked as if she were many miles away. Rebekka felt a sudden twinge of guilt. Had her family ignored her today and not paid her enough attention? Ruth was in her early twenties, and had become irreplaceable to the Davidson family. She had overheard Mor asking Ruth on several occasions if she wanted to return to the little coastal town where her mother lived, in view of the circumstances.

"Do you want to leave? After all, there's a fair amount of risk if you remain with a Jewish family." Mor had mentioned this several times.

Ruth's answer was always the same. "No, no, I want to stay. This is where I belong right now with you. I just feel so bad about this country and all the people who are suffering. I have been with you since Miriam was a newborn. You are my family as well."

"Do you miss your family today? Do you think about your mother and your sisters?" Rebekka asked.

Ruth looked back at her, saying, "I am okay. I am not crying for myself, I am crying for the country."

Rebekka was astonished. Ruth was right. Rebekka said, "I think the people of Fagernes managed to outfox the German soldiers. They probably had no idea of the importance of this day and therefore no expectation of the meaning of May 17th."

Ruth turned to her, smiled a little and hugged her. "You are right, you outfoxed them. Good for you."

She may have been right. As soon as the parade was over, the soldiers "woke up" and went into action. It was evident they had been given orders, although a bit late. People were told to leave, and not to linger on the green or on the street. This was a great victory for the Norwegians who had experienced their first May 17th under a German regime. They felt they had indeed outsmarted the enemy to celebrate the day.

The second thing that happened that day would also remain a permanent memory. When Frank and his parents arrived to have a celebratory dinner at the farm up in the hills, thanks to an invitation from the Davidson family's hosts, another surprise was announced. Some friends had uncovered an old batch of firecrackers, which they wanted to utilize as soon as the sun set. "Let's scare these foreign creeps out of their minds and show them how we celebrate Norway's finest day" was the message.

After dinner, everyone got into a buggy pulled by two horses to reach the neighbor's farm where the fireworks were waiting. They were running a little late and sat close together. A feeling of happiness spread through the group all enjoying a brief respite. Miriam insisted on sitting on Frank's lap.

After a few minutes, they heard a thunderous sound. The fireworks had already commenced. Unfortunately, the horses reacted with a quick jerk. One jumped into the air, throwing off the balance of the buggy and the relatively large group of passengers.

Frank was taken by surprise and let go of Miriam, who fell onto the bottom of the buggy. She rolled quickly toward the other side, only a second or two short of falling onto the road or landing in front of the rear wheel on that side. The travelers screamed. Frank threw himself onto the floor, grabbing onto the two-year-old's pigtails, which were bouncing in the air. He dragged her back from the buggy floor, and delivered her into the arms of her mother. Both child and mother cried out loud—the younger of the two from having been picked up and brought to safety by her pigtails, and the older, from fear that her child might have been permanently injured.

The rest of the group remained silent, each one shocked at having witnessed a potential calamity. The silence was broken by Frank's comment, "Guess I saved her life."

A true statement that no one could deny. However, no one dared or wanted to comment that perhaps the arms of a young teenage boy might not have been the safest place for an active toddler to sit under the circumstances.

As if by silent agreement, the group in the buggy turned around, returned to their homes and never witnessed the fireworks.

Chapter Four

Far, Please Listen

Harald was sitting at his desk, looking out the window. His homework lay next to him, untouched, as he found it almost impossible to concentrate. The school assignment was boring and unimportant, and he felt low, angry and restless. Come to think of it, he hated math. He just couldn't master it. The teacher kept droning on and it was impossible to understand what he was saying. There were so many other important issues to discuss and learn about right now.

Most of all, it was hard to figure out why and when this strange mood had come over him. Nothing had really changed lately. The days went by despite the war, but today it felt worse. Was that what they called depression? Was this a function of the war as well?

There were still a few things that intrigued him and caught his attention, and frankly, he felt these questions and issues were equally as important as his homework—much more important actually.

School had started again after the month when they all stayed home. His history teacher, Mr. Welhaven, had started a discussion group twice a week right after school. It was elective, and the first subject was the history of Germany under Bismarck. Twelve boys and three girls had signed up. These meetings had been taking place for the past few weeks in a regular school-room. No school officials seemed to object. The general title of the course was quite neutral, but as the course continued, much time was spent discussing the present political situation in Europe. Most probably, the Nazis had no clue what it was about.

Harald found the subject fascinating. The teacher brought up various situations going back as far as 30 years. Reading assignments for each ses-

29

sion were voluntary. When the discussion got fairly heated, Mr. Welhaven allowed each participant a chance to voice his/her opinion. Everyone played a part and had to justify his or her own position. The discussion was lively and in depth.

Harald was thinking about his Uncle Leonard who loved history and always made a point of being familiar with both former and present political parties. Harald vividly remembered two years ago when he had discussed this with his uncle, and Harald often took books out of the library to see how and where his uncle had acquired all his information.

However, when Harald went home, he often felt as if he got a slap in the face. Not a physical slap, but the way his father reacted, made it feel like it. His father refused to discuss any of the various historical situations which had contributed to this war and which were discussed in school. "Why did Germany try to take over Norway? Was it because they would be trying to take over England?"

Every day his father would ask him how school had been that day, and Harald would begin to tell him. As soon as he tried to explain the various opinions and what he thought the outcome would be, his father would smile. He smiled the way a father smiles to a small child who has recently learned to ride a two-wheel bike, or managed to learn more than four verses of a patriotic song by heart. But did he actually ever listen to Harald expressing his own points of view and arguments? Never. He just wasn't interested—at least not in Harald's opinion.

The first time Harald had asked him directly whether he understood why they were at war, and what he felt the Norwegians could do to end it, his father walked away. A minute later, he was actively looking at his business list of merchandise, the schedule for the chamber of commerce meeting that week, and even when the next wrestling matches were scheduled.

Once Harald confronted his father directly but even then, it was clear that his father was not interested in any conversation about this topic.

"Please let's not discuss this issue now. Your mother is very concerned and I don't want her to get any more worried. Believe me, I am getting all the information I need from my business acquaintances. I am certain that the war will be over soon; the allies will win and put the country back to where it was before."

He was sucking on his pipe, which he tended to do whenever he wanted to be left alone.

Heaven only knows what he is smoking, Harald thought. It certainly doesn't smell like pipe tobacco. His father continued, "As far as we are concerned, being the only Jewish family in town, this shouldn't be much of a problem. I am well respected, don't you know that? You may recall that Sweden is neutral and I was born a Swede. They would never target a Swedish person."

Harald thought for a second. "You were born in Sweden, but you decided to become a Norwegian citizen. You are no longer Swedish. Do you think that being a former Swede will override your present nationality? It doesn't make sense."

At this point it was clear the conversation had come to an end. His father sounded annoyed. "It's not for you to worry about. Focus on your school-work, and I'll let you know if and when the situation changes."

His sister, Ingrid, a few years older, had listened to the conversation. She was more outgoing than Harald and avoided any dispute with their father. She was first of all interested in music and arts, and ignored the political situation as much as possible. Ingrid had a habit of resenting Harald when he asked questions that couldn't be answered or their father chose to ignore him. Instead she went to the piano and started to play.

Harald stopped, realizing he wasn't getting through, and decided it would be best to change the subject. He attempted to speak casually to his father again.

"By the way, I heard something else today that you may or may not know. One of the people in my class said a major person from the Gestapo office in Trondheim has been appointed head of the Aalesund Police Station. This puts all the local police forces under the command of The Gestapo, and the Norwegian policemen will be collaborating with the Germans only. His name is Thomas Gyldendahl, and someone in my history class told me he is a dangerous and evil man. He has made it no secret that he hates Jews. They aren't serious, are they? I hope they're just exaggerating."

"We are the only Jewish family in town. Why would they worry about us? You know most of the families in town, don't you?" The father answered. Harald continued.

"It seems weird that some of these men who now support him are the same people we have known for years and years and who we trusted and depended on less than a year ago," Harald added, looking at his father.

His father looked up and nodded, "Yes, I am aware of this situation," he said. "I don't want you to worry about it. However, the Norwegian resistance forces are working to change things, and I am sure we will be able to succeed and be back to normal soon."

"I have heard about this man and we need to be very careful." He stopped and looked at Harald. "I know this man is opinionated, stubborn and ex-tremely anti-Semitic. This doesn't bode well for any of us, but I don't want you to worry. We will avoid having any contact with the police station. I heard that he has relatives here in town, but I don't know who they are."

"I know there is going to be a major reorganization in the police depart-ment here in town. But this is not for you to worry about." He stopped suddenly, looked at Harald, got up and walked away.

Chapter Five

The Pendant

OSLO, JUNE 10, 1940

Rebekka's family finally succeeded in establishing a daily routine while in the small mountain town. Rebekka made a few friends and started to feel more at home. The schoolwork eased up slightly once she could follow the curriculum. She even became used to the dialect, and occasionally caught herself using a few of the local expressions. Her artistic aptitude had become well known, and this made her feel more secure. But she was still homesick for Oslo, for her school, and most of all for Kari.

She missed Far terribly and thought of him every day, but stopped asking about him because she didn't like Mor's answer. "As soon as I hear, I'll share it with you. No news is good news."

It was clear that Mor didn't want to speak to her about Far.

At the end of June, Mor unexpectedly gave Rebekka a big hug when she returned from a visit to the village. Her eyes were sparkling and it was clear that Mor was very happy. She was looking directly at Rebekka and her voice had a totally different intonation than it had the past two months.

"Finally, Bekka, I have some good news! We are returning to Oslo and what's even more important, Far is joining us as well. A co-prisoner, who was just released, brought a note from him. I got so excited when I read the message, that I hugged him. Poor man was probably in shock."

"Far wrote that we should start planning for next week, but he will get back to us in a few days. He is okay, but it has been a bad experience. Let's go for a short walk, and I'll tell you everything I know."

The news came as a surprise to Rebekka, who was staring at her "new" mother. She hadn't seen Mor this happy for a long time. She wasn't sure what to think. Would Mor's mood vanish in a few minutes and would she become introverted and serious again? Rebekka knew that Mor's disposition had a tendency to swing. Being the oldest daughter in her large family, she was used to taking charge, making decisions and yes, telling others what to do. She was outgoing and friendly, but could get angry at any small, insignificant detail. To be fair, she was also known for remaining cool and collected in times of crisis. She was the tallest of the sisters, with dark brown hair. Rebekka was getting used to her own red hair, now that she had started to study the science of genetics. Frank's mother, for example, had jet-black hair, and was almost a head shorter than her sister Sarah, Rebekka's mother. Rebekka was also tall, which she assumed was inherited from her mother.

As usual, Rebekka stared at the pendant hanging around Mor's neck. Rebekka couldn't imagine her mother without this memento. As the two of them were walking, she glanced at the pendant hoping for assurance. Mor really was in a good mood. How the pendant could guarantee this, she didn't know. But somehow she felt better looking at it.

Was this Mor's good luck charm? Had it contributed to keeping Far safe?

She never asked Mor if she believed in the power of the pendant. One thing she knew though was that she hadn't seen Mor without that particular piece of jewelry since the invasion.

She was speechless while Mor continued talking about their return to Oslo, and asked if she had heard right. Mor looked at her with a gentle expression, saying, "I know how hard this has been for you, but I really didn't know how to make it easier. I was worried myself and the one thing I didn't want to do was lie to you. So I said nothing, which was easiest for me, but it may not have been the best for you. I am so sorry. But now I would like to tell you a little more about Far's time as a soldier, and what happened once he and his co-soldiers were arrested. He was taken prisoner only three weeks after he had joined the local military force. He will be released in about a week and we will be returning to Oslo!"

Rebekka had a hard time believing it. She kept staring at Mor. "How do you know? Are you sure? Have you seen him? When will I see him? Are you sure we are leaving?"

Mor looked at her, then started speaking slowly. "Sweetie, I have a story I would like to share with you. Do you remember about a week ago just after I fell and injured my arm?"

Rebekka nodded.

"Once Far had been away for several weeks and I didn't hear from him, I became concerned. I was worried and depressed. I started taking walks into the center of town alone, trying to find out what had happened to his battalion and where they were stationed. Initially, the locals were reserved and tried to avoid me—that made me feel even worse.

"But as soon as I identified myself and mentioned my husband's name, their attitudes changed quickly. Clearly your father is known in the area. He had been stationed in this county during his military service as a young man, prior to the war. I knew he had been very comfortable in this particular group, but I never realized how much they cared for him.

"The biggest surprise was that many of them are customers of our store, in Oslo, buying clothes for their kids. They told me Far would call one or two of his friends to alert them when he received some good quality pants, ski jackets and sweaters. They would check around to see who needed outfits for their kids as there aren't too many stores carrying this type of merchandise. He never told me about this.

"I then found out that the batch of soldiers from this particular area had been taken prisoner just a few weeks after they had signed up. They were kept in custody in an old building, which had been converted to a temporary prison.

"Once all this information had been revealed, I just couldn't stop. Little by little, I put the various pieces together, and that allowed me to establish the general location of the prison. No one could tell me exactly where it was located, but they implied that it wasn't too far away.

"I thanked everyone who had shared their information with me. Most of them also had a husband, son or cousin who had volunteered, and they, like me, were concerned. Nothing could stop me, Rebekka. I had to try to find him. Not even an injured arm was going to prevent me from locating Far. Do you remember my arm was in a sling? I think I have myself to thank for that fall. I was a bit preoccupied returning to you from the village that day, and I wasn't careful enough. Let this be a lesson for you, young lady!"

She smiled, reminding her daughter that despite this personal and unusual story, she hadn't forgotten to whom she was speaking. Rebekka was flabbergasted. She had difficulty remembering her mother ever expressing this much emotion, and even smiling. Mor spoke as a friend, not as the strict, serious parent she had lived with since the invasion.

"I was determined to locate Far, one way or the other, and decided that I had to find him on my own. No power in the world could stop me—or almost. I felt I had no choice. I left you and Miriam with Ruth knowing that you would be well taken care of, and I promised that I would be back in a day, or at the most two days. I left the next morning. You may remember that I borrowed Elisabet's bicycle once more, despite the injured arm, which really hurt. I told her I had to make some inquiries in the next town over about our store in Oslo, wondering what I should do about ordering new inventory. After all, the store has been run solely by the three employees while we were here. That was just an excuse, of course. I didn't tell the truth because I was afraid people would try to prevent me from going. It could have had dangerous consequences.

"Just before I left, I made a quick stop at the local physician's office, underplaying the severity of the pain in my arm. The doctor, tried to prevent me from leaving—especially on a bicycle. Reluctantly he gave up and wrapped my wounded arm in a sling. Apparently, it was not the first time this general practitioner had come face to face with a strong woman. He shrugged his shoulders and returned to the room full of waiting patients."

Rebekka and her mother were walking along a path next to bales of newly cut hay. The smell was fresh and invigorating. Rebekka didn't remember ever experiencing this wonder of nature before. She expressed this thought to her mother, who suggested that they sit down for a few minutes on an old, dilapidated bench located beside the hay field.

Mor stretched her legs and smiled again. Rebekka listened to each word, anxiously waiting for the next phase of the story. She didn't realize that she was holding her breath.

"My only clue was to try to locate a converted old building, which had been taken over by the Germans. How many could there be of this kind in the area? I was lucky, very lucky. I did something that you must never do, unless it's a real emergency. I got a ride with a farmer who was going in that general direction to work in his field. He was willing to give me a ride, putting the bike in the back."

A cat appeared from behind the bench and jumped into Rebekka's lap. She stroked the cat's soft fur, while Mor continued the story.

"Naturally, I asked him about the area and if he had any idea where this prison might be? First, he was hesitant, but little by little he shared what he knew. I have come to the conclusion that in a time of crisis, war or other emergencies, people, good people, want to help. Well, this farmer was a gem. He gave me whatever information he had."

Rebekka had an image of her mother in the passenger seat of the truck. A thought struck her. She was still carrying the light shoulder bag which she had taken to school, and as usual, she had her sketchpad at the bottom. It had been lying there for a few weeks, as Rebekka hadn't been in the mood to draw anything. She took it out of the bag, no, she ripped it out of the bag!

She decided to draw her Mor in the truck, speaking with a stranger who helped her find Far and the prison where he was held. Afterward she couldn't help sketching a few of the beautiful bales of hay, framed by the blue sky and the radiant sun, all right in front of her. Without even being aware of it, she included the bench, with her mother in a relaxed position, sitting next to a young girl with red hair. The cat was sleeping in Mor's lap.

Mor said nothing, allowing her daughter to duplicate the surroundings onto the pages in her book.

"Mor, please tell me about the ride in the truck," she said.

"Little by little this wonderful man was able to locate the building, which was rumored to be used as a prison. He made several stops along the way, asking everyone. He had a slow, understated manner. But he always got answers. It turned out he knew just about everyone. He took me to the neighborhood, but left me about two kilometers from the actual site. He felt that I might be more successful if I arrived alone. He was probably right.

"When he stopped his truck and reminded me not to forget the bike, I really didn't know how to thank him adequately. At that point I also realized I had forgotten to ask his name, which he then reluctantly told me. I was so fortunate."

"So you did get his name?"

"Yes, I'll tell you what it is when I get to the end of the story.

"Strangely enough, I wasn't scared. Well, maybe a little, but I tried to hide it. I probably should have been, since I had no idea what I was getting involved in. I approached the prison camp. I had tried to find a good excuse to present to the guards to make sure I got in. However, I couldn't think of anything satisfactory. Finally, I decided to adopt an arrogant attitude, which I hoped would be the most effective way to get through to the German soldiers-to intimidate them and it worked. You know we grew up speaking a lot of languages in my family, and I declared, in fluent German, that I had arrived to consult with my husband, Mr. Martin Davidson, about his business activities in Oslo. Would they please make certain I was brought to him immediately? They just stared at each other. Neither one seemed to have the authority to make a decision, yes or no.

"And here is the funny part, at least now that it's over. It wasn't funny at the time, but rather frightening. Far told me he heard this story when the guards came back inside. Apparently, the soldiers weren't really taken aback by my attitude, clearly failing to notice my arm in a sling and that I was holding on to an old bicycle. They were mostly alarmed by the pendant clock hanging around my neck believing it was a mini camera, which I intended to use for political espionage or something similar. As a result, their behavior was reasonably civilized!"

Mor paused for a second and looked into space, putting her hands on her neck, stroking the watch. Rebekka felt like a small child hearing a fairytale, and couldn't wait for Mor to continue.

"Can you believe it? This gift from your Grandpa? The last thing he gave me. It may have saved my life, or at least, helped me along. I'll never take it off, I promise you.

"The two guards rushed into the office where Far was, assisting the colonel interrogating various farmers. I learned later that very few of the local prisoners spoke German. When the commander realized that Far was quite fluent, he was immediately ordered to serve as an interpreter.

"At the door, the two outside guards whispered a few words in German to one of the Norwegian Nazis. Fortunately the significance of the suspicious pendant was lost in this dialogue, because this guard casually shouted out loud to the crowd sitting in the office.

"'Hey, Davidson, there's a broad here to see you!'"

"Oh, Mor, weren't you afraid to walk into the prison? What if they decided to keep you there?"

Rebekka's brain was spinning. Mor smiled and kept talking.

"Your father is no stranger to my ability to think quickly or make up excuses, but he was speechless when he saw me at the door. We were allowed to speak privately for a few minutes, when Far first asked about you and Miriam, of course. Next we actually did make a few decisions regarding the store. And then he told me that most probably he and the other prisoners would be released in a few days. Strangely enough, he found the commander to be a relatively easygoing man. He had listened to Far when he tried to explain that most of the prisoners desperately needed to get back to their farms to deal with the spring planting.

"After a few minutes, I was asked to leave and I had enough common sense not to push my luck and stay longer. I got back on the bike again and returned to you."

Rebekka had stopped drawing, and stared at her mother. "Is that the end of the story?"

"Just like Far had predicted, the Norwegians had to surrender to the invaders this month. There were too many German soldiers. The prison was dissolved. So that is it. The men will be released in a few days. We hope and pray that the war will come to an end soon. But right now we are looking forward to being together again as a family in our own home where we belong."

"Mor, what was the man's name?"

"I am almost afraid to tell you, thinking you won't believe me. But it's the truth, Rebekka. The man's name was David Martinson. Believe it or not."

Rebekka gazed at her mother, almost speechless.

"That's the reverse of Far's name, isn't it?"

She kept staring at her mother.

"Mor, I love you," was all she was able to say as she put her arms around her mother. She had come back to her—and so had Far.

Chapter Six

An Unfulfilled Dream

AALESUND, SEPTEMBER 15, 1940

The spring and summer of 1940 came and went. August had already passed, and fall was waiting around the corner as any other year. The inhabitants of Aalesund, however, felt that they were living in a different world, or at least in a different country. Rumors circulated constantly about bombing, arrests and other major calamities. Everyone asked questions; there were few answers. The selection of food was rapidly diminishing, save for vegetables and fruits, and of course the ubiquitous herring which was consumed by everyone everywhere.

Like other families, Ingrid's parents were trying to adapt to the new way of life. They pretended to ignore the enemy who was appearing more and more frequently on the streets. Leyla continued to volunteer at the local community hospital, while her husband worked even harder to find merchandise for the store.

Ingrid often thought about how quickly this strange atmosphere had descended on their town like a heavy, grey cloud with no indication of what would come next. She spent more time at the piano as if this part of her life was a shelter. The school day was limited, as were extra activities. Music had always been her primary focus, allowing for no other distraction. These days she felt permanently distracted.

"It feels like the attack on Norway has destroyed my ability to concentrate," she said to her friend Margarete. "Thoughts keep reappearing whenever I least expect them. Do you have any idea what I am saying? I have heard that several of the local men have vanished. Disappeared. Where are they? Were they drafted? Are they fighting? Are they in prison? Or are there even more serious possibilities that we haven't yet heard of? We don't know why they are gone. It feels like we are all in limbo. My parents won't talk to me about it."

Her best friend Margarete made a habit of spending time at Ingrid's house while the latter was practicing. This time spent together had started several years ago. Margarete was a master knitter, with the ability to create the most beautiful designs. Her talent and skills were known all over town. This took time, and an atmosphere of quiet harmony was perfect. Hours would sometimes pass, with Ingrid at the piano and Margaret knitting row after row. Each would concentrate on her own project, with no need to speak, except for mutually agreed upon short breaks. Not a bad solution for two talented and ambitious young women.

Ingrid had just turned seventeen and had participated in all kinds of musical activities at school, including plays and an occasional musical. In fact, the school's music teacher had just approached her asking about providing piano music for the newly-planned musical. Ingrid's instinct had been to turn him down, feeling that perhaps she should make better use of her free time. The feeling of guilt when she was away from practicing was hard to shake. But at the last moment, she had accepted the invitation, hoping the reverse—a partial break from the long hours at the piano—might help her relax a little.

A few days earlier Ms. Loevberg, her piano teacher, announced that she would like a meeting with Ingrid's parents, preferring it to take place as soon as possible. Ingrid was given no hint of the topic.

Ms. Loevberg, a formal, fairly reserved woman, was somewhere between forty and fifty. Once invited in, she kept her coat on, sitting on the very edge of the first chair she could reach. She looked uncomfortable, as if she was afraid to bother Ingrid's parents. She spoke slowly and concisely and made it clear that she didn't intend to waste their time—or her own. She had something specific to discuss.

The room was tense as Ingrid's parents grew concerned. They had assumed the lessons were going well, at least according to Ingrid.

"I feel Ingrid has reached a stage in her musical skills where she would benefit from more challenges," Ms. Loevberg said in a serious, almost apologetic voice. "I feel I have nothing more to teach her, and both she and I, for that matter, may be wasting our time. Have you ever considered allowing her to locate a more advanced piano teacher, possibly in Oslo?" she asked.

The last few words were delivered in a firm voice, making it clear that in her opinion, another local teacher was not even worthy of a discussion. When she was done, she heaved a sigh of relief, made herself more comfortable on the chair, and unbuttoned her coat. This confrontation, which is how she must have thought of it, had been difficult for her.

Ingrid's parents were astonished. They had always suspected that Ingrid had exceptional musical talent, but they weren't prepared for this. Neither of them had any experience with a musical instrument and felt that Ms. Loevberg was responsible for practically all of Ingrid's success. The fact that she was considered the most competent piano teacher in town was beyond discussion.

The Rosenbergs thanked her profusely and said they would discuss it. Within a few days they had located the name of a highly-respected piano teacher in Oslo, who might consent to take Ingrid on as a once-a-month student provided she fulfilled the necessary requirements. His name was Fritz Hertzberg. It was made very clear that Mr. Hertzberg was only doing them a favor as he was quite busy and didn't take on just anyone as a student!

The arrangement had been negotiated through a friend who was an acclaimed Oslo musician and was therefore able to get the maestro's attention.

They decided to combine the upcoming audition with a visit to Leyla's mother in Oslo, hoping to see the rest of the family as well. They might even try to time the visit to coincide with the Jewish holidays.

Ingrid was petrified when she heard of the piano teacher's dramatic suggestion. What if the master teacher didn't like her playing? What if he was just "throwing his friend a bone" in agreeing to hear her play? Well, she wasn't going to worry about it. She was going to practice and practice, and do the best she could. For the first time in several months she was feeling a little excitement. Something new might be coming her way, to offset the grinding feeling of bad news.

And besides, something else had happened. Something relatively insignificant and unexpected. But it was enough to make her feel good. When Margarete left their joint "work session," she casually called out, "Who was the tall, striking 'elderly' man who you were speaking to for so long at the school musical last night? He must have been at least nineteen. When were you planning on telling me about him?"

Ingrid smiled to herself, uncertain whether she should get involved in this conversation or not.

"He is just a guy who loves music and is involved in the amateur theater. He heard me accompany the cast and was very friendly. His name is Arne. That's all I know." She was hoping Margarete hadn't noticed how she was blushing.

Her friend snickered and said goodbye as she let herself out, carrying the big bag of yarn, needles and patterns.

Chapter Seven

Are Jews Different?

OSLO, SEPTEMBER 30, 1940

When did this happen, Rebekka thought to herself. She kept digging through a box labelled *winter/spring clothing, RD*. Nothing fit. Everything was too small. All her skirts and dresses had gotten shorter. Come to think of it, she had worn nothing but shorts and blouses while in the mountains, even in school. She must have grown during that period. She hadn't thought of that!

The weeks and months since their return from Fagernes had gone by very quickly. It was already the end of September. The delayed startup date of her new school had finally been announced. Rebekka was trying on last year's pair of boots, primarily because they were packed on top. Same with her shoes.

"All the stores are out of boots and shoes, as well as clothing," her mother had told her.

It seemed as if they had just returned from the stay in the mountains. Time had passed quickly there, especially when she got more involved at the local school and made a point of doing well. It all came to an end in the final days of June when most of the young families with children returned to Oslo. The hysteria over the bombing of the capital had subsided. Damage had been minimal, if one could even speak of it in those terms. The initial fear had been triggered by rumors that England had plans to bomb Oslo to prevent Germany from taking over.

The brave Norwegian soldiers who tried to defend their country against the Gestapo had to surrender in the middle of June. There were too many enemies and too few soldiers. The small local prisons were full of Norwegian fighters, including Far. But now the prisoners had been let go, and the prisons were closed. At least for the time being.

Far had joined them at the farm before they returned to Oslo, and Rebekka was thrilled to have him come back safely.

She was overjoyed when told they were going home. Everyone had said their goodbyes and promised to keep in touch. Once they were in the car, there was a noticeable silence. They were glad to return to where they belonged, yet uneasy as to what awaited them.

They looked forward to being reunited with friends and relatives, living in their own apartment, sleeping in their own beds. Beyond that, they knew that much had changed.

When they finally reached the apartment, it felt strange. Rebekka was the first to notice it. "Mor, what happened to our big radio in the kitchen? The one that's always on. Did someone steal it? Was anyone here?"

Mor didn't answer, but kept on walking from room to room. Was she looking for other missing things? Far came in behind Rebekka and stopped.

"We were going to tell you but the timing wasn't right. Sorry. In the middle of May the Norwegian Police, now working for the Gestapo, passed a law that all radios belonging to Jews should be confiscated. I suspected that they would come here despite our being away. Most probably the janitor let them in. Damn, this is disgusting." He was furious.

Rebekka didn't bring it up again. She knew better. Far's mood didn't improve. He stood in the living room talking to himself. "And tomorrow I have to deal with a business in which I haven't put a foot in for three months. Heaven only knows what is left of it. I wonder how the 'personnel' of four ladies has managed. I have no idea what's waiting for me or where to start looking for new merchandise. Most of what was in the store had been sold and nothing has been replaced. The entire business will need to be rebuilt with new inventory from new sources, if I can even find some. I've been told that it's getting increasingly difficult."

He didn't mention the present political situation in Oslo with his family, which obviously must have been on his mind as well. Rebekka could see from his expression that he was quite agitated.

Mor was not much better. She worried about everything and everybody. She also kept talking to herself.

"I haven't seen my mother or any of my sisters and brothers since early April. I am also concerned about where I can get food to feed my family. It appears to be even harder in the city than in the country, where bartering food was much more common."

Ruth said nothing at all. She hadn't heard from her boyfriend for a long time, and she was concerned.

It was a rather sad family that went to bed that night, despite being back in their own house.

Kari had returned to town as well and she came knocking on the door the next morning. Ingrid was thrilled to see her best friend. "Kari, I have missed you terribly. I had no one to talk to." They exchanged experiences and realized that they had spent the two and a half months in a rather similar way. New schools, new kids, another dialect, which was hard to figure out initially. The two friends had plenty to discuss and made plans for the rest of the summer, which still remained, although they realized that July and August would pass by all too quickly. Before they knew it, it would be time to go back to school.

More news and changes awaited them. The leftover days of June and the month of July had gone by quickly. They were ready to start the upper school, which was scheduled to start on August 25, but only a few days later a change in plans had been proclaimed! Notices were sent to all parents announcing that the starting date had been postponed three weeks until September 21. Supposedly, there was a shortage of utilities, as well as books and equipment. The most serious problem was the big turnover of teachers, who the Nazis claimed had left town or suddenly retired.

Rebekka reacted violently to the news—speaking out loud to anyone she could see. Far had just returned home and responded to her strong reaction.

"They are not telling the truth. They are giving all kinds of fake explanations. I have heard through a friend whose father has been reading one of the illegal papers that their main reason is something very different. A good number of teachers are refusing to teach the new curriculum which is being forced on them. It's full of propaganda about Germany and criticism of the content in the old books. Some of the teachers have quit, and the rest of them are being threatened with termination unless they adapt. Two teachers have already been arrested because they exhibited an angry reaction. Apparently this situation is the same all over the country."

"That's the real reason why the opening is delayed and can only meet three times per week, four hours per day. Many students have had to move from school to school each week. But the proclamation states that this is due to lack of staff, books and utilities at the local educational institutions. Far, what can we do?"

Rebekka's voice expressed anger while speaking.

Far listened carefully, but had no answer, and it was clear that he had additional problems on his mind. "I'll do the best I can to get some information, but I doubt it will do any good. Your job is to get ready for the official opening day and work hard. Be ready." And this time, he walked away without any further comments.

Rebekka got her hands on some used books in one of the local bookstores. Kari inherited her older sister's books, and, by luck, a friend of the sister wanted to sell three of her used books as well, which Rebekka bought.

Rebekka and Kari were among the close to one hundred students starting at their class level. Chaos and confusion prevailed. Some of the classrooms didn't even have enough desks to accommodate the overflow of students, many of whom had been transferred from another school district. And this was the school that she had looked forward to ever since she was six years old, Rebekka thought to herself.

In addition she had her own shortage. She needed clothes, mostly shoes.

One morning in late October, Rebekka was struggling to get ready for school, trying to ignore the morning darkness. The cold and gusty weather was not helping. The days were getting shorter and it felt as if the wind would never let up. She shivered while brushing her teeth, looking in the mirror. The darkness at sunset was even worse, as the new laws enforced covering all the windows with blinds that had to be kept closed, making it even darker. If her downcast feelings were solely a function of changes in the weather, well, that would have been a separate issue. That she could deal with, knowing that eventually the weather would change. But it was more serious than that. Everything had changed, not only the weather and light.

Under ordinary circumstances, this new school would have made her very happy, providing more of an intellectual challenge. German and French classes had been offered the previous year, but were now temporarily cancelled. Math was more complicated, but didn't scare her. Boys and girls were in the same classrooms, a new experience. However, the routine was helter-skelter and teachers and substitutes varied from week to week. Occasionally students from another school would attend who had prepared different homework.

Later that same afternoon, Mor asked her to go over to Frank's house to look at a pair of boots which most probably would fit her. They were "almost" new. Rebekka wasn't thrilled but agreed to go.

Frank, normally a daily guest at her house, had stayed away for the first few weeks after they returned from the mountains. Rebekka wondered if he was afraid or embarrassed, worried there would be repercussions after the potentially serious accident involving Miriam. Her parents, however, never brought it up. She was not comfortable mentioning it either, finding the entire episode fairly confusing.

She felt nervous as she approached his house, wondering if he would be there, and if so, how he would react. His mother had told her how busy he was with some kind of political group, studying history. She also heard that he read a lot, hoping to excel in this section, which consisted of a number of older members as well.

Entering the house she found herself half wishing Frank would be out. Hopefully he is at one of his intellectual and selective gatherings, she thought. Sometimes she really liked being with him, and sometimes she found him a little overwhelming.

His mother greeted her warmly as usual, and had even baked a small batch of cookies. "An old schoolmate from the country made a surprise visit and brought me a pound of butter and a bag of flour, and I remember how much you used to enjoy these cookies. Please bring some home for Miriam and Ruth as well."

Rebekka had almost forgotten how good her aunt's cookies were, now that the ingredients were just about impossible to get a hold of. She tried on the boots sitting on the floor. They fit well, and she was relieved they didn't look too bad at all. She gave her aunt a hug and made a mention of how surprised she was that they looked so nice.

The moment she said it, she felt terrible. War in Norway and a shortage of food and clothing, and she was worried how the boots looked? She knew she was blushing. "What I meant was . . . ," she started, but her aunt just smiled and told her not to worry.

After a while, Frank appeared. As usual, he hastened to report details of all the activities he was involved with. He didn't mention the unfortunate episode with the horse and buggy on May 17th. Little by little their conversation almost became relaxed, like before. However, he was speaking faster than usual. While listening to him, Rebekka noticed he was biting his nails again after having stopped for a while. She wondered why he was looking everywhere else in the room, but not at her directly.

He seems nervous being with me, she thought, beginning to feel badly for him. She decided to look at him directly and try to put him at ease.

"I've missed you. Where have you been all this time? Miriam is constantly talking and she is getting harder and harder to stop, which I guess is normal for a two year old. We think she's left-handed, by the way!"

Frank's face lit up and she could feel him relax. For a little while he said nothing. Then he asked her a few questions about her new school, what she was studying, and then he burst out, "How is your friend Kari?"

"She's fine, and we see each other all the time. I missed her a lot while we were in the mountains. Why don't you stop by one day to see her yourself?"

Was it her imagination, or did Frank's face turn red? Suddenly he exclaimed, "Did you tell Kari about the, eh, incident with the horse and buggy?"

"Why would I?" she said, and saw that he calmed down.

A few minutes later she was ready to leave. She grabbed the new boots, thanking her aunt again. True to his character, Frank grabbed her arm as she reached the door, indicating that he had a "trump card" to share with her, just like he used to do a few months ago.

She recognized the familiar expression on his face. He had acted as the self-appointed expert on everything, and it was clear he had some news to spring on her. She decided not to get involved in another one of his stories, and excused herself, saying she had to go home. He tried to make her stay. "I have heard that your Uncle Leonard is being watched by the police. They think he is involved in the 'underground.'" She looked at Frank for a moment, trying to understand what he meant, but he said nothing more. "I need to go," she uttered and walked out.

Walking home, she had a hard time dismissing Frank and his comments. Was he intentionally trying to scare her? Or was her favorite uncle really in some sort of danger?

She recalled that her mother had asked her to stop by the fish store to look for fresh carrots and possibly some fish stock. She had almost forgotten. She hurried in the direction of the fish market and grabbed the door handle.

She was inside the door when she was practically knocked over by a young man, roughly two years her senior. She had turned thirteen few months earlier. He was wearing a navy knit hat, pulled all the way down over his ears. He looked angry, as if he resented her coming into the store before he had a chance to get out. He pushed her aside with his shoulder as if he intended to hurt her. She stared at him. She remembered him from school, before he graduated a couple of years earlier. She remembered his bad acne. She had wondered if that was why he always looked so angry and unfriendly, because his expression was always the same. He hadn't changed. Now he made her feel as if he didn't like her, although she didn't even know him! It was creepy, she thought, his being so rude. Once he had left the store, she forgot about him. She got her items and hurried home.

The next morning she thought back to the dialogue with Frank which still bothered her. She kept replaying it in her mind. Rebekka finished her morning routine, getting ready for school, which included putting on the new-old boots. Despite the comfortable fit the same feeling of ambiguity remained. She was sick of feeling low and angry. She was ashamed of the old hand-me-downs she was expected to wear. Rebekka was also angry with herself, recognizing that she was behaving like a spoiled brat. Her country was at war. Thousands of people were starving. Families were separated; children were missing their fathers who were fighting at the front, many of them never to return.

The stores had less and less food to offer. Chocolate was a thing of the past. Meat was a rarity. It was fish, fish and more fish. Long lines were forming outside each store. Much too often the people at the end of the line never even made it inside. Her family was lucky, as their friends and hosts from the mountains kept sending them packages whenever they slaughtered one of the cows.

Why does everyone keep saying the war will soon be over, she thought. It's almost November, and it seems to me that things are just getting worse.

Gulping down some cereal and milk in the kitchen, she shouted to Mor, "I am late for school. Have to hurry. Yes, I am wearing the new boots. Yes, they do fit." She really was in a hurry and needed to leave. Ruth was dressing Miriam in the bedroom, and Mor was on the phone.

"Don't forget to take your cod liver oil!" Mor shouted from the living room, but Rebekka ignored her. She hated the slimy, tasteless oil which every Norwegian child had been instructed to take. The idea was that it contained vitamin D, which would provide strength to growing bones and compensate for the severe shortage of food. Quickly she slipped out the door, getting into the elevator and pulling her red knit hat down around her face.

Wearing a traditional red knit hat with a tassel had become a new fad, which rapidly spread all over the country. It was the topic of conversation everywhere. The red knit hat had become an implicit token of being a *"joessing,"* a Norwegian patriot. She had also been alerted that very soon the Germans would come to realize that this innocent red hat was a symbol of the resistance.

The appearance of more and more people of all ages donning this specific hat would no doubt alert the invaders that it served a specific purpose, beyond keeping the inhabitants' ears warm! She felt better and giggled a little to herself. It did feel good to be on the red hat team.

Deep in thought, she almost collided with a neighbor when he entered on the next floor. Her eyes immediately landed on his minute paper clip, proudly displayed on his lapel. She had heard that this was another way of showing allegiance. A paper clip in this position worn as a decoration was a similar innovation to inspire camaraderie and togetherness. I wouldn't even have noticed the paper clip if I hadn't been familiar with the symbolism, she thought, smiling broadly to the neighbor from the third floor, half whispering, half saying, "Good morning."

By the time Rebekka reached Kari, she felt much, much better. Her friend's expression of admiration was evident as she noticed the old 'new' hat. Her face lit up. "I went through all our drawers and boxes containing winter clothes, looking for a hat like that. Mother said that she would rip up an old red sweater and knit one for me today."

Rebekka looked at her friend closely. She felt strangely affected and inspired. Kari's eyes had attained a bluish tint. Her cheeks were red, and she seemed short of breath. She looked like someone who had experienced something exhilarating—as if she had been given a gift of some kind. Rebekka kept staring at her. Kari's level of enthusiasm at that moment was high, but for what reason?

Is this what they called having the morale boosted? Was the promise of a newly red knit cap enough to make her friend feel empowered? Did she feel like she was doing something important, or at least worthwhile?

Kari walked in the direction of school and Rebekka had a hard time keeping up with her. Kari's gait was faster than usual, and her body moved as if generated by a machine. Rebekka understood. They had both become empowered. She had been encouraged by the red knit hat, having recognized the neighbor's independent message about allegiance. Kari was excited about her mother offering to knit a hat just for her which she could use to encourage and inspire other patriots. If this intoxication could be spread around the country, it might help everyone, she thought. Eventually it might even reach the people who were suffering in cold houses and get adequate food. The people who had been separated from their friends and relatives might feel stronger while fighting for freedom. How? A feeling of solidarity and fellowship with a responsibility towards helping others might go a long way getting their country back.

She wanted to help distribute this feeling of togetherness. She involuntarily touched her own red knit cap, feeling strength might be transmitted to her with a mere touch.

As they continued their walk to school, Rebekka remained quiet. A snapshot had suddenly appeared in her mind bringing back the conversation with her father while in the mountains, before he joined the initial resistance fighters.

Rebekka recalled how her father had explained the importance of his joining his friends from the military service days. At the time, it had been hard for her to understand why he would volunteer, without being forced to. She had also wondered why he seemed almost excited about it, rather than being frightened. Unexpectedly she was able to put herself in Far's position, fully grasping what had prompted him. Was this loyalty? Had it been boosted by his friends? Or was it something even stronger, which she hadn't yet fully understood? Now that he was back in Oslo with her and the rest of the family, unharmed, she was overwhelmed with pride and admiration. Yes, now she did understand what he was trying to convey to her at the time. Was this maturity on her part or was it something else, something that was related to allegiance and love of their country? Or was it a combination of both?

Far returned home every day adhering to his daily routine. However, life was now more complicated, even though he was no longer engaged in battle. He had to try to make ends meet by looking for new merchandise, even though the quality of the items differed considerably from earlier. She heard him mumble to her mother. "I heard today that Jewish lawyers have been forbidden from practicing law. I just cannot figure out what they want from us?" He stopped for a minute and left the room, not waiting for an answer.

Life was to change once again, proving that nothing ever remained the same. On a cold and dark evening at the beginning of November, Far returned from the store. Contrary to his usual calm and positive attitude, it was clear that something bothered him. He immediately entered his office and closed the door, without speaking to anyone. He remained there until the group of usual resistance men arrived around 8 pm. At that point Far reemerged to greet them politely, although the expression on his face made it clear that something serious had taken place. He spoke in a subdued voice. Mor knocked on the door, which was also unusual. The door opened quickly, and she disappeared into the small sanctuary as well. After a few minutes, she reappeared moving quietly. She put dinner on the table, but refrained from speaking to Rebekka or Ruth. Miriam was already in bed for the evening.

Ruth watched her carefully, mindful that something bad had taken place. Rebekka overheard Mor speaking to Ruth in a subdued voice, "No, we have no more news. My husband is trying to have it confirmed. Three of the Haakons contacted him today informing him that it took place around three o'clock this afternoon."

Rebekka knew something serious was being discussed. She didn't react to the mention of the "three Haakons." Haakon was the name of the king of Norway, and the resistance men all used this name as a general alias. No one was to know their real names. In the event one or two were arrested, they couldn't be forced to pass on names of people involved to the enemy. I wonder if that has already taken place, she thought. She turned to Ruth, asking, "Do you know what has happened? Everyone seems very serious." But Ruth only turned her back giving the impression she hadn't heard.

Rebekka was about to find out. Around 9 pm the doorbell rang fiercely and incessantly. By chance she was standing next to the entrance door which she opened. One of the regulars, a man a little older than most of the others, was waiting outside but this time he didn't even say hello. "Where is your father?" was all he said.

Far came out of the office, staring at the man. He said nothing, just stood still and waited. The man looked at him with a pained expression. "I have the confirmation." His voice was almost impossible to hear, as if this message was difficult and traumatic. His voice shook, and perspiration ran down his forehead. "My son was there in person because he had an appointment with the doctor."

Rebekka's pulse quickened. The only doctor he could have been referring to was Uncle Leonard. Something was wrong, she thought, very wrong.

"He was examining a patient, when two soldiers threw the door open abruptly, my son told me. The two Nazis ignored the receptionist, stormed into the examination room, and announced the purpose of their visit. 'We are looking for Leonard Davidson. You are to be brought to Victoria Terrace, which is the Gestapo headquarters.'"

Her uncle was much too familiar with this place to waste any comments on these two soldiers, Rebekka thought to herself.

The visitor continued, "The doctor was in the examining room, remaining totally calm, realizing fully well what they wanted. He kept his composure throughout the entire confrontation. His only comment prior to leaving with the two Nazis was to ask, 'May I reassure my patient that his medical complaints don't represent any danger to his life. The right type of medication can ameliorate his problem. May I suggest that he contact Dr. Engebretsen?'

"The patient finally dared to move and get dressed, having remained frozen and with fear on the examination table.

"After that, Leonard removed his white lab coat, put on his jacket and overcoat and followed the two men arresting him."

Far said nothing after the visitor finished the report. It seemed as if all his strength had left him. His face had turned gray. Rebekka was behind him. She could see him but wasn't sure if he realized she was there. She was leaning against a small, decorative table, afraid she might faint or fall. Her stomach was doing summersaults and she found it hard to stand. He has been arrested, she seemed to hear her brain telling her. Just like the people Frank had talked about in the mountains. So this time Frank wasn't trying to impress her without knowing the facts. He *had* heard some threatening news and this time he was right. The image of the two men forcing their way into her uncle's office, announcing that he was being brought to the Gestapo headquarters, kept replaying in her mind. She could essentially see him taking off his lab coat. She had difficulty breathing.

A voice inside her head kept trying to get her attention. There you go, Rebekka. You have been complaining that the adults never told you anything, and how much this annoyed you. Well, that's over. From now on you will probably hear much more than you want, and it's not going to be good.

Chapter Eight

Grandmother's Story

The meeting between Ingrid and the renowned piano teacher turned out to be awkward and at the same time highly successful. Both reached independent conclusions within the span of a few minutes. The prominent musician, despite having agreed to give the young girl from Aalesund an audition, was formal, even borderline arrogant. The parents were sitting quietly in the back of the room.

"So you are the 'Wunderkind' from Aalesund whom I am supposed to hear. I will certainly listen to you play. I promised my friend, Maestro Weisman, to evaluate your skills. I owe him a favor. I also must tell you that the competition here is fierce. You have no idea how many youngsters come here hoping to be appointed the next prodigy and march directly into the Academy of Music. I have forgotten what you have chosen to play. Please tell me again so that we can get started. I will give you maximum 15 minutes."

Ingrid's hands started to sweat. This was not what she had expected. She knew that he would be strict and demanding, but . . . he really expected her to fail. She gave him the name of the piece that she had rehearsed for the past two months. And she was prepared. At least she felt she was yesterday. Her heart was beating fast. A voice in her head interrupted her thoughts. Go ahead, Ingrid. You know you can do it. Do your best and ignore this person who has never heard you play. She moved around on the seat making herself comfortable and waited for the Maestro to finish his own recitation, which consisted of explaining why he was in Oslo.

"I am really from Berlin where I have spent my entire professional life. It's the center of music in Europe, in case you didn't know. Frankly, I consider Oslo almost uncivilized, compared to where I grew up. Why am I here? Well, it's because of Mr. Hitler who is trying to change Europe. As soon as he comes to his senses, and allows Berlin to return to normal, I will return."

However, after about 15 minutes of listening to Ingrid play, the atmosphere in the dreary room, which held nothing but a grand piano, quickly changed.

Ingrid had finished. While playing she had forgotten where she was or who was listening. She was in charge of the piano, the music and her own skills. The environment made her feel as if she was in the middle of a fairytale, or perhaps even an operetta. She focused only on the music that poured out of her hands and brain.

The maestro got up from his chair, walked around the room, wringing his hands, saying nothing for a couple of minutes. The parents observing this exaggerated farce-like scene were getting uncomfortable, not knowing what to anticipate.

Finally the maestro spoke. "Aber Mensch," he exclaimed in German. He had a tendency to fall back on his native language when emotional. "Why didn't anyone tell me that the girl has real talent?" He directed this question to the parents with an almost offended manner. He ignored the fact that a number of people had tried to tell him exactly that, but he had refused to listen.

When the maestro calmed down, he approached the parents quietly, ignoring the pianist. "Your daughter has an enormous gift for music." He turned to Ingrid, using a very different tone of voice. "Have you ever thought about making music your life—making a career of playing the piano?"

Instead of being intimidated and embarrassed, much to her parents' surprise, Ingrid paused for a second, replying in a strong voice, "Music is *already* my life. My biggest fantasy since I was a small child was to make it my career."

A long-distance phone conversation was arranged between Ms. Loevberg and the Maestro. She was formal and professional as expected and the Maestro was likewise, without failing to describe his credentials and superior experience in Germany. They reached a satisfactory agreement. Ingrid would have classes with the Maestro once each month, and Miss Loevberg would supervise her practice in between.

The maestro still had to have the last word.

"You must continue with Miss Loevberg until you are through with your formal schooling in Aalesund, or whatever the little town is called, in June of 1942, roughly 18 months away. I, and only I, will assign the pieces that you should work on. You must be diligent." When he used the word diligent, it was clear he also considered himself a master of the Norwegian language.

He pronounced the word like it had several e's and i's. "The plan will be to apply to the Academy of Music in Oslo and focus on your future as a pianist. But you have a lot of work to do first."

Her father, Isak, was an outgoing person by nature with a great sense of humor. When he retold this story to others, he would embellish the details. He described the maestro as not only emphasizing the long physical distance between Berlin and Aalesund, but also highlighted the cultural contrast between the two areas.

When they left they thanked the Maestro profusely for his time and for evaluating Ingrid and inspiring her at the same time. No sooner had they reached the street, Isak turned to his wife and the new star, as he thought of her, expressing himself and said in a strong, happy voice, "Let's go buy a piano!"

Ingrid and Leyla stared at him and Leyla said, "Why? We have one already. Is there anything wrong with it?"

The wife and daughter hadn't seen this spark in his eyes for a very long time. His smile got even larger, if possible.

"Just follow me. There is a reputable piano store just a few blocks away. They are expecting us. I was hoping that your playing would impress the professor of Music, but I wasn't sure. I had heard that he had extremely high standards. So I was nervous. If all goes well, you will graduate in June of 1942, and as we all have dreamed about, you will attend the Academy of Music in Oslo. You have demonstrated that you are serious about your future and choice of career and have committed yourself to reaching your goal. The small upright piano at home will prove inadequate if you are to grow as a professional musician." The smile never left his face when he declared this plan.

"This type of piano is expensive. Besides, it's heavy and large. It would be quite costly to ship the piano all the way to Aalesund for this brief period of time—less than two years and then back to Oslo when you move. In addition, shipping a piano might cause damage. The owner of the store from which we may buy the piano, offered to keep it safe for the duration, until Ingrid would move to Oslo.

"I have heard that Bestemor has asked if you would stay with her here in Oslo when you are ready. Well, my ladies, what do you think of my idea?"

Ingrid couldn't help herself. She threw her arms around her father and shouted out loud, "You are the smartest and best father in the world. I promise I will practice and practice and make you proud!" She turned to her mother to get her reaction. Leyla was smiling as well.

Once they completed the piano transaction they remained in a happy mood and headed for the Davidson house where Uncle Martin's family lived. Several members of the Davidson family had already gathered. Ingrid's fifteen-year-old cousin, Rebekka, who was known for always carrying around her sketchbook, had changed quite a bit, and was showing signs of becoming an independent adolescent. Still fairly quiet, she now appeared to be reserved rather than shy. She seemed to pay careful attention to the general conversation, nodding occasionally, but didn't speak much. Ingrid felt like Rebekka was studying the adults' faces while listening, as if trying to memorizing their conversations by heart.

Rebekka was seated next to Ingrid's brother, Harald, who would turn sixteen in a few months. Ingrid was suddenly struck by the similarity between the two. It wasn't a physical resemblance, but they appeared to be equally observant. It seemed that they were trying to remain outside the conversation, more as observers than participants. It felt as if they had created a barrier between the rest of the relatives and the two of them. The other guests talked about the disquieting school situations, about the teachers who had escaped to the country because of the occupation, and other incidents that had upset the educational process.

Bestemor sat quietly, listening. She had always been reticent by nature, and was comfortable in that disposition. She was short, with dark deep-set eyes, framed by dark shadows on her eyelids and below her eyes. Her four sons had inherited this feature, as had Ingrid's mother. Bestemor had an affinity for navy or black dresses, which she always wore, adorned by a small white lace collar. The family was so accustomed to this that they barely noticed it anymore.

However, Bestemor was unusually quiet that night, even considering her normal demeanor, of refraining from speaking unnecessarily. Bestemor was born in Germany but had grown up in Sweden, a classic example of how Eastern European Jews had moved around during the nineteenth century. The story, which her children's generation told, and which probably was accurate, was that her husband, their grandfather, had swept her off her feet as a very young woman. Ingrid looked at her, trying to picture her as a young girl in Sweden and a young bride coming to Oslo. The story of how she fell in love with Bestefar had been told and retold. Ingrid used to love hearing it when she was a little girl, and on occasion still thought about it.

Grandfather Leib Davidson, known as Bestefar, was an admirer of the beloved Norwegian poet, Henrik Wergeland. The poet had worked persistently for many years, trying to repeal the article of the Norwegian constitution which prohibited Jews from entering. He was the author of two beautiful poems, named "The Jew" and "The Jewess," which had been read by most Norwegians. Wergeland passed away in 1848 and never saw his passion and mission in life come to fruition in 1852. He was considered the great hero and protector of the Jews. Bestefar Leib, was born in Russia and symbolized the story of a foreign-born Jew who chose to settle in a newly "opened" country looking for a place to escape ethnic persecution. Bestefar arrived 16 years after the law was changed.

In 1878 Bestefar initially settled in the North for several years. This was an undeveloped area in Norway, and he started from the bottom with a small business of his own, providing merchandise to people who needed what he had to sell. The family legend continued, stating that despite how hard he had to work to make a living, his priority was to learn to speak Norwegian immediately, spending every possible Krone for this purpose. He was successful and became a Norwegian citizen in 1892, one of the first Jewish settlers. Time had come to find a wife and settle down, having lived by himself since he arrived in Norway, a country of new frontiers.

In Gothenburg, Sweden, known for its active orthodox Jewish community, he was introduced to a young but shy lady by the name of Henriette. It was love at first sight, at least on his side. He found her lovely, bright and sensitive. She was protected by four older brothers who eventually found the stranger from Norway to be an acceptable candidate for marriage, despite the fact that it involved moving to yet another country.

Throughout the years Bestefar's children and grandchildren would encourage him to tell this story as often as possible. When he passed away, members of the next generation asked Bestemor to continue telling the story.

That January evening at dinner she was resisting, saying that she was tired and out of sorts. However, the entire family insisted and finally she gave in. Her voice was a little monotonous initially, and she was clearly preoccupied. Nevertheless, she warmed up when she saw the faces of her children and grandchildren listening intently.

"You have no idea how nervous and torn I was when I waited for the daily train from Oslo. Bestefar, the unknown man who had settled in Norway, had announced to my father that he would like to make an official visit to the family."

She smiled. "It was clear that he was going to ask for my hand in marriage. My parents were pleased, but my four brothers were still skeptical, as they knew nothing about him. I wasn't sure. I was only 20 years old and, frankly, a little scared. We had moved twice since I was a little girl and I felt that finally I had found a country where I belonged. Gothenburg was a big city, and I had a number of friends in the Jewish community.

"I was uncertain whether I should risk moving to the Land of the Midnight Sun with the exceptionally cold climate, high mountains and very few Jews. What if he wasn't as nice as he seemed? I didn't know much about him, and what little he had told my father and brothers didn't really register in my mind. I never had a chance to think. My parents had said that they wouldn't force me, but what if they changed their minds? He had announced he was coming to visit me again. I knew I had to make up my mind, or possibly risk disappointing my parents and brothers. After the first meeting he wrote that he was coming to town, and I knew why.

"I was trying to be brave. I told my parents that I wanted to meet him at the train alone. I wanted to speak with him directly, without my brothers interrupting and my parents supervising. They objected, but I told them that if I was going to move and live in another country, I needed to get to know a future husband before I said yes. They reluctantly gave in.

"I don't even know how I got to the railroad station, but I know I got there early. I became increasingly nervous. What was I doing there, meeting a stranger? Finally the train arrived. He was the first one to jump off the train, wearing an elegant suit and a straw hat. He ran towards me, handing me a bouquet of lily of the valleys, which he had been holding during the entire trip from Oslo. He was polite and well spoken, and more charming than I had realized when he came to the house the first time, attempting to win over my father and my four skeptical brothers. I was spellbound. The rest is history. I learned then that he had been one of the first Jewish settlers in Norway. And now look, there are close to two thousand Jews altogether!"

On occasion, she would expand on the story. "He was such a modest man. He was heavily involved with establishing a formal Jewish Congregation in Oslo. This finally came about in 1891, and Leib was naturally invited to sign the original charter in the capital. It turned out the signing was scheduled for the date when Leib was going to Gothenburg, Sweden to marry me. He had the choice to choose between passing up being one of the original signers of the document, or asking his father-in-law to postpone the wedding. He had no difficulty making the decision, and took off for Sweden in plenty of time for the nuptials. He would always tease me and reassure me that the decision was the best one he had ever made."

Grandmother smiled like a young girl when she told the romantic story. "Of course, I agreed! Imagine if he had postponed the wedding! My brothers wouldn't have allowed him to marry me at all!"

Theirs had been a happy marriage, which lasted close to 65 years, and they raised nine children, four boys and five girls. One of the young girls died during the influenza epidemic in 1918. Leib Davidson died in 1933.

Ingrid continued to look around the room. For some unknown reason, today she felt estranged by her Oslo relatives. The conversation seemed muted, almost forced. She was glad that Uncle Martin, Rebekka's father, had encouraged Bestemor to tell her story, because most of the adults focused on discussing issues related to the changes in Norway and potential problems for the Jews.

The only person who talked nonstop, if one could call a toddler a person, she thought, was her little cousin Miriam. Ingrid calculated she must be around two and a half years old, having her personality already clearly established, speaking loudly and rapidly and in constant motion, to everyone's amusement. Sitting on a high chair she threw all her utensils on the floor, one by one.

"Is she left handed?" Ingrid exclaimed. She had never come across a left-handed person in her family. The uncle responded with a big smile, "And how! She refuses to use her right hand if she can use her left! I don't know where it comes from. No one else we know has this characteristic."

Ingrid's face turned red, and she exclaimed, "I am left-handed!" For now that was as far as the similarity would go. Perhaps this new little cousin would also have dark, curly hair, just like her cousin from Aalesund, she thought.

Ingrid turned to her brother to see if he had heard. It was a joke in her family that she preferred to use her left hand. However, her brother was busy. He was engaged in a deep conversation with Rebekka, giving the impression they were old friends. The two cousins were talking as if they were alone in the room. Her brother was staring at a sketchbook, which he was trying to conceal under the table. Her younger cousin was turning the pages while expanding on the content.

To Ingrid's relief, the meal was nearing the end. Frankly, this family gathering hadn't been what she had expected, in view of the happy events earlier that day.

Something was off, she felt. She saw tears running down her grandmother's face, and Uncle Martin went over to put his arm around her. He whispered something in her ear, which Ingrid failed to hear, but her uncle had a gentle expression on his face. All she heard was, "Please don't worry, they will let him go once they have questioned him and found there is no reason to hold him. This has happened time and time again."

Suddenly it struck her. Of course. The Gestapo had arrested her uncle. That was the cause of the subdued atmosphere at dinner. The unexplainable pain in her stomach seemed stronger and more intense. The rumors from Eastern Europe—the target was Jews. What did it mean? It meant that the persecution of Jews had reached her world and family.

Chapter Nine

Icy Spots

OSLO, FEBRUARY 28, 1942

The sun was bright. The heavy snow made the pine trees bend to the ground, greeting the skiers on the trails. It was a perfect Sunday in the middle of January. Correction. It smelled, felt and looked like a perfect day. Of course it wasn't. No day was perfect anymore.

Rebekka was the first to reach the top of the hill. She stopped and turned, waiting for Kari and Frank to catch up. They were not far behind. She stretched her arms and legs, which felt good.

"It's hard to believe we're at war," Frank said, as he and Kari caught up with her, "when you see nature looking so incredibly beautiful." He paused. He then turned quickly to Kari, implying that his statement was directed specifically at her. Kari blushed, making her entire face turn an even darker shade of red than already evident from the cold weather and strenuous exercise. She tightened her hands around her ski poles, pretending she hadn't heard.

The chemistry between the two was quite obvious to Rebekka. It was also clear that neither of them wanted her to notice. Rebekka sighed. Frank was always the flirt; using any opportunity to let Kari know how much he really liked her.

The wind cooled her skin, reminding her that her body heat was from exercise and not from the sun despite its strength. It was time to get back on the trail, ending the brief pause and the few seconds of rumination. Rebekka's body responded immediately as she grabbed her ski poles, making her feel like a finely-tuned machine. Every muscle worked, allowing her to move forward with even strokes. Perspiration ran down her forehead, and her nose was dripping. She smiled to herself and kept moving.

Gradually the wind increased, which was an alert that it was time to consider returning home. They had been on the trails for the past three hours, going up and down across existing tracks. Most of the snow-covered surface was packed, yet occasionally the skiers would come across random pieces of ice, hidden by nocturnal snowflakes, or where the snow had been shifted by the wind.

In her mind she could hear Far's voice repeating the same message since she was a small child. "Always watch out for icy spots, the enemy of the snow."

However, Rebekka was getting a little annoyed, having to manipulate the trail by herself again. It's just like Frank to monopolize every special moment, she thought. He had invited himself when he heard the two girls had made plans. She knew that Kari admired his unusual mannerisms, and that was probably why he tried so hard to play the "big charmer."

It annoyed her much more than was warranted. She realized her mood had changed altogether. Why, she asked herself? Suddenly she was about to start crying, and she had no idea why. She tried to reverse this sudden mood change by looking into the wind. Ice may be the only enemy to watch for when dealing with snow, she thought to herself, but unfortunately enemies were not limited to snow. Living in the shadow of an enemy had become a daily routine. The more time passed, the worse it got. Gradual yet steady arrests of Jewish men, closing of Jewish-owned businesses, confiscation of radios, acute shortage of food and clothing, more bombing and fighting. Many brave young men fighting for their country were lost, regardless of their religion!

It wasn't Frank she was angry with, although he was annoying. His giggling was beginning to irritate her. The day had started in such a wonderful way, but it was strange how the word *enemy* kept popping up in her head, taking control of her thoughts. First on her mind was always her uncle Leonard, making her wonder how he was being treated in prison or wherever he was being kept.

She turned to Frank before she had even thought about the ramification of her words and heard herself say, "Why do you always make a joke out of everything? Are you afraid to allow the conversation to touch on anything serious? Have you entered into a pact with yourself to only bring up pleasant events? Have you considered placing everything sad and scary in your pocket and closing it with a zipper? You didn't use to be like that. Just after the invasion the only thing that you wanted to discuss was war and tragedy."

Her sudden, angry outburst got through to Frank who stopped and stared at her. "Rebekka, what's going on?"

She kept moving on the flat trail, but she no longer had the energy to force her body to work hard.

"I keep thinking about my uncle. More than a year has passed, and not a word. No communication whatsoever. Far has been in touch with an active spy system claiming Leonard spent several months at Grini prison outside Oslo, an awful place. Afterwards he was sent to Northern Norway.

She stopped and felt a shiver run through her body.

She needed to say what had bothered her the past few weeks or rather months. And she was afraid to bring it up. But now she had. She felt that the time had come.

"Tell me, Frank. I am sure you and your parents must experience the same. Don't you get up every morning and wonder if today is the day when we have to make a decision about escaping to Sweden? Or should we wait? And what may happen if we do wait? Your parents may not talk about it to you, or even to themselves. This is how all of the Norwegian Jews are living these days. We don't know what is waiting around the corner."

"And there is much more . . . ", she whispered reluctantly.

Frank didn't answer. For once. Kari appeared close to tears.

"Stop Bekka, please listen," Frank said, catching up with her. "I purposely don't bring up the war to you, or anyone else for that matter. I'm just too scared. If I allow myself to worry as much as I should, I'll probably fall apart. I've wanted to bring up your uncle's name many times, but I was afraid you'd get angry."

Rebekka stared at him, not knowing what to say. Kari joined them and asked gently, "Rebekka, do you know what happened to his fiancé?"

"As for Synnoeve, I have heard rumors that she is in hiding trying to avoid being arrested. Far has decided not to look for her, for her own safety." Rebekka paused, looking into space. "We all hope she got away. These days, the less you know, the better off you are."

The temperature was dropping quickly. It was close to 4pm, time to hurry before darkness set in. Frank and Kari both gave her a hug. Being able to express some of her fear and apprehension had made her feel a little better, and she no longer felt isolated and helpless. The three moved quickly along the trail, reaching the official end of the particular slope, winding up near the train which would bring them back to the city proper.

The routine at the train station was always the same. Once the skiers had removed their skis, each pair was placed on the metal tracks outside the train. The poles could be brought inside. The compartment was full of passengers. People of all ages had taken advantage of the gorgeous Sunday weather and snow.

There were no seats available, forcing them to stand, supporting themselves by holding on to the straps dangling from the roof of the train. The air emitted a unique odor that Rebekka always associated with the end-of-day skiing. She recognized it as kneaded leather, resulting from hours of straining to hold on to the straps on the poles. The mixture of perspiration oozing from the skiers and their ski sweaters was unavoidable as they crammed together on the moving train.

She felt tired, especially after the verbal exchange, and she opted to remain quiet. Frank was animated and kept talking, mostly to Kari. He was joking, and she was smiling at him. The connection between them was clear to everyone around, and they did make a nice couple, Rebekka thought. Frank was tall and thin, with his mother's dark brown eyes. He had a full head of thick, dark curls, the only genetic connection he shared with his red-haired cousin. Kari's long, blond hair, together with her vibrant deep green eyes made her look like a stereotypically beautiful Norwegian young woman.

Rebekka's glance drifted around the compartment, wondering if there were any other girls around Kari's age with her exceptional coloring and looks. Her gaze fell on a young man, standing exceptionally close to Frank and Kari; closer than necessary, despite the crowd. Was he trying to overhear their conversation?

He must have been around seventeen. There was something familiar about his face and she thought she had seen him somewhere before. At the same time, she was overcome by a negative reaction, although she didn't understand why. The young man was tall with reddish brown hair, cut quite short. His face—unfortunately for him, she thought, was covered with acne. He didn't seem to know her, or at least he didn't let on, if he did. However, he was quite focused on eavesdropping on Frank and Kari.

Rebekka was mesmerized by the intensity of his staring at Kari. He never cracked a smile when Frank joked, as opposed to many of the other people in the full tramcar. Rebekka tried to ignore him, but found his closeness uncomfortable. The term "fanatic" went through her mind as she watched him, but she shrugged it off. She was probably just tired and perhaps a little jealous in general, she thought, having felt like a third wheel for most of the outing.

When they arrived at the final stop, the crowd of Sunday skiers emptied out. The three friends moved along with the rest of the large crowd, stopping only to retrieve their ski equipment from the outside of the train. Their next target was the short flight of stairs from the train platform to the street level, as the station was underground. Without warning, the intense and overly attentive young man swiftly made his way over to Kari, who was waiting her turn. Putting his head close to her, he whispered something in her ear.

Kari, taken by surprise, turned quickly to face him, and said carefully and reluctantly, "You live in the same building as my family, don't you? You live in the entrance next to ours. I may have seen you in the courtyard? I didn't hear what you said."

The intruder didn't introduce himself, nor did he confirm or deny her observation. He leaned towards Kari once more, trying to pull her closer by putting his arm around her neck. Kari moved away from his grip, as best she could in the crowd. At that point he exclaimed out loud, for everyone to hear,

"How can a beautiful girl like you hang around with two damn Jews? Don't you realize they are the reason why Europe is at war. They are going to destroy our country and they killed our Savior!" Kari stared at him in disbelief, unable to move. She looked like she had been hit and was about to start crying. The surrounding crowd stopped and watched. Frank instinctively grabbed Kari's arm as well as her skis and Rebekka grasped her other arm. The three walked quickly up the stairs, checking over their shoulders to make certain they weren't being followed.

Silence prevailed. They just kept moving, staying close to one another. Kari was crying quietly, glancing occasionally at Rebekka. The two cousins, however, refrained from talking—mostly because they were at a loss for words. The intruder was nowhere to be seen.

At the appropriate street, they split up. Frank stared at Kari for a second. It was obvious he wanted to say something but didn't know what. Being speechless must be a new experience for him, Rebekka thought, and instantly felt guilty. Frank left for home, saying good-bye in a low voice.

The two girls carried their skis over their shoulders, and walked down the half frozen, half-melted sidewalk. "Do you remember what it was like when we had street lights?" Rebekka uttered nervously, "When we didn't have to rush home to avoid being hit by a car?" Kari remained quiet, still lost in her own thoughts. Rebekka was hesitant to say anything else, so they continued in silence, side by side. When they reached their own neighborhood, Kari gave a quick nod, and hurried off to her house. For a second or so Rebekka thought about following Kari to her door to make certain she got safely inside. Hadn't she said the intruder lived in the same cluster of buildings? However, she decided against it. Her instinct told her she might do more harm than good.

Rebekka crossed the street to reach her own building. Just before she went inside, she looked back toward Kari's building. She couldn't help it. There was no sign of her friend.

It struck her. "Of course!" She realized why the offensive guy seemed familiar. She recalled the unpleasant incident in the local fish store last year. She had recognized him as having attended the same school as she did. He was the boy who bumped into her on her way into the fish store. He had pushed her when he left, deliberately trying to hurt her. Now he was wearing the uniform of the young Norwegian Nazi team, which had made it their priority to show off in groups whenever they had a chance. When she saw him almost one year ago he didn't wear a uniform.

She felt awful. The pleasure of the outing was long gone, and she doubted she would even tell her parents of the incident. They had enough on their minds. There was nothing they could do about it, anyway. She felt uncomfortable in the now damp ski clothing and couldn't wait to get inside.

As she entered the door to her own building and got into the elevator, she felt a little uneasy. Why should she react now, she wondered. The unpleasant episode at the station was behind her and she was just about home. She tried to make herself relax while waiting to reach her floor. "A premonition?" she thought, remembering her teacher discussing the meaning of this particular word. Putting the key in the door, she entered. She was about to call out to announce her arrival, but something stopped her.

The light in the narrow hallway seemed subdued and almost made it feel abandoned. Where was everyone? Her parents? Ruth? Miriam? It was unnaturally quiet. Within a few seconds, however, she heard a muffled sound emerging from the den.

Someone was crying. It was a low, yet piercing sound, as if someone was trying to suppress the emotion. Who? The she recognized the source of the weeping. It was Mor.

Rebekka froze, not knowing whether to move or stay still, whether to enter the room or not. The sobbing subsided for a moment, and she could hear Far's voice, speaking in a low, slow tempo. This by itself was unusual, as he was known for always speaking fast, actually too fast, people said. The pace of his voice made her even more concerned, and she tried to hear what had made Mor so upset.

"I know these times are difficult," Far continued. "It is understandable. However, you know as well as I do, we need to remain calm and weigh the situation. We can look at our options and decide what to do. We have a number of friends and acquaintances who will keep us informed about the present status, changes in aggression and what we can do on our own and together. Please. You have always been a levelheaded woman. Try to calm yourself down, if you can, and then we can talk about the various possibilities.

"We need each other. We need each other's support. We have two children we need to protect," he continued. Rebekka remained transfixed behind the door to the den.

Mor said, "I just don't understand. Do you think we should try to get to Sweden? I know I bother you too much with this, but I keep wondering what's next for us. The two soldiers rang the doorbell and knocked on the door, screaming and threatening. They didn't even know which one of my two brothers they wanted to arrest. As long as they could bring back two Jews, it didn't matter. Can you imagine how my mother must have felt, experiencing this at her age? How can we continue to live through this?"

Far's answer came immediately. "This is exactly what I was referring to. The Gestapo must have learned that there were two single Jewish men living there and decided to question them. They are totally paranoid and see treason in anything connected to a Jew. That's why they wanted to get him. You can call it a fishing expedition. They were not sure who was who in the house, so they took both men. But as you know, they were released the next day. That's what is important now. This is proof that the Gestapo may not even know what they are doing next. They are looking for a needle in a haystack, trying to uncover something they can blame on the Jews. Your brothers are both okay, and back home with your mother."

"And what about the forms that we're being forced to fill out? It feels like we're being marked for slaughter," Mor continued. "The Gestapo has already stamped a J for Jew on our legitimation cards."

A pause followed, while both took deep breaths. Rebekka felt increasingly uncomfortable, eavesdropping on the conversation, and needed to tell them she was there. She pushed the door open gently. Her parents looked up at her in surprise.

As soon as the mother saw her daughter, she immediately put a handkerchief to her face, wiping her eyes and turning away. Her right hand was holding on to the watch pendant.

Rebekka remained by the door, unsure what to do next. She focused on Far in his easy chair, his regular position when he was concentrating. As usual, he was in his shirtsleeves wearing suspenders. He was smoking a cigarette and leaning toward his wife.

With a quick glance at his oldest daughter, signaling for her to sit down, he continued speaking to his wife, "The order to complete this form is what we have dreaded for a long time. We knew it was coming. The Germans are known for their fastidiousness. Right now it's not clear how they will try to take advantage of these forms where one copy is designated to each individual member of the Jewish congregation. The forms may mean nothing, but we'll find out. In the meantime, we will do what they say, and not cause any havoc. That wouldn't be worth it."

"So we have to fill them out because we are Jewish, and not because we are Norwegians, is that what you are saying?" Mor, now in a more challenging voice, stared at her husband. He remained quiet. She repeated the question and added "Please answer me."

Eventually he nodded, and stood up. "Let's end this conversation, dear. There is nothing further to discuss. As soon as I hear any more, I'll let you know."

He turned to go into the living room, but not until he had taken a look at Rebekka who remained sitting in the same position, "Why don't you get out of those clothes? You must be hungry."

Mor remained immobile for another minute, and then she got up as well, turning to her daughter, "Do as your father says. Do you have any homework to do?" Her voice was now back to normal.

Chapter Ten

Cousins Connect

AALESUND, APRIL 28, 1942

Dear Rebekka,

Sorry I haven't written for so long. I can hardly remember when. I don't like writing letters—actually, I never write at all. However, since you live so far away, and as I really would like to hear how you are doing, I can't think of another way to reach you.

When my parents suggested I accompany them to Oslo a year ago, I had no particular interest in going. Well, I went along because they rather insisted, but I wasn't that enthusiastic. Now I am so glad I went with them because you must realize I have never had a cousin, or any other relative whom I feel I have something in common with. The only relative I really care for is my Uncle Leonard who is my big hero. You remind me of him, and to think he is your uncle as well makes it easier for me to write to you. Actually, I am not even sure exactly what it is I mean, but I want you to know I am so glad we have become friends.

That was the easy reason why I haven't written. But there is another reason as well. Something sad has happened. Do you remember my favorite teacher, Mr. Welhaven? I am sure you do. He is a great teacher and I have been lucky in that I have been assigned to his classes for two years. I am quite familiar with his political and intellectual positions. He doesn't say he likes Jews directly, but I feel he shows it in the way he discusses the curriculum. He expresses the need for people to be liberal and tolerant of different ethnic and religious choices in life. And yes, I know he hates the Germans.

Believe it or not, he was arrested and sent off to prison. It's incredible. The Gestapo and the Nazis who make decisions here in town claimed that he was sabotaging their plans. He kept bringing up the strength of Norway, their long history as leaders and how they had prevailed over Sweden, Denmark and other European countries for several hundred years. We all know that's true. Well, these maniacs who have decided to alter Norway's history wouldn't put up with it and sent him off. I have heard that this is taking place in a number of schools around the country. Do you know anything about it? It's so sad and I miss his voice so much. When he taught, it was always interesting assignment.

I admire my sister's skills at the piano, but I can't understand how she can sit and play for hours and hours on end. Do you know that she has been going in to Oslo for music classes once per month? How can she not get bored? She really has no other interest but music. She hangs out with a bunch of girl-friends who are not interesting. If you ask one of them about what happened in Germany that made it possible for Hitler to gain control as quickly as he did, they will probably stare at you and say, "I don't know, but I need to go home now as I have a lot of homework to do." They also act as if they can't survive alone and need to be in a group at all times. They dress the same, which for the most part consists of ski sweaters they have knitted. Big deal, I say. Anyone can knit a ski sweater if they try hard enough. What do you think? Do you knit as well?

Besides all this talk about my sister, I have discovered something new about her. She has a boyfriend. His name is Arne, and he is about two years older. I think they met while participating in the school play, or maybe when he graduated this spring. I am not sure. He is tall and I guess the girls think he is good looking because he is both an athlete and a top student. I have seen him waiting outside the school at the end of the day. Not right in front, but across the street, indicating he doesn't want anyone to see he is there. On two occasions, I have seen him walking with my sister when I rode by on my bike. They were so involved with each other, I don't even think they noticed me. I didn't say anything to them. I am waiting to see how long she is keeping this a secret.

By the way, she is supposed to graduate this June, but there is some trouble with the high school's last grade. Because of the shortage of teachers this past year, the students haven't had enough hours in history and civics, and there is a good chance they will have to continue going to school at least a few hours per week until November, just for these two subjects. Otherwise they can't graduate. What a mess. And here Ingrid had already applied to the Academy of Music in Oslo starting in August. Well, I hope she can start in the New Year.

Of course your sister is just a little kid, but your time will come as well, when your sibling will start demanding to be number one in the family. Maybe you will be different. You were not afraid of ignoring all the chatter from the other cousins and didn't feel you needed to make small talk. I both like and envy your ability to focus on your sketchbook. What a fabulous solution to avoid idle chitchat. I just don't have the patience to listen too long. So many people I meet seem to talk just to hear themselves speak, and there are so many other things to focus on right now. However, as I said, you are different.

Many years ago, we had a wonderful dog named Pluto. He was my best friend and companion. He slept on my bed. I would have long talks with him when we went for walks, and he always stayed close to me. When he died, my parents said I had become too old to have a dog as a best friend, and that the time had come for me to learn to socialize, because they felt I was too shy.

I am not shy, nor am I afraid of people, but I'd rather be alone than with people I find boring. Unfortunately, there are quite a few of them. I like to read and watch movies, especially news reels because they help me understand what is going on in the world. But I am not sure if they allow documentaries anymore.

Right now I am feeling rather low. Two full years have passed since the invasion, and no matter what the rumors, I see no sign of this horrendous war coming to an end. German soldiers are all over town, and in the outskirts. They all look alike to me. They have blonde or brown hair and walk with a stiff gait. They stare ahead most of the time, as if they want to appear invisible. They show no emotion or life. They all wear the same grey uniform, complete with a steel helmet on their Aryan heads, tall black boots, a rifle hanging over their shoulder and a hand grenade on their belts—quite a sight. Sometimes I think about throwing a snow ball at one of them to see how they'd react!

I presume the intention is to intimidate us. Don't they realize the only reaction they are able to provoke within us is hatred?

I wonder where they eat and sleep. Do they ever think about all the innocent families that no longer can feed their children properly? Kids who have no recollection of eating meat on Sunday, or a piece of bread with sliced sausage.

Even though Aalesund is right near the water, the only fish caught is herring, of which there is plenty. At least that's all we can get our hands on. I am getting sick of eating herring, regardless of how my mother tries to prepare it. Good fish is very hard to find in the stores because each storeowner only gets a small supply compared to what they used to get before the war. But I assume you are used to that as well!

Yes, we have ration cards, but they don't get us far. What about rolls and homemade bread with cheese? Not to mention all the wonderful chocolate that used to tempt us in the candy store windows. Now the only thing we can count on if we are lucky is potatoes.

Last fall large crowds of people went into the woods and picked blueberries, raspberries and whatever they could get their hands on. The berries were canned and stored for the winter months. More and more people are raising their own vegetables, such as turnips, carrots and anything that will grow. Hey, do you know there are people who have started breeding rabbits? My friend's father did. Suddenly there are rabbits everywhere, just like they say. That certainly is one way to get meat. However, rabbits eat a lot of grass, and people with small properties pick up bunches of grass that grow along the roadside to feed their new "house" animals. I bet you wouldn't be able to raise rabbits in your apartment in Oslo?

The owners of the farms around here sell their produce to whoever has the money to come and buy. You wouldn't believe the prices that are being paid for a single, tiny piece of red meat, or a chicken. If a buyer has a lucky day and happens to get his hands on more products than he needs for a few days, he tries to barter with others. This is a daily activity. For those who drink coffee, you can forget it. The coffee is made from some dried weeds called chicory root and rye. Apparently, it smells similar to coffee when it's heated. My parents drink this garbage, and so do many of my parents' friends. There they sit, small groups of people, holding on to their cups, relaxing, pretending they are drinking coffee. I think it's a little weird. But I guess they miss holding a cup of coffee while talking to each other.

Fortunately for us, my father still has some merchandise in the store that he uses to barter with occasionally, so I guess we are slightly better off than most. Whenever my parents hear of some type of food available, for example, they send me to get it. Never Ingrid. They tell me to carry boxes or bags of clothing or anything they can think of. I sometimes get a little annoyed, because last time I looked, Ingrid has two hands as well! But they are so worried about her hands being hurt or injured that she has to be careful all the time. I do understand, but sometimes I think they are getting a little carried away. She uses her hands to eat, doesn't she? As well as for carrying her schoolbooks. Even to ride a bike, and fix her hair. Anyway, this is kind of boring for you.

Did they confiscate your radio as well? I would imagine so. I wonder why they bother. All the information on the radio has been censored regardless, so there is nothing but propaganda. The most exciting part is when we hear from the resistance people who manage to listen to English radio, and if they are lucky, they get the real news—and write illegal newspapers. People are very careful with whom they show and share these small pieces of paper with. I have, however, been told this has a very good effect on our morale, in that it creates togetherness to tolerate this madness until the war is over.

By the way, did you know the first people they confiscated radios from were the Jews? Now they take everyone's.

Here I ramble almost like you live in a foreign country. I am sure you have the same situation in Oslo, the capital of this subdued, but not surrendered country. Do you wear a red knit hat? How many paper clips do you have?

Yesterday I walked home from school and saw three German soldiers painting a garage door. Someone had managed to sneak by and paint a large H-7 sign on the green door. Do you think our King Haakon the seventh realizes his sign is now the most popular message in this country? I was laughing a little when I saw they needed three men to paint the door. I may have smiled too much, because one of the foreign "visitors" gave me a dirty look. I just kept walking casually along. Well, maybe, I was walking a little faster than usual.

Our school now has twice as many students as before the war. The high school has been confiscated to house the soldiers. Therefore we only have half a day of school and we have to double up. Some of the students resent this and complain when they are given twice as much homework as before. You have to be a total idiot not to understand why. Therefore, my friend and I take turns doing our homework together.

There are no more official sports activities. That's forbidden as well. Why? I don't know, but we meet in secret without uniforms and pretend it's just a pickup game. It's sort of gives you a strange feeling of rebellion in a way, to still keep score. Mostly we play soccer and basketball.

Rebekka, please don't think I am a sissy, but I worry about Uncle Leonard all the time. At first, everyone thought he would be released after having been questioned. Now he has been held for almost a year and a half. My father told me Leonard was sent up North to work on a railroad. Why and how could this happen? He is such a wonderful human being. He is smart, considerate and decent. What are they doing to him, and what do they want from him? And what about his fiancé? Mor calls Bestemor as often as she can to see how she is doing. But Bestemor refuses to talk about it. She seems to pretend it hasn't happened. Does your father talk to you about the war?

I haven't told anyone, but I am looking for contacts so I can get involved in the resistance work. Don't know if I am too young, but there has to be someone who can use me. I can deliver illegal newspapers, I can bring messages. I'll do anything to help. If they can keep our uncle in prison, then the least we can do is try to support his principles and beliefs. I think about him every day. I think I can trust you, so please don't discuss this with anybody. I have a strong feeling someone I know is involved in this activity. I can't explain it, but my instinct tells me he is. Well, there is nothing wrong in my sharing it with you, anyway. One of my friends told me I should be careful when I write letters in case we are being censored. I haven't heard about this, so far. I have heard talk about books and songs being looked at, but I have no personal experience. Well, I just x-ed out a line above with a black pencil! It contained private information.

When I have a chance, I'll approach him to get his opinion about the mail being censored. I keep thinking about what I should say. Wish me luck.

My parents don't think I am old enough to deal with this. What does age have to do with it if that's the way I feel? We are the only Jewish family in town. Maybe I am just being sensitive. Rebekka, please write to me. I am so grateful you are my cousin, but also that you are my friend.

Sincerely,

Harald

Chapter Eleven

The Blueberry Tooth

OSLO, MAY 7, 1942

Dear Harald:

Thank you for your letter. I was glad to hear from you. It has been quite a while since we wrote to each other. It's amazing. You write just the way you speak, so I can almost hear your voice when I read. Sometimes you are funny, sometimes you have things on your mind which you need to resolve, and other times you just write what you think.

School is terrible. We don't know from week to week how many days we are supposed to show up, since the schedule changes so often. We are bombarded with homework, which I guess I can understand, but we never know what teacher is going to be there. I started a new school last fall which was three weeks delayed. A few of our best teachers have also been arrested and sent to prison. Why? Because they were brave and not afraid to speak up against the invaders who are trying to take over the curriculum and change the values and doctrines of Norway. At least this is what they tell us. For instance, we have, or rather, had, a most fabulous history teacher. He could make just about any event in history come alive. I used to love his classes. It was something in his mannerism that made you sit up and take notice, and before you knew it, it seemed that you were living and experiencing that very situation or event. Well, it appears he was a little too outspoken, and didn't want any outsiders to come and tell him what to teach and how to teach it. The final result was that he eventually was thought to be too independent, and unwilling to adhere to the altered curriculum. His critics felt his independence to be too "dangerous" and before we knew it, one day he didn't show up. We heard he was sent off to prison along with many other "treacherous" and independent good Norwegians. I think of him every day. Sometimes I even think I hear his voice and can imagine the energy in his face.

When I read about your teacher, Mr. Welhaven, I think of my history teacher as well. I wonder if history teachers are more apt to being arrested. Especially if they refuse to teach how important and wonderful Hitler is.

Therefore, I try to keep my mouth shut and concentrate on my homework. They can't punish me for that, or can they? I have also spent a fair amount of time drawing. As you know, I am trying to sketch the various episodes and situations I experience, and actually even some I just hear about. I have even attempted to create the scenario outside your family store, the way I was told it looks. I think it came out okay, if you will allow me to use that description. What I mean is I felt I was able to portray your faces—yours, Ingrid's and your mother's in my mind. It felt as if I was present observing you while drawing. For some reason, it helped me feel good. As for your father, I just couldn't "see" him, which makes me feel bad. I don't know why I found that so hard. Maybe because I don't know him well, and perhaps because he didn't have any of the Davidson traits! I'll try again some other day.

However, I promised you I would focus on general news in this letter, for lack of a better word. At least the story I'll tell you has a successful conclusion.

The other day I was the indirect source of a near serious episode, unrelated to the Germans. It turned out to be pretty bad, but it could have been much worse.

I am not quite sure if you have met my family's housekeeper and nanny, Ruth, who has been with us for several years. She is fairly young and really nice. We think of her as a member of the family since she's been through everything since the invasion. Ruth is very close to my mother and loves Miriam, who she has cared for since she was a baby. Miriam is now four, and controls our family. She is very noisy and talks a lot for her age. She has curly hair just like me, but hers is dark brown. Why in the world did I have to inherit the genes for red hair? By the way, do you remember when you saw her a couple of years ago, that she is left-handed, just like your sister? See, you and I have more things in common than we thought? Joke! Oh, yes, one more thing. I just read that the Latin word for being left handed is "sinistra," which historically means a person who preferred to use his/her left hand was evil! Thank heavens that has changed!

A couple of weeks ago we were at the large park, St. Hans Haugen. Ruth asked me to keep an eye on Miriam, while she went to the fish store to buy dinner. I realized she might be gone 15 minutes or one hour—I am sure you know what the markets are like these days. Any sighting of food products will generate a small army of people waiting in line, considering themselves as having won "a prize" if they are able to buy something other than herring or fake meatballs prepared with heaven knows what. This park is where Ruth normally takes Miriam in the morning to a playgroup with 15 other kids and two nannies for a couple of hours, while Ruth gets some housework done. Mor sometimes helps Far in the store when they are busy, and she also helps her mother who recently lost her husband, my grandfather. When the weather is nice, Ruth takes Miriam back to the park in the afternoon so she can run around some more. Sometimes it's fun to watch her, but at times it's annoying, seeing a wild kid who needs to burn up some of her energy. Did I say spoiled? No, I didn't, but I sort of wanted to.

As I mentioned, Ruth left to find some dinner, leaving me with the little monster. Miriam was to stay with me at the playground. A group of kids of various ages ran around in circles. I placed myself on a bench where I could see Miriam, and pulled out my sketchpad.

I kept looking up and saw a small cluster of kids running and screaming, trying to see who could laugh the loudest and make the most noise. I found them a little irritating, wishing they would turn it down a notch or so. I was trying to sketch an argument, which I had with my cousin Frank who still insists on bossing me around. You don't know him but he is my mother's sister's son. He is a year older than me. He is considered very bright and a quick thinker and normally we are quite close. On occasion I have heard my parents say they felt he was "too grown up for his age," and a little spoiled. This seems to be a common criticism for any child without a sibling. I always thought this assumption was unfair. Still I think of him as a bit of a "pain in the neck" on occasion, especially when he feels he has earned the right to lecture me. I had decided to draw him in the middle of trying to convince me that he was right and I was wrong about some issue that's long forgotten. No big deal. I was just thinking of him at that moment.

Then I noticed a handful of German soldiers in their grey uniforms forming a small cluster around the kids playing on and around the fence. They were smiling, which was unusual and annoyed me. Who gave them the right to smile to Norwegian kids? Shouldn't they just go back to their own kids in their own country and smile at them? Normally these soldiers usually just stare straight ahead, perhaps afraid to make eye contact with the Norwegians, as I am sure you know. I just heard yesterday, by the way, there is an organized group of Norwegians all around the country which keep an eye on local girls who fraternize with German soldiers. If they know this for a fact about one of "our" girls, they keep a sharp lookout for these women, catch them without hurting them, and cut their hair really, really short. This is supposed to be a signal for people to realize they are traitors against their own fellow citizens.

Back to the park. The small batch of kids had been climbing and walking on the low fence, which separated the large play area from the sloping green lawn, on the other side. Suddenly I heard a loud scream. I recognized the voice; it belonged to my sister.

I ran towards the kids and adults, who were quickly congregating by the fence. There was Miriam, being lifted off the ground, on the opposite, hilly side, by a German soldier, of all things, trying to help. Miriam was crying, no, screaming, with blood pouring out of her mouth. For a second I thought she was going to be angry with me for "allowing" this to happen, but strangely enough she wanted me, and no one else, to hold her. The soldier gave her to me, of course, but neither he nor his companions stayed. It seemed they wanted to be sure Miriam was okay before they left. In retrospect, it's slightly strange to think of, isn't it?

One of the adults who was trying to soothe Miriam claimed afterwards that I screamed almost as loud as my sister.

"Oh, no, please, my baby sister. It's my fault. I had promised to watch her!!! Is she all right? Please tell me she is all right? Why is there blood coming out of her mouth?"

I have to admit I have no recollection of this statement, but it's probably true.

Instead, in answer to my question, a number of clean handkerchiefs appeared out of nowhere and willing hands tried to stop the flow of blood. Fortunately at that very moment Ruth appeared, carrying a grocery bag full of food, which she immediately dropped on the ground. At the sight of Ruth, Miriam started to sob loudly once again, and threw herself into Ruth's extended arms. Suddenly there was no need for me, the big sister, which I can understand, but frankly, it made me feel even worse, if at all possible.

I have to be honest; I felt like a total failure, in every sense of the word. Someone in the crowd summoned a taxi, quickly bringing the three of us to the pediatrician whose office was much closer than the emergency room. By the way, it seems I also automatically grabbed the grocery bag with our dinner, including the potatoes, which had fallen out and were spread around on the grass at the foot of the fence.

When we reached the physician, the bleeding had subsided, and the little patient reluctantly consented to opening her mouth for examination. A dentist next door was contacted to assess possible damage. Ruth and Miriam disappeared into his examination room.

Ruth, who had accompanied the small wounded athlete, reappeared with the dentist who was holding Miriam's hand. Smiling at me he said, "Please take your sister home and make sure she doesn't climb on any more fences." Ruth was smiling as well and Miriam had stopped crying, so I felt a little less scared.

The dentist continued, "There is a 50% chance the injury might cause Miriam to lose the tooth. If the tooth remains, it will most probably turn blue, due to blood having bled into the injured tooth. Regardless, this problem will disappear when she gets her permanent teeth in a couple of years."

He then turned to the owner of the tooth. "You may end up with a special front tooth which is very, very unusual and only happens to very brave and very smart little children who have had an accident. It's a magic tooth. Therefore, you need to promise to take good care of all your teeth, brush them every day and never, never try to climb up on anything high until you are at least twelve. This tooth will be called a blueberry tooth as long as you keep it."

Miriam absorbed all the new information with amazing concentration and said, "How does the blueberry get there? Do I have to eat lots and lots of blueberries and blueberry jam on good bread? And I like blueberry pancakes. Ruth, will you make them for me every day? And maybe I don't have to swallow that terrible cod liver oil which you make me take every morning, anymore? I don't think it's good for blueberry teeth."

Fortunately, what was left of that day passed uneventfully despite my concern about how my parents would react. However, it turned out I was more or less ignored once they heard Miriam was fine. Mor actually hugged me instead of chastising me, saying, "Let's put it behind us. We know you are reliable, most of the time. Remember that little kids move quickly, which is why they have to be watched."

Miriam was the recipient of a lot of kindness and attention. A couple of mother's sisters, as well as her special aunt, Tante Marie, came by, all making a big fuss over the little patient. She is a lovely woman who has no children of her own. For the most part she is shy and quiet, but possesses a special talent for communicating with children, and is therefore one of our favorites. She came here from Germany a few years ago.

Upon arrival, she handed a large package to Miriam who tore it open immediately, making it clear that no other part of her body had suffered any damage during the accident. Inside the package was a beautiful small silk umbrella in a myriad of colors. The unexpected gift was acknowledged by a happy scream, exhibiting the front tooth which hadn't yet reached the blue color predicted by the dentist. The umbrella was opened immediately and paraded around the house for everyone to see, and successfully managed to outshine the excitement of the fall.

Since then Miriam has insisted on being lifted up to inspect herself in the mirror, in an attempt to proclaim to the entire world that she may have a magic blueberry tooth. As luck would have it, she got her wish. About one week later, the tooth did indeed change color and took on the shade of blueberry. Therefore, she now is the proud owner and promoter of her mouth, which has all white teeth with one exception.

Well, I was trying to distract you a little, by telling you about my failure as a responsible babysitter.

I wonder if you have experienced what I am going through right now? I feel I am being treated as a person with no maturity or common sense, at least not one the adults, will trust. They seem to think I am old enough to be responsible and patient, at least most of the time. However, as soon as something serious or difficult happens, I feel they are censoring what they tell me. Do you ever feel like that? I turned fifteen last month but I still feel like that. I am assuming your sister is very close to your mother. I don't think I have ever told you that I got a big kick out of seeing how much your mother and my father look like our mutual grandmother.

I would like very much to hear from you soon to see how you are managing under these difficult circumstances. I have been told there is no local censoring of domestic mail so far, at least. Regardless, I don't worry about the censor. I'm not writing anything that isn't true.

Your cousin, Rebekka

Chapter Twelve

Isak Is Arrested

AALESUND, MAY 12, 1942

Today was a beautiful day. Ingrid's piano teacher in Oslo had assigned her a new piece to work on. It was complicated but she knew she could master it. Despite endless hours of practicing, she still felt it needed more work. She was due for another piano lesson in the capital in eight days.

Chopin op 10, no. 3, also called Tristesse, was quite a challenge. Ingrid had been at the piano for half the day, repeatedly working the most difficult parts. Her neck was tight and her wrists ached, and she needed a break.

Her hands flow over the keys, and, yes, it was beginning to sound like Chopin. The romantic melody was emerging slowly, just as she had hoped. She could both hear and feel the full richness of the basic tunes amidst all the accompanying notes.

At that moment, she felt a presence in the room, and turned her head, while continuing to play. In an easy chair across the room was Arne.

She stopped playing, facing him and turned to him in surprise. "I didn't notice you coming in."

The past few months had been extraordinary, despite the lingering general unease. She had befriended this wonderful young man, Arne Friberg. She had admired him at theater performances and concerts, but never had a chance to speak with him. His entire presence fascinated her. He was tall, with dark brown thick hair, which always looked like he had misplaced his hairbrush. However, it suited him. His face was not exceptional but she had memorized his features. He was two years her senior. What fascinated her most of all was the alertness in his eyes, as if he was eager never to miss any detail, absorbing anything that he felt interesting and different. His teeth were perfect, and he had the most incredible smile she had ever seen. Yes, indeed, she had studied him carefully, both intimately and from afar.

A few months ago, the local theater group had begged her to join them as their accompanist. It didn't take her long to agree, as she knew that Arne had one of the leads. The chemistry, which she now realized was the right term, had been instant. It seemed they could never run out of things to discuss, and yes, now they were a couple, spending more and more time together. She found herself thinking of Arne almost all day, and it was just about impossible to focus on other issues without her thoughts being interrupted by the memory of his face and most of all his voice.

Arne got up from the chair. "I've been sitting here for 15 minutes. Your mother was nice enough to invite me in. I could see you were concentrating and I didn't want to disturb you. And this is the first time I've heard you play classical music, yet another aspect of your remarkable talent."

His voice lowered a bit, almost to a whisper, as he continued, "I can't stop thinking about our conversation last night. I needed to see you again to tell you I won't let anything happen to you. You are too important to me. I've something to tell you."

He paused and appeared a little nervous, allowing Ingrid to respond. For a few seconds she just stared at him, as she wasn't sure how to react. She tightened the belt on her light blue bathrobe. She hadn't even dressed yet, having gone right to the piano.

She and Arne had talked for hours the night before, and for the first time she had opened up and spoken about her feelings and anxiety about being Jewish. She had shared a number of things with him, including her night-mares, which seemed to occur more and more, as the news got worse. Arne had urged her to speak about it and as she felt increasingly closer to him, she told him of her reaction to fears that she had never earlier confronted, not even to herself. He had held her and listened intently.

One of the topics she had talked about to Arne for the first time were her thoughts about being Jewish.

"When it comes to anti-Semitism in this country, actually in most every country in Europe, there is no such thing as preventing or not allowing anyone to do anything. The Gestapo is prepared to hurt, harm and control all the Jews. That includes my family and me.

"I think we are on the verge of being beyond help from those who care for us. Do you know how many people have told my parents that we should escape? They allow Norwegian Jews and other Norwegians who have a need to escape the enemy to seek shelter in Sweden or England. But Far doesn't want to leave! He keeps saying he is Norwegian and this is where he belongs. There is no logic, no rules that The Gestapo has to follow. The key element in this war is hatred of the Jews."

The conversation from the previous night had stuck in her mind. She closed the lid to the piano. The euphoric sensation she had just experienced, if only for a few minutes, was behind her. Neither Arne's feelings nor Chopin's incredible music would help this situation. She waited for Arne to start speaking, but he remained quiet. It was clear that he had something to share with her, but didn't know what to say. She said nothing, allowing him to begin.

Arne looked overwhelmed. His initial efforts to speak had taken a totally unexpected turn.

He sat down on the bench next to Ingrid. His expression changed and he bent his head, cupping his face in his hands with his elbows resting on his knees. She had never seen him like this. He was totally different from last night.

"Arne, what's wrong?" Ingrid finally asked, staring at him. When he looked at her, he was on the brink of crying. They both remained staring at each other for a few seconds. She had no idea what to say and was waiting for Arne to continue.

He was shivering slightly and she put her hand on his knee, hoping to help calm him down. Finally Arne took a deep breath and said, "I've something important to tell you. Please don't think there is something wrong between you and me, well, at least not directly. You could even say that it's much worse. I've been trying to share this with you for the past several weeks, but I haven't had the courage. I was afraid you might be upset and not want to see me anymore. And the thought of losing you is unbearable."

He paused, looking at Ingrid, and said, "Considering our conversation last night, I feel I need to tell you what's bothering me. I believe you have met my father, or at least he says you have. He said he met you at one of the theater performances. He was born here in Aalesund, while his father, Andreas Friberg, grew up in Trondheim. He married young to a local woman, and they had a son named Thomas. Grandfather had problems with alcohol and had a difficult time keeping a steady job. The marriage suffered and Thomas grew up spoiled and nervous and had a hard time getting along with just about everyone. When he was nine his parents divorced and my grandfather, Bestefar, as I call him, moved to Aalesund where he had a friend, who helped him get a job. Eventually he married my grandmother. I was told that he started a new and sober life. This has never been a secret in our family. The son, however, remained in Trondheim with his mother, who tried to raise him the best she could. When he was around twelve or thirteen years old, she died suddenly. Bestefar invited, no, begged Thomas to come here to live with him and his new family, but Thomas refused, saying he hated his father and he moved in with some relatives in Trondheim. He even took his mother's maiden name.

"To make a long story short, my grandfather did well and achieved a respectable position here in town and has been successful. My father was the only child from the second marriage. Far tried in vain to get in touch with his half-brother on several occasions, but Thomas was bitter, and felt that his father had abandoned him."

Ingrid kept looking at Arne, wondering where this story was leading.

"In the late 30's we heard that Thomas had joined the Nazi party and had become increasingly involved in the Nazi organization. When the war broke out, he was a natural choice for a high-ranking position by the Gestapo, and made an official statement that he had finally found 'the way.' He was excited about building a career with the enemy, stating that his own family had let him down. I've been thinking of nothing else the past few weeks, feeling I had an obligation to tell you. Thomas has now been appointed the new head of the local police in Aalesund. Yes, Ingrid, I am sure you have guessed who this half-uncle is, and yes, he is here in town. He is offensive, rude and feels passionate about supporting the Gestapo. He is clear that he hates Jews and makes that known everywhere."

Arne stopped a minute, catching his breath, while watching Ingrid's reaction.

"Why are telling me this? You don't even know him, right?" she asked.

Once again, Arne covered his eyes with his hands. "I wish it were that easy, Ingrid. It seems that my father feels so badly about his father having abandoned his first born son that he feels obligated to try and be a 'brother' now that they live in the same town. They are not close, but Thomas is invited to our house for every special occasion. Far feels he is able to ignore their opposite political opinions, which of course includes Far's love of Norway, but it's almost as if Far has taken on the guilt which his half-brother poured over his father for years. I think Thomas is taking advantage of Far's name and contacts to propagandize at every opportunity. I am staying away from him, but it's a difficult situation. I've heard that he's even trying to change his name from Gyldendahl to Güldenthal, which he feels has more of a German sound."

Ingrid stared at Arne in disbelief. She too was overwhelmed by the news, and it took a minute or two until she realized the significance of what Arne had just revealed.

"Oh, my God," Ingrid said, as the reality finally hit her. "It's him! He is your uncle! Oh, no!" It felt like a load of bricks had fallen on her. How much worse could the situation get, she wondered?

"Arne, I can't believe it," she cried out again, "I may have failed to tell you about my father's experience with the Nazi police force just a month ago.

"Far was forced to meet with them and found himself being questioned by two high-ranking Gestapo officers, with the aid of the new head of the local police—your uncle, I guess. He was horrifyingly impolite and he threatened my father. He made it very clear that our little buzzing town was being thoroughly monitored, due to its proximity to London. There are rumors of refugee traffic between Aalesund and England. Far was questioned for an entire day with nothing to eat or drink. And then he was forced to return the following day. Most of the interviews, if this aggressive questioning could be called that, was focused on his store. They wanted to know all about sales and merchandise, profits and expenses, staff and operations, implying that he had been involved in illegal activities, which is ridiculous.

"Far answered as best he could, which wasn't easy, as he had no idea what they were looking for. He insisted that the success of the business was due to hard work.

"When he returned the next afternoon, he was bombarded with more of the same questions. It was clear they were attempting to see if they could trap him into providing different answers from the day before. Finally, they let him go after demanding the rights to inspect all his books and records. How I wish that we had just escaped at that point to a neutral country, but he wouldn't listen, saying he had done nothing wrong."

Ingrid was sobbing when she finished speaking.

Arne looked at her with tears in his eyes, not knowing what to say.

"Ingrid, I don't care what you are. I love you, regardless if you are Jewish."

What was intended as a complement, hit Ingrid like a slap in the face.

"What are you saying, Arne?" she said, staring at him. "Do you realize what you just said?"

She stared at him still waiting for him to speak. She thought to herself, if he had only said, I love you because you are you, and therefore I love you because you are Jewish. But that's not what she had heard.

"Being Jewish is not an illness, Arne, it's our religion. In the Bible we are referred to as God's chosen people!"

Both were interrupted by an insistent fierce ringing of the doorbell, accompanied by banging on the door. It didn't stop. Whoever was there was certainly in a hurry. She heard Mor race through the apartment, calling out, "Ingrid, I am in the middle of finishing the dinner casserole. Don't you think you have practiced enough for today? I don't understand why you couldn't get the door," Mor called out as she hurried to open it.

Before Mor had a chance to utter a single word, there were loud frantic voices from the two women standing there, both speaking at once, quick and animated, with a definite sense of urgency—even hysteria.

Ingrid heard the agitated voices and joined the women at the door.

"There are at least four police cars," one of them said.

"They were holding him by the arms—two of them—pushing him into the first police car. There are people everywhere, they keep coming! People are lined up in front of the store, but the police and the Gestapo are trying to keep them away! The store's personnel are outside, in their shirtsleeves, just standing there, not knowing what to do. They were told to get their coats and leave. But they are afraid to reenter the store, and they are just standing there waiting with the others."

"Who are you talking about?" both Ingrid and Leyla screamed, although deep down they already knew the answer.

Leyla and Ingrid grabbed their jackets, quickly joining the bearers of the alarming news. One of them had an old car which could barely run, and it was waiting downstairs. Arne followed them down the stairs, logging behind as if he was afraid to interfere.

When they reached the bottom floor and the door, he called out, "Ingrid, I'm coming with you."

She didn't even notice. She got into the car with Leyla and the two women. Arne remained behind, holding his bike. Ingrid had a fleeting look at him through the car window. Numb all over, she felt farther away from him than just a few feet. She felt she had completely entered another world—a world with no room for Arne.

At least not now.

In less than six minutes, they reached the center of town and the main street where Rosenberg Magasin was located. The crowds were huge with more and more people arriving. Ingrid ran as fast as she could in the direction of the store entrance and confronted one of the guards. "What is going on here? Where is my father and why has he been arrested? He has done nothing wrong!"

She barely noticed the tears pouring from her eyes.

Leyla had caught up with her, but remained quiet, unable to believe what was happening. She held on to Ingrid's arm. It was clear that she needed support.

Small groans escaped from her mouth, while she stared at the store's display windows. Ingrid followed her gaze.

On the main store window facing the street next to the entrance a shocking, but no longer surprising image, had been painted. A large, black swastika covered most of the glass window.

Their eyes automatically landed on the soldier next to the window who was in the process of painting something in oversized letters.

It took Ingrid only a few seconds to identify the four letters—J U D E— the German word for Jew, as she knew too well.

Once more she tried to communicate with the police officers, several of whom she recognized and one of whom was a customer in the store, but they ignored her. She desperately tried to get the attention of the two Gestapo officers overseeing the vandalizing, but to no avail. They all pretended not to see or hear her.

She turned towards Mor who remained motionless, not uttering a word since arriving on the scene. Ingrid also stood still for a few seconds, trying to force herself to stay calm, wondering what she should or could do. Her heart was beating at an incredible pace and her hands shook.

She looked down and realized she was wearing her light blue worn bathrobe, partially covered by her outer jacket. She was also wearing her red and grey slippers. She felt suspended in space, invisible, an outsider looking in.

"Mor, Ingrid, when . . . how? Tell me, tell me!" A sobbing scream was coming closer.

Within a fraction of a second two arms were around her neck and she felt, rather than heard, the sobs.

"Where is Far? Where did they take him, and why? Why?"

"Harald, I know nothing. We just got here. Far has been," she paused, and then made herself say it, "arrested!"

She looked into her brother's eyes, trying to force both of them to remain calm. "The car must have left just minutes before we got here. I think he's being held at the police station."

She ended with the undeniable fact.

"The store has been closed."

She turned to her mother who was very pale and rigid. Her eyes were fixed on the entrance to the store and the guards who were lined up.

Intermittently people from town who had congregated would attempt to talk to the guards, asking questions. Some tried to convince the guards that they were making a big mistake and they perhaps had misunderstood the situation. The guards remained stiff and unresponsive and asked people to move back from the entrance. If the crowd tried to stay too long or came too close, the soldiers raised their guns in what was clearly meant to scare people away.

Ingrid was panicky. She was petrified looking at Mor's immobile face as she was clinging to her daughter. On her other side, her brother also appeared unable to control himself and was weeping. She tried to suppress the panic and focused on being strong, saying to herself, Ingrid, you need to be in control here right now. It's up to you to help your mother and brother.

She continued aloud, "Mor, I don't think there is anything more we can do right now. I think we should go back to the house so I can get dressed, and you can get something to eat. Then let's go down to the police station to see if we can get some information."

Mor didn't object, just moved a little, indicating she had heard her. Harald stared straight ahead.

The few people who had tried to speak to them, to express their empathy and allegiance, moved as if they had heard her as well, and began to walk away.

The trio slowly left the area. Somebody offered them a ride, which they accepted, without even looking from where the invitation came. Ingrid grabbed Mor's arm and helped her into the car. She turned around to see if her brother needed any support. From the corner of her eye, she saw him. His fists were closed, and he looked like he was about to attack someone, anyone. She also caught a glimpse of Arne on the opposite side of the street, standing by himself. He looked distraught. She hadn't meant to hurt him; she just had been overwhelmed. She raised her hand in a quick motion to him, before she turned to grab her brother, the last one waiting to enter the car.

Harald was not walking towards the car. He had suddenly stopped and was staring in the opposite direction, having caught a glance of a young man in a Nazi uniform standing next to the now locked and boarded up entrance door. Harald knew immediately who it was. He recognized the young boy in his class who had verbally attacked him at school two years earlier during the day of the invasion, on April 9, stating that the Jews were responsible for the war. The hostile classmate stared back at Harald once again, reminding Harald of the encounter.

Ingrid put her arm gently around her brother, turning him around. Harald entered the car.

Chapter Thirteen

Persecution of the Jews Begins

OSLO, SEPTEMBER/OCTOBER 1942

"Rebekka, what time do you get home from school today? I have to go to the dentist, and I may not be back in time to get Miriam to the playgroup at 12:30. Do you think you can manage?"

Mor's voice was not to be ignored. Rebekka was standing in front of the mirror, getting ready for school.

Ruth had been gone for almost two weeks visiting her mother at her small town on the coast. She didn't really want to leave. She felt she should stay with Rebekka and her family, but Mor had insisted she needed some time off.

Rebekka could still remember Ruth when she finally left two weeks ago. She was reluctant, almost in tears. "Please, don't forget to sing her favorite song about the little mouse who wanted to live in the city, not the country. That's a sign the light is about to be turned out and she has to go to sleep. When she asks about the blueberry tooth, please tell her it will be there the next morning as well. She knows that I'll be back in 14 evenings and 14 songs. Maybe you can make a chart for her showing how many stars will make 14 days . . . and . . . "

Finally Ruth grabbed her suitcase and got into the elevator. Rebekka missed her as well. It was quiet in the house without her; even more quiet than usual.

Mor's voice sounded again, interrupting her flashback to Ruth's departure.

"Rebekka, did you hear me? Please answer?"

Rebekka mumbled, "Yes, I'll do it. I'll get her at 12:30."

"Good, thank you, sweetie. That's very helpful."

The rain was beating against the windows, which certainly didn't make her feel any better. Was four-year-old Miriam right when she asked, "Are the clouds crying?" Frankly, it felt like the weather was trying to tell her this was reality. Life was gloomy and wet, just like the rain. She might as well get used to it.

Rebekka continued looking in the mirror, fixing her hair. Her face was going through changes. It seemed as if a stranger looked back at her when she sporadically confronted her image. Not only was she growing taller, even her face had taken on a different look. She looked thinner and her cheeks less round. Her nose seemed a little longer, but that didn't bother her. She reluctantly admitted to herself that her eyes were getting bigger, and she sort of liked the way they looked now that she had turned fifteen. Strange, she thought.

The other positive thing was her hair color. She saw the irony in such a ridiculous thought, but she couldn't help it. She had a vague suspicion that it now had turned a tiny bit less red, well, maybe even a darker shade of brown, which pleased her to no end. It suddenly hit her—Would she look more Jewish if she had dark brown hair than if she had red hair? What a strange thought!

Her cheeks flushed. A feeling of shame, yes, actual shame, overcame her at this thought, and she stopped scrutinizing her face.

She had also grown quite a bit taller this year. She suspected that the larger boots, inherited from Frank's mother, would very soon be too small.

She tore herself away from the mirror, realizing she now had to rush to get ready for school. She was scheduled for morning classes, which would be over by noon. She needed to have some cereal and juice before she left, and she went into the kitchen

She would keep a careful watch on her thick mane of hair, which was how Far referred to it, on those few occasions when he had time to speak to her and would touch her hair. It had a tendency to get thicker and more curly depending on the weather which was even less often.

Actually, that very morning he was eating breakfast while she was getting ready for school. He seemed relaxed. The first thing she noticed was the absence of his regular grey suit, which he wore almost every day to work.

"Hey, Far, I like you in your sweater and ski pants. Are you skipping work today, planning to go hiking?" she said as she poured a glass of juice.

Far grinned, and looked at her briefly before he glanced at Mor.

"No, we are doing some work in the store today—going through the inventory to see what we have available. I'll be going back and forth to the stockroom, and thought I might be more comfortable in casual clothes."

"Well, I guess that's why you aren't in a hurry to leave. I was wondering," she said.

Normally he would leave the house to open the store which was still in business despite a lack of merchandize before she left for school. However, this morning had been different. He hadn't seemed to be in a hurry. Even Mor seemed a bit different. Was she relaxed, just like Far? No, not really. Was she tense or distracted because he was sitting at the breakfast table so long? No, on the contrary. She kept offering him more juice, coffee and bread. But her expression was tight.

Far rose from his chair and came over to hug Rebekka as she was about to run out the door. He whispered in her ear, "Have a good day, Sweetie; you know how proud I am of you. Try to enjoy school despite these hard days. Good days will return soon."

A little ominous, she thought, as if he is telling me a secret. He then put his hand on her head, touched some of her thick curls, twisted them a little around his fingers and said, "I wonder where you got those thick curls from?" repeating his regular joke once again about her "mane." Everyone knew she had inherited her father's thick hair.

As she walked down the stairs, she was a little annoyed that he had messed up her hairdo, considering how hard she had worked to make the long layers of the new dark, red-brown hair lie quietly in a small bun in the back. However, she was pleased Far had paid that much attention to her.

Classes went quickly. Most of the time was spent assigning homework and independent projects. As Rebekka walked out, Kari caught up with her and said, "Do you want to do some homework together?"

"Fine with me, but I have to pick up Miriam at the park first."

Rebekka was not really in the mood to work on her homework that day, but didn't want to say no. It also might be nice to have some company while watching Miriam until Mor returned. Kari seemed a little off, which was quite unusual. It sounded like she didn't want to go to her own house. They settled down in the dining room, spreading books and papers all over the table. Miriam was thrilled to see Kari and brought a lot of noisy toys.

"Kari, am I glad you are here. I am a bit at loose ends. Homework is the last thing I want to focus on. Can you think of an excuse for not doing it? Something else we can talk about?" Rebekka said.

Kari looked at her hesitantly, as if she were unsure whether she should open up or not.

"I don't know. What I do know is that I am not in the mood for math problems either. I know your family so well and know what you are afraid of. I can't blame you. I worry about you, your family and little Miriam who has no memories of birthday parties and ice cream and being with happy people. Even to you I find it hard to speak about it."

Rebekka was stunned. Gone was Kari, the student who always made homework her favorite activity. Who was always in a good mood, and who tried to see the positive in almost everything. Kari's eyes seemed misty and it was evident she was holding back tears. Was Kari dealing with fear and apprehension as well? Rebekka hadn't anticipated this reaction from her friend. She was the secure, gifted Norwegian girl, who didn't have to worry about being Jewish and being on "Gestapo's black list."

Kari continued, "I just heard that my friend Gunnar's brother John who you may remember was on the soccer team last year, dropped out of school two months ago. He joined the resistance fighters and got into trouble almost immediately. He was shot and killed two days ago. I haven't been able to tell you. Rebekka, he was nineteen! No one is safe. Not even if they hide in the corners and pretend they are not interested in freeing Norway."

She hid her head in her hands and sobbed. Rebekka grabbed Miriam, who stood next to them, and took her in her lap, giving her a pen and some paper to try to distract her. She felt ashamed, but didn't know why. It hadn't even occurred to her that Kari was also carrying around constant fear and sadness.

Kari continued, taking a deep breath, "I haven't told you that my father has moved out—he has gone into voluntary hiding. He has been involved with an illegal newspaper—one that tries to tell people the truth about the status of the war and its progress. He was warned two days ago that the Nazis were beginning to monitor him. From what he's been told, they aren't ready to arrest him yet, because they don't know enough, and feel that if they arrest him now, they may not get the information they think he has.

"I don't even know where he's staying. There's more. My sister Anne Marie saw him briefly yesterday, walking quickly up Main Street. It was clear that he saw her as well, but didn't acknowledge her. Anne Marie was in shock. She wanted to scream at him. She had to stop and tell herself to calm down. Can you imagine, not being able to speak to your own father?"

Kari stopped; she needed to collect herself. "We have no idea when he will be returning." Rebekka stared at her again in disbelief. The vision of Anne Marie stopping in the midst of several people passing by, went through her mind—some pushing one another to get through, some avoiding her. Anne Marie was probably wearing her signature green coat which made her stand out from the others. Somehow, Rebekka could even visualize Kari's father, a very tall man walking in the opposite direction, staring straight ahead, avoiding even a glance in the direction of his daughter. He had a habit of keeping his arms crossed behind his back when he was in a hurry. That's how well she knew him.

"Kari, I don't know what to say—it's horrible! I didn't know. You must feel terrible. When will it end, if it does end? It makes me finally understand the meaning of the word 'maze.'"

Kari quickly gathered her books and put on her ski jacket. She was having a hard time trying not to cry. She mumbled as she left, "I'll see you tomorrow."

Miriam had fallen asleep, and Rebekka walked around restlessly, not knowing what to do with herself. A little while earlier she had heard Mor return with Aunt Charlotte, Frank's mother, and she could hear them talking in the kitchen. She gestured that Miriam was taking a nap, and didn't join them. Rebekka needed to be alone.

She had a strange sensation that today wasn't going to be a calm day. And within a few moments the doorbell started ringing.

It wasn't a calm ringing—not two short beeps, or one long, which members of the family would use, to indicate who they were. It was an irate hand guided by a mind in a hurry.

Rebekka ran to the door, wondering if there was an emergency, but to her great surprise she found her cousin Annika waiting at the door. Annika wasn't really Rebekka's cousin, but rather Mor's first cousin. She had just turned twenty-two and she and Miriam shared the same birthday, April 21.

Rebekka was fond of Annika—they both enjoyed and admired each other enormously—despite their age difference, or perhaps because of their age difference?

Annika had finished her comprehensive education last year. She had landed a wonderful part-time job, which she adored, in an advertising company. She had also started dating the boss's son, which was a subject of conflict in the family, since this unusual looking hockey player wasn't Jewish. Annika's mother had told her sister, Rebekka's grandmother, that he was arrogant and a bit too self-absorbed for someone that young.

On this particular day Annika wasn't interested in making conversation with Rebekka. She was quite agitated. She made her way to the kitchen and closed the door. Rebekka was left standing in the hallway, uncertain what to do. She could hear loud voices and she wasn't sure if she should enter or not.

Rebekka circled the apartment. The sight of her books on the dining room table reminded her of the painful conversation with Kari, and she decided to join the three women in the kitchen. Her pretense was looking for her sketchbook. When she opened the door, it was clear they didn't notice her, or didn't care whether she was there or not. Annika stood by the door, hands on her hips. Her head was held high and she was clearly upset.

"What have you and your sister, Charlotte, told my parents about the situation of the Jews? Why did you have to scare them? They are beside themselves."

She was definitely addressing Rebekka's mother. "When I came home today, I found this envelope addressed to you. On it was a note for me to bring it to you personally. And that's why I am here. Because of your interference and your hysteria about the future, my parents have been admitted to the hospital, just like your mother. They will remain there for one week to ten days until they can be smuggled out to Sweden. I am not allowed to visit them, and they told me to stay in touch with you so you can arrange for me to escape as well. I think this whole thing is ridiculous, but I guess I have to deliver the letter to you. My boyfriend keeps telling me that this is Norway; we are Norwegians and no one is going to touch us."

Rebekka was unfamiliar with her grandmother having been admitted to the hospital for the purpose of escaping to Sweden. She looked at Mor with surprise. Mor nodded to confirm that it was correct. She also made it clear that this was neither the place nor the time to discuss it.

Sarah stared at Annika during her outburst. Rebekka noticed the same tired expression on Mor's face that had been there for the past few weeks. It was clear Mor had been through this with Annika before. She was now trying to muster the energy to repeat everything again, trying to convince Annika that the danger ahead for the Norwegian Jews was real.

Mor made one last attempt. "Your parents have gone under cover at a local hospital and my mother is there as well. The physicians are supposedly admitting them for observation and diagnostic exams. Some of these physicians have arranged for an ambulance to pick them up in about ten days, pretending to transfer then to another hospital. The ambulance, however, is a special large truck involved in transporting elderly citizens over the border."

Rebekka didn't move; she sat quite still and tried not to show her surprise. Why hadn't anyone told her about her grandmother having already started her escape? Once again she realized that the adults avoided telling her what was going on.

Rebekka's mother took a deep breath, while looking at the young, attractive woman who was so sure of herself that she couldn't even listen to another opinion. It was evident from Annika's expression that the truth still hadn't sunk in.

"Annika, please don't repeat this information to anyone. Not even to your boyfriend. Especially not to your boyfriend, because it sounds like he doesn't believe the severity of the situation. If the story about the hospitals gets out, it may have a direct negative effect on many people. Your own parents may be in danger. Please promise me."

Annika stopped snickering long enough to listen to her cousin's explanation and plea. For a second she stood quietly and looked into space, as if actually considering the other version of reality. She wrapped the strap of her bag across her shoulder, buttoned her leather jacket, and turned to face Sarah directly.

"Okay, I'm leaving. Yes, I promise I'll not mention your fantasy to anybody, including my boyfriend. Actually it's embarrassing. I'll take care of myself. I hope my parents will be able to get to Sweden safely if that's what they want."

With those words she walked out of the apartment without looking back.

Rebekka stayed in the kitchen after Annika left. She whispered, "I was wondering if I left my sketchbook here?"

Neither Mor nor her aunt answered. That very moment the telephone rang, as if on cue. Saved by the bell, Rebekka thought. Mor grabbed the receiver. Mor seemed relieved with the interruption as she didn't want to elaborate on the conversation with Annika any further.

She watched her mother's face while trying to guess who the caller was. It didn't take long. She was speaking to Ruth. With just a minute or so of listening, Mor took charge of the conversation. "You need to take some time off; you have had no vacation for a whole year. I'm not sure if you are safe here with our family. Please stay another few days."

Rebekka found herself listening intently. There was something in Mor's voice that made her slightly uncomfortable. She sounded evasive, as if she really didn't want Ruth to return at all.

Mor continued. "Listen, Ruth, things are not getting any better; they are getting worse. No, no decision has been made about leaving. Not yet, but we are considering it. A number of people are contemplating the need to escape."

Mor paused while listening intently to Ruth's answer. Rebekka watched her closely as did her Aunt Charlotte. They heard the front door slam in the background; Annika had left.

What exactly did her mother mean? Escaping? When? How would they escape?

Rebekka had visions of her entire family running up a road in the country, faster and faster, with Miriam crying and wanting to be carried.

Mor was holding the phone tightly and tapping rapidly on the table surface with the other.

Rebekka turned around. Frank's mother was more or less curled up on a chair by the table. She was deep in thought with tears running down her face, listening to her sister on the telephone. Eventually Mor hung up. She sat down, poured herself a cup of coffee surrogate, which she held with both hands. Mor's hands were shaking and the cup spilled over.

"I was unable to convince her of the reality. She insists on returning to her boyfriend. I really don't know what to do. I can't forbid her." Mor said this out loud to no one in particular.

Her last sentence was interrupted by an angry message from the enemy, it seemed, since at that very moment an air raid siren erupted. All three looked out the large kitchen window where a cluster of Mosquito Combat planes were coming in through the city. The appearance of the rain in favor of the blue skies with a few clouds almost felt like a direct insult to the little group gathered in the kitchen. Had Mother Nature decided to facilitate the arrival of enemy planes?

Rebekka said, "Mor, do we have to go to the air raid shelter?" assuming that her mother would ignore it, as usual. She was right. Mor shrugged her shoulders, grabbed her cup again, and drank more of the ersatz brown fluid.

Finally she had become aware of her daughter's presence, at least for part of the conversation.

"No, it's not necessary."

She lowered her voice, although it was unclear whom she was addressing. It felt as if she were speaking to herself again.

"We have other more serious problems to deal with than an air raid."

She took a deep breath and leaned towards her daughter.

"Rebekka, have you finished all your work for tomorrow? Maybe you could take Miriam for a short walk. I have a fair number of things to do and work out."

"Mor, if you are so busy why are you trying to convince Ruth not to come back? I don't get it. And Miriam really misses her. And I have a history paper coming up."

"Okay, dear. I understand. I do appreciate all the help you're giving me. There are many things that need to get done, and I think there will be more decisions to make during the next few weeks."

She looked at her sister with a questioning expression seeking permission to go on. Aunt Charlotte shrugged her shoulders, which both Rebekka and her mother interpreted as a "go ahead." Rebekka wondered if Mor was trying to make a decision about letting Ruth return, because they were thinking about escaping.

Aunt Charlotte started speaking. "A close childhood friend of mine worked for the Norwegian police prior to the war, before they were taken over by the Gestapo. She has held this position for close to 20 years, and has intentionally stayed even though the Gestapo has taken over. She feels that she might do more good by staying than leaving. Her name is Signe Falk and she has called me several times a week with news informing us of the impending activities at the Gestapo Headquarters. This is an extremely important mission. She has been doing it for weeks. Unfortunately, lately the news that she transmitted has not been very good."

It wasn't clear to Rebekka exactly what her aunt was leading up to, and she was reluctant to ask. Finally, turning directly to her aunt, she decided the time had come to bring it up. "What are you saying exactly?"

Aunt Charlotte looked up, attempting to remain calm. She had a tendency to stroke Rebekka's arm while speaking to her. She was an affectionate woman, quite artistic as well as creative and loved to cook and bake. She was the most religiously observant member in the family. She worshipped Frank, often expressing that she wished she had more children, especially a daughter. She put her arms around her niece.

"More and more rumors are emerging that a mass arrest of Jewish men is near. A number of men are contemplating going into hiding and escaping to Sweden, but they don't yet know when to leave, as it can't take place without help from a resistance group. There are rumors that all Jews will have to register and report to the police every day to ensure they don't leave."

Rebekka felt like something had hit her on the head. "Mass arrest?" The words scared her. Her thoughts went to Harald and the story of his father, as well as Uncle Leonard who had been arrested more than a year ago. No one talked about them. Had they mutually decided not to bring up the missing relatives? Did they feel if they avoided speaking about them, perhaps providence would leave the prisoners alone, without being hurt or tortured. All she could think of at this moment was that her father might be among this "mass" of Jews. She would have to speak to him about . . .

Suddenly she froze.

"Mor!" she screamed. It felt as if she were looking at a clock, which had implanted itself in her brain. However, contrary to a regular clock, this one went backwards more and more quickly. She knew immediately when it would stop. It would stop at eight o'clock this morning. Of course!

"Mor!" she screamed once more.

"The ski pants, the sweater! Far left this morning to hide from the Germans, didn't he!"

Chapter Fourteen

Where Is God's Part in This?

AALESUND, OCTOBER 17, 1942

"These candlesticks were a present from my parents when Far and I got engaged," Leyla said out loud. Ingrid and Harald didn't bother answering, having heard it many times over. This had become a Shabbat evening ritual. The old candlesticks, complete with new white candles, were waiting on the white tablecloth as always.

"Praised be our Lord, King of the universe, who has sanctified us by your commandments and allowed us to light the Sabbath candles," she started.

For the previous Friday nights, since her husband's arrest, Leyla had started to light the traditional candles. Previously they had only celebrated this day when it was convenient. Now it had become Mor's Friday evening priority—her anchor, it seemed.

She added her own personal prayer, in a much lower voice, apologizing for mentioning a personal wish. "And please, dear God, let us soon see the safe return of my dear husband and the children's father. And please bless all the Jews who right now are suffering from bigotry, anti-Semitism and hatred."

She handed a glass of whatever red juice she had, pretending that it was Shabbat wine, to both Ingrid and Harald, urging them to join her in reading the prayer. Thereafter followed the breaking of a small loaf of bread, which she had either managed to buy or barter. Her face relaxed a little, and a peaceful look settled on her pale face, which seemed more emaciated every day.

Ingrid had developed an antipathy to her mother's newly observed weekly ritual. The more Ingrid was forced to attend, the worse she felt. Mor's composure during the prayers had the exact opposite effect on the daughter.

99

Ingrid failed to understand why this ceremony was that important. The new reliance on religion was out of place, she felt. What good could a Friday night ceremony with prayers do? Money had become a serious concern. It never used to be. Now that the store was closed, there was no income. The Nazis had depleted most of their bank accounts.

And now she expected God to help them. It didn't make any sense.

I wonder where God is in all this? she thought. Initially she had tried to analyze the "fairytale of her childhood," the presence of God, as she had come to think of it. She was staring at the small, dainty wine glass. She worried she might accidentally crush it in her hand. She took a very, very small sip of the juice, trying to convince herself that her participation was minor if she only took a little sip. She almost burst out laughing. But the sense of levity didn't last. She was indeed conflicted.

She didn't feel like saying, "Please God," a prayer which came naturally to most people. She had decided that bringing God into this horrible situation would make her thoughts and hopes even more complicated than they already were.

Did she believe in God? Yes, of course she did, more or less, the way any teenager or adult would feel, for that matter. She hoped God was real, as she had been taught ever since she was a small child. At least she wasn't prepared to deny the possibility, although miniscule, that he was real.

When she was younger, she always felt that this was one aspect of her life she could share with her non-Jewish friends; in other words, she wasn't different. And now she wasn't quite sure anymore. Why else would her family have been singled out? She knew the answer; it was because they were the only Jewish family in town.

So her conclusion had been easy. God had nothing to do with the arrest of her father and other Jews. If she were to connect the evil which had taken over their existence with the supreme spirit that ruled the world and humanity, how could she justify believing in God if He was connected to Nazi evil?

She couldn't hold it in anymore. The words poured into her mind, and she wanted to shout them out load. Automatically she pushed her chair back, and started to get up. Even now she was torn, not knowing if she should leave the table or stay. Leaning forward she held on to the tablecloth—careful not to spill the juice—and screamed at her mother.

"How can you pray to God asking for help to bring Far back? Do you really think God will help?" As she continued, she saw her brother out of the corner of her eye. He was immobile, showing nothing, staring at her as if she were a total stranger who had joined them at the table. Was he in shock? Perhaps it was fear? Despite his reaction, she couldn't stop.

"If God could help, why would he have allowed the Nazis to arrest Far?"

Mother stopped immediately, staring at her. It was clear Ingrid had upset her enormously. Yet she didn't try to stop Ingrid's frenzy.

Ingrid continued, still out of control, "How do you dare to call on God? Aren't you afraid that God will be angry at you for connecting Him to this horrendous, evil behavior of the Gestapo and the Norwegian Nazi helpers?"

Ingrid finally stood up straight and pushed her chair in under the table. She felt as if she could only express her desolation in segments. Her mother remained silent, allowing her daughter to rid herself of the repressed anger and sorrow. Slowly, very slowly, unsure whether she would be welcome, Leyla walked around the table toward her firstborn, whispering in a barely audible voice.

"Sweetheart, I don't dare *not* pray to God. It's the only thing I have left to believe in at this point."

Ingrid couldn't tolerate the situation any longer. She jerked back so violently that one of the dining room chairs toppled over, with a loud bang. Mother and daughter stared at each other, both in pain—both unable to speak.

Ingrid turned and left the room, not knowing what to do or where to run.

She felt restless, needing to get away. Every inch of the apartment reminded her of Far. His desk was neat; everything was perfectly organized, not like when he had used it. It was clear her mother had straightened the papers. Far always had a thousand things going on at once, dropping papers on the floor. The phone would ring and within a minute or so, he would be in deep conversation with a friend discussing the athletic club, the chamber of commerce or a civic issue with which he was involved. More often than not, a colleague or a friend would stop by, unannounced, just to chat.

He was musical and full of energy. On occasion he would grab his wife around the waist while she was preparing dinner, making her dance with him. She pretended to be annoyed at the interruption, but never failed to join him. Ingrid recalled how she would watch them smiling at each other. She would sing along or even clap her hands. She had been told she had inherited Far's personality, or at least his musical ability. Looking back now, it seemed a lifetime ago.

Everything had changed. There was nothing remaining of their uncomplicated and easy life. Even her school and graduation plans had changed. She was supposed to have graduated in June several months ago. Instead of applying to the Academy of Music in Oslo, she was taking a course in typing and shorthand at a local business institute. Three times a week she had to run back and forth to her old school. Not because she hadn't been prepared, but no, because the school couldn't find enough teachers. Thank heavens the school nightmare would be over in a few weeks, so what? The dream of moving to Oslo and studying music was gone, at least as long as the war was continuing.

She needed some fresh air. She grabbed a jacket and ran down the stairs. Once outside she felt refreshed. Their apartment house was situated along the upper part of a hilly area, and she could see the fjord from several vantage points. She had been told that Aalesund had one of the most beautiful views in the country. As she started to climb the hill, a feeling of calmness came over her. She started to feel free, which was strange, since she also felt guilty about having hurt her mother. Deep down she knew her mother would understand what she meant. She allowed herself to breathe in the fresh air. The twilight would last for a good part of the evening.

For a second she thought about her brother, who had witnessed the conflict. She worried about him. He had always been fairly reserved, and now he was almost a recluse. He refused to speak about his schoolwork or his friends. It appeared the only thing that kept him going was reading. Not necessarily school assigned reading, but history, world history. She wondered if he were somehow trying to find a solution to the present political situation that maybe someone had overlooked. In particular, he wanted to read about anti-Semitism. He seemed obsessed. One day she was so frustrated that she had said to him, "Are you trying to find some undiscovered loophole that you can grasp, analyze and eventually present to the new powers of the country, to prove how they are wrong?"

Of course she hadn't expected him to answer. And of course he didn't.

How he could keep on reading about the same issues, over and over, was beyond her understanding. She took a deep breath and promised herself that she would try to engage him in a conversation.

She stood still, looking at the water and the surrounding mountains, which seemed almost close enough for her to touch, yet she knew they were kilometers away. This particular place was just as beautiful as when she was much younger. She would come here with her friends, bringing blankets to sit on the grass-covered knolls, eating sandwiches and giggling. She always thought of it as her favorite place to laugh, rest and dream.

Unexpectedly, the stillness ended, broken by a gentle voice that was familiar, very familiar. Her name was being whispered behind her, softly, "Please forgive me for disturbing you. I know you want to be left alone, but I have something I need to tell you."

Turning around she found herself face to face with Arne, whom she deliberately had tried to remove from her mind.

The lack of communication had been her choice. She no longer tried to understand why she needed to separate herself from him. Initially he had tried to meet her at the end of the school day, but most days she had arranged to leave early, consciously trying to avoid him. She never told him why, she just needed to be alone. All she knew was that it involved Far's arrest.

"Arne, I can't believe you are here! How did you find me?"

Had she ever realized how blue his eyes were, and had he gotten even better looking?

"I was trying to find you, so I went to your house, hoping I would see you. I didn't have the nerve to ring the doorbell. Your mother appeared out of nowhere. She said she had seen me through the window and she didn't know where you were. She thought you'd gone for a walk up the hill. I remember you telling me about this place."

Ingrid remained motionless, letting him speak, and eventually moved a little closer.

She felt guilty for having told him that she didn't want to see him the last time they met. She didn't even try to explain how confused she felt. At that moment she recognized the great joy she felt seeing him standing so close to her.

"Ingrid, I just saw your father," he blurted out. His voice was harried, feeling that he needed to justify his presence immediately. "Please don't be angry with me for being here. I've tried to respect your wishes, but it's been hard. Besides, I have something to tell you, and I'm not sure if you will consider it good or bad news."

Ingrid said nothing. Her father? She only wanted to hear what he had to tell her.

"Yesterday I saw him walking down Main Street with six other prisoners outside the police station." He paused, lowering his voice. "Their feet were chained together," he said.

"I've been told that a decision was made two days ago that they'd be sent out each morning at seven o'clock, forced to carry out manual labor just outside of town. It will probably start next week some time. Supposedly they'll return around five o'clock in the afternoon when they go back to the police station where they are being kept.

"I don't know how long they will stay here in town." He paused a few seconds, before he continued. "He appears to be in relatively good shape, Ingrid. He looked tired but otherwise unchanged. I just needed to tell you . . . "

His voice dropped still feeling unsure of how she would react.

Ingrid looked at his conflicted expression, and said, "Arne," moving towards him, "Thank you so very, very much. I've been hoping that someone would hear something about him. I can't believe it would be you!"

She continued, "He is here? He is here in town, although in prison. I can't believe it! Mor went down to the police station several weeks ago to ask about him, and one of the guards told her he was sent away the day after the arrest, and they refused to tell her where. And now you tell me this entire time he was right here in town. Imprisoned, yes; but still here in town."

This was more than she could bear. Her knees went week and she became dizzy. Arne moved to support her, and she threw her arms around him.

"Listen to me, Ingrid," he said, "This is why I had to find you. I was informed confidentially by one of the policemen at the station—who has to remain nameless—since he knows your family. Please don't ask his name. Believe me; it would have terrible implications for him and his family, as well as your father, if they realize you know him and that he has been giving you information. He knew that we, eh you . . . " Arne hesitated, not knowing whether to go on, "He knew that you and I are, were very close."

Ingrid pressed her body close to him. "No, no, I believe you. I know that you would never come here to tell me if it weren't true. Please help me so I can see Far and talk to him. Our lives have been unbearable for the past few weeks, not knowing whether we will ever see him again or not."

Arne briefly withdrew a little from her arms. She could see that it wasn't out of choice, but that he needed to make certain that she fully understood the seriousness of what he had told her.

"You can't go near the police station or try to reach him. They are prepared to send him away. Right now he is safer here than anywhere else. Please promise me you agree with this?"

She stared at him; eyes filling up with tears. "I promise to do whatever you tell me if I can see him . . . " She paused for a few seconds.

"Yes, I promise," she added. Her eyes showed a hint of optimism. "I think I have an idea."

"Ingrid, you promised."

"I can't tell you about it. Please trust me."

Ingrid kept looking at him. He turned and looked at a tiny fishing boat down in the harbor. For a few seconds neither of them spoke. He turned back to Ingrid and said. "Ingrid, I am still worried about you."

Ingrid and Arne were still standing at the highest area of the hill where they had met only a few minutes ago. Arne felt torn. One part of him told him not to push her and risk losing her confidence. On the other hand, he was also worried that she would get involved in something much more serious than she could realize. He looked at the little fishing boat which was turning in towards the dock in town. He had a perfect view.

He was seriously concerned about her safety and her new plan to see her father which she didn't want to share. Her eyes had an almost dream-like expression. He sensed that she wanted to be alone, but he needed to ask her again to promise she wouldn't share this information with anyone, not even her mother. She reluctantly gave him her word. He also made her promise they would see each other again, when she was a little less preoccupied. This was easier to handle. She had a strong urge to see Arne again as well; first she needed to put her plan into action.

While Ingrid and Arne clung to each other for a brief moment, he whispered once again, "Are you sure you don't want to tell me about your plan? I really would like to help you."

"Yes, I am sure. Thank you. I need to do this myself. Please trust me." She stood watching him until he was out of sight. She did indeed need a couple of minutes to process the past few minutes and how Arne's news had initiated her own thoughts.

Chapter Fifteen

Arrest of Jewish Men

OSLO, OCTOBER 25, 1942

In retrospect, Far's decision to go into hiding before the mass arrest of the men would always symbolize the beginning of Rebekka's life as an adult. Not just the regular—run of the mill adulthood—but also the phase of her life when she no longer took her parents and family for granted.

She had become intensely aware of the fact that anything could happen at anytime and anywhere.

A couple of days after Far had left, Mor came into the room late at night. Rebekka was reading and Mor sat on the edge of the bed, gently stroking Rebekka's hair. Did Mor have something terrible to tell her? Fortunately, she was wrong.

Mor spoke in a low voice. "I think I need to share some of the new information with you for two reasons. First of all, you are almost an adult, and secondly our situation is becoming increasingly dire. When Far left last week, he took shelter in an empty apartment along with his brother Fred. How do I know that? It was planned for several weeks, and perhaps in a few days or so I'll tell you where it is.

"It's within walking distance of our house, but that's all I can share with you now. In addition to knowing that Far is hiding with Fred, you know that their other two brothers have been arrested. Uncle Leonard was arrested early on because he was involved in resistance work. Their older brother, Max, attended a meeting arranged by the Jewish congregation a few weeks ago where they discussed how to organize their resistance and make plans to escape to Sweden. That was all the Gestapo needed to hear—everyone present was arrested and sent to prison. You know all this, don't you?

"Two of *my* brothers are also hiding in the same apartment as father. The resistance people have told the four men to remain in seclusion until the appropriate manpower and means of transportation become available to bring them to neutral Sweden and freedom. Believe it or not, the men have been instructed not to walk on the floor during the day, if possible, to prevent anyone in the building from hearing them. There's always some risk involved in hiding in other people's apartments. Some people are nosy and like to report information to those that just shouldn't know."

Rebekka remained quiet, listening intently.

"When the rescuers are ready to pick them up, they will contact the men in hiding through me. When exactly is not yet known—hopefully, as soon as possible."

Rebekka didn't even think of asking for more details. She was afraid her mother would stop sharing this vital information if she interrupted her. The concept "as soon as possible" had taken on a totally new significance these days. It reminded her of learning and understanding the concept of "infinity" when she was a small kid in school.

She stared at Mor, trying to visualize the four men tiptoeing around an empty apartment.

"What are they doing all day?" The words fell out of her mouth, but she had to ask. After she asked, she felt silly.

"They do a lot of reading and tell each other stories and jokes. They are trying to keep their spirits up, considering all the great challenges that lie ahead. So must we, sweetie, and now it's time for both of us to go to sleep."

Mor got up and left the room. It was apparent that revealing this information hadn't been easy.

Deep down Rebekka knew there was much more going on, and that she was still being kept in the dark to some extent. She also felt if she didn't ask too many questions, the reality and potential danger might seem less severe. If you don't say it out loud, it's less likely that something bad will happen. True or not, she didn't know, but it made her feel better.

Every day around five o'clock in the afternoon Ruth would start preparing an enormous package of carefully wrapped sandwiches, letting it sit waiting on the kitchen counter. Rebekka had once tried to find out who the recipients were, but she got no response. It was clear that it was more than one person. Naturally, she had a suspicion, and didn't want to ask if it was prepared for the four men in hiding. So far she wasn't sure if even Ruth knew for whom the mysterious food packages had been prepared, and if she did, perhaps she didn't want to discuss it. There was no denying it, family interaction had completely changed.

Every night around eight or nine, once it got dark, her mother would put on her heavy coat and say, "I am going for a walk. I need to drop something off at my sister's."

No more. And then she left.

She carried a small flashlight in her pocket, which would give her minimal protection against the few cars still on the road. There were no streetlights, as strict orders had been issued by the enemy to cover all windows with heavy inside blinds as soon as the sun went down. The official excuse was that if any plane overhead was trying to bomb the city, lack of illumination would protect Oslo's inhabitants. However, this didn't prevent Mor from leaving and returning every night.

One particular Wednesday evening was no different. Mor had just left. Ruth was reading a book, and Miriam was fast asleep. Rebekka reluctantly pulled out her math book ready to tackle an unavoidable task—homework. This particular Wednesday evening in late October was no different in that respect.

She settled in at the dining room table, her favorite place to do her homework. She opened her book and tried to figure out what to do. The time was 9:35 pm, exactly.

Within a few moments, the doorbell rang. The person on the other side of the entrance door totally disregarded the late hour of the evening. His or her purpose was solely to make certain that the sound was strong and clear, forcing whoever was inside to rush to open the door, she thought.

She was right. She opened the door. It wasn't a social visit. They were intruders. She was face to face with two unknown men, wearing matching dark raincoats and hats. There was something intimidating about them, which strangely enough was generated by the absence of comments or action. So far. They seemed equally uncomfortable communicating with her, perhaps because of her age. For a second or so all three stood still, staring at one another. Eventually the men lifted their right hands in the direction of their hats, as a token civilized sign of greeting. The man on the left cleared his throat, and said, "We would like to speak with Mr. Davidson. Is he available, please?"

Rebekka stared at them. Who were they? And what did they want? Should she answer? Should she slam the door on them, or should she call for Ruth?

At that very moment the elevator stopped on their floor and Mor emerged. She stopped as if transfixed. It seemed like a long time but in reality it was only a few seconds. She walked around them and entered the apartment, while gently pushing Rebekka aside. She remained at the doorway, facing the visitors, but made no sign of inviting them in.

"I am Mrs. Davidson," she finally said in a firm voice. "What can I do for you?"

Rebekka was mesmerized. She had never heard her mother speak with this tone of voice. She sounded like a stranger. If she was surprised at the visit by the two men, she certainly didn't let on. She acted as if she knew them, or at least that she had anticipated their appearance. Rebekka's immediate thought was that the two men seemed intimidated by Mor's voice. It seemed impossible, yet they had changed their expressions a little, scowled less and seemed a little less threatening.

"Ahem," the taller man said, "we are from the Oslo Police. We are looking for Mr. Davidson."

Rebekka grabbed on to the little table in the entryway for support. She felt slightly faint, but couldn't take her eyes off Mor who remained totally calm.

"He is not here," Mor responded. "I haven't seen him for several days. He's away on business. He is trying to locate more inventory for the store. I don't know when he will be back." This was delivered in rapid order; without emotion. "Is there anything else I can do for you? It's late and we need to go to bed." She paused and stared at the two men.

For a second Rebekka was afraid. Are they going to search the apartment, she thought, almost in a panic. Both of them, perhaps inadvertently, took a couple of steps backwards. Another few seconds of silence ensued. Then they tipped their hats once again, turned around and disappeared into the waiting elevator.

Mor remained motionless. Closing the door, she turned slowly to Rebekka. "It's late. All is well. Please go finish your homework and then we'll speak tomorrow. Let's stay calm. We are fine."

The next day arrived. The surprise visit of the night before seemed like it had never happened. Rebekka went to school but had a hard time concentrating. It felt as if she were watching a movie in her mind—somewhere in the middle—not knowing how it would end.

The school day went fast and she was back home around noon. The telephone rang a few times. Several of the resistance men came by, only to speak to Mor for a couple of minutes, leaving just as quickly as they came. What were they looking for? Getting information or giving information? It was hard to tell. Mor looked drawn and tired. Ruth was pale as well and hardly spoke.

Rebekka walked around the apartment, moving her book bag into her room. She could hear Mor's voice on the phone. It was getting louder and more agitated. It was impossible not to hear the conversation. She was speaking to Aunt Charlotte.

"I've been trying to reach you all morning. Where in the world have you been? Don't you know that I was half out my mind when I couldn't reach you? Do you realize how close we were to losing our husbands and brothers last night? Have you heard anything about where the arrested men are being held? One of the resistance men stopped by early this morning, wondering if the police were here late last night, but primarily he wanted to tell me that the little group in the 'you know where apartment' was intact. No, I haven't heard from them. I know they're all right. It was a great relief to have this confirmed by the young 'Haakon' who came. I'll see the little group this evening as usual. What do you mean? Of course I'll still go there.

"Thank God your husband is safe across the border. What have you told Frank? Does he understand the situation? Rebekka opened the door for them last night right before I got home, so she must have figured out why they were here."

Mor's voice stopped for a minute, as she listened to her sister. She started walking around in the library, opening cabinet doors and drawers, and pulling the telephone cord with her as far as it would reach.

"Yes, I am still here. Keep talking. I'm trying to see if Martin has hidden any cigarettes somewhere. I haven't had a smoke for six months but today I really need one. Did you speak to mother, and is she okay? Well, I am glad that she is not alone. You know, I still dream of father, even though he has been gone for two and half years already. Perhaps it was a blessing in disguise he didn't have to experience this war. He went through enough during his childhood in Russia."

Mor looked everywhere, behind pictures and in boxes, searching in vain for hidden cigarettes. In between, she stopped so she could concentrate on what her sister was saying.

"I heard that more than 375 men were arrested. I wonder if they also arrested the boys who have turned fifteen, just as rumored." Mother paused and cried suddenly. "Frank! Did you ever think the mix up with his French birth certificate, might protect him? Oh, my God. If they knew he is almost sixteen! I don't even want to think about it."

She continued, "I don't need to be told not to listen to rumors, Charlotte, I know, I know. But that's what the secret message from the police station contained. And the young resistance boy who was here this morning said that he heard all the men who were arrested were being held just outside of Oslo in a large prison, and will be transferred somewhere else tomorrow."

"What!! The Rabbi and the Cantor were among those arrested? Oh my, how horrendous. The Gestapo will never let them go."

The doorbell rang, and Mor called to Ruth asking who was there. When she heard, she asked Charlotte to hold on.

Turning to Ruth again, she said, "Is Rebekka all right? Maybe she could go and pick up Miriam from the park. Thank you."

She went back to the phone. "Martin's niece stopped by to bring me a sweater for her father. You know he is with Martin as well, don't you? She went to the kosher butcher this morning and the store was full of women, even though there was no food. Someone said that all the families—I mean the women and children—are now frantically trying to find good people to help them escape, but at the same time they are afraid. Why? Because they feel that if the Gestapo hears about them escaping, they may take it out on their husbands or sons in prison. And they are afraid—afraid of not having enough money to manage in Sweden, as well as leaving their homes behind. Someone told my sister-in-law that the synagogue has been closed, and the Torah scrolls have been hidden. That's a blessing, right? Still, who knows when we will have a chance to go there again—it won't be for a very long time.

"I need to go. Let's agree to contact each other if we hear something new. It would be best if you came here, and also," she lowered her voice and whispered in French, "I don't know for sure, but I am not totally convinced the telephone is safe. I haven't even thought about this until now!

"No, I haven't heard anything more about our departure date. It may take weeks, I imagine. First the men need to be brought across. Please don't forget to include us in your prayers. Yes, yes, of course I'll pray as well. You are much more observant and will do a better job. Take care of yourself. We need each other. I don't know what I would do if anything—no, I won't let myself even think like that."

Mor hung up the phone and stared into space.

Then she sat down, looking exhausted. Rebekka felt that perhaps she should leave her mother alone for a while. She could think of nothing to do, so she filled a glass with water and handed it to her mother. She sat down at the dining room table, pretending that she was concentrating on her homework.

Nevertheless, when Ruth returned with Miriam a few minutes later, Mor asked Rebekka and Ruth to join her in the kitchen. Her face was drawn, and it was evident that she was tired. She spoke quickly and without much emotion.

"I need to talk to both of you. Rebekka, I have chosen to think of you as an adult because the news I have just received pertains to adults only. I have watched you these past weeks, and I am very proud of the way you have managed the unexpected changes in our lives."

She stopped and paused. Rebekka noticed a small twitch at Mor's left eye. Clearly, this conversation was significant, and Rebekka began to feel nervous.

Mor started again.

"Rebekka, those men were here last night to arrest your father. I knew that it was just a matter of time before it would happen. Thank God, Far went into hiding in time. He and your three uncles are waiting for the resistance people to take them to Sweden and safety. I hope it will happen soon. I will not relax until I receive a message telling me that they have made it.

"Within the next few weeks, we'll be leaving as well. There is a band of resistance people who have agreed to help us escape, but there is a large number of other people ahead of us. The first groups to be brought across the border are the men in hiding, because the Gestapo has targeted them. You are old enough to understand how dangerous this situation is.

"You aren't to discuss this with anyone, you understand that, right? Nobody, at all. Not even Frank or Kari or even with your aunts. The less we talk about it, the better off we are. As soon as I know more, I'll let you know. Try to go about your normal day-to-day routine."

Rebekka listened to every word Mor said. She felt paralyzed. Mor seemed to be done with her, at least for the time being, and she turned towards Ruth. It was obvious that she had a hard time starting the conversation.

"Ruth, I know what I am about to say is no surprise to you. You still have the option to leave, either to go back to your mother's house or perhaps consider staying with a friend or an acquaintance somewhere else. I would imagine the first place they would look for you would be in your mother's town."

Ruth was just looking down at her lap, and didn't seem at all interested in Mor's arguments. It appeared that her mind was set. She didn't even let Sarah continue, but interrupted.

"I have already told you, I am staying with you. I appreciate your telling me about the choices, but I feel that I belong here." Tears began to run down her normally sweet and stable face. "I haven't, I haven't told you something that happened recently, as I didn't want to give you anything more to feel sad about. When I was home last month, my mother told me that my childhood boyfriend, whom I always felt I would marry one day after having spent some time on my own, was killed in a car accident this summer. He was in a jeep with four other soldiers; the driver was shot by the enemy, lost control and went off the road. He was only twenty-three. And now he is gone. And besides, you need me. Miriam needs me. I want to help. It is my choice so please let me stay."

Mor stared at her. "Ruth, dear, why didn't you tell us? I wish we had known. If you feel that you are part of our family, you need to let us share your difficult times as well." Mor paused again, and continued, "How I regret that you find yourself in this predicament after having given us three years of your life. I hope you realize how much you mean to us. Unfortunately, I also need to tell you something else. We both know your life is in danger, especially if you choose to remain in Norway after we leave. Your association and exposure to our daily routine for the past three years have automatically merged your life with ours, and therefore you are at risk, just as we are. The enemy will think you are familiar with names, places and people who have helped the Jews and who are about to help us. You will most probably be arrested if you stay and they find you." Mor stopped speaking and it became quiet, as there was nothing else to discuss. "It is probably best that you leave with us, but it has to be your decision."

Mor was holding Miriam on her lap. She bent her head and planted a big kiss on the child's head. "Is there anyone here who would like to go back to the park and speak to the ducks in the pond?" Miriam started to jump up and down. Mor, looking at Rebekka, whispered in a low, slightly nostalgic sounding voice, "When you were two, we would take our stale bread with us in a bag to feed the ducks. Now we can't even get enough bread for it to get stale. Let's all go. No, Ruth, I think you should stay here and rest for a little while."

Ruth however insisted on coming along and within a few minutes the small entourage of duck lovers returned to the big, beautiful park where they could extract a small period of pleasure despite all the bad news.

Making their way up the street towards the park, Rebekka looked around. As usual people walked up and down the main street. Some were holding on to their small children, carrying grocery bags with whatever they managed to purchase that day if fortunate. Not many of them smiled or seemed relaxed.

Rebekka couldn't help thinking about Mor's telephone conversation that morning. Did Mor know that she had been eavesdropping, more or less by chance? The number 375 stood out in her head—men and boys. She wondered where these Norwegian Jewish men, just like her own family, were held prisoners. Were they cold, hungry, scared and concerned about their families worrying? And how did their wives, mothers and daughters feel? They had been left behind to worry, at least so far. Rebekka shivered when she thought it could have been Far, if he hadn't gone into hiding. It could have been Frank. She remembered having heard that he was born in France where his parents had lived for a year. His parents had never reported that his Norwegian replacement birth certificate had accidentally recorded him as having been born one year later. If they had, Frank might have . . . she didn't want to think of it anymore.

Chapter Sixteen

"Where Is Everybody?"

AALESUND, OCTOBER 26, 1942

Dear Rebekka

I feel I had to write to you. All kinds of rumors and stories are circulating here in town. Someone told me that all the Jewish men who were not in hiding have been arrested by the Gestapo. Is this possible?

I know that it may be dangerous to write letters that are too personal, especially if they consist of information and names, so this is a very short note.

As you know, my father was arrested in early May and our Uncle Leonard hasn't been heard of for at least a year.

I haven't heard from anyone. And if Mor has, she hasn't shared it with me.

Do you remember those friends of my uncle, the doctor, who had a bridge club? I am trying to see if I can play with them. I am trying to keep busy.

Please let me hear from you. Soon.

HARALD

Chapter Seventeen

Tante Marie

OSLO, OCTOBER 28, 1942

Dear Harald,

I was happy to hear from you as I was worried about you and your family as well. There isn't much to be happy about these days.

Everything you asked about is correct. Your Uncle Martin and his brother are away on a joint business trip trying to locate merchandise and are hoping to do some early skiing.

Something very scary has happened. It's on my mind all the time so I decided to write to you.

I don't think you ever met our friend Marie Kaufmann. She came to Oslo from Germany in the thirties after her parents and husband lost their lives under very difficult circumstances. She had a brother in Oslo who worked in my grandfather's store. He had convinced Marie into join him in Norway Oslo. She became very close to Mor and we considered her a family member. Miriam adored her. Aunt Marie would sing to her in German, and I think she was the only person who was allowed to speak or sing in that language. Do you remember the story of the blueberry tooth which Miriam acquired from a fall? Marie bought Miriam the striped, silk umbrella, which became her favorite toy.

Her brother was among the Jewish men arrested recently. Marie became deeply depressed as it brought up all the terrible memories from Germany. Her hope had been that the war would never reach a country this far away.

Harald, she took her own life! Can you believe it? She gathered all her medicines into a glass and swallowed them. Mor found her when no one answered the door to Marie's apartment.

She left a note saying that she no longer wanted to live. All the Jewish men have been arrested. Either they are in prison or they have escaped.

I am not sure if you are familiar with the Jewish cemetery in Oslo. It's strictly Orthodox and everything has to be carried out according to specific rituals. Ordinarily, only the men are in charge, but now Mor and her friends had no choice. All the men were gone. A handful of women went to the cemetery late at night, prepared a grave, bought a coffin and made certain she had a traditional Jewish burial. I am so upset and feel so sad. At the same time, I am so very proud.

I hope this terrible war will be over soon. I think of you and your family all the time. I have even started to pray to God for better days. It's a little embarrassing to admit, but it cannot hurt. Do you think I am silly?

Thanks for listening, I mean, reading. Rebekka

Chapter Eighteen

Ingrid's Plot

AALESUND, NOVEMBER 2, 1942

Ingrid was looking at herself in the mirror—something she had avoided doing for several days. It was time to finally try on the white dress her mother had put aside for her several months ago. Mor had been hoping Ingrid would wear it for the graduation ceremony and the subsequent party. Ingrid had refused to even talk about it. Well, the tide had turned.

It looked quite good, she thought. The sleeves were a little tight and perhaps the skirt could have been a bit longer, but in general it fit her, and yes, it made her look good. This was something she hadn't thought about for months. Today was November 1—the day before her big plan was to be put into action.

Ingrid thought back to the day roughly two weeks ago when she had met Arne at the top of the hill, when he surprised her with the news about her father being in town. Yes, Far was still in prison; he was here and not shipped off to an undisclosed location that no one knew about! And now she had an idea that would enable her to see him in person. She hadn't shared how this would take place with anyone. Not with Arne who had informed her where her father was, and not with her mother. Ingrid had promised Arne to keep his information strictly confidential as several people would suffer if it became known.

She was totally consumed by Arne's news, along with his unexpected appearance on the hill. She hadn't seen him since the day Far was arrested. Her idea of how to take advantage of the news about her father kept spinning in her mind. It felt as if her secret plan was all she could think of, day and night. She was fixated by the chance of seeing her father again.

Far is in town. I am going to see him! That was all she could think about.

Ingrid had raced home from the hill that evening, so preoccupied that she barely escaped falling. A pebble in the road resisted her worn and stretched sport shoes, causing her to trip. It was a miracle she avoided a serious accident, as two cars passing by narrowly missed hitting her.

I need to slow down, she reprimanded herself. Her head and heart were still racing.

She had just completed the two final exams which was the reason the final exams had been postponed until November. She had attended all the classes and now she was done. She decided to ignore all the annoying feelings she had about the delay. Now the work was done, and it was a necessary part of her carrying out her plot. Passing the exams and attending the subsequent graduation were all necessary aspects of her strategy. The final tests had been given last Monday and Tuesday.

Today was Friday. The big event was to take place tomorrow, November 2.

Once again, her thoughts wandered back to the unexpected meeting with Arne. She was worried Mor would read the news written all over her face when she returned home. Fortunately, it was quiet and no one was around. When Mor finally appeared, she acted as if their horrible fight had never taken place. Only a small nod acknowledged Ingrid's return. Nothing else was said. Harald was half sitting, half lying on the floor in front of the sofa, which had become his favorite reading place. Ingrid hesitated for a second, but controlled the urge to tell him.

He seemed relaxed and involved in his heavy history book, so she didn't interrupt him. He was holding the book quite close to his eyes, and she remembered that just before Far had been arrested, there had been some talk about Harald needing reading glasses. This topic appeared to have gotten lost in the major changes that had taken over their lives.

Harald had been wearing one of Far's sweaters. She had wondered if the sweater made him feel closer to Far. Should she tell him that sometimes she put her nose close to Far's sweater to try to discern his scent? Sometimes she would even be afraid to hold Far's clothing too close for fear his scent would disappear.

Today, she was afraid to even mention Far's name as her new and exciting plan might make Harald notice something in her face. So she kept to herself.

The first major challenge was to make an excuse to Mor explaining why she had changed her mind about going to the party. This event had been planned by Tante Sofie, Mor's best friend.

Ingrid recalled a conversation in this very room, roughly a month earlier. Tante Sofie had been visiting Leyla. Sofie, a local, single woman was a responsible civic and educational leader in town. The two women had been close friends for many years. Sofie had been a major support since Far's arrest and essentially their only connection to others in town.

The two women were having a cup of coffee, or something which they convinced themselves was coffee. Ingrid, studying in a nearby room, overheard snippets of their conversation. For the most part, Ingrid left the two of them alone, feeling it might serve Mor well to have another adult with whom she could share some of her fears. Their conversation had been rather monotonous, until Ingrid heard some mention of a party, which naturally caught her attention.

"I feel so bad the graduates won't have their traditional dance, as they always had before this wretched war. Do the Germans have to destroy everything that's traditional and pleasant for the new generation? If we could only think of an alternative."

Ingrid's ears had perked up, curious how Mor would respond. However, Mor remained silent. There was nothing to say.

Suddenly the guest interrupted herself and continued in an exceptionally animated and hearty voice. "Oh my, am I a fool!! Wait, wait. It's just so simple. Why should I complain about this? I can give a private party at my house. It's *my* house and I can invite anyone I want. Let those . . . "

She stopped quickly; looking around to make certain no one would hear her derogatory language. "Let those damned foolish soldiers and Nazis worry about it . . . they can't stop me. I need to leave, Leyla. I need to go home right now, get organized and prepare invitations for each of the students who are graduating."

She got up in a hurry and tripped on a small stool near the sofa, luckily without falling. Ingrid had been amazed at the excitement in her voice. Her face had a determined expression. Sofie pushed her partially brown and grey hair to the side and was out the door, her unbuttoned coat swinging around her, already concentrating on her new task.

Tante Sofie was what was called a "no-nonsense women," who also dressed in a very dull manner. Generously speaking—one could call it a 'no-nonsense style.' However, Ingrid and her family adored her.

Superficially, one would wonder what Sofie and Leyla had in common. Sofie was outspoken and on occasion opinionated, while Leyla was quiet, mild mannered and more of a negotiator than a rabble rouser. A special affinity between the two continued to grow. The two women had spent much time together discussing religion and other interesting topics.

Leyla remained on the sofa, taken aback by Sofie's hasty exit.

"What do you think, Ingrid?" Mother had called out, knowing Ingrid was listening, "Do you think it will work? You will go, won't you? What a generous offer!"

"Yes, Mor," she had responded, "it is, but I don't feel like going. I just can't do it. It's going to be hard enough to attend the ceremony when most of the other fathers will be there. No, I won't go."

Ingrid had gotten up and walked out of the room. She wasn't going to attend the party. The topic was closed.

That was before the news from Arne changed everything. First of all she was forced to tell Mor she had changed her mind. Not only did she want to go to the ceremony as well as the party, but she also needed to give a plausible reason *why* she had changed her mind. That was the hardest of all. Lying was difficult.

This very morning she had approached Mor. "I need to speak to you. This has been a complicated time for us and I appreciate that you haven't criticized me for that unpleasant conversation at the Shabbat dinner. I have given it a lot of thought and of course I know our existence is just as hard for you as it is for me these days. Please forgive my outburst." Mor didn't answer. All she did was hug her daughter.

Ingrid took a deep breath, not knowing how to continue, and then exclaimed, "Mor, where do you keep the white dress you saved and hoped I would wear to the graduation party? I'd like to try it on and see if it fits as I'm thinking about going after all."

If Leyla was surprised, she managed to hide it. Like most mothers, she wasn't unfamiliar with the necessity of treading lightly around her children. When she got up and crossed the room in search of the white dress, Ingrid noticed how thin Mor had become. Leyla's sweater was almost falling off her. Ingrid felt a sudden pang of guilt. How could she have missed that?

For a second she toyed with the idea of sharing Arne's news, then again, she remembered her promise. She wanted so much to tell Mor Far was in town, but concluded that it was impossible at this point. She felt her mother would try to prevent her from carrying out her plan, or cause some other problem out of anxiety. She decided to wait until the party was over, when she hopefully had seen him. Besides, and this was most important of all, she had promised Arne not to do it, because if it got out, it might have dangerous ramifications for other people involved. Yes, her mind was set.

"Here it is. Let's see if it fits you."

Leyla casually handed her the dress. Ingrid took the hanger, feeling she was holding a piece of fine china, and that she didn't really deserve Mor's kindness.

"Pressed and ready," was all she managed to say. Looking at Leyla, Ingrid began to realize how badly Mor must have wanted her to attend the party. For a second she felt terrible, having failed to let Mor know the real reason for changing her mind.

"I think I've changed my mind. Yes, I have definitely changed my mind."

Pausing again, she continued, "I also need money to order my graduation cap. It has to be paid for in two days. Can we afford it?"

Ingrid noticed a quick, almost unnoticeable shadow cross Mor's face. Ingrid wasn't sure what it meant exactly, but it could be one of several reasons. Had she, Ingrid, been that obsessed with her own pain these past weeks?

"Of course we can. This is something we've been looking forward to ever since you were born."

"Will you come with me when I pick it up?" she whispered. Feeling ashamed, she secretly hoped Mor would say no. It was getting harder and harder to keep her plan a secret.

Leyla looked at her, shaking her head, "No sweetie, I just can't do it. Please, forgive me, but I do want you to get your cap. You have earned it and you should have it."

The entire week seemed like a lifetime, despite the remaining two finals. But tomorrow was November 2 which she had dreamt about night and day for almost two weeks. And she was ready.

Ingrid barely slept a wink that night, counting the minutes until she could get up and put her plan into action. The graduates and their families gathered in the school's auditorium, as other classes had done for many years. Ingrid found it hard to relax, her excitement intensifying. Despite this important day and ceremony all she could think of was how it would be a means to an end. She forced herself to sit still. The ceremony passed by in a blur.

She heard snippets of the headmaster's speech, but found it difficult to concentrate on what he was saying.

At one point she became aware of the crowd becoming surprisingly quiet. Why? She looked around. The girl seated next to her gave her a quick jab in the side, "Ingrid, get up. This award is for you! How can you sleep . . . ?"

The headmaster repeated his last sentence, and she quickly managed to walk to the lectern, shake hands with the music teacher and the headmaster, grab the diploma, and return to her seat. She felt as if she were in the middle of a dream. Out of the corner of her eye, she caught a glimpse of Mor and Harald, both applauding louder and harder than anyone else.

She managed to stay alert during distribution of the diplomas. Everything seemed a blur. Once all the parents and siblings had congratulated the graduates, the crowd walked slowly down to Tante Sofie's house, a couple of kilometers or so away. Ingrid walked by herself. She noticed several graduates looking at her, and she ignored them. She suddenly felt quite nervous. What if the police had changed their minds? What if they had sent the men somewhere else? What if . . . .?

She tried to reassure herself that if there had been any major changes, Arne would have found out and contacted her. She didn't have a choice. She had to move forward.

The atmosphere at Tante Sofie's house seemed subdued. The young recipients stood in clusters attempting to make polite conversation, feeling slightly unsure about this unusual celebratory format. Sofie gave a small speech to the graduates, explaining why she felt this special day shouldn't be ignored, despite the seriousness of the status of the country. She said the achievements of her guests, after so many years of education, were significant, as they were at the threshold of adulthood and their energy, skills and contribution were of particular importance for their country in war and peace.

Her words were appropriate and some of the solemnity of the moment was broken. Finally, the students began to acknowledge the significance of the celebration, and started to enjoy the moment. The hostess served her famous honey cake and some type of mild alcoholic punch, with which she announced a toast in their honor.

Within a few minutes the young people began to relax, looking at each other all wearing caps with the long tassels attached to their right shoulders. The girls looked sophisticated dressed in white. The boys, decked out in their suits, actually looked like young men.

One of them exclaimed, "Don't know about you, but this monkey outfit certainly is not mine, and I'm not so sure if I'll ever buy one! My mom dug it out of the closet. She mumbled something about it having belonged to her brother, Jan, who left for America about 20 years ago. I wonder what he wears when he has to get dressed up for serious events!"

A chain of giggles passed through the crowd.

"Me too. I think my dad wore this when he was married or something like that. It wouldn't fit his arm now . . . it wasn't a total loss because I found 100 Kroner in the right pocket and Far said I could keep it!"

The girls weren't quite that outspoken. Some of them had kept their dresses from their confirmation ceremony just a few years earlier, or had altered a dress that had belonged to an older sister.

As the atmosphere became more relaxed, the students began to circulate. This was the perfect set up for Ingrid's final step. Close to 4:30 pm, she excused herself with a forced smile, as she slowly and deliberately started circling the large room. Gradually she moved in the direction of the outside wall, which consisted of windows and a double door leading to the balcony. She positioned herself for a minute or so with her back against the French doors, waiting for just the right moment, simultaneously testing the door handle to see if it was open or locked. She was in luck. The knob yielded immediately. Gently she pushed the door open, just wide enough to slide through, and quickly closed the door. Hopefully no one had seen her.

She took a deep breath as her master plan began to materialize. Nervously she fumbled with her hair, making certain the cap was firmly in place and the long tassel extending from the top of the cap was still attached on her right shoulder. Fine, as her parents would say, when she asked them how she looked.

She moved across the balcony floor, until she was almost leaning over the banister. From that point, she had a perfect view of the Police Station across the street, as well as the entire length of Main Street. Once again, she reassured herself this was the only street any pedestrian would use to reach the Police Station. This specific group of men, who were forced to walk all the way from the outskirts of town after heavy labor, would be no exception. They would have to pass by the balcony to return to the newly-established prison awaiting them.

She didn't know when this would happen; she was prepared to wait as long as necessary. She almost lost track of time, because she couldn't stop thinking about Far. If everything went as planned, he would pass right below and make eye contact with her, if she was lucky. Around 5:15 pm she glimpsed some shadows moving in her direction, although still far away.

She willed herself to remain calm, telling herself over and over that she might be mistaken—but she wasn't. Holding her breath, she watched the shadows grow larger and clearer until there was no doubt in her mind. It was a group of men walking closely together. She recalled Arne's gentle voice telling her the prisoners would probably be chained together at the ankles, indicating there was very little flexibility in the individual walking space among them. It also became clear that one German soldier was in command of the men up front, and another soldier, holding on to the leash of a large dog, was in charge at the rear.

As the prisoners approached, Arne's prediction was confirmed. The eight men were indeed linked with ankle chains. Could it be? Yes, it was.

Ingrid saw only one person. Her heart started beating faster, and she had difficulty breathing. By a stroke of luck, Far was the second man from the right, allowing him to be quite close to the balcony, as opposed to the other side, closer to the Police Station. She leaned even closer to the banister while repeating to herself, Look up, Far, please look up.

She was afraid if she said even one single word out loud, she would attract the attention of the guards, which would probably result in a number of highly unpleasant consequences for the men. She needed to get his attention silently.

Please look up, please look up, she prayed.

And perhaps it was indeed magic, because it worked. When the prisoners were just a few yards away, Far lifted his head and stared up at the balcony. His expression was instantly transformed from gloom and obvious fatigue to delight. He stopped, nearly causing the man next to him to trip. The man followed Far's glance, causing a chain reaction of missed steps among the hostages. Perhaps they were all alerted by a secret signal, because they slowed down and attempted to continue walking in an almost stationary manner, while concentrating very carefully so as not to alert the guards.

With eyes that revealed parental love and adoration, Far came to a full stop, dropped his arms on either side of his body, bowing forward—a gesture of respect, admiration and love. He was saluting his daughter and her new educational status. This was perhaps a moment which he had dreamed about and anticipated since the day she was born.

Father and daughter exchanged glances for what seemed like a very long time, yet at the same time, it seemed like only a fraction of a second. The group then continued slowly down the street until it reached the police station where they quickly, much too quickly, disappeared from sight while Ingrid tried to force herself to keep the image in her eyes and heart.

Chapter Nineteen

Next—Women and Children

OSLO, NOVEMBER 3–25, 1942

Life went on, out of necessity. Most of the Jewish women in town continued to follow a makeshift routine, for lack of a better word. The rumors and nightmares persisted, and each family attempted to prepare a long-term plan or in some instances, two.

Rebekka's family was no exception. They waited for good news. And they were fearful of bad news. They learned the meaning of the expression "to live in limbo." The most surprising was the realization that life still went on, day by day, hour by hour.

And despite knowing they were in line to be brought to Sweden, no one spoke about it. Everyone knew it was a matter of time.

November 4, yet another young man from the underground, unexpectedly knocked on the door instead of ringing the doorbell. The batch assigned to the Davidson family seemed to consist of five or maybe six men. Occasionally one failed to show up for two or three weeks, and no one commented on this. It appeared to be an unwritten law to ask no questions, although it was impossible not to wonder. What happened to the one with the red hair, and the scar on his left wrist? Had he escaped to Sweden, or had something terrible taken place? Rebekka never dared to bring it up, only hoped that he would "check in" to reassure them that he was still in action.

The messenger who arrived that day had been there several times before. He was around twenty years old, well built, with strong muscular arms, that belied his boyish face. One might even wonder if he ever needed to shave. They used to call him "Haakon with the smile!"

The attractive young man asked politely for Sarah. Rebekka noticed that he turned his head briefly in the direction of the kitchen, as if he wanted to see who was there. Perhaps he was looking for Ruth, Rebekka thought, nodding briefly to the visitor after he flashed his beautiful teeth and exceptional smile.

When he saw Mor, he got right to the point. "It appears the milk truck arrived at its destination very early this morning. All four milk containers were intact with no leakage. They were removed from the large cardboard box which had been used for protection and were delivered to the designated dairy. You will most probably receive a list within the next few days as to where the milk can be purchased."

He stood still, waiting for Sarah to confirm that she understood the coded message. She looked at him, holding her breath. At that point he couldn't help himself, and broke into a large smile. She covered her mouth with her left hand, and said, "Thank you, God. Thank you, thank you!"

Oh, thank you, God, Rebekka immediately thought as well. This must mean that Far and her three uncles had arrived safely in Sweden. There were two armoires in the apartment that were chosen to get them down the stairs and out of the house without being seen by anyone. The armoires were loaded on to a large milk truck and stayed there until they finally arrived at the targeted location at the Swedish border.

For a few minutes, Mor's face had taken on a slightly softer look, and she seemed to give herself permission to breathe normally. Rebekka was watching her intensely. Mor was thirty-eight years old. Rebekka wondered what was the source of her strength and perseverance. Was this a gradual development within a person when faced with adversity? Did this strength and skill grow? And what about Ruth? She was in her early twenties. Where did she get the ability to make the decisions of the kind that she had recently? She didn't even seem to hesitate whether or not she would escape with them to Sweden. Was it fear or a strong moral perception to automatically discern what in life was right and what was wrong?

Rebekka realized she was late for school and rushed to grab her coat and backpack. Running out the door and entering the elevator, she found herself standing opposite "Haakon with the Smile." When they reached the ground floor and walked into the street, he gently touched her shoulder, asking, "Do you have a second, Rebekka? I have something I want you to know."

She looked at him in complete surprise. She had never spoken to him directly, as she always stood next to Mor, or sometimes Far, when he was still around. She became aware of her surroundings. They were standing in the middle of the sidewalk. People were passing them on either side and cars were driving by. She just stared at him, and muttered a cautious, "Yes, of course."

He signaled for her to move a little to the side so they were closer to the wall and would be less obvious to people passing by.

"Listen, Rebekka, that's your name. Right? I know who you are, and I have noticed that although you say almost nothing, you listen to everything I report. I have something else that I should tell your mother, but it's bad news."

He paused for a few seconds, studying Rebekka's face as if convincing himself she was okay so he could continue. "When I saw the relief on your mother's face about the arrival of the milk cartons, I didn't have the heart to tell her the second part."

He looked at Rebekka briefly to see if she had understood what he meant by the "Milk Cartons." He must have been satisfied that she knew because he continued. "And unfortunately there is nothing she can do about this new situation. We have just learned that Leonard's fiancée, Synnoeve, was arrested yesterday and placed in a prison outside of Oslo. They have been looking for her for a while, and she was very cautious once he was arrested. It appears her emotions got the best of her."

Rebekka was staring at him, without speaking.

"Yesterday she decided to pay a visit to Leonard's mother's apartment as she had heard rumors that her future mother-in-law had escaped. Perhaps she was looking for a note or a letter or something about Leonard that had been left behind. Big mistake. His mother—Mrs. Davidson, your grandmother, had indeed been picked up and whisked out of Oslo safely by an ambulance two days ago, managing to fool the Gestapo and their bloodhounds. The Nazis were furious and decided to watch her place around the clock in the event that Synnoeve or someone else decided to come by to pick up some personal belongings. As luck would have it—or actually in this case, very bad luck, they arrested the beautiful and committed fiancée."

Rebekka took a deep breath. She wasn't quite sure whether she should be flattered that he had chosen to share this important news with her, or whether she felt uncomfortable. She stood still and continued to listen.

"Please, are you willing to relay this terrible news to your mother when she has a calm moment, and explain why I couldn't do it this morning? She'll probably hear about it from other sources as well."

His eyes were riveted on Rebekka and she didn't dare blink or move. He continued speaking.

"We have also heard that the Gestapo have started to send many of their Norwegian prisoners on to prison camps in Germany. Are they running out of space here in Norway, or do they have other plans?—that we don't know. They have sent two ships full of men and women."

He paused and turned a little to the side, shielding his eyes. He remained quiet for a short while and then continued. "It's a terrible world, isn't it?" he said.

"Synnoeve's younger brother was my best buddy when we were in school. He volunteered a short time after the invasion, and was shot just two weeks later. He was the main reason I got into resistance work."

Rebekka said nothing, as she didn't know what to say. She had heard that most of the men in this cluster of passionate and active Norwegian patriots had developed the art of not displaying emotion, but occasionally even their sadness was too much to bear.

She gently put her hand on his shoulder as a small token of sympathy. He whispered softly, "Thank you for helping me, I appreciate it." He then turned and was gone.

Life was about to change—forever. Actually, it already had. The regular calendar had been replaced by one single question, "When are we leaving for Sweden?" Winter was coming, and it got a little cooler each day. The leaves were gone and the first snow was around the corner. Every other day some-one dropped a casual remark. "I just heard that my friend who I used to play bridge with each Wednesday couldn't make it yesterday. No, I don't know where she and her kids are. She didn't tell me." Looks were exchanged, but no words. The same comments were dropped about a sister-in-law, a cousin with two small girls, the elderly woman who used to run a flower store.

Around the third week of November, Mor entered the kitchen and asked both Rebekka and Ruth to sit down; her signal that she had some news. Her voice was unusually serious. They gathered around the kitchen table, each sitting at their regular places. Rebekka wondered why all serious events had to be discussed in the kitchen and not in any other room? Perhaps they already had become used to the severity of an impending talk and felt more secure at their regular seats? Rebekka sat down, holding her sketchbook, which she hadn't touched for a few weeks. Ruth stood leaning against the kitchen counter. Sarah was in constant motion between the coffee pot and the telephone, with an occasional tapping on the table or the counter. She used to smoke, but there were no more cigarettes to be bought.

It was obvious Mor had something on her mind, but gave the impression of being hesitant. Finally she got started. "I just met with Signe Falk, whom I have mentioned before. She is our contact at the Gestapo. She continues to alert us in secret. She has bad news. She and seven non-Jews are going door-to-door warning Jewish women who are still around to make plans to leave as soon as possible. "The ground under your feet is beginning to burn,"" she said. "This is as serious a message as we can get.

"She told me that sometime tomorrow or the next day a large German ship will dock in Oslo harbor. The ship is slated for transport back to Germany once it's full of as many Norwegian Jews as possible. All the Jewish men and boys presently held in prisons will be brought down to the docks. They are also planning on arresting women and children at the crack of dawn on November 26 for the same purpose. For that reason it's imperative that we either go into hiding or manage to get across the border to Sweden where father is waiting for us."

Silence prevailed when Mor stopped. Rebekka and Ruth didn't dare move. Mor rose and crossed to the stove where the coffee pot permanently sat. She heated up the water and brewed something that certainly wasn't coffee. The only thing this ground coffee surrogate had in common with coffee was its name. It hit the spot, nevertheless.

She poured three cups so each one had something to hold while attempting to digest the news and the rescue plan. Despite looking tired and drawn, Mor was determined to complete the briefing. "I have already made arrangements for my mother, her sister and brother-in-law, Annika's parents, to be admitted to a local hospital tonight. They will stay there overnight. The Chief of Staff, an old friend of the family, has arranged for them to be transferred tomorrow afternoon by ambulance to another hospital, which has more room and better facilities. However, this is just an excuse. The ambulance is not going to bring them to another hospital, but will bring them directly to Sweden. This is being done because elderly people may be unable to tolerate the strenuous travel and walk through the woods to the border of Sweden."

Mor stopped speaking and stared into space, "Listen, both of you. This is going to be serious and maybe scary. Let's not say anything else right now. I am sure you have enough to think about."

Rebekka and Ruth sat still, wondering if Mor was going to continue speaking.

"Here is what I would like to do. Please get up." The other two kept looking at her. "Let's move into the library. I am getting sick of sitting around the kitchen table discussing serious issues. This is bad enough. Come with me."

Rebekka and Ruth stared at her in disbelief but eventually got up from the table.

Mor sat in front of the fireplace. Her face took on another expression. Clearly the time has come to make a major decision—hopefully the last phase of this horror, Rebekka thought. Mor seemed almost excited, or at least calmer than earlier. She turned around and opened the screen to the fireplace where they could see the outline of three pieces of firewood. As far as Rebekka could remember they hadn't had a fire for the past two years, as access to firewood was just about impossible. Mor noticed her astonishment and said,

"Yes, Rebekka, time has come to use these logs that we have been saving for a special occasion. Today is just that, although not a happy one. I decided to think of today and tomorrow as special days in our lives. They will symbolize our future in Sweden where we will be able to live free from looming dangers. I want you to remember them for the rest of your life. We are going to fight back."

A few minutes later the logs were lit, sending out beams of light into the small library. Rebekka recognized the unique smell of the logs which she hadn't experienced for so long.

But Mor had more information to convey. "Frank, his mother, and two or three women will leave for Sweden tomorrow afternoon, Wednesday the 24th, guided by the same unit that will attempt to bring us across the border the following day, Thursday, November 25 at 5 pm. Our group will consist of the four of us—you two, Miriam and me. We need to be ready exactly at that time and we'll hopefully be brought across to Sweden in the same manner as the ones leaving tomorrow. I have been able to hide some of our silver and some old sentimental things like family pictures. We will leave everything else behind and place our lives in the hands of God and the Norwegian resistance."

Rebekka was in deep thought. She felt totally overwhelmed. Sweden? Where would they live? What about her schoolwork, and what about her friends? What about Kari? It occurred to her that maybe the Swedes might not be as nice as they expected. What could she bring along and what would happen to all her things that she couldn't bring? Was Mor serious? Should they leave everything in their apartment behind? Their clothes, their books, their furniture? What about Miriam's toys?

Ruth and Rebekka sat still, neither saying a word, just watching Mor. No one knew what to say or do. They were fascinated by Mor's new attitude. Finally she asked, "Do you have any questions? You must have some questions."

"What are we going to tell Miriam?" Ruth asked gently.

Mor hesitated for a second and then continued. "I suggest that we follow our regular daily routine. We need to think of something to tell her to explain why we are leaving the house. As far as I'm concerned, there is no reason why she shouldn't go to the park in the morning as usual."

Ruth volunteered to speak with Miriam. "I'll tell her that we are going on a winter vacation to the country to pick potatoes!"

"Great idea, Ruth," Mor exclaimed.

She got up again, but this time she was smiling. "Ruth, if you find any good food hidden in the pantry that we may have put aside for a special occasion, now is the time to get it out." However, a small shadow covered her face. "I really doubt that there is anything there at all."

"Don't worry," Ruth said with a slight spark in her eyes, "I'll look. What about Annika, have you been able to reach her today?"

"I can't reach her. I need to try again. If we can convince her, she could leave either tomorrow with Frank and his mother, or with us. But I can't get a hold of her." Mor got up and went back to the kitchen to call again, but as before, there was no response. The library was warm and cozy, clearly the kitchen was their work center.

Rebekka started thinking about the danger involved in the escape. She tried in vain to push these thoughts away. At least she didn't tell anyone how she felt. She got up slowly and stood absolutely still, holding on to the back of a chair. She looked eager to leave the library and the fire. She had a strange sensation. She felt she shouldn't relax too much, to let her guard down. It felt as if remaining in the kitchen might postpone the inevitable, or at least keep them safe.

Wednesday arrived, and the calendar showed November 24, the scheduled departure day for Frank and his mother. Nothing was said, there was nothing more to say. The waiting had ended. Rebekka went to school, and thought of nothing but the two who were getting ready to escape. Frank and his mother were to leave at 3:30 pm, when they were being picked up by the get-away car.

Mor was quiet throughout the day, and Rebekka was afraid to bother her. She did however hear her on the phone with Annika.

"Listen, sweetie, this is serious. Your parents are on their way to Sweden. I promised your mother that I would speak with you. There is still room for you to come with us."

Evidently Annika persisted in saying no. The conversation continued until Mor stood with the receiver in her hand, saying out loud to no one, "She hung up on me. What more can I do?" She walked out of the room, but Rebekka couldn't miss the expression on her face; the exhaustion and frustration were apparent.

On the way home from school that day Kari brought up the subject of her father, who had been in hiding, away from the house for several weeks. She confided that her father would stop by the house late at night. He would enter through the courtyard in the back of their apartment building, which was facing another street, walk through several small sheds, and come through the kitchen stairway. He would stay for a few hours, speaking with his wife and his daughters. He would take a short nap in his own bed before leaving early in the morning when the streets were clear. Rebekka listened to the fear in her friend's voice, not unlike what she experienced herself.

Finally Rebekka couldn't take it anymore. She felt she might burst. "My father has been gone for one month." She couldn't hold it in. She cried, "He is in Sweden. He's safe now, but he was hiding in an empty apartment for three weeks. Frank and my aunt are leaving today, in a few hours. We are leaving soon, because the Germans are planning to arrest the Jewish women and children."

Kari looked at her in disbelief. Rebekka continued, "We, we . . . " she was unable to continue—it felt like she was choking, "We are actually leaving tomorrow, and I am not supposed to tell anyone. We are leaving for Sweden. Please, please, don't tell anyone, you have to promise me."

Kari couldn't take her eyes off her friend and remained quiet. She put her arms around Rebekka's neck and hugged her.

"Of course I won't. I'll think of you every day, and I'll be here when you return." She turned around abruptly and walked away. Rebekka could see she was trying not to cry.

Rebekka walked around the block. She didn't feel like going home quite yet. Everyone appeared to be on their way somewhere. Well, for them it probably was just a regular day. There were the usual lines at the grocery store, and the streetcar was full of people. A few soldiers were walking from one place to another, and some youngsters were laughing and joking. War and suffering didn't exist for them—at least not at that very moment. A couple of small kids ran in front of her.

I wonder what it will be like when we return, she thought, not knowing how long they would be gone. Would Miriam remember the park and the wonderful ladies who played with her every day from 11 am until 2 pm? Would her classmates move on to other schools, and would she ever see them again?

She reached her house and went in. Now it felt like a calm day. There didn't seem to be anything left to discuss or worry about. The decisions had been made. The dinner that day was light and unexceptional. Mor was quiet and lost in thought. Ruth had prepared a number of small dishes, which she put on the table.

"Are you trying to use up whatever's left in the pantry?" Rebekka said to Ruth, half as a joke and half seriously. No response. She excused herself and spent some time going through her clothing. Would her clothes fit when she returned? She had pulled out a couple of heavy sweaters and her ski pants, which she had been instructed to wear tomorrow. She put them on a chair, organized her schoolbooks and a few personal letters, and put them in her desk drawer. At the last moment she took out a batch of sketchbooks which she had worked on ever since the invasion. She tied them together and put them at the bottom of the backpack as Sarah had instructed her to bring only essential items. It made the bag heavier, but she couldn't stand leaving them behind.

Then a thought struck her. She felt slightly dizzy. What would happen to their apartment while they were gone? Their furniture and their belongings? Her clothing, her books? Would another girl sleep in her bed and even try on her clothes? Who would these tenants be? Would they be nice people who needed a place to hide, or would they be Nazis and Germans who wanted to settle into a good apartment? The more she thought, the worse she felt. There were no answers—that much she knew.

She got up from her desk, and walked around, feeling very tired and sad. She quickly pulled off her clothing, put on her nightgown and got under the covers. Maybe if she went to sleep, these disturbing thoughts would leave her.

Being the end of November, it was already dark. The blinds on the windows were down, and the noise from the street was subsiding. She felt herself relax, getting ready for a full night's sleep, despite her internal turmoil. Suddenly a loud thump was heard on the front door. And another. It was clear that it came from the outside. She heard Mor get up and say, "Who could that be?"

The knock was repeated once more before Mor was able to reach the door. Whoever was responsible for making this noise was in a hurry; one might even say desperate. She heard Mor call out, "Who is it?" Rebekka was unable to distinguish the answer. A few seconds later the door opened and she heard Mor scream, "Oh, my God. What happened?"

Rebekka couldn't stay away. She had to see who was at the door. Dressed in her pajamas and bare feet she slipped into the dining room, hiding behind the door that faced the hallway.

The man waiting was in great distress. His face was pale, his eyes bloodshot. He was soaking wet with perspiration, he was shaking. He took one look at Mor and started sobbing.

She let him in and took him in her arms.

It was Frank.

Chapter Twenty

Leyla Gives In

AALESUND, NOVEMBER 25, 1942

"Ingrid, have you taken leave of your senses? Do you realize what could have happened to you? These are not toy soldiers—they are mad men!"

Harald couldn't remember ever yelling at her—at least not this intensely. He kept staring at her, needing to convince himself that he had actually heard correctly. It was too incredible.

"If the wrong person had been there, you would have been arrested and sent off to some women's prison. I shiver when I think of you being foolish enough to make your way inside the police station at this time in our life."

He shook his head, trying very hard to remain calm.

Harald had just returned from school and couldn't find his key. Actually, he hadn't even looked for it, depending on Mor to open the door as usual. Like most teenagers, he had a key, which he chose not to use; instead he just banged on the door with his fist. Today though, when he didn't get the expected response, he decided to ring the doorbell once. Twice. No answer.

He had no idea what was going on. Reluctantly he dug through his pockets, found his door key and let himself in. Just as he had expected, Mor was indeed there, but she was talking on the telephone.

Actually, she wasn't speaking at all. She was listening while the person on the opposite end talked non-stop. His mother wasn't sitting down on a chair as she normally did; she was moving around in small circles limited by the length of the telephone cord.

Her free hand was busy fiddling with her apron, which she always wore over her street clothes, and today it was protecting her dark brown dress, which meant she had just returned from some committee meeting in town.

It hadn't taken Harald long to realize this was not a pleasant phone call, she was upset and agitated. Occasionally she answered with a "yes," "no," or at best, "you don't understand."

Harald tried to figure out who was on the other line. Mor turned in his direction. Choosing to ignore him, she continued to listen intently to the other party—not saying a word.

When the conversation eventually ended and she hung up, she still didn't move but remained in the same position. It took her a couple of minutes to regain her composure and finally acknowledge her son.

"Did you have lunch at school?" she asked. Harald knew that this was a ploy to postpone the inevitable so he didn't answer.

"Who was on the line?" he said. Nothing more and nothing less.

She relented and answered, "That was your aunt in Trondheim. This is the second call I've had today from my family." She took a deep breath to get herself ready to convey the message and said, "They are all telling me that we need to get out of town, and try to get to Sweden or even England. They are already in hiding and will leave within the next few days."

"Have you talked to Ingrid about this?" he asked. "I have no idea what you're waiting for. You know several people in town have been encouraging us to do the same."

She seemed to purposely ignore his comment, and she continued, "The situation in both Oslo and Trondheim is deteriorating. Your father's childhood friend, Max Goldberg, a dentist in Trondheim, has been arrested along with 11 other men. They're being held in a prison nearby. Several of the resistance people involved in helping the Jews have also been arrested, and the cantor has been shot. I don't know where things are worse, in Oslo or in Trondheim." She paused again; trying to avoid her son's piercing glare and expression. "Well, what do you think we should do?"

With that, she broke down and started crying, allowing the tears to run down her cheeks.

He became acutely aware of his mother's distress. His goal was to explain calmly and realistically that it was time for them to think of alternate ways of living and that they needed to leave town. Move. Escape. He really didn't know what word he should use, not wanting to scare Mor more than necessary, or maybe he was trying to avoid scaring himself as well, if truth be told.

Actually, he did want to scare her, just a little bit, but he wasn't sure how to accomplish this. Her initial reaction was exactly what he had expected.

"Don't you understand, Harald? How can I leave? What will happen to your father if he is released and we are gone? Can you imagine him coming home to an empty apartment, with no business and no family? You know how distracted and absentminded he is. Who is going to take care of him? I'm sure the only thing that keeps him going is knowing we're here. I can't do it, I just can't. Please understand me. Oh, my goodness, I just don't know what to do."

It was at that very moment that everything escalated. The apartment door opened and Ingrid burst into the room, wide-eyed, as if seeing them for the first time ever. She was obviously agitated, in some kind of heightened state. Her red jacket was unbuttoned as were the top two buttons of her white blouse. Her cheeks where red as if she might have a fever, and she was perspiring. She had difficulty breathing, having run up three flights of stairs. She had just gone through an emotional experience, which she frantically tried to share with them—but they couldn't understand a word!

Harald, already in a mood of intense concentration, approached her, ever so gently, afraid that she would pull away from him. He took her hand and whispered, "Please sit down and tell us what happened, but take your time."

He looked around the room hoping to find a clue on how to reach her. Finally, he decided to go into the kitchen, returning with two glasses of water—one he gave to Ingrid and one to his mother. If he had been able to carry a third glass, he would have brought one for himself.

When she had caught her breath, Ingrid said, "I did something I never thought was possible. I have no idea where I got the idea from and what made me do it. I was downtown walking past the police station and suddenly it dawned on me what I should do."

"I opened the door, and strangely enough no one tried to stop me. There were two young officers sitting at the counter. I decided to try to fool them. I bent over and said in a low voice 'Please, I am terribly sick to my stomach, I think I am going to vomit. May I please use the bathroom?' They were so surprised that they didn't know if they should say yes or no! I think they were worried that I would vomit right there!"

"One of them pointed towards a corridor in the back, and I walked very quickly around the corner and entered the bathroom. Once I got there, I really didn't know what to do, so I flushed the toilet and ran the water for a long time. I even washed my face!"

"I opened the door, pretending I was lost and went in the wrong direction. You may not believe this but at that very second four men came out another door and one of them was Far. I stood still, frozen to the spot, with no idea what to do next, or which way to turn. I then actually felt so sick to my stomach that I almost did vomit for sure. Far saw me and grabbed my arm, and do you know what? He was angry with me."

She stopped, and started to cry.

"He asked what I was doing there, and I answered that I didn't know. That's exactly how I felt. He half pushed me in the right direction towards the counter with the two soldiers, whispering quickly he would be sent to northern Norway tomorrow at 7 am by boat. He said, 'Tell Mor that all of you must leave the country as soon as possible. Please listen to me!'"

"And that's the last I saw or heard. I ran out past the counter and the men. Past a police dog sitting in a corner. Strangely enough, no one reacted. I ran and ran, and didn't stop for a second. I was afraid to look back, worried the police officers or the dogs would be coming after me. They did follow for a while, but fortunately they stopped after a few minutes. Perhaps they didn't know what to do with me."

She grabbed the glass and quickly emptied it. Her brother took it and filled it up again. Both he and his mother stared at her, speechless.

It was then that Harald no longer could control himself, and exploded. He couldn't believe that Ingrid would be that careless and risk causing even more problems for them. He felt faint and it was liberating to scream at her.

Her mother got up from the sofa and crossed the room. She put her arm on Ingrid's shoulder, while she said, "If he is to be transported tomorrow morning, we have to be at the dock at 6:30 to make certain we see him—if only for a few seconds. After that we need to contact some of our friends to see if it's too late for us to escape, or if we can still make it."

Chapter Twenty-One

The Wrong Train

OSLO, NOVEMBER 25, 1942

Thursday, November 25, 1942, the designated day for the Davidson family to escape, had finally arrived. Rebekka found it difficult to abide by her mother's request to go about her normal activities, such as attending school.

What for? She thought. I won't be there tomorrow. I'll be in Sweden, or . . . she decided not to think any further.

She recalled the excitement of the previous night with Frank's unexpected return, and that prompted her to focus on her bizarre dream. In her night-time vision, she was walking through several train compartments, looking for Frank. Everyone in the compartments looked identical, but Frank was missing.

She dismissed the dream and rushed into the kitchen. There he was, in person, sitting quietly. He didn't even look up.

Was he avoiding her? Was it possible that he was embarrassed about having taken the wrong train?

Should she mention his unsuccessful escape or wait for him to say something?

She stopped by the kitchen table, unsure whether to sit or stand, not knowing what to say. It appeared that Mor had the same thought.

"Did you get some rest, Frank? It took me quite a while to fall asleep. But you are here now, and we're grateful for that. You must be starved. I think we have a few eggs left over. We've tried to save them for special occasions, considering that we won't eat breakfast here tomorrow, I hope that you and Rebekka will finish them. Whatever we don't finish today, we'll take with us on the trip." Mor's voice was relaxed as if nothing unusual had taken place or was about to do so later in the day.

The trip? Rebekka thought. That was a generous name for the plans in store that afternoon. She said nothing, just waited for a response. Frank looked up, sending a quick smile Rebekka's way. It dawned on her that perhaps he was as shy about speaking to her as she to him.

He put his fork down and folded his napkin meticulously, as if he were present at a formal family dinner.

He took a deep breath and looked at Mor first and then at Ruth, who was clearing the dishes.

"Do you want to hear what really happened?" Frank finally said.

No one answered as it was obvious they couldn't wait to hear the details.

He started speaking slowly but gradually his voice took on more emotion. "The trip in the car was uneventful. I was sitting in the rear of the small van, behind the passenger seats, which were jammed full with four women. My seat was small and crude and couldn't accommodate anyone else. I had taken a little nap and had just awakened when I heard the guides giving out instructions.

"After about two hours we were told that we were nearing the station. That's where we were supposed to leave the car and get on the train. Just when the guides stopped, they became aware of a group of 10–12 German soldiers standing in a cluster on the platform. This unexpected appearance came as a surprise and alarmed everyone, including our guides.

"Clearly this wasn't a good situation and the guides' concern was evident even before the driver had turned off the engine.

"My mother had been told to sit in the front between the two men, being the smallest of the five women. Fear and slight panic erupted when the guide on mother's side started to speak. 'Listen carefully, everyone. We have a bit of a problem here. Obviously you have noticed the group of enemy soldiers waiting on the platform—for what, we don't know. Maybe they're just planning to get on the train, or maybe they have another agenda. Our fear is that the sight of five dark-haired women together might alert them that you are Jews on the run.'"

Frank paused and looked at the women in the kitchen who were holding their breath.

"Everyone in the car stopped speaking immediately to listen, and they were very upset, to say the least. Then the driver himself took charge, and told them once again to listen carefully. 'Here is what we suggest you do. Please split up. Walk up and down the platform until the train arrives and try to enter the train one by one, or no more than two together. If you can, try to look casual and relaxed.'"

Frank paused for a few seconds once more and looked around the kitchen before he continued. He touched the breadbasket sitting on the table in from of him.

Rebekka asked gently, "Were you able to relax?"

"Yeah, that would be easy, right?" Frank continued, in a sarcastic voice, looking at her. He grabbed a slice of bread, which he pushed to the side. Rebekka wondered if he was trying to bide his time to avoid crying. None of the three sitting around the kitchen table uttered a word.

"Neither of the guides spoke to me directly, and even if they had, I just couldn't have heard them because of all the noise." Frank continued. "Well, I guess I kind of heard them, but I didn't understand what they wanted us to do, and especially what I should do, sitting by myself behind two rows of seats.

"I tried to reach my mother but couldn't with all the noise and conversation. It was impossible to get her attention with all the chaos and agitated banter among the women. Or maybe she tried to reach me, but couldn't be heard."

For a second Frank's voice got a little shaky, as he was close to tears again.

Frank, crying? Impossible, Rebekka thought. Then she felt guilty considering what he must have gone through.

"Honestly, it got quite confusing. The women were upset. I was very scared. When we were told to leave the car—which was behind the platform—everyone fought to get out first. The women scattered, trying to board the train alone. I forgot to tell you that another train had just come in to the station. The guide told me to leave the car immediately. All I could see were arms, backpacks, and a little pushing. I didn't see Mor. I wondered if she had to wait for the guide next to her to get out first, or perhaps she had already left the car and was waiting for me."

Frank stopped speaking again, needing to catch his breath, or perhaps he needed to regroup a little to stay calm.

"I kept looking around, but couldn't see Mor. I felt panicky. I boarded the train the closest to me, as I thought the guides had instructed. I think I assumed Mor was there already. I don't even know what I was thinking. I just got on the train. By myself. Then I realized I could see two other trains through the window. At that point I got totally confused. Where was my mother? I looked around the compartment but couldn't see her. I really don't know why I had ended up there, I have no explanation. I just thought that's what I was supposed to do, and I was scared, really scared about having done something wrong.

"As soon as I moved to go down the steps to leave, I felt a jerky movement. The train was starting to leave.

"For a minute I hoped I could get off at the next station and catch another train back. No such luck. I was on a non-stop train going in the opposite direction, heading back to the Central Railroad Station in Oslo.

"I sat down at the very end of a compartment and spoke to no one, trying not to show how scared I was. I had no idea if they would feel pity for me or report me to the first Nazi they could see on the train. Two hours later, we reached Oslo and fortunately the train stopped. I was the first one off. I had no ticket, of course, and when the train conductor approached, I jumped off and ran. I ran away from the conductor, from the station and from the soldiers walking around the Oslo station.

"My legs would only move in one direction, that is, toward your house! My hope was that you and the girls hadn't yet left. I remembered you were scheduled to leave on Thursday. That's today, right?"

He grabbed a glass of water sitting right in front and drank.

"I sobbed all the way to your house. I don't think I started breathing normally until I got here, Tante Sarah.

"My mother must think I'm dead. Oh, my God. I wonder how she is."

Here he stopped for a moment, and said, "When I was little, she always told me that if I ever got lost and couldn't find her, I should ask for my Aunt Sarah. That's when she taught me your last name was Davidson. I felt I was hearing her voice as I ran towards your house. Do you think she remembers that?"

Mor remained silent. She patted Frank on the shoulder and whispered. "I hope so. I'm sure that's what she will think about as well. You did the right thing. You'll see.

"Rebekka, please get ready for school. Once again, it's vital that you attend today as usual. We need to stick to a regular routine so no one will suspect anything. As for me, I'll phone Annika, my stubborn cousin, one more time to see if she has changed her mind."

Looking at Frank, she said calmly, "When you have finished your breakfast, you may want to take a shower."

Turning to Ruth, who had been in the kitchen getting organized for the day, she said in a soft voice, "I know you have lots to do today, but Frank's clothing needs to be washed. No, wait! Come to think of it, forget it. Let Frank go into my husband's closet and pick out any clothes that will fit him, are comfortable and will keep him warm for the trip.

"Frank, we are being picked up at 5 o'clock. After you have taken a shower and picked out some clothes, please go into Rebekka's room and stay there. Don't leave the room, and don't call for me. I don't want anybody to find out that you are here. That's the way it's going to have to be. I hope the guides won't object to another person in the car."

For a second Rebekka thought about Annika. What if she changed her mind and decided to join them after all. She kept it to herself certain her mother would know how to deal with that as well. Rebekka got up slowly, still uneasy about leaving the house. Then—knowing Kari was waiting downstairs, she rushed out the door.

Chapter Twenty-Two

The White and the Black Raincoat

AALESUND, NOVEMBER 25, 1942

"How do we know the prisoners will really leave tomorrow morning at 6:30 am? And how will we get there?"

Leyla could hear her own voice shaking.

She was looking out the window. She felt Ingrid place her hands gently on her shoulders. The fjord could be seen from their house, which overlooked the city. Was she talking to herself or to her children? Was she thinking aloud, she asked herself?

"Mor, I saw Arne a little while ago. I told him I visited the jail, without an invitation and nearly got caught. I can still hear the dogs running after me; though not for long. It seemed like an eternity! He was just as shocked as you and Harald. He will try to verify that the prisoners really are to be sent out tomorrow. I'm meeting him again in about 30 minutes. He will also try to find other options for you, me and Harald. We need to start somewhere. Most probably he will come back with me when I return."

Ingrid had more or less regained her composure since the traumatic experience at the police station. Then something else had also taken place. Besides seeming quite collected, Ingrid appeared different in some complex way, which was hard to decipher. She was more self-confident, more determined. She couldn't make things happen fast enough. For some reason it made Leyla apprehensive.

Why would she want to bring Arne home today when there were so many personal issues to address? Her daughter's voice had a new undertone, making her sound assertive, and at the same time, she also seemed hyperactive. This was an unusual combination. It felt as if Ingrid had taking charge of the next step for her family. Leyla had finally reached the decision that leaving

145

Aalesund was essential considering the political climate. All their thoughts were focused on how and when the next phase would be played.

"I'll be back later this evening; I don't know when," Ingrid muttered quickly as she slammed the outside door behind her.

Harald looked up briefly. As usual, he was calm, concentrating on two separate atlases and speaking in a low, meditative voice, either to himself or to his mother. It was hard to tell whom he was addressing, "I am looking at the routes to Sweden."

Leyla didn't interrupt him. She gently touched his head, not unlike the gesture her daughter had made to her a few minutes earlier. She felt the only person who needed to be informed about the family decision, was Sofie.

"She is the only person I trust in this situation. There is nothing anyone else can do, regardless."

Walking towards the telephone, she wondered whether it was safe to discuss this type of urgent information on the telephone.

She grasped the telephone, "Hello, Sofie," she said. "I hope your cold is better. Did you take my advice about sleeping with a hot towel on your chest to loosen the congestion?"

She was wondering how her friend would react to this bizarre comment, since this topic had never been brought up.

However, Sofie was a perceptive woman and a quick thinker; she responded swiftly. "Thank you. I am feeling much better. I would like to return your heating pad, which helped quite a bit. I was thinking of bringing it over today. Will you by any chance be available if I stop by around four or so?"

Thirty minutes later Sofie was knocking on Leyla's door. Her face was serious as she walked inside, sat down and addressed her friend, "What's going on?"

Leyla gave a quick rundown of the dramatic day, ending with the family's decision. She was quite relieved to share this information with Sofie and started shaking slightly while providing the update, including Ingrid's careless experiment earlier in the day.

"Where should we go and how? Do you have any suggestions about who I should contact? Will it cost money? I have almost nothing left. They have confiscated everything. I don't even know what we will need, besides clothing, food and passports. What should I do with the few things left here in the apartment?"

Sofie in her straightforward manner reacted immediately.

"I am leaving and will be back as soon as I can. Wait here until I return. Let me see what I can find out."

She turned in the doorway on the way out while putting on her coat and hat.

"I'll drive you to the docks tomorrow morning to see the prisoners off, regardless of what other plans we come up with."

Harald looked up, saying something that sounded like, "Great, thank you. Mor, my sister and I appreciate your support and help." He knew that Sofie's instruction was partially aimed at him as well, but he had nothing else to share. He was still obsessed with the various escape options.

Late afternoon and early evening passed slowly. Leyla and Harald didn't speak. The process of waiting had become a full-time activity, it seemed, absorbing all their energy and thoughts. Leyla was the only one to move around. She walked restlessly from one piece of furniture to another, touching each piece. She felt like she was saying good-bye to the items that had been part of her life for many years and besides, it gave her something to do with her increasingly fidgety hands.

With a deep sigh, she realized there wasn't much left of value to worry about. She had sold pieces one at a time. They had needed the money. If her children had noticed, they certainly hadn't mentioned it. She found a medium-sized empty box in the closet in which she placed some silver trinkets that she had kept since her youth and from her wedding. Her symbolic Jewish pieces, which she only took out for the holidays, were placed in there as well. She closed the box and wrote "Sofie" on top.

The few pieces of jewelry she had received through the years were put into a small cloth bag, which she planned to bring along, thinking she might have to trade them in for cash. She wondered how she would be able to withdraw what she had left in her savings account, when she remembered there was next to nothing in it. Fortunately, she had a habit of keeping some cash hidden in the house, and for a brief second she felt happy knowing she had the foresight to make that decision. There certainly wasn't much else to be happy about that day.

The hours went by—in keeping with the November darkness outside. No sign of Sofie and no news from Ingrid. Leyla sat in the twilight, once again thinking about her husband. That was all she could do now. She worried about his health—his aching feet and back—his frequent headaches. Stress headaches, he called them.

By chance, Sofie and Ingrid, followed by Arne, all arrived at the same time. It was clear that Ingrid and Arne were in charge, together, as one unit. Sofie sat down next to the young couple. She had said nothing since she entered the apartment. She hadn't even looked at Leyla. Leyla started to wonder if this was just a coincidence, or if it were some sign of agreement Sofie, Ingrid and Arne had reached.

Only one lamp was on, with minimal light coming in from the street. Leyla had failed to pull down the blinds on the two windows in their living room, as instructed by the police. It wasn't done intentionally. However, could it be interpreted as disobedience? Let them come and complain, she thought. What else can they take from me? My husband is gone and we are planning on leaving our home. Regretting her disobedience, she got up and closed the blinds. It might be better not to challenge destiny.

Arne initiated the conversation by asking everyone to gather around including Harald who was still sitting by himself. It was clear that Arne had something specific to impart to them. His voice was firm and assertive. Ingrid kept staring at him as if seeing him for the first time. Her love and admiration were obvious. Leyla's gaze moved from her daughter to Arne. There was indeed something different about him today. Not just his voice. Not just his gestures. Not just the expression on his face.

Like lightening, it struck her. Arne had become an adult. His mannerism had changed because he had changed. He was taking charge. He was going to tell them what to do.

Even Harald put aside his maps and books and paid attention.

Arne cleared his throat. "Sorry it took so long for me to get back to you. It was difficult to verify the information which Ingrid learned today. But it's accurate.

"This is what we know. The bastards have made plans to ship Mr. Rosenberg and seven other prisoners off to northern Norway tomorrow morning. I apologize for my language, Mrs. Rosenberg, but I can't think of other words to describe these people. They all are to board the regularly scheduled ferry, which leaves every day for Aandalsnes from dock three at 7 am. The difference is that tomorrow morning the ferry will have no passengers other than this group. I have heard that once they reach the docks at Aandalsnes, the prisoners will continue north by train, ostensibly to do manual labor. The plans for the first part of the journey are definite, but we have no additional information beyond that."

Arne's voice was clear and calm, pausing between each sentence, making certain that everyone heard. Leyla was silent and listening intently. At times, her thoughts drifted, focusing on her husband, worrying if he had enough warm clothing, both for the ferry ride and later. She was overcome by loneliness and fear, despite the presence of her two children. Parents are supposed to protect their children, not the other way around, she thought. She tried to stay in control but was unable to prevent the tears from rolling down her face. She grabbed a handkerchief, trying to concentrate on the next piece of information.

Arne continued, "My contact person," he paused, without divulging the name of the person in question, "feels there is no reason why you shouldn't go down to the docks tomorrow morning to see Mr. Rosenberg off if you want to. Hopefully you'll at least have a chance to wave to him."

Leyla looked up. For the first time in the past fifteen minutes, she stared at Arne, listening intently. She was fixated, waiting for him to continue. Only her hands were in motion, bending and unbending.

"There will be other relatives seeing the prisoners off as well. That's all we can tell you. Ms. Sofie has offered to drive you there. To be on the safe side, I suggest that you get there by 6:00 tomorrow morning."

Silence filled the room.

Arne repositioned himself and continued directing his questions at Sofie.

"Tell me, do you own a raincoat?"

Everyone looked at Arne, and then at each other, wondering if they had heard right.

"Yes, a raincoat," he repeated.

Sofie pointed to herself, to confirm that she had heard correctly, before she replied.

"Yes, of course I do. It's black and very practical," she added, although no one had asked about the color. "I don't wear it very often. It's long and has a hood, and . . . why do you ask?"

"I'll get to that in a moment."

"Mrs. Rosenberg, Harald, and of course Ingrid," he said, inadvertently sending a glance at Ingrid with an inordinate amount of tenderness. "You have, although unbeknownst to you, a very good and caring friend who is working at the local police department. Yes, he is with the opposition, and he is working with the police by choice, having intentionally chosen this position. It's extremely risky and dangerous, but it gives him a chance to secretly help his fellow Norwegian citizens."

Arne continued, telling them that he obviously couldn't divulge the person's name. He was sure they would understand why that was essential.

"When Ingrid turned to me today asking if I knew of any contacts who might be able to help your family get away, I promised her I would ask around. I didn't tell her I already had one contact.

"I have spent several hours today with my brave friend, and we finally came up with a possible solution."

Harald was listening attentively. He straightened his back, holding on to the chair armrest. He stared at Arne. Finally, he spoke up, "What in the world does this potential solution have to do with Sofie's raincoat?"

Under normal circumstances that might have generated some laughter, but that wasn't to happen today. On the contrary.

"You have just heard about the transport of the eight prisoners tomorrow. The ferry service normally runs in the morning and in the afternoon. Due to a number of misunderstandings and confused plans, the ferry that ordinarily would bring regular passengers from Aalesund in the mid-morning was canceled for tomorrow. Another ferry was scheduled and booked for later in the day, around 5 pm. Just by chance, the police failed to notify the steamship authorities that there would be no need for a ferry in the mid-morning, since there would be one leaving at 5 pm. But you're going to be on the mid-morning ferry.

"The ferry should arrive tonight, and return to Aandalsnes tomorrow with no one onboard except for Mrs. Rosenberg, Harald and Ingrid and the captain and one or two men, and a few significant cartons."

Leyla began to feel overwhelmed by the details, and had difficulty following Arne's description. He had a lot to say and he said it quickly. She struggled to keep the facts straight in her mind, as he painted an almost incredible scenario. She noticed that Ingrid, on the other hand, was looking at him with large, trusting eyes.

Had she lost her daughter to this young man already? She had just turned nineteen. What would happen to her musical future? They had been assured that Ingrid had exceptional musical talent, and the plan was for her to study at the prominent Academy of Music in Oslo. The grand piano that Isak so proudly had decided she would need was bought and paid for, waiting for her in Oslo. Now what would happen? For a quick minute she forgot that Ingrid was about to leave town with her and Harald.

She felt too shy to interrupt Arne to tell him to slow down.

Leyla listened as he told them that the captain of the ferry had offered to help them.

Leyla turned to look at her son. He was biting his nails, which she hadn't seen since he was a small child. How could she have missed that? She worried that she hadn't paid enough attention to him lately, especially since he had alienated himself from his friends ever since his father's arrest. All he did was read European history. He gave the impression he was content being by himself, and that his research, as he called it, was a priority, but she hadn't even discussed what it was he was reading. She didn't even know if the reading material helped or supported him, or if it made him even more anxious.

Harald desperately needed a haircut and Ingrid had made fun of him by offering to put a bow in his hair. After that he allowed her to trim a little off the back. Were they afraid to ask her for money to go to a barber, and had they realized their cash was running out? Just about every member of her family in Oslo and Trondheim had already left for Sweden. Only she had refused, worrying that Isak would miraculously return and wonder where they were. And now it might be too late.

The droning voice continued telling them to bring a backpack large enough to hold clothing for a couple of days, medication and necessary personal items, and to wear sturdy, comfortable shoes. "Warm sweaters and trousers. Don't make it too heavy. You must be able to carry it by yourself whenever necessary."

Leyla had tuned Arne out several minutes ago. She wished he would stop talking, although she realized that the instructions were necessary.

She flashed back to her childhood. How strange! She was playing with her two older sisters. They were teaching her how to stack cards on top of other cards. They were making a house of cards, they said. The house got larger and larger, and it became increasingly harder to place the thin pieces of cardboard. Leyla inadvertently sneezed. To her great surprise and disbelief, the entire house of cards collapsed, right before her eyes. Her two sisters laughed out loud, while Leyla burst into tears. The shock of seeing all their efforts and skills falling apart right in front of her was more than she could bear.

She recalled the sensation and subsequent shock, which she hadn't thought of for many years. Unexpectedly it made her feel her real house of cards had collapsed in the same manner. Her husband had been taken from her without any notice. She had no idea what his future held, how he felt at this time, and even whether he was in reasonable health. Her two children had changed as well. Ingrid was becoming independent and Leyla felt she was slowly losing her—not physically, but definitely emotionally.

Her son was also withdrawing. His loneliness had become more and more apparent, and it was clear he was quite isolated, at least from his contemporaries.

Arne was still talking. Well, she couldn't blame him, although she found it hard to focus. Their lives were at stake and he was only trying to do what he felt was right, Leyla thought.

"You may have to spend most of the time in the ferry's hold until no one else is in sight, on land or in other boats on the water. You can't be seen. The captain will let you know when it's okay for you to walk around. Approximately two hours into the voyage, in the middle of the fjord, he is expecting to meet a large freighter which will bring you on board and facilitate your escape to England.

"I realize you had hoped to go to Sweden, but in view of the present situation, you should take advantage of this opportunity as soon as possible.

"This may be your best chance," Arne continued, looking directly at Leyla. He must have noticed that she seemed preoccupied.

Harald repeated, "The raincoat?"

"The raincoat? Oh, yes. I mentioned the raincoat. Bear with me. If Ms. Sofie will wear her black, long raincoat and you, Mrs. Rosenberg, will wear your striped raincoat, which Ingrid has told me about, we may be able to gain a little advantage. When you arrive together to see the prisoners off in the morning, most people will notice the coats, and the one with the black and white stripes worn by Mrs. Rosenberg will be especially hard to miss."

"We will attempt to keep you inconspicuous for at least one hour or so after the first ferry has left and before you board the next ferry. Sometime during this interim, the two of you should exchange raincoats."

Both Leyla and Sofie looked at him, as if asking what he had in mind with this strange idea. He continued, "In the event that one of the policemen notices a woman in a striped raincoat still at the docks sometime in mid-morning, he will probably remember this woman from earlier in the morning as Leyla Rosenberg."

"We will assume that the police will not focus on Miss Sofie who will wear a black coat first thing in the morning. This will make it considerably easier for Mrs. Rosenberg in the newly acquired black version to get on board the second ferry, albeit with our help. I hope this is not too confusing."

Chapter Twenty-Three

Annika's Mistake

OSLO, NOVEMBER 25, 1942

When Rebekka went downstairs to meet Kari, she found it hard to make conversation. She was still thinking about Frank and his experience and it was difficult not to mention it. Kari noticed something was on her mind, because she was quiet as well. However, Rebekka kept remembering the specific instructions not to let Kari know this was the day earmarked for their escape.

Rebekka remembered that she wasn't the only one concerned about her family. She wondered what if anything had happened to Kari's father, but was afraid to ask. As far as she knew, he hadn't returned home yet. She was eager to ask, but she felt this was the wrong time.

Rebekka looked up and down the familiar street where they had walked back and forth to school for so many years.

And tonight we are leaving for an unknown future, she thought.

Halfway down the street they could see the bus stop, which had been there for years. The large, grey bus passed by and came to a standstill just in front of them, letting people off, while two men and one woman waited to get on.

Her eyes fell on the sign in the front, left window next to the driver, displaying a street name, indicating the final bus stop. She had never noticed this sign before. But where had she seen that particular name before? It was familiar.

It took her a few seconds to recall the street name where Annika lived with her parents. Then she remembered. Annika's parents had been smuggled out of the country about a week ago with her grandmother, Mor's mother. Together they had been taken by an ambulance, which had brought them across the border to Sweden. Annika was by herself! And Annika hadn't answered Rebekka's mother's phone calls for the past two days.

Rebekka started running towards the bus. "Please forgive me; I just remembered I have an important errand to run. I'll stop by to see you later this afternoon!" she called out to Kari.

Rebekka climbed onto the bus just as the door was about to close, barely missing being caught in it. The last thing she saw was Kari's astonished face, staring as the bus moved up the street. There would be no school for Rebekka that day. Or the next.

Fifteen minutes later Rebekka found herself outside Annika's parents' apartment on the third floor.

She was contemplating whether to ring the bell and risk scaring Annika, or knock on the door, indicating that it was someone she knew.

She opted for the doorbell. She wasn't even sure if Annika was staying at the apartment, since she hadn't answered her mother's last few calls.

Two minutes passed without any sign that Annika was home. Rebekka began to be a little concerned.

What if someone "bad" had been there to arrest her, for some strange, unknown reason? Maybe they had heard about her parents' escape, not unlike what happened to Uncle Leonard's fiancée.

She was considering leaving, when the door was flung open, and her cousin's voice exclaimed, "Rebekka, what in the world are you doing here?"

There she was, the young woman everyone had been concerned about. Annika looked healthy, actually more than healthy. She looked beautiful! She was wearing a multi-color silk robe which looked brand new. Her hair cascaded down her shoulders in waves, and she looked confident.

"Mor has been trying to reach you, but she got no answer. She's very worried. We're leaving later today, crossing the border to Sweden, and we would like you to join us. Please, Annika, reconsider. It's not safe here anymore for Jews. We have been alerted that there is a very good likelihood that women and children will be arrested tomorrow."

"Rebekka, I have already told your mother that I don't believe in this." Annika rolled her eyes. "It's not going to happen; it's just a plot to scare people. The Norwegians need to accept the German visitors. Our liberators have big plans for Norway, and people need to live according to the new laws."

Annika's voice stopped short, bordering on sounding irritated.

Rebekka couldn't absorb what Annika was saying. She stood in the entryway, trying to understand what she heard.

At that moment, to Rebekka's great astonishment, a young man, also wearing a bathrobe, appeared behind Annika. He didn't say hello or introduce himself. Instead, he placed himself right behind the young woman, wrapping his arms around her waist. He was tall, not unlike many Norwegian men, but had dark eyes. He had a small moustache, perhaps trying to draw attention away from a weak chin.

Annika reluctantly said, "This is my boyfriend Hans, whom you may have heard about. He is more familiar with the political situation in Norway than anyone in our family, if not in Norway. He has assured me that I am safe, and I trust him. I want you and your mother to leave me alone."

Hans interrupted her and said in a rather self-assured, arrogant voice, "I'll never let anything happen to my Annika. She belongs to me."

A few seconds passed as the couple stared at Rebekka, and vice versa. No one moved and no one spoke.

It was clear to Rebekka that her presence was anything but welcome, and that she had been invited to leave, which is what she did.

She ran down the two flights of stairs, eager to get as far away from the unexpected confrontation as possible, heading for the bus stop to go home. Her stomach was upset. She feared that she might be sick right then and there.

During the ride home, she could think of only one thing. How could she have done something this stupid, and did she have to tell her mother, or should she keep quiet?

Then another thought struck her. Mor had told her not to talk about the plans for the family's attempted escape with anyone, and now she was responsible for letting Annika's boyfriend know that this was the exact day they were leaving. The implications of his comments were scary. Rebekka was afraid. The more she thought about it, the more incredible the situation seemed. What side was he on?

The trip home seemed to last for hours. Her stomach got increasingly worse, and she couldn't wait to get to her apartment and the bathroom. Ruth opened the door for her, indicating that Mor was sleeping.

"The guide has insisted that she get some rest, as the plans for this evening may mean missing an entire night's sleep. I'll try to do the same in a little while as soon as I'm finished with my work. What is wrong with you? You look ill."

Ruth followed Rebekka, who had disappeared into the bathroom without speaking. Rebekka was afraid Ruth would hear her, and wasn't surprised when she found Ruth waiting by the bathroom door with a bucket and a damp cloth.

"Rebekka, what's wrong? You need to tell me. Here. You vomited, didn't you?"

"I can't, it's too terrible. I don't know what to do," was Rebekka's only answer. Finally, sitting on the bathroom floor, she started sobbing and gave Ruth a word-by-word account of her visit to Annika's house.

Ruth paused for a few seconds, and responded with a low and gentle voice, "Well, I am glad that you decided to tell me. You must feel terrible, but I'm sure that everything will be fine. Let me go and get your mother. I am sure she is done with her nap."

She returned in a few minutes with Sarah. Rebekka had to repeat the entire episode, including all the details. Mor stared at her intensely and focused in particular on the boyfriend's comments.

"Well, I am quite surprised and don't quite understand the circumstances either. I wonder if that's why her parents left without telling me in person. They must feel awful. They were probably too ashamed or confused to even speak to me. My goodness!

"Although I am actually annoyed with you for taking the matter into your own hands, I am also proud that you felt confident enough to try to help.

"I really need you to help me a little today. Would you go to the park and pick up Miriam, as Ruth has enough to do. And perhaps on the way home you could tell her that we are going away today. Use your imagination. Ruth, as you know, has an idea."

Rebekka stood still. A great burden had been removed from her mind. She wondered if she should stop by to see Frank, who was ensconced in her room. She concluded it might be better to leave without speaking to him. She had experienced enough upset for this early in the day, and would probably benefit from a little tranquility. And she wasn't ready to discuss Annika's situation with Frank yet either.

Thirty minutes later she was on her way up the street towards the play area in the park.

She crossed the street to the fenced-off area where the toddlers were playing. At the gate she introduced herself to the two ladies in charge of watching the kids. "I am here to pick up my sister Miriam."

Miriam, who was swinging back and forth, was quite surprised to see her sister, rather than Ruth. She grabbed her backpack and waved good-bye the way she always did.

Within a few minutes, the two siblings were on their way down the street, with Miriam as usual hanging on to her sister's left hand. She jumped up and down with her dark braids bouncing.

Time had come for Rebekka to tell Miriam a credible story to justify the changes that were waiting for the rest of the day. The point was to avoid alarming her.

"I have something to tell you, Mimi. We have decided to go on a little family vacation—you, me, Mor and Ruth. It's been kind of quiet around our house the past few weeks and we need a little change. How would you like to go on a trip to the country? It's getting cold and there is not that much we can do outside until the snow comes when we can ski and go sledding. But we have thought of something we can do.

"All the farmers have been growing potatoes for people to eat during the winter. Soon the snow will cover the ground. We are going to pick potatoes.

How would you like to go to Hadeland, where we can all help the farmers pick potatoes?"

Miriam, who probably only understood half of what her sister said, found the idea intriguing. She kept on jumping, while talking about how she was going to pick potatoes. By the time they reached the house, Miriam was ready to announce the details of their trip to Ruth.

Rebekka, however, was distracted by the sound of Mor's voice on the telephone in the adjoining room.

"Yes, I realize we have one extra person in the car. No, of course I didn't know this when we made these arrangements. Don't you have a list that shows my nephew's name with the group that left yesterday? Yes, that's it. He left around 3:30 pm, then he returned here around 10 pm. Yes, that's the one. I imagine you have already heard what happened.

"As I already explained to you, he accidentally got on the wrong train, which brought him back to Oslo—fortunately, I would say. I really don't know how else to describe the situation. Yes, I do realize that it's going to be tight in the car, and we appreciate your accommodating us.

"Regarding the other incident—which I told you about earlier, it has to do with my cousin's young daughter and her friend Hans—no, I don't know his last name, but based on the conversation, it obviously has made me a little more apprehensive. I just thought I should inform you. Wait, wait, I think his family owns an advertising company in town. Would that be of any help?

"Would you consider leaving an hour early, in case they try to . . . ? Naturally I'll leave it up to you. We'll be ready whenever you decide. We trust you and depend on you. At this point, there are not many choices. Please feel free to contact me if necessary."

Mor turned towards her two daughters and gave Rebekka a big smile, making it quite clear that she was working very hard at keeping her family as calm and relaxed as possible. Sarah was known for being a highly energetic person; notorious for resolving their ups and downs. She could become highly agitated by relatively minor issues, and be difficult to calm down. However, she was also a level-headed person when handling major issues and crises. This day was another test of dealing with difficult predicaments and even potential disasters. Perhaps this was the reason that she had always been the sibling in charge of her large family, or perhaps that was exactly how she had developed these skills? What came first, the chicken or the egg?

By 4:30 pm, they were ready—or as ready as they would ever be. Miriam was dressed in her winter snowsuit and boots, since they were expecting to be outdoors the entire evening and night, most probably until the next morning. Rebekka was told to dress in appropriate warm clothing as well, and did just that. Frank was wearing the same outfit as he wore during his ill-fated journey the previous day, having turned down the offer to wear his uncle's clothing. A big satchel was filled with sandwiches and drinks—enough for a couple of days.

Each of them carried a small, tightly-packed backpack. Miriam was allowed to bring one small doll and blanket. Rebekka didn't feel like speaking. She added an extra pair of heavy socks, some underwear and heavy gloves to the pile of filled sketchbooks as well as two that were still blank. She had also thrown in two pencils.

The resistance people had already given Mor preliminary instructions, as the two guides leading them had stopped by for a few minutes the day before. Rebekka had only spoken with them previously, but as usual listened in silence. The younger of the two guides had stated, clearly, "Experience has taught us that the escape car should never wait in front of the house. You will be surprised how many nosy people have nothing better to do than to look out the window. If they suspect the car may be waiting to take a family to a secret destination—in particular, if the family is dressed in warm sports gear, carrying bags—they will not remain silent.

"They may try to gain an advantage by notifying the police or The Gestapo.

"The car is large and black, and it will be waiting on the next block, around the corner. It will be parked outside the butcher store, which closes early these days anyway. The driver will be there. All you need to do is to open the door and get in, slowly, carefully and quietly. Keep your bags in your laps. Do your best to keep the small child as quiet as possible. Whisper, sing or talk to her, to distract her. Any questions?"

No one responded. The guides nodded and left, calling out that they would return in a few hours.

"It's 4:30 exactly. Are you all ready?" Mor walked through the apartment, looking at Ruth, her two children and her nephew. She gave out repetitive directions on how they were to leave the apartment. Her voice was shaking a little. This was ignored by the others. Ruth and the two girls were to leave by the back stairway, which was next to the kitchen door. By walking down the three flights of stairs, they could exit the building directly through the rear courtyard and reach the street through the short tunnel-like walkway. This walkway was used by the few car owners, just like Far, who had garages at their disposal.

The two resistance guides would use the elevator together with Frank. "The boy will go with us. We will not take our eyes off him as long as we are together. We will make certain that he'll be safely delivered to Sweden," the older of the two announced.

Frank looked embarrassed and intimidated. The tall, younger guide smiled gently and winked at him. They left through the front door and entered the elevator as agreed on. Ruth left with the girls. As they were about to walk down the back stairs, Rebekka suddenly stopped.

She whispered in Ruth's ear that she would meet her and Miriam on the sidewalk downstairs. Then she joined her mother.

"I didn't feel right leaving you alone here, Mor. I also want to say good-bye to our home for Far."

She had no idea where the last sentence came from. The words just popped into her head and out.

Mor looked surprised, but said nothing.

Rebekka stood in the doorway, trying to create a mental image in her mind, looking at the various rooms she could see from her vantage point. Mor put her arm around her waist and gently moved her out of the apartment.

Finally, she put her hand on the entrance door, closing it gently and firmly. Rebekka looked at her mother, who was busy with the upper lock on the door, which they only used when they were planning on being away for more than a day.

Mor was mumbling something to herself, but Rebekka could still make it out. "I'm sure 'they' will get inside as soon as they realize we have left. They will enter like hungry wolves. Let's make sure that we at least make it hard for them."

Rebekka said nothing. A response seemed unnecessary. But Mor's comment led her to another thought.

"Mor," she said, "You have forgotten something."

"What?" Mor asked.

"You are supposed to kiss the mezuzah before you leave your house. For luck. The Lord will keep an eye on you."

The mother stared at her daughter. "You are right. Your grandfather would have been so proud of you." Quietly she raised her hand to her lips and then with her fingers touched the mezuzah which had been attached on the outside doorframe.

Entering the elevator without looking back, Rebekka closed the metal door. Mor pointed to the down button, indicating that Rebekka should press it, not unlike the routine they had when Rebekka was a small child.

When they reached the bottom floor, they casually walked out the front door, and turned right in the direction of the walkway leading from the back of the building. They waited two more minutes for Ruth and Miriam. Approximately ten feet further up the sidewalk the two guides were waiting, on either side of Frank.

Miriam ran towards her mother. "Mor, I whispered all the way, just like Rebekka told me. I was very good. And Ruth whispered. We have to be very quiet so that we don't wake up the neighbors who were taking a nap. But I don't like those dark stairs. I was a little scared. Next time I want to go in the elevator."

Rebekka leaned over her little sister and praised her. "I'm sure Ruth will tell me you were the best of all. Now you and I can see who can whisper the softest. I'm worried that you may win."

They walked slowly and casually along the sidewalk to the next block, quite aware that if they ran into a neighbor or two, they would make a point of saying hello, pretending they were just going for a walk.

At the light, they crossed over to the next block, rounding the corner, out of view of their own building. They were getting closer to the butcher store, where their escape car was waiting. The street was slightly narrower than their own, with a number of people walking in both directions. Rebekka fell back a little, allowing Mor, Miriam and Ruth to walk ahead of her. She was increasingly anxious. The mere possibility of being separated from the others, if only for a couple of meters, scared her.

Was it Frank's story that morning that frightened her, she wondered?

She could see Frank with the two men walking on the sidewalk ahead of her.

Calm down, Rebekka, all is well, she kept repeating to herself.

A large car was visible 8–9 meters down the next street. Their car. The car that was waiting for them. It was parked on the street next to the butcher. She felt a little better and looked up for a second, just in time to almost bump into a tall man walking towards her.

"I am so sorry," she whispered, immediately assuming that she had been clumsy, and looked up.

However, the man whom she had bumped into was no stranger. He was very tall and serious looking. It was Kari's father. He was wearing the same dark gray overcoat as the last time she saw him, complete with his gray hat with a black ribbon. Rebekka guessed that he was planning a quick visit with his family, who lived across the street. She knew that he would appear intermittently, and usually without alerting his family in advance. He would enter through the door on the opposite side of their building, walk down some stairs and through a few unlocked doors in the basement. She remembered his routine. He would stay for 15 minutes and leave. Officially, he was still in hiding.

The two on the sidewalk exchanged glances, but neither spoke.

Oh, how she wished she could ask him to tell Kari that she was leaving that day, but she couldn't.

His nod was so quick, she almost missed it. All she could do was lift her left hand a couple of inches and offer a very small wave, hoping it would be enough. He blinked his eyes once, flashed a hint of a smile, and moved on.

That was all Rebekka needed. Suddenly she felt so much better. She knew that Kari would get her greeting.

She reached the car, opened the door and slipped into the back seat, next to her mother, Ruth and Miriam. Frank was already sitting in the front seat between the two guides. She was ready to start a new life. Deep down she knew she would return one day. When—she didn't know . . .

Chapter Twenty-Four

The Last Glimpse

AALESUND, NOVEMBER 25–26, 1942

Leyla was unable to fall asleep. Once Arne and Sofie had left, she walked around the apartment touching pieces of furniture and knick-knacks hoping to gather strength from these familiar treasures. For Leyla they symbolized her entire married life, ever since she left Oslo to live "far away." Every piece had a history, which she would take along, if not physically, yet in her heart and mind.

Just before Sofie left, Leyla had given her the box containing her silver and a few other valuable items. She also scooped together all the framed pictures, tying them with ribbons. Sofie had pressed the box to her chest, saying, "I'll keep it until this is over."

They exchanged glances. There was no need to define "this." Their thoughts remained unspoken.

"I'll be downstairs tomorrow morning at 5:45 am," Sofie said casually and walked out.

Leyla had taken out various items she felt would be useful, including suitable travel clothing, in addition to packing a small bag with medicine and personal items. On top of the pile was her old black and white raincoat. Her thoughts were wandering. Both the practical ones and the emotional ones. Eventually she drifted into a light twilight sleep, only to wake up every hour checking the time.

Ingrid and Harald said goodnight, pretending they were going to sleep as well. Ingrid appeared relatively calm in view of the impending plan and the long day, which she had just put behind her. Harald was stoic as usual, showing no emotion. It was unclear if this was a natural attitude, or a function of significant effort.

163

However, by 5 am they were all dressed and packed. True to her word, Sofie was downstairs in her car at the agreed-upon time.

It was still dark and rather difficult to see. The trip down to the docks went fast, a little too fast. All four were quiet, staring out of the car window. Their thoughts were the same. None of the three wanted to talk about Isak—father, husband and friend.

A number of solemn-looking people were already waiting by the ferry.

It feels like a funeral, Leyla thought to herself. She stopped herself before she said it out loud. Some of the people waiting were holding hands. An occasional face was familiar, but in general, the other spectators were strangers. Clearly, the prisoners were from a wide area around Aalesund. No one spoke. No one made eye contact.

Ingrid and Harald stood close together, giving each other both physical and mental support. At first Sofie stood next to them, then found herself stepping back, standing instead by herself, behind them. Close enough to touch, if necessary. Was this an involuntary movement on her part, she thought, making sure they wouldn't be taken away from her as well?

They waited. At exactly 6:30 am, a large police van pulled up. Several soldiers emerged, two of whom held on to police dogs, as they walked slowly towards the waiting ferry. The soldiers' commands to the dogs were loud and crisp, a daunting contrast to the quiet, helpless crowd waiting to see their loved ones. When the men emerged from the van, a gasp arose from the bystanders. Twelve men walking four by four. Their ankle chains clanked. The prisoners were dressed in regular clothing, mostly of worn pants and threadbare jackets, of which some fit and some didn't. They all stared straight ahead.

Leyla tried desperately to see her husband. It was still dark, the men walked closely together, out of necessity. They all seemed middle-aged, thin, wearing a variety of worn, thin knit caps. She thought she saw Isak. He had a special way of walking—holding his head totally straight, while moving his arms.

The prisoners reached the end of the dock where the gangway had already been extended to facilitate boarding the ferry. At that very moment, as if by command, the twelve men turned their heads to the right, facing the assembled group, which stood speechless, eyes wide open, afraid to miss even a second of seeing their loved ones being brought away. Many of the prisoners lifted an arm, a hand, trying to send messages with a sign. The man she thought was her husband suddenly moved his head in her direction.

Yes, it was him! Isak! His eyes penetrated hers!

The men stopped for one second only, and then continued on to the waiting vessel. The police officers with the canines formed the final section of the procession.

Leyla held her breath. She felt if she moved ever so slightly, the vision of her husband would vanish forever. She didn't exhale until he was on the vessel, still as part of the group, their feet linked together.

When the last glimpse of his back and head disappeared, she turned to her children. It was obvious they had seen him as well. Their expressions said it all. To her surprise, they were holding hands.

No one moved or showed signs of leaving. It had started to rain, but most of the observers seemed unaware, frozen in time. The departed ferry took off with their husbands, fathers, sons and brothers to an unknown location and destiny. Eventually the cluster of friends and relatives started to move.

The Rosenbergs and Sofie were among the last to walk back up to the street level, next to the other docks. No one spoke. It was almost eight o'clock. Ingrid and Harald walked slowly in the direction of the street, under the pretense of returning home. Leyla and Sofie took their time, stopping intermittently to look back at the water, where the ferry was increasingly hard to see.

Once the four had crossed the street, which ran parallel with the water, they caught sight of an old model black car. It had stopped in front of the sidewalk. A stranger wearing a black knit cap and glasses sat in the driver's seat. Rolling down the window, he extended a newspaper, shaking it briefly. It gave the appearance of someone getting rid of some sand, letting it disappear. He withdrew the paper and closed the window.

This was the signal the group had been waiting for.

The three Rosenbergs and Sofie quickly got into the car, all squeezing into the back seat. The driver turned, having removed his hat and glasses, revealing his face. It was Arne.

"Lock the doors; we are going for a ride," was all he said, as the car slowly crossed the cobblestone street.

"Mrs. Rosenberg and Sofie, this would be a good time for you to exchange raincoats," he said.

Sofie slipped into the striped white and black coat, giving Leyla the black coat.

"You will find that your backpacks are now in the trunk. They will be brought aboard your ferry by some other men. Don't worry about them."

"The next voyage is scheduled to leave at 10 am, a little earlier than originally planned. Any questions?"

Evidently not.

This time Leyla listened carefully to the instructions. This didn't prevent her from observing her daughter while Arne spoke. Poor child, she thought. This must be hard for her. In addition to the other trauma they were experiencing; seeing her father being sent away as a prisoner, waiting to escape from the only place that she had ever lived, and also saying goodbye to a young man who meant a lot to her. The chemistry and affection between the young couple was becoming more and more obvious.

The car circled the center of town, primarily on small, residential streets. A few minutes were spent waiting in a small park, while the passengers stopped at a local cafe to buy coffee surrogate and some dried crackers to make the time pass faster.

Around 9:30 they were once again back at the dock area. A ferry could be seen waiting perhaps 20 meters to the right of the one which had come and gone. Arne stopped the car.

An unknown man greeted them, his arms full of raincoats worn by dock personnel during bad weather. He shoved the coats quickly into the back seat and instructed Ingrid and Harald to put them on, including the hoods. They followed his instructions immediately, as best they could in the overcrowded back seat. If they were surprised or apprehensive at this unknown part of the plan, they said nothing. Leyla, however, could see how pale they had become but she decided to remain silent. Ingrid reached out, placing her hand on the back of Arne's head, running her hand down his cheek and neck, pausing briefly. He didn't move, just stared ahead. The siblings left with the stranger. The last thing Leyla could see through the car window as they resumed driving was her children closing the new raincoats.

Leyla suddenly felt dizzy. What was she doing? Perhaps it was a mistake to let Harald and Ingrid go off on their own. What if something went wrong? What if one of the "helpers" made a mistake and went left rather than right? What if one of the policemen was keeping an eye on them in secret? Her mind raced, thinking of horrendous things that might go wrong. Her first thought was to call out to them, tell them to come back, where she could keep an eye on them—just like she used to do when they were small.

Another ten minutes passed. Leyla forced herself to look in the other direction, adhering to the original plan.

"Now, ladies, it's your turn," Arne said.

"Mrs. Rosenberg, please start walking towards the right. Keep along the sidewalk until you reach the dock that's visible from here. I assume you saw the ferry. There's a little gray shed on the right side, can you see it? When your reach the shed, open the door, enter and wait until someone comes to bring you on board. He will not speak to you and you are not to address him. Just follow my instructions.

"Ms. Sofie, you can stay in this car, and I'll let you out a little farther up the street. Your car is parked in front of the bank. I hope you have your key. The spare key which we used will be put in an envelope under your door later this evening."

He paused.

"I wish you and your family good luck, Mrs. Rosenberg. We'll meet again under happier circumstances."

Leyla started walking, slowly. She concentrated on each step, thinking of nothing except finding the gray shed. Her heart beat quickly, and she felt a little faint. The image of her husband, as one of the prisoners a couple of hours earlier, moving his arms, kept recurring in her mind. She could still see his face when he turned towards her. He had given her the striped raincoat for her birthday a few years ago. Maybe the coat had made it easier for him to see her in the crowd of people? Would she ever be able to tell him about the exchange of raincoats?

Her thoughts returned to the children. She wasn't going to allow herself to worry about their safety in getting on board the ferry. She had confidence in the good people who were helping them. Everything was going to work out all right. Many, many Jews had already escaped. Soon, maybe by tomorrow or the next day, they would be safe. She had to think positively.

She reached the mysterious shed, letting herself in. It was empty. She stood absolutely still. She remembered her husband.

Isak and Leyla had exchanged glances for only 30 seconds, but that was enough for her to see right through to his heart. He was thin, much thinner than she had ever seen him. The special spark in his eyes, which had fascinated her when she first met him and ever after, was no longer there. His eyes were dull. His hair was gray and thin. Yet she still felt he had looked right into her soul. She had felt that he was greeting her and saying goodbye, both at the same time.

Her ruminations were interrupted as the door opened, and she found herself face to face with a man she had never met before. He was tall, almost bald, with some bruises on his face, yet he looked kind. The door closed behind him.

He muttered, "Come with me." She turned to follow him. He stood with his back to her, his hand on the door, which was still closed. A very loud alarm—perhaps a car horn pierced the air.

The man smiled at her, opening the door just enough for both of them to get outside. "This is our signal," he whispered. "They are creating a distraction, to keep attention away from us. Come, quickly."

He grabbed her hand, pulling her along. "We don't want the Nazis to see you boarding the ferry. Let's run."

Within a few seconds, she was aboard the ferry, facing her son and daughter. She felt an immediate sense of relief and willed herself to remain calm. She could hear that the alarm in the distance had been turned off. She could also see a few police officers approaching Sofie, who was wearing the black and white striped raincoat. The counterpart, Sofie's black coat, was now on Leyla's back. It appeared that the trick had worked. Sofie was waving her arms, appearing to be arguing with the policemen surrounding her. A warm feeling of gratitude to Arne, Sofie and their colleagues went through her.

The man from the shed was also on board. He introduced himself as "Fredrik," and said, "This is not my real name but you can use that if you need me. I'll be your contact person in every aspect of this voyage. If you have any questions, let me know. I'll answer the best I can. I am sure you are familiar with our general plan for you and your family." Leyla nodded, thanked him and said no more.

Ingrid and Harald were lying on the floor of the ferry on what appeared to be two beds made up of several blankets. A third bed was next to them. It was clear her children were quite uncomfortable and apprehensive. Her mother's instinct kicked in. She tried to force a smile, and whispered, "So far, so good."

Fredrik looked at all three as he was speaking. "It's crucial that you not be seen from the shore or from any small island along our path. This ferry is scheduled to run unoccupied, and sighting people on board will very quickly generate conversation. Please, Mrs. Rosenberg, will you be kind enough to join the other passengers right there on the floor."

Leyla bent down, trying to make herself comfortable on the blanket bed, which smelled of dust, dog hair and sea salt.

She tried to be funny, despite her state of mind. "Well, at least you don't have to worry about me falling out of bed."

Finally, she was rewarded with a slight snicker from her two children. She was amazed she was able to make a joke at this time, when so much was at stake.

Another man appeared, much younger and quite thin, almost emaciated. A nametag attached to his sweater indicated he was employed by the Aale-sund/Andalsnes Maritime Society. He offered them a hot drink as well as some dry bread. Considering they hadn't eaten a regular meal for close to 24 hours, it tasted good. They thanked him and devoured the snacks. He was chatty, "I have heard that you are Jews. How does that feel now that we are at war?"

The three on the blankets were astonished and didn't answer. Fredrik, their contact person, reached out, grabbing his arm, advising him in no uncertain terms to get back to work.

"Torgeir, please leave our passengers alone. I am sure that you mean well, but this is neither the time nor the place to discuss religion, the politics of Norway or its invaders."

It was hard to lie still—doing nothing—not even think! The ferry started to roll. Leyla attempted to settle down on the third "bed," and she raised her head to look out onto the fjord. White tops were visible on the water. She put her head down again. There was nothing she could do, beyond waiting.

Fredrik sat down on an anchored seat next to Leyla, and attempted to review the plan for the rest of the voyage.

"As you may have discussed with my friends in Aalesund, we have had some success helping people cross over to England. Today we are planning to meet a large freighter at a specific place in the fjord. We are supposed to make contact by radio when we get a little closer. The plan is for the freighter to lower a small boat for the three of you to board, and from there you will be brought onto the freighter. This won't take place until later in the day."

Leyla stared at him and thought to herself how easy it all sounded in theory. If only it would work.

"I can't begin to tell you how much this means to us. Frankly we don't have many more options left . . . my husband . . . ," she started, but was unable to finish the sentence. The tears welled in her eyes.

The increased rocking of the ferry had the same effect on all three family members. Within a few minutes they fell asleep, despite the uncomfortable accommodations. No one had slept much the previous night.

Around two o'clock in the afternoon Leyla woke up with the realization that several hours had passed. The motion of the ferry had increased enormously and she felt herself feeling a bit queasy.

The boat rolled from one side to the other, exacerbating her already upset stomach. Her daughter lay on her side, far from feeling well.

Fredrik made an appearance in an effort to tell them the weather unfortunately had surprised them by changing from regular winter activity to a more severe weather situation, and actually had taken a turn for the worse. For that reason they had been unable to contact the freighter. He was convinced it was only a matter of time until they would succeed.

The three passengers were beginning to feel uneasy. Ingrid sat up for a minute, put her head in her hands, trying to hold back her tears, "Here we have worried about the Gestapo, soldiers and the Norwegian police, but none of us gave any thought to bad weather."

"What if we can't meet the freighter?" Harald said. His anxiety was obvious. He twisted his hands, trying not to bite his fingers. Harald was usually the last one to be apprehensive. Leyla tried to calm him down, using the little energy she could manage to muster.

"Let's not worry about it yet. Weather can change very quickly," she said, trying to find a comfortable position on the floor.

Fredrik brought Leyla a heavy chair which could be attached to a hook on the floor. After some effort she was able to get up slowly and sit on the chair. Ingrid remained silent; it was clear she was worried. She was mumbling to herself, "After all that we went through to get here. I can't believe this."

"I'll keep giving you updates on the weather every 30 minutes," Fredrik said. It was clear from his tone and expression the situation was getting more severe. About an hour later he approached them, looking very serious. "The freighter is not responding, and we have drifted for the past hour. As much as I understand the ramifications of my decision, I have to tell you that we need to turn around and head back to Aalesund. At this point it's a matter of safety for everyone involved."

The passengers were incredulous. "What about our plans? What about the chance to escape and get to England? What about the Gestapo and the Nazi police officers who have been fooled, and most probably are furious now?"

They stared at Fredrik, unwilling to accept his decision. He stared back. Ingrid was sobbing and unwilling to discuss the situation. Silence ensued. Fredrik turned around, ostensibly to tell the captain to turn the ferry around, and follow the wind back to Aalesund. The decision had been made.

Leyla tried to stifle her tears. At the same time she did whatever she could to prevent the rocking waves from making her vomit. Harald had crawled over to a bucket nearby where he was able to get some relief. Right behind him was his sister, and finally his mother.

Three hours later they docked at Aalesund. They disembarked, carrying their backpacks.

Arne and Sofie were waiting at the dock, a little farther back. She was still wearing Leyla's black and white raincoat. They had been informed about the unfortunate change in plans from an unknown liaison at the police station.

Arne's face was immobile. He stared straight ahead, making every effort not to exchange a glance with Gyldendahl, his uncle, who could be seen a few meters behind the other two. The latter intentionally alternated his gaze between his nephew and the small gathering of passengers embarking in the pouring rain. A large smirk played in the older man's face.

Harald and Ingrid put their arms around Leyla while disembarking. There was nothing to say. They followed Sofie and Arne and walked slowly towards Sofie's car. The escape plan had failed, and Leyla was acutely aware that they now had moved into another phase of danger.

Up front, also attired in a large raincoat, between two young police officers holding not one, but two umbrellas, was the portly man in his mid-fifties, with a small moustache, Gyldendahl. His face broke into a vicious smirk, while raising his voice.

"Welcome back, all three of you. Your presence in Aalesund has been missed. We will make certain that you never leave us again. From now on, you should expect to see a police guard at your house 24 hours a day, until we decide your next place of residence."

The gloating look on the face of the heavy-set man left no doubt. None of the Rosenbergs had ever met him in person. However, all three knew that this was no one but the infamous Mr. Gyldendahl. The chances of getting away were getting smaller moment by moment.

Chapter Twenty-Five

The Yellow Sign

OSLO, NOVEMBER 25–26, 1942

Rebekka had asked to sit by the window. She remembered getting carsick when she sat in the middle of the back of her father's car several years ago, and from then on she always requested a window seat. The fact that this trip might result in more serious discomfort than nausea was quite an understatement, but no one objected. Ruth was in the middle with Miriam more or less on her lap, and mother sat by the other window. Frank was in the front between the two "pilots."

The sidewalk next to their waiting car was crowded with people on their way home, having finished their workday and other activities. The passengers in the car, however, were eager to get on the road.

But not so fast. The driver, a stocky middle-aged man, had something to discuss with them before leaving. His voice was calm and confident. He failed to introduce himself. He cleared his throat once before speaking and his message was delivered in a distinctive voice. Rebekka felt it sounded like a rehearsed speech, which he had given many times in similar situations. He had a message to deliver, and it had nothing to do with his name, or how his passengers were feeling at that particular moment.

"Here we are. Before we start this chancy journey, it's important that we all agree. The journey has to be defined as a matter of life and death. There are no promises, beyond that we will do everything in our power to get you to Sweden safely. This is not our first trip. We know the route, and we have a network of other devoted, competent people also waiting to help you. Nevertheless, the ultimate decision about proceeding has to come from you. You need to put your lives in our hands."

Rebekka turned to Mor whose face showed very little emotion, as usual. Her eyes were open, staring into space, at the back of the driver. She was ready, that was clear.

"Are there any comments or questions?" The driver continued.

Finally, Mor answered, "No. We trust you."

"Fine, let's get going."

No one spoke as the car made its way through the Oslo traffic. Their target was the main road leading in the direction of Sweden. The only sound was Ruth's soft voice singing to Miriam. The child fell asleep almost instantly.

The driver turned out to be a man of few words, maneuvered calmly along the road. Once he had delivered his initial message, conversation was kept to a minimum. The less the passengers and the guides knew about each other, the better it was. For safety reasons most of the resistance workers didn't give out their names, Rebekka had been told. If the passengers wanted to address them, a temporary name was made up. Rebekka found this a bit uncomfortable. How could they make up a name, out of nowhere? She preferred to speak about them as "the short blond man with the scar over his right eyebrow," or "the dark guy with a strong dialect from Northern Norway." If she had to speak to either one directly, she would try, "Excuse me, Sir," or something like that.

Rebekka had heard stories about cars being stopped by soldiers at corners or red lights, if the car seemed overly full of people holding luggage, bags etc. It didn't happen often, but there was always the possibility. Rebekka found it almost impossible not to think about it. The rumors said if this happened, both the passengers and the driver would be arrested, especially if it turned out that the passengers were Jewish. She sat quite still, keeping her face down.

Once the car had reached a major road outside Oslo, the traffic subsided a little. There were fewer traffic lights and the traffic moved a little faster. The driver started to debrief his "passengers" about the plan for the next few hours, in addition to the strategy for the evening and night. The women and Frank listened intently.

"We will be traveling by car for another two hours or so, until we reach a designated railroad station which connects with the southern part, in other words, closer to the Swedish border. The place is called Oerje. You may be familiar with the general area. This is where we will part ways," he said.

Rebekka surreptitiously studied the man next to the driver who was sitting in the passenger seat. He was a bit younger and thinner, as well as good looking, Rebekka thought. He had a gold band on his ring finger, which he kept turning. Rebekka couldn't help but wonder why. Was he nervous? Was he thinking about his wife? She was wondering what his wife looked like. Did she mind that he was doing this type of work? Had she told him to stay at home instead? Rebekka's imagination was running wild. Until that moment he hadn't said one single word. As if reading her mind, he spoke. She was so deep in thought that she jumped when she heard his voice. She felt her cheeks blush.

"The railroad station is small and the train will only stop for a few minutes. It's imperative you get onto the train. Don't speak to each other and avoid drawing attention to yourself or anyone else. We are familiar with the incident which took place yesterday and only hope that the mother of the young man has arrived at her destination and is waiting at the border for him."

He paused, turning slightly towards Frank. For a quick second Frank turned his head as well and looked at his aunt. Why? Rebekka wondered. He was blushing. Her mother said nothing and Frank turned back to his initial position. Was he embarrassed, or did he need to make a connection with his aunt, Rebekka thought. There could be a variety of reasons.

"We are stopping at a different station. It's highly unlikely there will be cluster of soldiers waiting to board the train there. If, however, this should turn out to be the case, we will drive you to the next station." The driver suddenly interrupted his younger colleague, giving the impression that this topic was closed.

"We are discussing this now because it's imperative that you appear as relaxed as possible. I would suggest the following scenario. Ruth, we would recommend that you enter first with the little one and her older sister. We will notify you when you have to wake the four-year-old so she is alert and not cranky. If you have a snack or a toy that would be a good time to give it to her. The more relaxed you appear, the easier it will be for the other two. You are young and pretty and definitely have the genetic look of a young Norwegian woman."

He stopped for a minute, giving the impression that Rebekka or her mother might have reacted negatively to this statement.

"What I mean is . . . "

"That's fine. We understand. Keep going." Sarah's voice made him relax and he continued.

"Once you are at the station, we recommend that Mrs. Davidson boards alone, perhaps aiming for the closest lavatory. I would lock the door and stay there until the train has left the station. And by the way, Mrs. Davidson," he hesitated for a few seconds, a bit unsure on how to express himself, and then continued slowly, "If I were you, I would remove the necklace you are wearing. It attracts attention, and there is always the possibility someone may have noticed you and your family leaving today. If the wrong person saw you, he or she may use the necklace to describe you to one of our Nazi citizens or enemies."

Rebekka felt like someone had slapped her in the face. Would a person really do something so horrendous as reporting their escape to the Nazis, and use Mor's pendant to identify her?

She turned to Mor whose face had the same calm expression as she had from the moment they had left the house and entered the car. She had already removed the necklace, and she was wrapping it in a silk handkerchief that she always carried in her purse. When she was done, she slipped it into her purse, and turned her attention to the driver.

"Thank you, eh, Mr. Driver. I can't begin to tell you how much I appreciate your thoughtfulness. It never occurred to me, and I thought I had been so careful."

The driver continued with instructions, as if the comment about the necklace had never been made.

"At that point, once you leave the lavatory, you can sit anywhere you want. Personally, I would check to see where Ruth and the children are sitting, and take a seat in the next compartment, near them. Not too far away, yet not too near."

He paused once more, and an almost indecipherable smile crossed his face as he looked at Frank.

"As for this young man, we think he has had enough excitement these past two days. Another team of pilots will be waiting for us at the station when we arrive, and they are ready to be your back-up guides during the train ride, although they may not necessarily communicate with you. They will meet us as soon as we arrive and see that Frank gets on the train safely. One will be wearing a red sweater and the other will have a gray and black scarf around his neck. Frank, you have to follow them and listen to whatever they tell you to do. Most probably, they will say nothing but hello. If necessary, they may engage in conversation with you. You will be safe with them.

"You will stay on this train until the final station, which is called Huldra Stasjon. Another car will meet you there. You will know which car because Frank and his two pilots will meet you on the platform to take you to the right one. Just follow Frank's pilots. They will tell you what to do next."

Rebekka had a sudden thought. Was it possible the Nazis were looking for a fifteen-year-old Jewish boy who had jumped on a train by himself? Had the story of his unexpected separation waiting at the platform circulated among the enemies as well? That didn't seem surprising. Had German soldiers heard about it and were they trying to find him? One part of her felt that she was getting too intense imagining she was living in a dramatic war story. Ha! Isn't that just what she was doing? If she had these thoughts, most probably Frank had the same. No wonder he seemed more withdrawn than usual.

Just as predicted the car ride lasted close to two hours. They reached the train station around 8 pm. Darkness had fallen and the air was crisp and windy. A light snow was falling, but didn't seem to accumulate. Rebekka was trying to see out the car window; it was practically impossible.

The station was located in a remote area, surrounded by fields and woods. Most probably, it was chosen for that very reason, as it didn't seem to attract an abundance of people. Only an elderly man could be seen on the platform. He was sitting on the only bench visible, reading a newspaper. He didn't look up when the car arrived, seemingly uninterested in scrutinizing any new travelers.

The driver looked at his watch and said, "The train will arrive within the next ten minutes. Are you ready? As soon as we hear and see the train pulling in to the platform, please exit the car immediately. No need to say goodbye."

"Enter the first open car in the order I gave you. Ruth and the two girls. Mrs. Davidson is next. Trust us with Frank. If you look to the other side of the platform, you will see two men wearing knickers, sweaters and ski jackets. They are our replacements who are here to accompany Frank and to be your guards and guides for the next leg of the journey. We wish you a successful and peaceful trip."

No sooner had he finished his instructions, than the train could be heard in the distance. Ruth started whispering again to Miriam and looked at Rebekka, who responded immediately by nodding.

She was trying very hard not to show Mor and Ruth how frightened she was when they left the car and started walking. Fragments from Frank's experiences the day before kept popping into her head. She almost envied Miriam who was holding on to Ruth's hand and laughing. What if the train started moving just as she was getting on? What would happen to Mor? What if someone had reported her, Rebekka, as having thick, curly red hair? Should she wear a scarf on her head or a hat? Since she had neither in her bag, she really had to stop worrying about her hair, or anything else, she decided.

Fortunately, the entire stressful episode passed quickly. By the time the train had stopped at the station, Rebekka, Ruth and Miriam were already waiting on the platform. They entered the train and found seats in a semi-empty compartment. Thirty seconds later Sarah did the same, although she went in the opposite direction past another compartment until she found a lavatory. Frank remained on the platform, obviously apprehensive, looking anxiously in every direction.

Two tall men, one wearing a red sweater, the other with a carefully wrapped scarf around his neck, joined Frank. Rebekka was scrutinizing the trio from inside the train through the compartment window. They were standing less than a meter from the train steps where she had entered two minutes ago. The man in the red sweater was introducing himself to Frank with a big smile on his boyish face. Something about him looked familiar, especially how he moved his hand seemed familiar.

"Good to see you. We have been waiting for 30 minutes. If you want to party with us, let's get on the train before we miss it."

Frank stared at him momentarily, reacting to the unexpected remark, although he figured the man was one of the two to meet him. He nodded and went with them. They entered the train at the same time as Rebekka, Ruth and Miriam, but turned in the opposite direction to another compartment.

The station appeared to be totally empty of people. The elderly man had already disappeared somewhere on the train, and wasn't to be seen.

As predicted, the first two guides left without saying goodbye, and in a few seconds she could see their car turning around—obviously on their way back to the capital—at the very same time the train left the station.

Rebekka felt better once she knew all five of them were on the train. Ruth and Miriam were walking through the compartment looking for a seat and a place to stow their backpacks. Frank's horror story from the previous day was still playing in Rebekka's mind, although she felt better knowing that they were all together. Now she was bothered by the young man in the red sweater. She knew she had met him before.

Suddenly it hit her. Of course, it was him. She knew it! It was the young man with the wonderful smile and the brightest teeth she had ever seen. He had come to tell Mor that Far had arrived safely in Sweden. "The milk cartons have arrived," he had said. They didn't know his name, of course. Ruth had named him 'Haakon with the smile.'"

He was quite young and very muscular. She had met him in the elevator afterwards when the two of them left the apartment at the same time. He had approached her when they reached the bottom floor and told her the sad news about Uncle Leonard's fiancée who had been arrested.

Rebekka wondered if he realized that Frank, who was being guarded by the two men, was her cousin. What a coincidence! Then she thought, it probably wasn't a coincidence at all. She had heard certain units were assigned to a certain family, which could be the exact reason he was here today, making sure Frank's second attempt would be completed without any major trauma.

Rebekka continued to walk through the compartment; she could see Ruth and Miriam up ahead. She reached them just as they were sitting down. Seating didn't present a major problem. The compartment was only half-full. Two rows of seats on their right faced each other, which seemed like a logical place for them to sit. The few people around them seemed to be half-asleep, minding their own business. After a few minutes while Miriam examined the unfamiliar surroundings and tried to look out the window, she announced that she needed to use the bathroom. This wasn't unexpected and Ruth got up from her seat.

"Let's see if we can find it, Mimi. Rebekka will stay here and watch your doll and our bags."

They walked in the direction of a sign, which indicated lavatory. Rebekka watched them go down the aisle. To calm herself, she looked around casually. Did the woman right behind her stare at her unnecessarily or was she just imagining it? At that moment the lady lifted her knitting, looked at it, and put it back into her red and green bag. She closed her eyes and leaned back, getting ready for a nap. Rebekka concluded that the woman was just bored and a little nosy.

The train shook a little and she opened her eyes, just in time to see Ruth. To her surprise, she saw a German soldier walking through the compartment in the opposite direction. Miriam kept saying, "Hurry, hurry." Regardless of who was purposely listening or not, no one could avoid hearing the dialogue, leaving no doubt as to what the four-year-old had in mind.

Ruth bent down, pushed Miriam gently in the back, and said, "Please excuse us, we are in a hurry!" The soldier smiled, and moved to the side of the aisle allowing the blond young woman and the small child with the dark curls to pass. Then he continued to walk through the compartment. Rebekka had followed everything, pretended she was sleeping, looking through her lashes. Her heartbeat felt louder and louder. The soldier scrutinized both sides of the aisle as he walked, seeming more interested in the woman with the knitting than the fifteen-year-old girl with a sketchbook in her lap, appearing to be sleeping.

Shortly Ruth and her little protégé returned. The soldier was gone, and Rebekka decided not to bring it up. He was gone, and that was all that mattered. Miriam described her achievements with a loud and proud voice, which had to be heard by everyone near them.

"Your mother is in the next compartment, sitting by herself," Ruth whispered gently to Rebekka, once they were seated. "She seems relaxed. Frank is in the same compartment, at the opposite end, next to the two guides."

For a moment or so, it appeared peace and tranquility would reign for a little while. Then, Miriam had a surprise for them.

"I am tired. When are we going to be in Hadeland?" she asked, as she was standing on her knees, looking out the window, seeing nothing but darkness and trees along the railroad tracks. The young, bright voice belonging to a small child penetrated the compartment, and Ruth reacted quickly. She looked around the compartment at the few people occupying other seats.

Why would a child ask when they would arrive at a place which was in the opposite direction?

Ruth's thoughts were written all over her face as if someone had shouted them out loud, and Rebekka felt that she was on the verge of panic. She had never before seen Ruth so apprehensive.

Rebekka leaned towards Ruth and whispered, "It's fine. Kids say strange things. Let me take care of it."

Ruth looked embarrassed.

Rebekka put her arms around her young sister and said, "Silly little girl," resorting to the truth, or at least part of the truth. "We aren't going to Hadeland until next month. Hadeland is in the opposite direction, so this train will not take us there. Tonight we are going to visit some very nice people who are our friends and who live on a big farm. They have cows and horses."

Miriam's eyes began to shine at the thought of cows and horses.

"If you lean really close to me, I'll draw some of the animals for you. Maybe you will get to ride on a horse or see a cow being milked."

Miriam quickly responded, turned around, climbed into her sister's lap, and followed eagerly as Rebekka's hand quickly, very quickly, depicted an abundance of farm animals in her sketchbook. The passengers around them seemed to be satisfied with this explanation. Whether or not they had even worried about the conversation in the first place, would never be known. The moment of danger had passed. Ruth's normal face coloring had returned.

Around 9 pm, the train came to a full stop at the final station, as announced by the conductor who walked through the train. This station was larger than the prior one, with three tracks and a couple of trains already there. Ruth and the girls waited until most of the people had left and started looking for Mor. Despite the darkness and the light coating of snow now on the ground, they could see the platform and surroundings, with no sign of a car and no reception team.

Miriam was awake and cranky. "I want my mommy. Where is Mor? You said that I would see her soon."

Rebekka tried to distract her. "Let's see if we can see 'soon.' Let's look on the floor, and let's look out the window. Let's look in Ruth's hat." Finally, Miriam was satisfied and started laughing. Mor had to walk through two compartments until she caught up with the three waiting passengers. She overheard Rebekka trying to entertain her sister, and snuck up behind both of them, planting a big kiss on the four-year-old's neck. "Here I am! You found me." Miriam screamed out loud and threw her entire body at her mother. Rebekka felt like doing the same, but instead had to be satisfied with a big hug. Mor took Miriam in her arms while also trying to hug the two others. "Thank you, thank you," she whispered to Ruth. "During this entire trip I thanked God for letting me be fortunate enough to have someone like you helping me."

The four got off the train and looked around the platform for Frank and his companions.

Rebekka spotted him in the middle of a bunch of passengers walking along the platform. Next to him were the two men who had kept him company during the journey. Frank lifted his arm slightly, signaling to Rebekka. "I see Frank. I think we are supposed to join him," she said in a reasonably low voice.

Once the other passengers had left, Frank's two companions introduced themselves as Tor and Leif, using the now familiar explanation that their names were only valid for the next few hours. The "red sweater" was Leif. They expressed concern that the next set of pilots hadn't arrived, but didn't seem too worried. "It could be anything. A rainstorm, a little snow, some car trouble, we have experienced just about anything. Let's wait 15 minutes or so, before we consider alternatives."

Mor didn't seem to recognize "Haakon with the smile," and neither did Ruth. Rebekka felt shy as she glanced in his direction. She was rewarded with a big smile, just as she had seen earlier. As he walked past her, he said in a low voice, "It's nice to see you again. So far, so good. I'm sure everything will work out all right." It made her feel a little calmer. She turned to Frank who had stepped back a little. He appeared preoccupied and didn't say much. Normally he would grab the first opportunity to start a conversation. She wondered if he felt a little embarrassed about what had happened when he went on the wrong train. Did he think that people would think less of him? She put her arm around his shoulders and whispered, "I am so glad that you're with us. You must be exhausted, having gone through so much these past days."

He didn't answer, but she saw a trace of a smile appearing on his face.

Suddenly Rebekka felt faint. Oh, my goodness, she thought. How could she! The first time someone entrusted her to deliver important news, she forgets. Forgets! Just like a small child or some thoughtless, self-obsessed individual. Seeing "Haakon with the smile" made her revisit their conversation. She had forgotten to tell Mor the story of Uncle Leonard's fiancée, which she had promised to do. How could she! She grabbed on to Frank with both hands, afraid that she was going to get sick right there on the platform. Frank reacted quickly, but instead of trying to support her and make her feel better, he immediately called for his aunt to come help. Mor ran to her daughter, frantically asking if Rebekka was ill. A white-faced Rebekka collapsed around her mother's neck, and began to tell the entire story of how she had failed to convey the message delegated by the young Haakon known as Leif.

"I am so sorry, I am so sorry," she kept repeating. Mor listened carefully. "Please let it go, Bekka Sweetie," she said. "I can understand how bad you feel; I would have felt the same. But to be honest, I heard about it a few hours after you did. Someone else in Haakon's group stopped by after you left for school, or should I say Annika's. The person just wanted to make sure I knew. I was aware Haakon had told you. There were so many things going on that day, which is why I decided not to tell you until you mentioned it. Please don't worry about it."

Mor looked around once again, making certain that there were no strangers near them. The platform was empty now.

"I am so proud of all the other responsible things you did, from taking care of your little sister and telling her about the potato trip to Hadeland, to standing quietly next to me when I was arguing with Annika. And yes, most of all, when you decided to stay with me when we locked up the apartment together. The special moment when you reminded me what you did remember—to kiss the mezuzah. You showed me to act as a proud Jew, at a time when we were in danger because of being Jewish. I'll never forget that. Wait until I tell Far about this. He will be so proud of you. Please let's put this behind us, and hope and pray that Synnoeve will be released."

Mor moved a little to the side and spoke in a low voice to the guide who called himself Tor. He seemed to be a few years older than Leif. Rebekka had difficulty hearing what they were saying. Mor gestured while speaking. Her purse kept moving on her arm. Rebekka couldn't help wondering if the pendant had kept its magic powers, now that it was wrapped in a silk handkerchief, and not hanging around her mother's neck.

It was getting colder and the darkness made the situation less than comfortable. Miriam had fallen asleep once more, and was being held alternately by Sarah and Ruth. It was dark.

Exactly 15 minutes later a covered truck appeared and stopped at the platform. The man next to the driver jumped out, looking around quickly. He approached one of the two guides who were standing next to the women. "Do you know if the flowers were delivered to my grandmother today?" he uttered immediately.

The guide standing between Rebekka and Frank, broke into a smile, replying, "*The flowers were a mixture of red, white and blue.*"

The two men shook hands and started speaking quickly. "The damn car broke down half way. It would take too long to fix it. We were able to walk to the farm, and borrow a truck. They are waiting for your people. Let's get on the road."

Inside the truck, the guide driving explained that each journey involving an escape with several steps and had its own code, one question and one answer, making certain that only designated people were permitted to ask questions and give orders.

The next stop was less than 15 minutes away, it was a large farm, which was referred to as a "Safe Farm." There were only a few with that designation, which meant that the owners allowed refugees to stop to rest before they started their long walk through the woods which would lead them to the Swedish border. The driver had explained the importance of the place, which opened their doors to refugees that needed to stop and rest and recharge their strength. He hesitated over whether he should go further, but eventually in a very few words, he said, "The farmer and his family are actively involved in resistance work helping people 'on the run' to succeed in walking a good part of the night to reach the Swedish border.

"If and when they are able to travel on foot far enough, they will eventually be rewarded by seeing a number of large yellow signs welcoming them to the Kingdom of Sweden. At these markers, there will be Swedish soldiers who will monitor and check the names of the people who cross the border."

Rebekka was surprised when they arrived at the farm just before 11 pm. It was located at the top of a hill full of pine trees. She had never seen anything like it before, and she had only read about estates of this size. When they got closer a woman was waiting at the entryway, who shook their hands and bid them welcome with a warm smile, as if they had been invited to a party.

Rebekka could tell from the woman's mannerism that she was the owner and hostess. She appeared to be around fifty years old and was fairly short. She was wearing a hand knitted maroon cardigan decorated with a traditional grey and navy design. The buttons on the front were made of pewter. Rebekka had never seen anything that striking, and found it difficult to take her eyes off her. The complicated, yet perfect design on her spectacular cardigan was repeated over the entire garment. It reached all the way down to her knees.

The wearer of the unusual garment seemed genuinely engaged in their arrival considering it was late in the evening. The first thing she asked was, "Are you very tired? You will have a chance to rest." She complimented Sarah on Miriam, who had awakened and was carried by Ruth.

Two men, standing about a meter behind, appeared to be servants. They stayed close to the woman, but didn't speak. Rebekka had a feeling that the two "servants" were also there to protect the hostess, if necessary.

The main building was large, and the host waited inside the large foyer, standing next to a pair of magnificently carved chairs, which obviously were at least a couple of hundred years old. The shiny wooden floor was covered with three traditional handwoven rugs, each in a different pattern. In one corner, the largest fireplace Rebekka had ever seen was lighting up the room and radiating heat. The host was in his sixties, with a large shock of grey hair, and a deep voice with a dialect from the Western part of Norway. He seemed more reserved and introverted than his wife, but his eyes were friendly and emanated compassion and warmth. Rebekka felt she had arrived at a place where she was welcome, despite the grandeur and the unusual sophistication.

The hostess encouraged them to take off their jackets and overcoats, and to make themselves at home. Her braids were worn on the top of her head, which gave her a highly sophisticated appearance. She was soft spoken, and pressed everyone's hand more than once. She even tried to shake hands with Miriam, who was too shy and tried to hide her face in Ruth's neck. She smiled warmly at Rebekka and admired her hair, which she found magnificent. To their astonishment the hostess introduced herself, leaving out her last name.

"My name is Hilde," she said, "and I always wanted to have thick red hair. It has been my dream all my life. I saw a movie star with red hair once as a very young girl, and I have never forgotten it." Rebekka couldn't think of a reply. All she could do was smile. Everyone was surprised that she volunteered her first name so quickly. They introduced themselves as well. Rebekka couldn't help but wonder if Hilde was her real name or a "temporary" name. She knew better than to ask.

Hilde led them into a very large room beyond the foyer which probably had been a ballroom at a different time in history. It was now furnished with two long tables and several chairs. A couple of cots were lined up around the walls, and soap and towels were available. A few windbreakers, two or three hats and scarves in various colors could be borrowed, and were arranged on a clothes rack along the wall. Bathroom facilities were also available. Another fire burned in a corner fireplace.

Rebekka found it all fascinating. The house was so big and the rooms were so beautifully designed that it reminded her of stories she had read in school of mansions owned by wealthy farmers many years ago, and of the parties they would give.

It felt good being inside—they were tired. The package of sandwiches and snacks brought along from Oslo was placed on the long table and the crowd devoured all the food within a few minutes. Coffee surrogate and milk were offered by servants. The guide who had sat in the passenger's seat during the trip to the house leaned over to Mor and said in an upbeat voice, "In view of the circumstances, and considering the car problems that almost prevented us from picking you up, I feel that the first portion of the journey has gone well."

All turned toward him, wondering whether they should answer or not, and if so, what they should say. Rebekka looked at Frank to see if he would respond, but he remained quiet. To her complete surprise Rebekka found herself saying, "How can we know if it has gone well or not? We don't know if anyone saw us leave and are out to get us. We don't know how we are going to get to Sweden. Are we going to walk or run? Drive or swim? No one has told us anything."

Frank looked at Rebekka and then at the guide, who had continued eating, but looked a bit embarrassed.

"I'm sorry, sir, but I think what my cousin means is that it's difficult for us to measure whether the trip has gone well. We are worried and frightened all the time. I am sure you mean well, however, it's almost impossible for us to share your optimism. I, for one, feel if I relax, something bad will happen. I don't know what happened to my mother after I left her last night. I don't know if she is dead or alive. I don't know if she continued on her journey with her group, or if she is trying to find me. She could be anywhere. My father has already escaped to Sweden. I have no idea where he is."

Everyone at the table stopped talking. It was a difficult moment. Frank's face was red and he appeared to have a hard time breathing. Mor got up and walked over to him. She bent down and hugged him; speaking gently. "I am glad you spoke up, Frank, remember you are not alone. I'll not let go of you until I know that you are all right. I have a good feeling that your mother will be right there at the border waiting for you. She is a strong person, and you are the most important person in her life."

Frank allowed her to hold him for a while, and then he sat up. "I'm okay, Aunt Sarah. It just felt like something exploded in me. It had to come out. Sir," he said, addressing the guide, who looked embarrassed that he had generated this reaction, "I apologize for being rude. I know you meant well."

At that point, the two guides, Stein and Petter, suggested it was time to move on. They were polite, respectful and helpful. No personal information was exchanged and no questions were raised.

The mistress of the farm had remained at a distance in the large hall while they were eating and resting.

"This must be a daily event for these people," Mor said to one of the guides, "Considering how many people have been forced to leave Norway and not only because of their religion. There must be hundreds of people stopping by here every day."

"Do you know how many people are risking their lives every day to fight for the country's freedom? Most of them eventually have to escape to Sweden as well to save their own lives," Stein said in a low voice.

The guides approached Mor, considered the head of the family and therefore in charge, and started to discuss the next phase. Rebekka listened attentively, keeping silent.

"We would like to get started in about 30 minutes or so. It's close to midnight." Petter, the guide who seemed to be in charge, announced. He spoke in a gentle, low voice, yet it was so clear that everyone could hear him. His wide shoulders matched his height, which must have been close to two meters. Two of his teeth were missing. Rebekka wondered how and where he had lost them. Was it because of a fight with a German soldier? Was it because he had to run too fast and had fallen? She had her sketchbook with her, thne realized that this was neither the time nor the place for her to pull it out. She would try to remember his face and see if she could portray the memory. Maybe later when they got to Sweden she would be able to draft a few lines. Suddenly she felt much better.

"The trip tonight will be my third in a week," Petter said, this time a little louder, as if speaking to the crowd in general.

All were surprised to hear one of the guides make a personal comment, the first of the day, and listened carefully. He suddenly looked away, and it was clear that his concentration was on Hilde. She had moved away, closer to the large doorway, while indicating that she would like him to join her.

"Please excuse me," he said, as he got up from the table; crossed the room, joining the hostess of the farm. The two of them were out of sight for a short time, after which he returned, looking relaxed, but preoccupied. The others, still sitting at the table, watched him, anticipating some type of message, which they expected would be serious. To their surprise, he didn't volunteer any new information.

As they were about to leave the large farmhouse, Stein approached Mor. "I guess it's time to tell you about the next phase of our journey. We will be walking through the woods for the next four to five hours, which you may or may not have heard. Depending on the weather and the moon, it may be quite dark. The good thing is no one will see us. We hope. We will be passing and possibly crossing some of the small lakes by boat." He turned to Mor. "Would you allow me to carry your little daughter in my large rucksack?" he asked.

"It's large and roomy, and I think that this would be the best solution for everyone. It will be cumbersome for you or Ruth to carry her for any length of time. I can assure you that this is not the first time that I have carried a passenger on my back, and this will allow us to walk at a steady pace."

Ruth looked at Mor, indicating that it had to be her decision.

"If you have made that many trips in one week, I am assuming you have carried many little kids in that rucksack during the past few months. I am sure she'll be safe and comfortable when she is told the two of you will play 'horse.' Thank you for offering," Mor replied.

Rebekka was watching her mother, who had been able to calm Frank down, and now make a decision about how Mimi would be transported. She was surprised at how collected she was. It was hard to believe this was the same mother who scolded Rebekka when she forgot to wipe her feet on the doormat after returning from school! Regardless, at least now she had learned they were all to walk for a long while. She got up from the table and looked for her coat.

They said goodbye to Hilde, who looked at Mor, and said hesitantly, "I want to wish you all the best on the journey. Will I offend you if I say that I'll keep you in my prayers, since we are of different religions?"

Taking her extended hand with both hers, Mor looked into the hostess' questioning blue eyes, "How can I be offended? You are risking your life to help us—besides, there is only one God. Thank you for your kindness and hospitality. Yes, please do keep us in your prayers." Hilde's husband was nowhere to be seen. Mor continued, "Please convey our gratitude to your husband as well."

Rebekka and Ruth also shook her hand. It was hard for both of them to stop the tears from running down their cheeks.

Miriam was tired and had been placed already in the rucksack, which turned out to be surprisingly roomy. At the bottom of the bag were the guide's raincoat, a flashlight, and a small first aid box. Rebekka also caught a glimpse of a handgun carefully packed in a heavy cloth. She said nothing.

It was midnight when they started walking. They crossed the far reaching fields behind the farmer's property, and within a quarter of an hour, they entered the woods. Everyone had been given a flashlight by the mistress of the farm, and they had been asked that only two people use it at a time, only when absolutely necessary, in order to preserve the batteries.

"When you reach Sweden, please return the flashlights back to the guides, so they can be used by the next batch of travelers," she had said. They promised to do so, feeling reassured by her optimism. Stein walked first, then Mor, followed by the others, and at the rear of the entourage was the second guide, Petter.

Initially, the path in the woods was quite narrow and it was difficult to walk steadily. Rebekka was tired and apprehensive. She had the same feeling of anxiety having to walk alone as she experienced earlier on the sidewalk while looking for the parked car. Once they had walked approximately a mile or so, to her delight the path became wider.

Instead of a narrow path, barely able to accommodate one person, the trail was now three times as wide, and it appeared to extend indefinitely, as far as the eye could see.

Petter explained, "This was prepared about six months ago by a group of 'Our Boys in the Woods,' as they are known. They felt widening the escape path would create a major impact on the speed of the refugees, and help people with physical difficulties, to walk and preserve energy. They were right; it has been a great physical as well as psychological improvement."

Stein suddenly fell into step with Mor, who was walking just behind Rebekka. Miriam was still fast asleep in the rucksack, so Ruth moved ahead to catch up with Petter and Frank.

Initially Stein was silent, in deep thought. When he started to speak again, he was hesitant.

"Sarah, I have something to tell you, which has caused me some apprehension, but I feel I should share it with you." Sarah glanced at him, didn't answer, and waited.

"I am sure you noticed my brief talk with Hilde just before we left." Next he took out a well-used handkerchief, wiped his forehead, and cleared his throat, "Mrs. Farmer," he paused, assuming that Mor was aware of his choice to revert to a fictional name. Rebekka immediately felt a shiver go through her body. She knew something urgent was coming, and she listened very carefully.

"Mrs. Farmer confirmed some very disturbing news from our Oslo network. It's now past midnight—the 26th of November. The news is no longer a rumor, but reality."

He paused and cleared his throat. "I am afraid that this date will be remembered as a sad day. Almost all the Jewish men who were imprisoned in various parts of Norway are now in the process of being sent to the docks in Oslo where a large ship, *The Donau*, is waiting."

He paused again, making sure that Mor and Rebekka kept walking while listening.

"Mrs. Farmer conveyed the news which she received about one hour ago from Oslo. Two hundred taxis have been ordered into service by the Oslo Police. These cars, manned with at least one German soldier each, will go to all the homes inhabited by Jews, arresting all remaining women and children. The families have been instructed to pack a small suitcase to hold their valuables, such as cash, jewelry and the like and enough food for three days. The taxis will bring them down to the docks and the ship. I wish to God that I didn't have to tell you, but I feel it's my responsibility."

Rebekka couldn't believe her ears. She couldn't imagine the taxis bringing women, old and young, and small kids through the streets of Oslo, forcing them on board and into the bottom of a large transport ship. She felt she could hear the crying. She wondered if the soldiers had come to their house as well. Probably, she thought. Did the enemies and the Nazis at the dock have lists on which they marked off people's names? Were their names on a list? Were their names read out loud? Was her name read out loud? She felt paralyzed but for her legs that miraculously kept propelling her along the path.

Stein continued. His voice hoarse and uncomfortable.

"The ship is scheduled to leave tomorrow afternoon bringing several hundred Jews out of the country to unknown destinations, possibly labor camps. One thing is clear; it will not be good for the Jews. It's still not clear where the ship is headed, but all the other information has been confirmed several times. Were you aware of any of this? Do you still have relatives and close friends who haven't gone into hiding and are remaining in Oslo?"

Mor hesitated and it was clear that she needed to digest the news. She then said "I had heard about the plan for the arrest from reliable sources, but I didn't know any details. And of course I didn't know whether this was rumor or reality, or when it would take place. We have tried to alert everyone we could. It isn't always easy to convince people that it's necessary. Our escape had been planned for a week. First our guides helped my mother, her sister and brother-in-law escape, and thereafter my sister, Frank and four other women to get away. I purposely scheduled myself and my children to go last. Oh, my God," she exclaimed suddenly, her voice slowly fading.

She stopped for a few seconds, speechless. Rebekka paused as well, and it became obvious that she had overheard the conversation. Frank and Ruth could be seen up ahead speaking with Petter. Then Sarah covered her mouth afraid to speak out loud. She signaled to Ruth, asking her to come and listen to the news. She quickly repeated Stein's story. As if reading each other's minds—the two women looked at each other half whispering and half speaking. Sarah gasped, "Annika! Oh, dear God."

They stood stock still for a couple of minutes. They had ran out of things to say.

Then Mor exclaimed. "What about Leonard? I wonder if they got him as well? I had heard that two smaller ships left earlier. He might be on one of those. As for Synnoeve, I don't think she was sent. As you know, she is not Jewish. Most probably she is in prison."

Slowly they forced themselves to continue to walk.

Fortunately, the weather remained stable. They were protected from the wind in the forest, and there was no ice on the ground. Rebekka kept thinking of what it would be like walking here once the snow and ice arrived. Strangely enough, she had started to feel more secure, in the company of the two guides. It felt as if their confidence had been transmitted to her. Miriam appeared to have settled down for the night, as she was sleeping peacefully in the rucksack. Rebekka had heard that some small children had to be sedated in an escape group, as any sound or crying could create a dangerous situation. So far, so good.

After two more hours in the forest, they found themselves near an open area; recognizing they had reached a small lake. Rebekka was exhausted. "It's the middle of the night," she said. "I hope we will get to the border soon, or I am going to fall asleep standing up." A circle formed around Stein who made it clear he wanted to speak to everyone. Even Frank listened. He was polite and helpful, and had offered to help carry Mor and Ruth's bags for a while.

"We need to make a decision. The water was frozen last week, and there is no reason why it shouldn't still be covered with ice. If we walk across the lake, we can save about an hour of walking time. The alternative is to walk around it, but that would probably take two hours," Stein announced.

"Is there any difference in the risk of being seen by anyone?" Mor asked looking at the lake.

The answer was slightly hesitant. "No, the risk is the same, regardless."

"We have to walk around the lake. There may be water on the ground, even under the snow and ice. Ruth isn't wearing boots, and Rebekka's boots aren't thick enough, and I don't think we should risk either taking ill. I think we should walk around the lake."

The leader looked at Mor. He gave the impression that he was about to challenge her, but must have changed his mind. It was clear her decision was based on fear that the lake wasn't totally frozen, and not due to lack of warm boots. The decision had been made, and they kept walking.

They reached the forest on the other side of the lake in less than two hours and kept walking. Somewhere around 4 am they reached another small lake, which was definitely not frozen. They stopped. The two men disappeared for a few minutes into the dense forest, only to reappear, hauling a light, long, rowboat. The boat was kept hidden in that area to be used when needed. The boat was put in the water and everyone was told to get in. If anyone was afraid that the load was too heavy, no one dared say it. The movement across the small lake went slowly, but steadily. The moon was full. Ordinarily the night would be considered beautiful with the moonlight falling on the water, but on that night, the extra light created additional danger of being seen.

"Please be very, very quiet. We are fine and we have colleagues hiding in this area who are watching out for us. You can't see them, but they are surrounding us. Unfortunately, we also know there is a family in this general area who are Nazi supporters, but we assume they are sleeping and not watching out for anyone. This won't take long."

He was right. Once they reached the other side of the lake, they all could breathe easier. They got out of the rowboat as quickly as possible, entering the forest once more. The path was narrower than before, but still adequate for them to make good progress. Later they became aware of some changes in the terrain. It was hard to tell what they were. Different vegetation? More trees? Closer together? Neither of the guides spoke.

At 4:25 am, exactly, Stein cleared his throat, indicating he had something to tell them, and his voice sounded somewhat excited.

"If you look to the right of the path, fairly far away, you will soon notice something sticking up between the trees. If you can't see it now, just keep looking, and tell me when you notice it. We will just continue walking."

He was holding a compass.

A few minutes later Rebekka was the first to announce she had noticed something yellow up ahead, and shortly thereafter Ruth and Mor echoed her. Rebekka's voice, however, had taken on a different degree of clarity as she shouted out loud, "I think I see a large sign! In the middle of the forest! It's a large, round sign, covered with yellow and green lettering. It's very tall!"

She started to run ahead of the others.

"I can read it! It says: Welcome to the Kingdom of Sweden."

Her voice was shaking.

"Is it . . . ? Does this mean . . . ?"

Rebekka tried in vain to get Mor's attention. She was walking behind her close to Petter. Mor smiled and answered, "I think so."

"Yes, that's it." Stein said. "Let's keep walking. We need to be on the other side of that sign first."

Stein's expression was enough to give her the official confirmation, but first he put strong emphasis on the word *other*.

The next few minutes passed as in a dream. Suddenly they were standing next to the sign, touching it. Rebekka read slowly *"Welcome to the Kingdom of Sweden."* She was afraid to move.

They all stood in disbelief, while the two men became very busy. A box containing something called a "walkie-talkie" would allow them to contact other soldiers, Norwegian or Swedish. In this instance, they needed to notify the Swedish authorities that they had arrived at the border, and ask for permission to cross over into Sweden. A number of strange terms and numbers were exchanged on the mysterious device. Immediately thereafter, a short dialogue followed. As the head of their family, only Sarah's name was given, and the conversation had to be limited. Every time a person spoke, the recipient on the other side couldn't speak, but only listen, and vice versa.

Finally, an official message arrived from the Swedish side. Luckily the Norwegian group didn't experience any difficulties understanding as the languages fortunately were quite similar.

"We have deciphered your location. Representatives from Sweden will reach you in about 30 minutes. Please wait and don't leave your position. Make certain that your passports are ready for inspection. Everything is routine . . . wait, one moment, please. Another message is coming from the sheriff that needs to be considered a priority. It is being sent to me on another line. Please stand by."

The members of the waiting crowd looked at each other, concerned. They waited breathlessly. Shortly thereafter the Swedish voice came back on the line.

"This is urgent and imperative. The sheriff has an important question. Please stand by."

The delay made everyone increasingly nervous. They held their breath, as Petter listened with the contraption pressed against his ear, until the message finally was delivered.

He responded into the device.

"I think you need to repeat this question once more out loud so the group and the specific person in question can answer."

A voice posed a question out loud in Swedish to which a chorus of voices next to the sign of Sweden screamed simultaneously and uncontrollably, "Yes!!! Yes! Yes!!"

The question that had come across the device consisted of eleven short words.

"Do you have the boy? His mother is waiting for him."

Chapter Twenty-Six

Where Do I Go Now?

AALESUND, NOVEMBER 26, 1942

The sky was grey. The street was grey. It was quite cold. The ski jacket he was wearing belonged to his father, as did the wool sweater and shoes. A couple of weeks ago his mother had taken a few things out of the closet while commenting on how much he had grown this year. It wasn't necessary to explain to whom they belonged. They both knew. The absence of his father permeated the room, and mother and son avoided looking at each other. He tried on a heavy windbreaker. It fit. "Thank you," was all he could muster.

His school had been divided into two daily sessions, one in the morning and one at noon. On that day, his classes were scheduled from twelve to three, and they had just come to an end. He felt slightly uncomfortable being at school. Many of his classmates heard about the failed attempt to escape, and were getting nosy. For the most part he kept to himself. The elective class discussion was scheduled for 3 pm with a substitute as Mr. Welhaven was still in prison. Some of his classmates had arrived, but the teacher was late. A handful of students were conversing, looking for news.

Eight kids were present, most of whom had brought lunches consisting of open-faced sandwiches. No one seemed to have anything specific to bring up.

Harald, sitting by himself, stretched his legs and looked out the window. He found the conversation slightly boring. He considered leaving and if there was anything to do instead, he might just have walked out.

"Hey, guess who I saw outside the police station last night? Gyldendahl. He definitely had some trouble walking in a straight line!"

The person bringing up this gossip, Rolf, was the son of a lawyer in town. The father had participated in the first round of fighting against the Germans, in Valdres. Harald remembered that his Uncle Martin, Rebekka's father, had taken part as well.

Harald wasn't close to Rolf, despite his friendly and charming personality on display whenever he felt like it. Rolf had a tendency to monopolize most conversations and always wanted the last word. He was a mouthpiece for any kind of scandalous and unsubstantiated gossip. Harald wasn't always comfortable in his company.

"Gyldendahl insists that he wants to live here in town to work hard for the New World, while enjoying the company of local relatives with whom he has reconnected."

Rolf suddenly got up, and started to walk around. It was clear he was trying to mimic Gyldendahl, and by pretending to carry a bottle of beer in his left hand, doing the Hitler salute with the other arm. Some of the boys started laughing.

"Great, who are his relatives? Do we know them?" Someone asked. Rolf immediately flashed his "holding court" smile; he had manipulated his audience exactly where he wanted them. "His nephew is Arne Friberg."

His listeners gasped.

"You must be kidding! The 'perfect' man in town? The star student, the athlete?"

Half of the crowd turned towards Harald, who obviously wasn't the only person aware that Arne and his sister were a couple. He pretended not to notice their stares, remaining silent.

The lecture on Gyldendahl continued, "He is a big beer drinker, and finds this especially helpful when he chooses to announce his new plans. His biggest frustration is hearing how many guys have taken off for England. One of his favorite ways of emphasizing this is holding his ever-present beer bottle up in the air, and attempting to scare the local resistance people by screaming, 'When is the next escape ship leaving for England?'"

Rolf didn't announce his sources, but he had no shortage of news. The laughter broke out among the crowd encouraging him eager to continue the conversation. At that moment, the substitute teacher interrupted. Having arrived ten minutes earlier, he had watched and overheard the gossip that was exchanged. The boys sitting in the corner of the room, had missed his arrival.

"This is not a proper conversation to have at all, and especially not at school. We are here for a reason—to help us understand what is happening to our country politically. You can show allegiance to your country through a variety of helpful ways. And you," he said, pointing to Rolf, "how do you think your father would feel if he knew you were broadcasting rumors and personal information?"

The boys sat down quickly, and the teacher introduced the topic for that day. Harald noticed that Rolf stayed quiet.

Shortly thereafter Harald left to see Dr. Nikolas Fjellstrand, his family doctor. Recently Harald had been visiting Fjellstrand's office twice a week. Rumors had it that the local police and The Gestapo were getting ready to move against Harald after the unsuccessful attempt to escape. The physician had come up with a plan which he hoped would at least delay the local police and The Gestapo from arresting Harald, if not preventing it altogether.

"Harald, listen carefully. We are facing some real trouble. A message was intercepted earlier this week which has been sent to every police station in the country announcing all Jewish men are to be arrested. A large number have already been picked up. This even includes boys who have turned fifteen. You just turned seventeen, Harald, am I right? We need to deal with this."

Harald stared at him incredulously, "Do you mean that I might . . . "

He couldn't even complete the sentence.

Fjellstrand ignored his comment, and continued, "Well, so far your name is not on the list. That's good. We don't know exactly why. Your age may have been recorded incorrectly. They know that your father has already been taken. We need to use this to our advantage as soon as possible. Because, believe me, they will find out, and this will happen soon. We need a plan to postpone the inevitable and get your family out of town."

Harald stared at the doctor.

The doctor continued, "We are going to make you 'sick.' I am going to explain that you are suffering from a chronic disease which requires ongoing medical supervision. According to the Red Cross Humanitarian Guidelines for Peace, you cannot be arrested if you are ill."

He stopped to see how Harald was responding. Harald sat quietly, his eyes wide open, listening carefully, then he asked.

"How can you do that? If they want me, won't they know where to find me? And what is the Red Cross Humanitarian Guidelines for Peace? How can that protect me?"

"There is something called Crohn's disease. It's a chronic stomach disorder, which may be dangerous but can be controlled, if treated appropriately. Patients who adhere to correct treatment often do quite well. I want to announce that you are a victim of this disease, needing to be seen regularly to monitor the progress. The stuff about the humanitarian guidelines, forget it! I made it up, hoping that it will take several weeks for them to investigate this law. Are you with me on this?"

Harald nodded, staring at Dr. Fjellstrand.

"All you have to do is to show up for pre-arranged appointments so I can 'see' you. It's a plot to fool the bastards." The physician continued.

"I'll make certain that the police department gets an unsolicited report about your condition in the event they start talking about arresting you. I will explain it to your mother. Leave it to me and trust me. Do you have any more questions, Harald?"

Harald shook his head, and whispered, "No, sir, and I understand."

He started to leave, with Dr. Fjellstrand calling after him, "Make an appointment for tomorrow or the next day!"

This afternoon's appointment was the beginning of the third week. During the short time at school that day, Harald had been lost in thought thinking of Dr. Fjellstrand's idea while the teacher brought up new pieces of information. This had happened several times. It had become hard to separate his nightmares from the realities of a normal day.

Leaving the school and gossip-hungry contemporaries, he made his way to the physician's office in the middle of town for a "routine" visit. Some routine, he thought!

He was still preoccupied with the story about Gyldendahl. Even a mention of the man's name triggered apprehension. The receptionist greeted him with a big smile, having become familiar with him. He was told the physician would join him in the examination room. Dr. Fjellstrand appeared, wearing his white lab coat, a stethoscope hanging around his neck. It was clear to Harald that Dr. Fjellstrand was planning to take this charade all the way. It was their secret, and no one in his office—staff or patients—were to suspect that a secret game was being played.

The physician asked a few questions which made no sense at all. Harald answered the best he could by alternating yes and no to the questions, as prearranged. After a few minutes, as Dr. Fjellstrand was about to leave, a knock echoed through the room. The receptionist announced in a loud voice that a Mr. Gyldendahl was in the waiting room, agitated, and insisting on speaking with him immediately.

Dr. Fjellstrand looked surprised, and for the first time uncertainty passed over his face. He looked down at his hands, trying to decide how to handle the situation. A few seconds later he lifted his head, and whispered to Harald, "Stay right here. I need to speak to Gyldendahl. I will get right back to you." Harald's heart skipped a beat, realizing who had arrived.

The doctor left the room, closing the door behind him.

Harald was frozen, not knowing whether to run. Gyldendahl's reputation was both feared and belittled by the local "good Norwegians." Now he was here in person, probably looking for him specifically! Was Gyldendahl planning to arrest him? Should he run, but where to? His legs were shaking, making it difficult to stand.

Harald's eyes fell on a small shelf on the wall, which shielded an opening into the waiting room. Through it he could both see and overhear an argument between Fjellstrand and Gyldendahl. The monster, the Nazi, the enemy! Right there in the next room!

"I demand to be present when you examine Mr. Rosenberg, to make certain that he is truly ill and that this is not a trick to fool me." Harald assumed that this unknown voice had to be the villain himself.

He placed himself by the wall opening. He could see the entire reception room, including the unattractive balding, overweight man who was raising his voice. Harald was paralyzed, afraid to move. He felt he was looking through a secret pair of binoculars, or maybe a telescope. He felt faint. He couldn't recall ever being referred to as Mr. Rosenberg. Did this mean that Gyldendahl thought of him as an adult and therefore he could arrest him?

He could hear Fjellstrand's response, delivered in a calm, polite manner, "I am sorry, I cannot do that, Mr. Gyldendahl," he said. "You must have heard of the Hippocratic Oath," which he then proceeded to quote in Latin in a loud and clear voice.

He said respectfully, "I am sure you don't need a translation into Norwegian. Most probably you are fluent in Latin with your educational background?"

The lack of response hung in the air, as Gyldendahl stared at him in rage. Gyldendahl finally chose not to respond to the educational challenge.

The physician continued politely. "Harald's condition, if treated aggressively, will preclude it from becoming a chronic disorder which will make it impossible to travel. It requires lots of rest to avoid getting physically exhausted, plus eating minimal, frequent meals. It's my professional opinion that my patient will recover within a couple of weeks if he adheres to this rigid plan. At the present time," he said, putting his glasses on, "hospitalization is not necessary."

Gyldendahl stared at him, trying to determine whether he was being told the truth or not. He insisted on waiting so he could verify that Harald was there. Harald, who was frozen waiting in the same place, could hear and see everything. The receptionist announced that Harald had left just a few minutes earlier through the back staircase.

Gyldendahl left through the front entrance, looking sulky and angry, while the regular routine of the office resumed. The last thing Harald saw and heard was a young girl around his own age who approached the receptionist and asked modestly, with great confidence, "Why did Dr. Fjellstrand recite the 'Guadiamus Igitur' in Latin, saying it was the Hippocratic Oath?"

The girl was given an open-ended compliment on her Latin skills, but nothing else was explained!

Harald had remained in the examination room as long as he could, afraid to leave without permission. After he heard the receptionist say that he had already left through the back door, he waited a few minutes and did exactly that to avoid a possible confrontation with his enemy.

Ironically, Harald, who just a short time earlier had been in excellent health, was beginning to feel sick. His stomach was nervous and irritated most of the day. As the day passed and evening fell, Harald kept thinking about the meeting with the physician and the threat from Gyldendahl.

He was just about to go to bed that evening when the doorbell rang. He opened the door and was face to face with two young German soldiers. He turned to his mother, who had been reading in the living room. "I'll speak with them," he said, trying to appear calmer than he was. He started worrying immediately that this visit had to do with him. And he was right. They looked quite serious. Perhaps they were nervous, as well, he thought. They mumbled something simultaneously, which he found inaudible. At the end of two repetitive, slightly incoherent statements, they managed to speak clearly.

"We are from the Aalesund police office. You are under arrest according to the laws of the Nazi party now in power. We have orders to bring you to the station, an order which applies to every Jewish male in this country who has reached fifteen years of age."

Harald's stomach felt like it was about to explode, which wasn't surprising. He was petrified. His mouth was dry and he felt acutely nauseated. He didn't have to pretend that he was sick. He was sick. His hands were clammy.

Fortunately, Dr. Fjellstrand had prepared him for what to say if the enemy tried to arrest him. Harald stared at the two, trying to suppress the intense fear that immediately engulfed him, while forcing himself to respond slowly and clearly.

"I have been informed that according to the International law governing the Red Cross Humanitarian Guidelines, you can neither arrest me nor remove me from my home, as I am suffering from a serious condition by the name of Crohn's disease."

He was surprised when he heard himself reciting most of Dr. Fjellstrand's words almost verbatim. He ended his speech by stating, "According to these guidelines I have up to thirty days to remain at my house in the care of an official physician."

The two men stared at him, making it clear that they were unfamiliar with the guidelines which he claimed restricted his arrest.

Harald therefore continued, "I will advise Dr. Fjellstrand to contact your office at the police station within the next ten minutes to confirm that you have been here in an attempt to arrest me, and that I am under his medical care. Thank you."

With that, he closed the door, locked it and went to telephone Dr. Fjellstrand.

He was concerned that the Nazi soldiers would break down the door, forcing their way into the house . . . and . . . He listened for a minute or so, until he finally heard them walking down the stairs and out the main door.

He contacted Fjellstrand immediately, describing the terrifying visit. The doctor reassured him that he would take care of it. True to his word, Dr.

Fjellstrand arrived at the police station at the crack of dawn the following morning.

The physician allowed himself to smile and display some humor when he informed Harald about the meeting prior to leaving for the hospital. "I showed up at the police station at 7:30 in the morning. The guy in charge, Thomas Gyldendahl, is known for his arrogance, rage and loudness. However, he is also known for consuming a fair amount of beer on a daily basis, and it was no big surprise that he was late. This was why I chose to appear at the police station at that early hour."

Regardless, Harald remained restless after Fjellstrand left. Now what would happen? Should he hide or try to escape on his own? He had no idea. He didn't want to go to school, he decided. He felt that he didn't belong there anymore. His mother was silent, moving slowly. Her face showed no emotion at all. Only her hands were busy, moving small knickknacks around, while wiping off imaginary dust. She had asked no questions about the surprise visit by the soldiers the previous night or the follow-up visit from Dr. Fjellstrand.

Harald was still torn about going to school. Was he wrong? Was there any purpose of attending as scheduled at noon? Could he sit still and listen to talk about math, Norwegian history and chemistry? Did it really matter now? Granted, life in Norway had changed for everyone, but it appeared his life had changed even more than the others. What would happen to him? He could feel his mother's eyes following him everywhere, yet she asked no questions. He was relieved that she didn't, as he had no idea what to tell her.

He had been told most of the Jewish men had chosen to escape to safety in neutral Sweden. He knew nothing about his relatives. Had they left and were they safe? Or had they been arrested? He felt isolated. Nowhere to go. No one to talk to.

He took a deep breath. It was hard not to obsess about the situation. Night after night for the past few weeks, he would go to bed, unable to sleep for hours, agonizing about the whereabouts of his father as well as his own future. He had stopped discussing it with his mother and sister. It served no purpose, he had concluded. They knew no more than he did. He had heard some rumors that his father was still in Norway. Rumor or truth, he wondered.

Finally he felt that he needed to get out of the house. "I'll be back in a couple of hours, Mor. I just need a little fresh air. Do you know where Ingrid is? I want to drop off my books at school this afternoon, as well as my Current Affairs article. Maybe I will stop at Fjellstrand's office on the way home. I feel that I need a little air. Are you okay if I leave you for an hour or two?"

His mother didn't object. It was still dry enough outside to bike, and besides, who knew, perhaps the bicycle might come in handy if someone tried to stop him.

What scared Harald most of all, he had to admit to himself, was the speed with which everything had developed. Only a year ago, actually less, he would never even have dreamt of a mass arrest.

As soon as Harald had thought one thing through, the other thoughts took over. What right did the enemy have to arrest him? How about freedom of speech? Freedom of religion? It was all quite confusing. He had written a couple of articles for the school newspaper. Was that the reason the Nazis wanted to arrest him? No, of course not. Now they wanted to arrest him purely because he was Jewish. At 17. Why?

Despite his nervousness on the bike, no one seemed to be looking at him. The atmosphere on the street was as usual. Teenagers, elderly couples and Norwegian men in their Nazi uniforms were walking around.

He reached the school and exchanged a few words with his friend Kristian Fredrik, making no mention of yesterday's event. He tried to pretend all was well.

By the time he returned home a few hours later, it was beginning to get dark. November and December were the darkest months of the year. His mouth felt dry and he was shaking, despite the lined windbreaker. Why did he feel something was off? A premonition?

Walking into the kitchen, he looked for his mother. He found her standing in the middle of the room, a terrified look on her face, staring into space.

"What happened, Mor?" he said, putting his arms around her, making her sit down. He forced himself to keep calm.

"I opened the door and two young uniformed men were waiting. Without a word, they pushed me aside and walked in. All they did was look around and say nothing."

"One of them walked over to the phone on the wall. No comment, no explanation, just grabbed it and tore it off the wall. I tried to object, but they ignored me. One of them laughed. The other pretended to throw it at me. I backed away and remained in the corner of the room, not knowing whether I should stay or leave. Eventually I thought it was better to stay still and do nothing. His partner bent over and swept everything off the coffee table and watched it land on the floor, laughing out loud. I remained in the same position, staring at him. They looked around the room. One of them said to the other in German, which I understood. "Oh, well, there's nothing worth having here!" And then they left, just as quickly as they had arrived."

Harald couldn't believe it. She had just stood there, immobile, and watched. It was probably the smartest thing she could have done. Most other women in her position would have tried to run away, and would probably have been hurt.

"Did they break anything of value?"

"No, we have nothing left of value. I've sold most everything out of necessity. The few valuable things I was concerned about were brought to Sofie's house before we attempted to escape on the ferry."

"You did everything right," Harald said. "I am so proud of you. Had you seen the two soldiers before? Were they the same ones that rang the doorbell last night?"

"Yes, they could be. They certainly wore the same uniform and were about the same age. I didn't look too closely last night as you were speaking to them and I was scared."

That was the end of Mor's bravery. She sat down on the sofa and sobbed.

Harald said, "I wonder if this was retaliation for not having been able to arrest me. They may have gotten into trouble for returning to the station empty handed."

Harald tried to think of ways to calm Mor down, but he didn't know what to say. As usual he gave her a glass of water, the only thing he could think of. He had given her quite a few glasses of water these past months, he thought to himself. Looking out the window he saw Fjellstrand and two other men approaching. He opened the front door, assuming they were on their way to see him and his mother. He was right.

"Harald, Dr. Fjellstrand and his friends are on their way," Mor said. "He called while you were out. I told them about the two soldiers and that you would be back soon. I meant to tell you immediately but . . . " She had a hard time finishing the sentence.

He let them in without a word. Shortly afterward three more men arrived, filling up the room.

The physician approached Harald immediately, using a gentle tone. It was clear the situation had deteriorated. He paused to allow Harald to calm down a little before explaining what had developed during the past few hours.

"Harald, we have to change our strategy, unfortunately. Things are getting serious, really serious. We won't be able to keep them away if they really intend to get you. We are trying to figure out how we can keep you safe."

One of the men, quietly smoking a pipe, had pulled away from the others. It was clear he was listening to every word. For some reason the smell from the pipe tobacco had a calming effect on Harald, or perhaps it was the man himself, although he had never met him before. The stranger stepped forward next to Dr. Fjellstrand, speaking directly to Harald. It was clear that he had something urgent to convey.

"Don't know if you have heard of a German ship called the *Donau* which docked in Oslo a few days ago. These are not rumors, but reality. Yesterday afternoon it took off with almost 700 Norwegian Jews; destination unknown.

For most people, it was a total surprise." He stopped speaking, not leaving Fjellstrand's side.

Harald couldn't believe the words from the unknown tall man. It was clear Fjellstrand knew him well and trusted him to take over the orientation. This was impossible! They had to be wrong. This couldn't be true! He turned to face his mother. He felt like a small child. He wanted to seek shelter with her, yet at the same time he wanted to protect her. He started moving around the room nervously.

Mor demanded his attention. "Please, Harald, stop. Listen to what he is telling us." Her voice shook. Did she know that man from earlier days, he wondered.

"They arrested women and children," the stranger continued. "Innocent people were awakened in the middle of the night and forced to leave their homes. Hundreds of taxis were waiting, full of police officers and soldiers, who brought them to the ship. They had no idea. Hard to believe, isn't it?"

The speaker hesitated, then continued, "Two smaller ships left on November 22 with about 60 additional Jewish men in each. That was kept a secret for the most part. I don't know the details yet."

"Most of the men who had been arrested on October 25, were kept in several primitive prisons near Oslo. They were brought to the dock directly from their holding places. Counting all men, women and children, around 480 people were forced on board when the ship left."

"The destination is unknown, but I can assure you, it's not going to be a pleasant trip."

Harald stared at the physician who had remained quiet. Harald had already heard snippets of the news whispered by two of the men who were sitting in Dr. Fjellstrand's waiting room. They had talked about a ship full of Jewish prisoners. He hadn't believed it. And now he heard that it was the truth!

"My father . . . ?" Harald asked carefully, looking at the stranger.

"No, we checked on that already. There were lists. Neither your father's nor your uncle's names were registered. I don't know where they are, but they were not on board the large ship."

"Some of the men transported from prisons around the country didn't make it to the dock on time, delayed by trains and buses. They are still incarcerated, being guarded in other facilities. That's all I know right now," the tall man said. His voice dropped. "I am so sorry."

Harald stood still, just staring at him.

The stranger continued, "We know this horror is hard to understand. In addition, they suspect we are using an illness to prevent them from getting their hands on you. Of course they are right."

"Several good people are working night and day to devise a plan to get you out of town, away from these damn monsters, but it will take time. Right now, it seems that the only way they will not be able to arrest you is if you are in the hospital. You will be admitted and we'll blame your medical problems. We need an excuse and have decided to remove your appendix to justify the admission. That's what we need to do. Please trust us."

Once again, Harald turned to his mother.

"I agree, Harald. If that's what they feel is necessary, we need to follow their advice. We cannot take any more chances. All my relatives," she began, trying to stop the tears that were running down her face, "All my sisters and brothers and their families have escaped, except for those who have already been arrested. I cannot get in touch with them. And Far . . . "

The stranger spoke again.

"We need to expedite this plan. I have just been informed that the trouble-makers, led by Gyldendahl, are so inspired by the ship full of Jews being sent off that they have decided to arrest any male Jew who has managed to avoid it so far. There aren't many left. Here in our town, Harald is their first and only target."

Harald walked over to the window, looked out and then turned back. He picked up an ashtray from the coffee table and turned it in his hand. Everyone in the room had their eyes on him, but no one spoke.

"Why are you all staring at me? What do you want me to say? I don't have a choice. The Gestapo and their brutes might as well have put me in chains. If you feel that you can get me out of this chain, by all means, do it, and quickly! Let me ask you directly—do you have any specific plans right now beyond admittance to the hospital? Anything at all? Well, let's get going!"

Chapter Twenty-Seven

On Neutral Ground

OSLO/SWEDEN, NOVEMBER 26, 1942

Rebekka didn't move while the Swedish sheriff and soldiers inspected the group's official papers. The new refugees were to be transferred to another place, only a few miles away. A flatbed truck had arrived, and they were asked to climb on. A pile of soiled blankets had been casually thrown on to the truck floor, and they were invited to sit down. They were told that at the next destination a small committee was actively working. Their job was to match the refugees with various cities where they could find employment and housing.

Mor was smiling and so was Ruth. Rebekka was still wondering how it was possible to switch from constant fear and anxiety to complete happiness in such a short time while thousands of people were still suffering and hoping to escape. However, when she looked at Frank and saw relief showing in his face for the first time in two days, she was overcome with joy. Her eyes filled with tears when she thought of Frank's mother, who was waiting for them nearby.

It was probably one of the most incredible moments of their lives. After a few minutes, the rattling truck stopped outside a primitive, one-story shack. One by one, they climbed off the vehicle and stood still, not knowing what to do, or where to go.

Frank said nothing, looking unwell, staring into space. He was pale and still, having said nothing since the episode at the border. Fortunately, his waiting period was to be short. The door to the shack opened and a female in uniform emerged, supporting the arm of a short woman who was almost unrecognizable.

Her eyes were swollen, most probably from crying nonstop for two days. Her hair was matted, her clothing wrinkled and stained, and she was shaking. Nevertheless, there was no doubt that the woman who approached Frank tentatively, staring straight at him, was his mother. As she came closer and realized this wasn't a dream, she half ran, half walked towards her son, who had been in her prayers for almost 48 hours. Just as she was about to collapse, she reached her goal, and sobbing, threw herself around his neck. He responded by leaning forward, arms extended. They remained in that position, motionless, until both of them accepted the reality of being reunited. It was impossible to hear what the mother repeatedly said to her son.

Finally she turned to the others, first embracing her sister. The two women spoke at the same time, each expressing their emotions, reliving their fears and worries. Both thanked the Lord in Yiddish, while expressing gratitude in Norwegian for the safe reunion between mother and son.

Eventually the sisters let go and Mor pulled out her necklace and kissed it. She had kept it hidden under her sweater for safety. The rest expressed their happiness and gathered around mother and son.

The first person to break away, looking in another direction, was Miriam. The man who next appeared in the doorway to the shack was no stranger to her. The four-year-old hadn't seen him for more than six weeks. Her screams of happiness were loud enough to make the others turn. She ran in his direction and threw herself into her father's arms, immediately followed by Rebekka. Mor was speechless and ran behind the girls, having had no idea that he would be there. The others followed her, expressing more prayers of thanks.

Martin Davidson explained calmly and quickly that he had learned from friends about the separation of mother and child, and tried in vain to locate the boy's father whom he had learned escaped across the border as well. Martin therefore requested permission to travel to the border area hoping to witness good news. However, at the same time he had prepared himself to be present in the event that the opposite would be the case, if the family needed a different kind of support.

Frank's father was located in a town about two hours away, and arrangements were made for him to come for them. Frank and his mother were to leave with the father when he arrived and were to settle in a small town called Lindkjoeping.

It wasn't easy to part with Frank and his mother. They expressed their gratitude over and over for the final chapter of their trip and naturally, they would meet again as soon as possible. The Davidson family was able to continue directly to Stockholm where Martin had already found a position.

Chapter Twenty-Eight

Immediate Surgery

AALESUND, NOVEMBER 26, 1942

Dr. Fjellstrand walked over to Harald and gently put his arm around his shoulders.

Harald responded by nodding and whispered reluctantly.

"What choice do I have? I'm seventeen years old! I can't drive a car and I'm not allowed to buy alcohol. I haven't even finished high school. How can they arrest me? This is insane. I don't understand it."

No one responded. Harald lifted his face, no longer able to hide his reaction. Standing, he stared into space, trying to ignore everyone and everything. This time the man with the pipe addressed Harald directly. His voice was firm, yet reassuring. He spoke rapidly.

"We'll admit you to the hospital tonight, Harald. Mrs. Rosenberg, you should expect hostile visitors tomorrow morning, looking for your son. Just keep telling them your son suffers from a recurrent, severe case of Crohn's disease. That's all you need to say and that he is in the hospital. This will give us approximately 12 hours to remove Harald's appendix. Obviously, they can't remove a patient from the operating table."

"So, young man, are you ready to give us your appendix to get you away from these rat-infested Norwegian traitors and their buddies?"

Harald's facial expression relaxed a little. He was fixated on this articulate and self-confident man, who exuded courage and integrity but whose name he didn't know and whom he had never met before.

Finally, Harald nodded gently and moved close to Mor, putting his arms around her and attempting to smile.

"Well, Mor, I guess it's time for me to say good night and to be on my way."

Harald went to get his bag in the adjacent room, and the other men started to leave. The only visitor remaining close to Leyla was Dr. Fjellstrand, who announced that he would take Harald to the hospital and start the admission process. He put his arm around her for a couple of minutes.

As he was about to leave the tall stranger hesitated and stopped just before walking through the door, still with the pipe in his mouth. He hesitated at the door and then turned around. Fjellstrand looked up in surprise. The man touched Fjellstrand lightly on the shoulder. "Nikolas, we need to speak in private. It has taken me most of the day to decide whether I should share it with you or not. I have decided that you must be told and you will have to decide whether Harald should be told or not."

Fjellstrand stopped and stared at him. "Okay. I am ready."

"I intercepted a telex message and wasn't able to decipher it until just before I got here today. I have learned, as you did, that two other ships also left for Germany in addition to the one on the 26th. The message contains a list of close to 50 names of men on board each ship. Three names jumped out at me. Two were Davidson and one Rosenberg. No first names." Fjellstrand's face went pale. "Do you mean?" "Yes," the other answered. "Who else could this refer to?"

They both paused. "There could still be other people with the same last names." Fjellstrand continued, "If you are looking for my opinion, the poor boy has enough right now. I think the best is to say nothing until we know the first names." The other nodded in agreement. "Well, then we think alike."

Dr. Fjellstrand was explaining to Leyla, "I heard of a plan that worked in Oslo a few weeks ago. Several Jews were hospitalized for various fictitious conditions. Arrangements were made to transfer them to other hospitals where they might ostensibly receive different treatments. The argument was that they had been diagnosed with different symptoms. However, the ambulance drivers who picked them up did exactly the opposite. They brought the patients to private trucks which stood prepared to bring them across the border to Sweden. We are trying to think of something similar, if at all possible."

Harald stood by the door to the living room, holding a small overnight bag in his hand.

"I am ready, I guess," he said in a barely audible voice. "Let's get to the hospital and remove my appendix while we plan the next step! That would give you guys a little more time, won't it?"

Just as Fjellstrand and Harald were about to leave, Ingrid returned. She was dumbfounded and frightened when Dr. Fjellstrand informed her of the newly-devised plan for her brother.

She immediately promised to keep her mother company when and if the enemy showed up. She gave her brother a quick hug.

The car ride to the local community hospital took just a few minutes, thanks to the quiet streets and lack of traffic. Fjellstrand seemed to be concentrating on something specific. Finally, he said, "Please, Harald, I think it would be advantageous if I entered by myself first. It will give me a chance to see who is on call for surgery tonight and tomorrow, as well as who is handling the reception and the registration. I wish I could explain this better, but the truth is that depending on the team on call, the plot may vary to some degree. Just give me about two minutes to check it out."

Harald was uncomfortable and apprehensive, but he tried to remain calm. His legs shook. He was cold and started to put on his overcoat. He even tried to smile but was unsuccessful. Dr. Fjellstrand left.

Harald stared out the car window, trying to distract himself. It was quiet for the first five minutes until an ambulance pulled up next to Fjellstrand's car and interrupted the silence. Harald stared straight ahead. No one appeared to pay any attention to him. He glanced carefully to his right. A couple of medical technicians emerged, lifting a stretcher from the ambulance. A small child lay on his back. Two adults, probably the parents, followed. Their faces were marked by concern. The woman cried. The man had his arm around the woman's shoulder, trying to comfort her. They moved from walking behind the stretcher to walking next to it, as if they felt this would speed up the arrival at the emergency room.

Thereafter, the parking area was visited by official police cars on two occasions, courtesy of the now Nazi police station. Harald looked away, trying not to exchange looks with the driver or his co-pilot. No alarm preceded them. The two officials walked through the entrance without greeting anyone. Harald wondered if there was a chance they already knew he had arrived. Hoping that he was wrong, he held his breath. He recognized that he was starting to panic and fought to keep his presence of mind.

The two soldiers returned to the car in less than five minutes, each with a cigarette in hand, and left.

Harald wondered if they were just making their rounds. Had they been bored? Perhaps they needed to use the bathroom? Harald's thoughts helped chase away the newborn traces of angst.

The second police car arrived shortly after the first. The two male visitors went inside and returned in less than two minutes, each carrying a cup of what seemed to be coffee.

A knock on Fjellstrand's car door interrupted Harald's thought pattern, and he jumped. He had forgotten that he had locked it. Fjellstrand got in and looked at him.

"We have bad news and good news. But the bad news is nothing compared to the good news. I have never met the receptionist before. She must be new. I think her name is Ilse. She didn't recognize me. I raced by her and called out that I was a physician and needed to speak to a colleague. I mumbled my name, but I doubt she heard it. I think I heard about this woman. I think she has moved here to be with one of the transfers who came with the new head of the local Nazi party. This is not good, however, we can't deal with it. We will try to stay away from her as much as possible.

"The good news is that the surgeon is a classmate of mine from medical school, a nice person. Mathiesen. He is relatively shy and keeps to himself. He mentioned to me the other day that he wants to help our country in view of the horrible present situation. This is good, very good. Maybe he will get his chance now. He's waiting for us on the second floor. Let's go, while the coast is clear. The new receptionist muttered something about having heard that they served almost real coffee in the cafeteria, so she was on her way out. Couldn't be better!"

He opened the car door and reached for Harald, failing to ask whether the patient was ready. The physician's secure attitude was just what Harald needed.

"Put your arm around my shoulder," Fjellstrand whispered, "in case someone is watching. Remember you are a patient in pain and I am going to bring you surgical relief."

Harald did as told, all the time worrying whether he walked the right way to convince a possible spectator. Evidently, all went well, as neither of the two employees stationed at the reception desk even looked up.

One of them was actually yawning, which wasn't surprising due to the late hour. The third employee, Ilse, whose name was recorded on the wall board as being on duty, was missing. The name was the same that Fjellstrand had mentioned as being new in the job, and being the girlfriend of one of the new police officers.

Maybe they did have good surrogate coffee at night to keep their workers awake, Harald thought to himself.

It might be to his advantage.

Within a minute or so, the two men were brought up in the large elevator to the department of surgery and emergencies.

Greeting them by the elevator door was a friendly man dressed in standard white and green hospital attire.

"Hello, Ketil, nice to see you, burning the midnight oil, are you? Meet my young friend, Harald.

"Harald, this is my colleague and friend, Dr. Ketil Mathiesen. We went to medical school together and by some miracle we both managed to graduate and end up here."

Dr. Mathiesen tried to make Harald relax. The tall, middle-aged stranger shook his hand. He came across as a kind man with a mild manner. A stethoscope was draped around his neck, which made Harald calm down a little. Why, he didn't know. Perhaps it put a touch of reality on this nightmare situation. The physician, who was almost bald, had narrow hands and long fingers.

Fjellstrand kept speaking as the three walked down the corridor into an examination room. He closed the door.

"Harald has been in my care for the past month or so, due to what I have conditionally diagnosed as Crohn's disease, and has been treated symptomatically. Despite this, his health has deteriorated and it's my opinion that we should remove his appendix."

Dr. Fjellstrand continued, expressing his opinion in a firm voice. The initial smile had left his face, and it was clear that he was all business. Harald couldn't keep up with the conversation fast enough, and finally, he just tuned out, only hearing a few words here and there.

The atypical, yet right-to the-point brief medical history, however, caused the night surgeon to pause, looking at his old friend. Obviously, the latter had understood that this wasn't the time to ask too many questions. Fjellstrand continued to briefly clarify the elusiveness of more details.

"It's also my wish that this surgery be performed as soon as possible, both for medical and psychological reasons, which I would prefer to remain confidential."

He stopped for a few seconds, looked around quickly, and whispered to his colleague, "Suffice it to say that there are also some political reasons involved."

Looking at Ketil, he wondered how he would react. Fjellstrand decided to present one last reason for his requested surgery.

"However, in addition to a rather acute surgical procedure, it's my opinion that an extended stay at this fine hospital would be of great benefit for Harald."

"This prognosis has been confirmed and agreed on by Dr. Myrdal, with whom I believe you are familiar."

Dr. Myrdal was one of the executive board members and a prominent doctor of the hospital. Even Harald was familiar with this famous name.

Dr. Mathiesen had stood absolutely still while Fjellstrand completed the medical history.

"I believe I am now in possession of most of the vital information related to Harald's ailment, including the acute need for the upcoming surgery, unless there is something more?" Dr. Mathiesen asked slowly.

Despite Dr. Fjellstrand's attempt to reassure him, Dr. Mathiesen seemed a little hesitant. He appeared uncertain whether the importance of his last question had reached the admitting physician, who remained quiet, or if he was unwilling to dispense any more information.

Dr. Mathiesen pulled up a chair and sat down next to the narrow cot, looking at the young boy who seemed increasingly uncomfortable. He paused for a minute and then turned to his co-surgeon and continued slowly,

"I think I understand the situation. I need this young man's full name and home address. I know his name is Harald, but I don't believe I heard his last name."

Dr. Fjellstrand and Harald both answered his question in unison, "Rosenberg."

The family name remained hanging in the air. Dr. Mathiesen took a deep breath, looked at Harald, and then back at Fjellstrand and said in a firm, confident way, "All right, then. When do you want to start?"

Within thirty minutes or less, the surgery had been outlined, planned, and the surgical team was getting organized. Harald was much less calm than he pretended. In addition to the natural anxiety due to the unwarranted surgery, he feared knives and needles, having never before been hospitalized.

Harald had a long history of becoming nervous when he received vaccines and shots for other types of medical care and tried to avoid them whenever he could. This time he reluctantly participated in everything the physicians told him was necessary. He tried very hard to mask his anxiety. The two physicians worked quickly and systematically in order to prepare him for the operation.

A young surgical nurse arrived and took the standard medical history, including a blood test and other various routine procedures related to the surgery. Her name was Agnes.

Her blond hair was tied at the back of her head. It must have been quite long as Harald could see several thick braids squeezed together under her white cap. A special pin, symbolizing her position and rank, was pinned to the cap. She had a beautiful smile and seemed totally unaffected by the late hour. Harald couldn't stop looking at her.

The nurse had a bright, friendly manner.

"I am so glad to meet you, but I'm sorry that it's here. I've heard about you and your talented sister through my nieces and nephews who attend the same high school as you. I'll try to explain everything to you which these doctors may forget."

She smiled at the physicians, indicating that she was joking.

"I hope we can become good friends now, because tomorrow or the next day you may not like me as I make you walk around the corridors, when you would rather stay in bed."

When she took his hand, he didn't object to it. She kept talking about other patients who had shared his phobia. Harald felt calmer immediately, although it was questionable whether it was her experience and kindness that helped him or the pure pleasure of holding her hand. Or maybe a combination of both. Regardless, with all the other fearful thoughts roaming around in his head, it was nice to have his anxiety slightly relieved.

Dr. Fjellstrand talked to the new patient for a couple more minutes, providing a quick, basic explanation of the steps needed to carry out a successful appendectomy.

"Stop, that's enough. I really don't need to know anything more. Just get it over with," Harald exclaimed.

"Let's make an agreement," Dr. Fjellstrand suggested, "If you will try not to listen to any conversation regarding your health, real or not, regardless if you understand it or not, I promise on my honor to share everything real that's related to your surgical procedure with you whenever you ask, or when I deem it necessary."

Harald was able to offer a quick smile. He nodded in keeping with the semi joke.

The surgery was completed without any complications. Harald reacted well to the anesthesia and woke up at the time they had estimated. After a brief stay in the recovery room, he was moved to a four-bed room, where there was no sign of any other patients.

Agnes was helpful, making certain that he was comfortable.

She showed him how to move the bed up and down, as well as finding the call bell, should he need help. The room was quite uninteresting. White walls, white beds, white sheets. The requisite table next to each bed held a number of glasses, bottles, and some type of container with which he was unfamiliar. He was quite sure, however, he would find out, if it became necessary to use it.

Harald became increasingly more alert and started rethinking the sequence of events which had unfolded within the past 24 hours. He still felt a little confused as to who had been present and in which order. He was, however, fully aware of why he was in the hospital and why he had been subjected to surgery. He tried to distract himself by looking out the half-open door to the corridor, wondering if his mother and sister would visit any time soon.

At that moment nurse Agnes knocked gently and walked in, leaving the door slightly ajar. Harald caught a quick view of at least one, maybe two men in uniform waiting in the corridor.

He tried to sit up. Agnes ran to his side and told him in no uncertain terms that he was not yet ready to move around without her assistance. He asked her, "Who are those men? Have they been sent to keep an eye on me? Are they afraid I'll try to walk out, right after surgery?"

His entire body started shaking. Was this what he had to look forward to every day in the hospital?

Agnes turned and addressed the guards at the door. "I'm sorry, but I need privacy so I can examine this patient who has just come down from the recovery room. Please excuse me," she said, and slammed the door right in the guards' faces, before they had a chance to object.

"Harald, are you feeling okay? No discomfort? No headache?"

After taking his blood pressure and temperature, she smiled and whispered, "All your vital signs are fine. I imagine you would feel even better if the monkeys outside the door would leave. I'm doing the best I can to get rid of them."

Harald watched her closely. Her voice had softened after the door was closed. "Your surgery went well, and you are now minus your appendix. But the rest of you is intact."

He tried to smile. She brought him a glass of water. "Drink it slowly— very slowly."

Harald paid attention to everything she said. There was something special about her. He felt that the two of them shared a secret. The content of the glass that she had given him was probably the best drink of water he had ever had. Within a few minutes, the dizziness subsided, and he even attempted to lift his head.

Agnes continued going through the regular drills, instructing her patient to take it easy, to stay in bed until told to get up, as well as other general directions. Harald was alert enough to hear her. A few minutes later he was sitting up, speaking normally. "Are my mother and sister here?" he asked.

"They are in the waiting room, and I'll tell them that you are as good as new. I also think you need to rest a little longer." Harald asked why. Agnes didn't answer, just went into action. "Let's wait ten more minutes. Just close your eyes for another ten minutes." She poured the patient some fluids, looked around the room and saw no one. She opened the door half way.

Within a period of two to three seconds, footsteps were heard and a man in a white physician's coat passed by the door, looking straight ahead. As he came into sight, Agnes moved quickly towards the opening and grabbed an envelope out of his hand, which she pushed into her pocket. The man didn't stop nor did he turn his head in the direction of either the room or Agnes.

She moved to the other side of Harald's bed and casually dropped the envelope on his bed. She stretched her arms and started to shake the bed cover, pretending it was messy. Within a second, the envelope disappeared under the cover.

Agnes gestured with her hands to get Harald's attention, putting one finger on her mouth and her ear, indicating that he should be quiet and just listen.

Harald, who had followed the entire show from the onset with great interest and even amusement, found her fascinating. He kept quiet, allowing her full freedom to shine as the self-appointed star. With a loud voice she asked if he was thirsty or experiencing any discomfort, making certain that the door was open and that anyone in the corridor could hear.

Then she turned to her "inside" audience, Harald, and said, "I need to keep going, young man. Many things to do. I'll stop by sometime later this afternoon. Get some rest and take it easy."

Glancing at the now open door, he noticed that the uniformed soldiers hadn't returned. Harald pulled the envelope out from under the cover.

"Dear Harald. I hope your surgery was a success and that you are on your way to feeling better. I am so sorry that you had to have your appendix out, but since it was giving you so much trouble, it will hopefully make your feel better. I'll stop by to see you later today.

If you get any unexpected visitors whom you don't feel too good about, please try to ignore them. They are only flunkies belonging to the other soccer team who have been told to visit you because the people who run their team are nosy about your general health. If they happen to get in your way at all, let me know, and I'll make sure they are prevented from bothering you. For now, do nothing.

All your friends on our team are looking forward to seeing you in action, and you know that we will be there to cheer you on. Just get better.

Best wishes from the entire soccer team.

Harald was taken aback a little when he first read the note, but it didn't take him long to read between the lines. He hid the letter under his mattress.

He was surprised when he saw more than one guard walking past the door again. He decided to ignore it for the time being. Clearly several guards were stationed around the hospital monitoring him. It was also obvious to him that Agnes was involved with the resistance people and had served as a link in getting the letter of encouragement to him. He was beginning to feel quite a bit better.

Shortly thereafter, Ingrid and Mor appeared in his room, with orders not to stay too long and not get him too excited. After a few minutes of standard post-surgery small talk, Ingrid decided her brother seemed strong enough to hear about their morning visit from Gyldendahl.

"He showed up at 7:30 am with an unpleasant knock on the door, and buzzing on the doorbell at the same time. Mor had stayed awake for most of the night, unable to sleep, so the noise was no surprise. I decided to let her deal with it. I assumed that perhaps the famous Gyldendahl would treat her better if he were alone with her. You should have heard her, she was incredible!"

Ingrid turned to Mor, making certain that she was listening, and turned back to Harald while continuing the past night's saga, "Mor positioned herself in the kitchen, right next to the entrance door. She pretended she had no idea who he was initially or why he was there! I never knew she had that type of theatrical talent. I was truly impressed!"

Ingrid spoke quickly in a voice slightly higher than usual, sounding almost hyperactive. Harald felt that she was trying to make him feel less anxious and worried. And maybe she was trying to sooth her own anxiety as well! He said nothing, letting her continue.

"Clearly he was trying to humiliate and scare her. Mor who had listened to all the discussions that took place the night before, had thought of nothing else all night but preparing herself to handle Gyldendahl, should he show up.

"That fat idiot just stood there asking Mor where you were. She wouldn't even let him in the door! He just stayed getting increasingly redder in the face. She told him you were in the hospital, having surgery. She must have been scared out of her mind, and the whole time she was standing there in just her robe. You should have seen her, keeping a hand on the door the whole time. She was terrific! Finally, he left. He wheezed his way down both flights of stairs."

Harald smiled despite the difficult situation, which didn't really warrant smiling.

"Not bad, Mor. I am impressed. I can just imagine you in your old, worn robe, scaring Gyldendahl. I wish I had been there."

Ingrid noticed that Harald seemed tired and realized that her mother also seemed tired. Not surprising, considering that she had stayed awake most of the night worrying about her son's unnecessary surgery and anticipating an ambush by Gyldendahl. She was now fast asleep in a chair next to Harald's bed. Ingrid had seen a visitor's waiting room at the end of the corridor, and now she got up and left the two alone.

Agnes, who was still monitoring Harald's post-operative recovery, returned to find mother and son both asleep and decided to leave them alone a little longer. She made intermittent stops in the room for the next hour and finally found Leyla sitting quietly, awake, in the visitor's chair. After having reassured her that Harald was doing just fine, Leyla retired to the visitor's waiting room where she would find Ingrid.

When Harald woke up a little later, he felt much more alert and impatient, and wondered where his sister and mother had gone. To distract himself he decided it might be a good idea to walk for a few minutes to restore his strength. He rang the bell and Agnes appeared. He told her his idea, and she had no objection.

"It's actually a very good idea. Right now I am busy monitoring other patients but if you promise to be very careful, you can try to walk alone. Stay close to my station, though."

Harald got up slowly and put his feet on the floor. So far, so good. He walked slowly across the room, feeling in control of his legs. Once in the corridor he hung on to the railing on his right side. He walked slowly, and remained upright for a few minutes. Then he felt a little weak, and decided to return to his bed. He had seen no sign of his mother or sister.

However, Harald did indeed have a visitor, but it wasn't the one he had expected. First, he thought that he was dreaming. Unfortunately, that wasn't the case.

Standing in the middle of his room waiting for him was no other than Mr. Gyldendahl himself.

A man in his early fifties, he was almost bald, except for a few strands of hair combed across his scalp to camouflage the shortage. To further downplay the lack of hair on top of his head, a narrow moustache was prominently displayed on his upper lip. It was difficult not to be reminded of the other political tyrant who apparently was among the first to introduce this style of facial decoration.

His eyes were small, his eyelids heavy and thick. A protruding stomach confirmed the general rumors circulating that Mr. Gyldendahl was an avid beer drinker, and the more he drank, the more he fantasized about being instrumental in achieving a joint victory over England.

With a vicious grin, he addressed Harald in a pompous voice.

"I decided to visit so you would get used to my keeping an eye on you, all the time, if necessary. When I saw you last, you were just getting off the ferry at night. You made it very clear that you weren't in a mood to speak with me. How rude!"

Strangely enough, despite the strict guard system, he had managed to make it up to the Department of Surgery on the third floor undetected. He got as far as the corridor just outside Harald's room. The combination of his arrogant demeanor, his uniform and the assistance by the Nazi receptionist whom Fjellstrand had recognized and managed to avoid when admitting Harald, had certainly helped him enter.

Harald had never spoken to this notorious and feared Nazi leader in person, but he recognized him instantly from having seen him when the ferry had to return to the dock in Aalesund as well as seeing him in the physician's office. The comfort level, which the recovering patient had briefly acquired, melted as a tiny patch of snow on a warm spring day. His mouth became even more dry than when resting in the recovery room.

"Well, here I am, making certain you remain in one place. As soon as you have recovered, we are going to have a talk, you and I, and I'll inform you what plans the new leadership of Norway has for people like you. So make sure you stay here."

His crude and arrogant voice was getting increasingly louder. For about ten seconds the Nazi leader and the young boy stared at each other, both unwilling to turn away.

Fortunately, Agnes had heard him. She rushed in to remove the Nazi leader from the room. She used all her female powers to distract him.

"Oh, I am so sorry, mister, sir, officer Gyldendahl. I would like very much to accommodate such a distinguished person as you, but I really can't.

Only family members are allowed to see the patient on this floor, a rule that is strictly in accordance with the hospital bylaws. If I let you in, I may lose my position, and you don't want that, do you? You seem like such a nice person, so I know that I can speak honestly to you. I'll remind Harald about your visit and make certain that he keeps his eyes open for you in a few days. I'll have to ask you to leave, and I'll convey your very best wishes for a speedy recovery."

She turned around just as quickly and raced down the corridor. Harald was sure there was no such restriction. By chance he had overheard this statement expressed by a friend whose father was a lawyer. The friend had explained that this rule only existed for patients who were in intensive care.

Gyldendahl stared at her with rage. For a minute it looked as if he was going to challenge her, but then he just turned around and left, mumbling something incomprehensible.

Chapter Twenty-Nine

I Need My Umbrella

OSLO/SWEDEN, NOVEMBER 26, 1942

While the Davison family said their final good-byes to Frank and his mother at the Kjeseter Camp, they became aware of a few similar houses nearby. The Camp was simply a clearinghouse that served as a temporary home for most of the families once they had crossed the border. A collection of volunteers worked day and night finding jobs and placements in a variety of areas where they could stay while the war was going on. Once an appropriate match had been found, they received an official permit to leave the camp and move on.

Martin Davidson had already found a job in Stockholm as well as an apartment, so they could leave immediately. One of the volunteers offered to drive the Davidson family to the train station.

The driver of the truck approached Sarah and her family, smiling and saying, "This time you only need one person to bring you to the station and you needn't be afraid. You can talk, laugh and hug each other. You can even speak out loud, if you wish."

When they settled on the train, Martin described his fifteen hours locked inside the armoire in the milk truck that had taken him across the border to freedom. Sarah finally had a chance to bring him up to date with the horrors that had taken place since his escape. She told him about the arrest of the men in October, and how they initially had been incarcerated in the eastern part of Norway. That same day as the family, including Ruth, had reached the border, more than seven hundred Norwegian Jewish prisoners were forced on a large German ship to an unknown destination. She was certain he must have heard of this. Two more smaller ships, also full of Jews, were sent to another unknown destination, although the rumors persisted that they were on their way to a place in occupied Poland called Auschwitz.

"Did you hear anything about my two brothers?" he asked quietly, but she only shook her head. She found it difficult to tell him she had heard gossip that his two missing brothers might be on one of the two smaller ships.

"What about my family in Aalesund?" he continued in a low voice. "I have heard nothing," she whispered.

He sat quietly without speaking for a short while. "I think I will send a letter to Leyla's friend Sofie to see if she knows anything. I will distort the content to some degree but make it clear enough for her to understand. I will sign it with Miriam's name."

Sarah told the story about Marie Kaufman and her tragic suicide. Sarah also described Rebekka's unexpected incident on October 25 when she opened the door to the two police officers who were looking to arrest him.

Martin turned and looked out the window. It had started to rain heavily. Miriam seemed fascinated by the downpour. "Mor, I didn't bring my beautiful umbrella that Aunt Marie gave me. It has stripes and is my favorite. Please call her and ask her to send it to me. It's in the closet."

Her request remained unanswered. None of the other four could think of an answer. They sat quietly.

Ruth was napping. Rebekka's parents continued speaking in low voices. She knew better than to disturb them. She clutched her backpack which she had on her lap. She was tired as well, but found it impossible to relax. Her thoughts were replaying the past 24 hours. If felt like they had left Oslo at least one week ago. She grabbed one of her sketchbooks knowing exactly what she wanted to do. Time had come to immortalize the experiences still fresh in her mind. She couldn't begin fast enough. Her mind went ahead of her hand. First, she drew herself trying to convey a message to Kari by waving gently to her friend's father. She could still hear the sound of the cars on the street just before they got into the rescue car. Then she saw the guides on the train platform who were practically forming a ring around Frank. She thought of Hilde and the beautiful mansion which was used as a shelter for refugees on the run, Miriam being carried in a rucksack, and finally, seeing the yellow sign at the end of the long road in the woods indicating their proximity to the Swedish border.

When she had recorded most of her memories, she put the book back in the bag and started thinking about her new life in Sweden.

Chapter Thirty

Recuperation from What?

AALESUND, DECEMBER 2–31, 1942

Harald wasn't feeling well at all. Despite the six days that had passed since the surgery, he had no energy. The brief healthy signs, which he had felt prior to Gyldendahl's surprise visit, were long gone. Trying to deal with the bewildering emotions and fear wasn't easy. He couldn't shake the image of Mr. Gyldendahl with his evil expression standing right in front of him threatening future difficulties. Every time he closed his eyes, the menacing face reappeared resulting in violent screaming. The man had really scared him. He felt frightened and lonely.

Although Harald had been exposed to Gyldendahl more than once before, he still felt physically ill each time he saw or heard the monster. The mere mention of the name Gyldendahl was now enough to make him shudder. He thought back to the day when Gyldendahl tried to get into the examination room where Harald ostensibly was having his Crohn's disease monitored. That was bad enough, he thought at the time. When he heard Gyldendahl screaming in Fjellstrand's office, Harald still felt safe, especially when Dr. Fjellstrand was ridiculing the Nazi. Even the episode when Gyldendahl stood at the dock waiting for the three Rosenbergs' return from the unsuccessful journey, had passed quickly in the dark. However, he never saw the malicious expression that went with the voice until now. It was scary. It struck him vehemently. Gyldendahl's face matched his voice. Both exuded evil.

Why? What exactly does this man have against me? Harald ruminated. Until recently he had been quite unaware that Mr. Gyldendahl and his underlings were actually working hard to arrest him. The reason was never quite spelled out, beyond Gyldendahl considering him a "genetic" enemy, a Jew, a mismatch according to the Nazis. But he was only seventeen years old! Did

219

Gyldendahl bear him some kind of a special grudge or was he afraid that Arne would end up marrying Ingrid and he would end up with a Jewish niece–he, who was a high-ranking Nazi focusing on getting rid of the Jews? No, that was too ridiculous—who would be that stupid and evil? There had to be some other explanation.

Harald tried to collect himself. A persistent voice from within was knocking, trying to get into his brain. "Harald, it's time to wake up! Don't be fooled. He has something really bad in mind." Harald tried to collect himself and relax. A walk down the corridor! Perhaps to get hold of some type of medication to counteract the sudden onset of both nausea and anxiety, if possible. The newly arrived cautioning voice refused to fade away and it persevered, appearing to have more on its mind.

Out of nowhere, he recalled a picture from an illegal newspaper, which he had come across several months earlier. It had depicted three Jewish men lying unresponsive in the streets of Berlin, having been shot to death by two German soldiers.

Harald stopped pondering, attempting once again to pacify his negative thoughts. "Quiet. This is the Aalesund hospital in Norway, and not Berlin, Germany," he muttered to himself as he kept walking.

Right now, the persistent voice and his emotional thoughts agreed on one thing—not to discuss Gyldendahl's confrontation with Ingrid or Leyla. They had enough right now.

In addition, he had an overpowering desire to deal with this himself, to limit the questions to Dr. Fjellstrand only. There was more of a chance running into the physician in the corridor, he thought, than staying in bed.

Lucky for him the corridor was almost empty with no one attempting to keep him away from the nurses' station. Only one nurse was on call at the counter where she skimmed through various folders and medical histories. He whispered gently, "Is there any chance that you might reach Dr. Fjellstrand? I am not feeling well."

The nurse looked up from her papers, shook her head, and continued whatever she was doing. She blew her nose in a white handkerchief. It was clear that she didn't want to be disturbed.

"As soon as he comes, I'll tell him to see you, Harald," she said. She offered to look for Agnes, but Harald had no desire to share his thoughts with the beautiful nurse.

A sense of loneliness swept over him. He had no one to talk to who could help him. He really didn't know where to turn. There was no sense discussing it with his mother and sister because there was absolutely nothing they could do about the situation.

Fjellstrand wasn't available and in some bizarre way Harald was relieved. How was this possible? He wanted to talk to Fjellstrand, but at the same time, he didn't want to. What if he asked Fjellstrand what he thought might be ahead, in the event that the escape plan didn't materialize? Was he afraid of the answer?

None of his friends had come to see him in the hospital, as they probably didn't even know that he had surgery. Besides, he really didn't want to see them, what would they talk about?

While walking back to his room, his thoughts drifted to Rebekka. He wondered what had happened to her family and how they were dealing with the present situation. They had exchanged a few letters earlier in the spring, but he had heard nothing since October when she had implied that her father was out of town. Harald wasn't exactly sure what she meant, but he had a strong feeling that her father had gone into hiding. Her last letter had sounded more cautious than earlier, and he had wondered whether she was afraid that the mail was being censored.

The more he thought about her earlier detailed and entertaining letters, the more he realized how he missed hearing from her. She would definitely be a person that he could communicate with comfortably. But did he want to risk sending her a letter? What if the mail was censored? Would it get her in trouble? Besides, according to his mother, everyone in the family had escaped to Sweden. So a letter addressed to Rebekka in Oslo wouldn't reach her anyway, if she was lucky.

Regardless, he still needed to tell someone how frightened he was. Rebekka!

He was going to write to her after all, he decided. Perhaps Fjellstrand would be able to locate her family. The worst he could say would be no. The image of the ship full of hundreds of Jews, men, women and children, departing from the docks, flashed quickly through his mind, but he ignored it. Something deep inside reassured him that Rebekka and her family were safe.

He had already started writing to her in his mind. He moved a bit faster down the corridor back to his room. He now had a purpose.

He had brought along a pad of paper when he was admitted, stuffed into his backpack. Why, he didn't know. Had that been a carry-over from Rebekka? He remembered that she normally carried a sketch pad with her.

He wrote for a long time. Unloading how he felt was liberating. Rebekka was the one person who was removed from most of the madness around him. He was a "temporary prisoner" in a hospital having agreed to unnecessary surgery, yet having to remain there to avoid being a real prisoner. And right now all the prospects of finding a solution to avoid going to prison seemed highly unlikely. He could trust her, her knew, and just the thought made him feel a bit rejuvenated. He kept writing as long as there were pages left in the pad. He fell asleep with the pad in his hands.

He had his first peaceful night of sleep in many weeks.

The next few days were quiet. The guards still rotated past his door, peeking in, but didn't speak to him. Harald made a point of staring back at each individual as they walked by. He felt that he was retaliating against them, if only in his own mind.

Mor and Ingrid came by every day or every second day. They took turns for the most part. But it was getting difficult to spend time with them because there was nothing "safe" to talk about. Ingrid had finished her secretarial course and tried to make small talk about shorthand and typing. One day he was about to ask her if she were still seeing Arne, then he decided to avoid dwelling on details. His mother was getting thinner and thinner and it made him depressed to see.

He had started eating solid food and was examined by Dr. Fjellstrand. "Exercise would be good for your Crohn's disease. It will help keep it under control."

For the past few days Harald had almost forgotten that he was supposed to recover from something other than having his appendix out. He was better physically, but more restless. The days were long and difficult. He was eager to feel well, feel normal. Living a normal life, as a free person. Even if his physical health would return soon, he had nowhere to go. He was stuck in this place, in a waiting pattern, at the mercy of other people. Two sides, one good, trying to help him, and the other, well, he didn't even want to think of what was in store for him. He had recognized that the quicker he recovered physically, the more risk was involved.

Chapter Thirty-One

Who Is Miriam Davidson?

OSLO/SWEDEN, DECEMBER 3, 1942

Dear Sofie:

I am taking the liberty of writing to you, as I have tried in vain to reach my sister, Leyla, and her family.

I am wondering if by any chance her telephone has been disconnected?

As I haven't had a chance to chat with Leyla for a long time, I would like to know how the family is doing. I would greatly appreciate hearing from them. I am even wondering if it is possible they may have chosen to travel in order to visit friends in another area.

If you have the time and the opportunity to contact me, I would appreciate it. My family and I have done some traveling as well, and for the time being we are visiting relatives in Sweden where we are celebrating a family wedding. I will include their address at the bottom of this letter.

I hope you are otherwise well. We remember our lovely visit to Aalesund a few years ago when we were entertained by you at your hospitable home.

Best wishes,

Miriam Davidson

C/o Mr. Hans Eriksberg

Polhelmsgatan 8

Stockholm, Sweden

46-07 33-15-19

Chapter Thirty-Two

The Wrong Side of the Floor?

AALESUND, DECEMBER 7, 1942

Harald looked out the window, studying the hospital grounds. It had started to snow. Soft, white flakes covered the ground, making the outside look idyllic and calm. What if he just left the hospital? If he could manage to slip out through an open door in the kitchen or in the basement? Somewhere. Would that be possible? It was December and cold outside. He had no idea where they had taken the clothing he wore when he was admitted. Could he find something else to wear? Maybe. Where would he go? He had no money. Could he go to his best friend and ask his family to hide him? They would probably be afraid to. And even if they said yes, wouldn't that be the first place the Nazis would look for him?

He had a vision of himself running from house to house in stolen clothing, with no food and money, being turned down by frightened people. No! This just isn't going to work.

For the first time, Harald had a roommate, but the new patient was less than friendly. He was opinionated, bigoted and loved to hear his own voice. Harald made a point of being polite and avoided getting involved in any discussion. Apparently, this annoyed the man, who was bored. First, he complained to Harald about the guards who were circulating in the corridors and who always stopped and peeked into their room, making it sound like this was Harald's choice.

Then he overheard the roommate complaining to his visiting wife.

"The Jew in the next bed just had his appendix removed, and he seems to be doing all right. But the German soldiers are here all the time, checking us out, and frankly, I find it annoying. The kid is only sixteen, and he doesn't want to talk to me about it. Strangers like that shouldn't be put in the same rooms as regular people. Maybe they should have rooms just for Jews, so we normal Norwegians, can rest and recover from illnesses."

Harald overheard the conversation and chose to ignore it. He decided to get out of the room for part of the day. Agnes had also heard the chatter between the patient and his wife and suggested that it would be good for him to walk around the corridors.

She continued, "His complaints have reached the hospital staff, and he demands that guards reduce the frequency of their checks. This was not well received by the police guards stationed in the hospital. Finally, they reached an agreement that the guards could only walk through the hallway once per hour and should avoid lengthy stops in the corridor."

After that the guards sat mostly in the visitors' lounge pretending to read the newspapers.

One day when Harald was alone in the room, Agnes brought him a meal. She whispered, "The police are not happy about the new rules to monitor the guards, and there are rumors that Mr. Gyldendahl will make surprise visits. In addition, a guard is always on call in the hospital lobby. Dr. Mathiesen told me in confidence that this guard spends most of his time chatting with his girlfriend, who is supposed to help visitors locate patients. That's okay with me. I can't stand him, so I won't mind if he is yelled at."

Harald was puzzled about Agnes. He was certain that she was involved in the resistance work and knew the reason why he had his appendix out. He concluded that even if she did know something, she wasn't about to share it with him. Every time he saw her, he had a feeling that he had met her before, or that she looked like someone. There was something in her mannerism as well as in her way of speaking. It kept bothering him, but he failed to figure it out.

The second week of December arrived, and the enemy seemed increasingly impatient. Gyldendahl and his subordinates developed a habit of showing up often and unexpectedly; on occasion they came several times per day. The soldiers were mostly Norwegian Nazis—or in some instances German soldiers. They were all very young.

Harald was beginning to have difficulty sleeping at night. Dr. Fjellstrand had no news and seemed low as well.

On occasion Harald almost resented seeing Mor and Ingrid come by. The conversation was strained. The issue of a possible escape plan was no longer brought up. It hung in the air like a perpetual question mark. It was ever present. Since there was nothing new to discuss, they took the easy way out, choosing to ignore it. Harald noticed that both of his two visitors were looking nervous. Ingrid was getting thin—very thin, which Mor made a point of mentioning often, to Ingrid's annoyance. Mor had developed a visible twitch in her eye, but luckily neither of her children brought that up.

In the middle of December Fjellstrand made a visit to Harald, sitting on the chair next to his bed. As soon as he came into the room, he closed the door softly behind him, and whispered, "Believe it or not, our friend, the beer barrel, is snooping around the floor today. I have no idea how he got up here."

Then he continued in an unusually loud voice, "Hello there, Harald. How is the redness on your incision that you complained about? Let me have a look. Let me put a 'Do not disturb' sign on the door. I just saw a glimpse of your roommate entertaining in the visitors' lounge. I want to make sure the door is still closed."

Harald could tell from the expression on Fjellstrand's face that this wasn't going to be a pleasant talk.

"I did promise you that I would tell you the truth," he started. "As for your general health, you're doing fine. As for our success in finding a solution to the situation, we have a big fat zero. We have considered several options, but so far none are good enough to be put into action. The risk is too great. We haven't given up, Harald, but we do need more time.

"And the issue of time right now is quite a challenge, as the Nazis are getting impatient. We have one more option that will hopefully allow us to keep you here, where you are safe, at least for a while. Listen carefully because this is complicated. When we decided to delay your arrest by removing your appendix, we recognized that we might run out of time. Therefore we did have a backup plan. When we closed up the incision in your abdomen, we didn't close it totally. We left a drain on the right-hand side of the opening, next to the stitches. The purpose of this scheme was to buy us a few more days if needed. Unfortunately, Harald, time has come to implement the plan in order to prevent your being discharged into the hands of the monsters."

He grimaced, stopped and looked at Harald to note his reaction to his language. Harald showed nothing but was listening intently. His knees started to shake.

"We will now declare that you have developed an infection in your stomach which will necessitate administering medication. In reality, it will be only water, but to them it will be something more serious. Please bear with us and play along, as this should allow us another ten to twelve days."

Harald put his right hand on the incision area as if he needed confirmation that it was still there. He was having trouble fighting back tears. He kept swallowing. Fjellstrand sat still, letting a minute pass. Then he continued, "Your mother and sister are waiting in the visitors' lobby. I have told them about the need to continue this farce."

Finally, Harald showed some emotion for the first time. "How did they react? What did they say?"

"They are okay, they understand the need, and will support anything that you decide on. They are only concerned about you. What do you want me to tell them? We are all in this together, Harald, but it's your decision. They will ask me the same about you. What about your feelings?"

Harald stared into space, and hesitated for a few seconds. He bent his head forward and tried to steady his hands. His cheeks were burning. Eventually he lifted his head, making a point of looking Dr. Fjellstrand straight in the eye, hopefully to eliminate any concern about this decision.

"Of course we need to go forward. We don't have a choice, do we? Please tell them that I'll play along. However, I don't want to discuss it with them directly. I don't want to talk about it. Will you tell them?"

Dr. Fjellstrand took Harald's hand in his. "Of course I will."

Once Harald was alone, he tried to get used to the new situation and the bogus game. He worried that he was beginning to mix up reality and play-acting. The almost chronic feeling of fear reappeared. As earlier, he felt a need to walk around trying to get rid of some of the recurring mental discomfort. This time he didn't ask for permission; he just took off down the corridor. He was worrying about running into Mr. Gyldendahl, but he decided to ignore it. He would circle the third floor twice, if possible.

The first cycle went reasonably well. The cane gave him good support. It felt good noticing the strength in the lower part of his body. He was careful to avoid bumping into others on the way.

At the end of the second cycle, down the end of the long corridor, he felt that he might have overdone it a little. He decided to turn at the next corner near his room, intending to get into bed and rest.

That would have been too easy! Suddenly a jolt hit his legs and abdomen, as well as the left side of his face. The cane tumbled and he fell to the floor but fortunately lessened the impact. He was partially successful in breaking the fall by extending his arms, and landed on his stomach. He immediately experienced intense pain in the right lower quadrant of his abdomen.

After he hit the floor, he pulled himself up slightly, trying to lift his head. The incision site throbbed, making it difficult to sit up. Next, he attempted to open his eyes to figure out what had happened.

The shock that awaited him was even more severe than the fall itself. To his great surprise and disbelief, he discovered that the person with whom he had collided was none other than his nemesis, Gyldendahl himself.

Harald almost fainted, not out of pain, but out of terror. The ache from the sutures seemed almost negligible compared to the fury and hate emanating from the other party's eyes.

"You stupid idiot, you damn . . ."—here the head Nazi had enough sense to control himself—"What are you doing?"

Harald saw a sample of the redness, which his sister had described earlier, coloring the other's face. The man seemed to have trouble standing up, due to the enormous rage magnified by his screaming. There didn't seem to be any major physical damage, at least superficially. Yet he continued screaming at Harald.

"You were on the wrong side of the corridor! Didn't you see me coming? How dare you be that careless? Wait until I get my hands on you, you . . . "

As he moved toward Harald, the recipient of his tirade curled up on the floor against the wall.

A crowd had begun to gather around the two and a few of the nurses arrived. Attempts to make the group disperse were in vain, as more and more people gathered. None of them made any effort to move.

Fortunately, Agnes had been within hearing of the incident and rushed to the junction of the two corridors, discovering the two involved. At the very same moment Dr. Mathiesen arrived and saw the situation. Pushing Gyldendahl ever so gently aside, he instructed three staff members to lift Harald off the floor, bring him to his room and place him on his bed. He left orders for Dr. Fjellstrand to be notified while he started examining Harald for potential injury.

Agnes ran back and forth between the corridor and Harald's room making sure Harald's pain was receding. Seeing Harald on the bed, superficially with less pain than during the first few minutes, she took it upon herself to give him a blow by blow report. She was so agitated and upset that she totally bypassed the standard professional manner for which she was widely known.

"Harald, you wouldn't believe what is going on out there. It's incredible. Mr. Gyldendahl is in the process of relating his version of the story to his four thugs who have formed a circle around him. He is shrieking and keeps repeating that the damn Jewish boy was on the wrong side of the corridor and is consequently responsible for the accident."

The last sentence was delivered with an apologetic, yet furious expression on her face.

"The four uniformed soldiers are standing, listening to him without uttering a word; most probably out of fear. Behind them is the receptionist whom Fjellstrand referred to earlier. I think her name is Ilse, and she is the girlfriend of one of the German thugs. Personally, I can't stand her.

"A second staff physician reached the site and asked Gyldendahl if he would like to be examined for potential injuries and perhaps have a general x-ray. Mr. Gyldendahl recognized this physician and refused his offer immediately in a condescending and cranky manner, then kept on moaning."

Agnes stopped to catch her breath and continued reporting the conversation between Gyldendahl and the physician, who said, "If you would like to rest for a couple of minutes, I'll take you down to the trauma section and the nursing staff will take you to a private, empty room where you can sit down quietly and relax until you feel comfortable."

Harald, now feeling a little better, started to pay more attention to her incessant report.

"Gyldendahl ignored the physician and pretended that he didn't know him.

"The physician repeated his offer. This time Gyldendahl stared him down in the in the face and uttered in no uncertain terms, 'I'll not let you touch me and I don't want help from anyone who fraternizes with Jews.'"

Agnes continued, looking at Harald a little hesitantly, as if she had perhaps said too much.

"This back and forth was so intense and loud that patients in all the adjoining rooms could hear every word that was said."

Once she realized that Harald appeared to be in reasonably good shape, Agnes made a point of opening the door to the corridor, allowing Harald to hear for himself.

The physician, who was rejected when offering to help Gyldendahl, was already walking down the corridor towards Harald. He appeared to have an afterthought, stopped, turned around, and once again addressed the head of the Nazi police.

"Oh yes, by the way. I regret to tell you, sir, that you are mistaken about the direction in question. The other party was walking on the right side of the corridor, as is the law, both here at the hospital, as well as when walking or driving on the road. Since you have been part of what is commonly referred to as a collision, I have to inform you that you, sir, you were walking on the left side, which caused this unfortunate accident. If you will excuse me, I'll now go tend to my patient who appears wasn't as fortunate as you, due to his present condition, recovering from major surgery."

Dr. Fjellstrand, continued down the corridor to check on his patient, who was sitting up in bed.

Fjellstrand pulled up a chair next to Harald, having reassured himself that the roommate wasn't there.

"I am glad to hear that you are okay, Harald. Dr. Mathiesen has assured me that you have no major problem. Luck was on your side. It could easily have been worse."

He signaled the need for privacy to Agnes, and as usual, she responded immediately. Harald's roommate was one of the many who had chosen to consider the incident in the corridor part of the afternoon entertainment, and refused to leave the site of the collision. The buzzing of unrequested comments could still be heard from frenzied voices. Agnes left Harald's room quickly, eager to get back to the ruckus in the hallway.

"The man is an idiot, Harald. Either he doesn't know the difference between left and right, or he's very ignorant, or most likely a combination of both."

"I hardly remember what happened. Dr. Mathiesen told me that I am all right. I hope you agree."

The tension in Harald's voice was clear when he spoke to Dr. Fjellstrand.

"Yes, you are fine. There is no damage to the incision and no sign of any other consequences, so please relax and thank your lucky stars."

"What about the drain in the incision. Has it moved?"

Fjellstrand paused for a second, shook his head, and looked directly at Harald, who answered his own question by saying that he actually felt better already. Some color had returned to his cheeks.

"The drain is small and hopefully hasn't been affected by the accident. I certainly hope so. Therefore with your permission we need to monitor the area for a few days to make certain that no damage has taken place. I want to be totally convinced the accident didn't reopen the wound. That is, if you will allow us."

Harald listened intensely, but nodded as he whispered, "Go ahead; once again, what do we have to lose?" A quick smile passed over Dr. Fjellstrand's lips as he winked at Harald.

Chapter Thirty-Three

Socks vs. Sugar

STOCKHOLM, DECEMBER 16, 1942

Ingrid was walking out the door of the Academy of Business and Commercial Education where she had just completed a course in business terminology, shorthand, typing and English and French correspondence. In her hand she had a diploma attesting to her graduation with high honors. All the teachers congratulated her as she shook everyone's hand and left. It was a bittersweet diploma to have earned. She had always known that using her hands would serve her well, but had never expected it would be on the typewriter.

As far as she could tell, her entire family in Oslo and Trondheim was in a state of flux. She didn't know what had happened to them. The correspondence was infrequent but she had heard most of her relatives had escaped to Sweden, including her grandmother whom she was supposed to live with had she made it to Oslo. The grand piano, which her parents had purchased two years earlier while visiting the capital, was still in storage at the large music store and it would remain there indefinitely. The mail was irregular and it was hard to tell what was going to happen next.

Her relationship with Arne had solidified. They were close and supported each other. He had learned much more about her extended family in Trondheim and Oslo and a little about what separated the Jewish religion from the Protestant. They could talk about almost everything. The only subject between them which was taboo, was his uncle, actually half-uncle, Gyldendahl.

Mor and Ingrid's daily visits to see Harald in the hospital had become routine.

A group of resistance people were trying desperately to think of some solution to get the three members of the Rosenberg family out of town. At this point the only solution they had come up with was to bide time. Nothing else. They had no choice—keeping Harald in a hospital bed was the only option.

Mor wouldn't speak about it and neither would Ingrid. There was only one priority in their life, and that was Harald's safety. No comments were necessary. One day at a time. They adhered to Dr. Fjellstrand's advice in every way.

Ingrid was engrossed in the same thoughts as she was every day. She was walking home to drop off her diploma and other papers prior to going to the hospital for the designated visiting hours. She would see her brother, and perhaps she would tell him about her certificate with high honors. She tried to walk fast because the December wind was cold and her feet were freezing. She had forgotten to bring her wool mittens and she kept her fingers in her pockets to keep them warm. When she was exhaling, she saw the cold air forming in front of her mouth which reminded her of happier days, when she was a small child and she and her friends pretended they were smoking cigarettes.

Life was monotonous. Every day was the same. She tried to convince herself to keep going, especially since she didn't know what was waiting for them around the corner. The memory of the ill-fated attempt to escape by ferry in bad weather was still vivid in her mind.

When she reached the apartment, which was now occupied by her and Mor only, she thought briefly of the days when Far would come home from the store with all kinds of funny stories which he shared with his family. As she opened the door, she called for Mor as usual. No answer. Her glance fell on a white envelope which had been dropped through the mail slot, landing in the middle of the entryway. The letter was white and she noticed the colors didn't match Norwegian colors. There had been a marked decrease in both general correspondence and bills during the past year. She bent over, grabbing the white, unexpected visitor.

The first thing she responded to was the weight of the paper. The paper used in Norway had been thin since the start of the war. This envelope was much thicker. Ingrid lifted the envelope and pressed it to her nose. It had a smell she couldn't place. It smelled good! It smelled fresh and clean. She didn't want to put it down. The stamp was unusual, but she recognized the word Sverige! The letter was from Sweden! She was holding a small piece of freedom in her hands! On the back was a printed seal which had been affixed with very small letters, stating the letter had passed through some type of approval for delivery in Norway.

Had it been censored? Here it was, in any case.

Turning the white tiny packet in her hand, she realized she had failed to see the name of the recipient. She was quite surprised when she read to whom the letter was addressed.

Herr Harald Rosenberg

Their local home address was just about the only thing which had remained unchanged.

She flipped the envelope over once again and was able to see very tiny handwriting on the back, which revealed the name.

R. Davidson
Per Lindstrømsveg 10,
Stockholm, Sverige

It was a letter for Harald from their cousin Rebekka! From Sweden. They had escaped! Ingrid's heart was beating fast. Her cheeks burned. She read the text on the front again, and then turned it around to reread the tiny handwriting on the back.

Her first thought was to open the letter immediately, right then and there. But reluctantly she realized it was intended for her brother and it had to be brought to him. She grabbed her coat, threw it on, and stormed down the stairs as fast as her feet could carry her. While on the street a few minutes later, a local bus was almost passing her. She waved her arms managing to catch the driver's attention. A short time later she found herself once again outside the entrance of the local hospital where she had spent so much time the past month. Today she was excited.

The lobby was almost empty and she had no trouble reaching Harald's floor. The tranquility came to an end there. No sooner did she get off the elevator than she noticed the abundance of nurses running back and forth. There must have been at least three times as many as usual. A young doctor spoke gently to a heavyset, bald man in his early fifties who sat in an easy chair. His face was turned in the opposite direction. She could hear that he was complaining and there was something that agitated him enormously. Whatever injury or problem he had encountered prior to Ingrid's arrival, certainly hadn't affected his vocal cords, as he was erupting with complaints in both Norwegian and German. Right behind him were four young soldiers in German uniforms, at attention, immobile.

At that moment he turned around and she saw the side of the angry patient's face. One of the attendants was trying to put a towel around the patient's neck. He barked, pushing the towel aside. Ingrid's instinct told her not to force her way past the assemblage. She turned away quickly, walked to the other corridor and circled the entire floor in order to reach her brother's room. She knocked softly and was let in. Dr. Fjellstrand stood next to her brother, saying good-bye to the patient. No one else was in the room.

Fjellstrand gave her a subdued nod, and an even more subdued smile and left. Ingrid was about to ask for details about the commotion in the corridor, but as soon as she had started to ask, Harald answered in no uncertain terms, "Please, don't make me speak about it. I was hurt accidentally, and I am fine."

The man who collided with me is an idiot." Ingrid knew better than to press him for the story.

She went over to the bed, trying in vain to keep a neutral voice. "There is a letter for you." She handed over the white envelope. He looked at it in disbelief and then stared at his sister.

Like Ingrid, he was hesitant opening the letter, turning it in his hand. He finally tore it open, having tried to make the surprise last as long as possible.

She took a few steps away from the bed, allowing him a little privacy to enjoy this unexpected communication. She had learned how close the two cousins had become through their correspondence. Once he put the letter down, indicating he had read it, he folded it in three, but failed to put it back in the envelope. He sat quietly, turning his face toward the window.

Despite his attempt to hide his reaction, she couldn't avoid noticing tears streaming down his cheeks.

She was unsure what to do next or what to say. After a moment, he handed her the letter, still without looking at her directly, yet saying, "Would you like to read it?"

"Of course I would, if you don't mind."

He handed her the letter.

Once she had finished reading, she returned it to him.

"Ingrid, if you don't mind, I would like to be alone for a while."

She got up, mumbling something about possibly coming back later in the evening with Mor and quietly walked out.

This time she decided to walk through the crowd of people in the corridor to avoid making a detour. She excused herself in a low voice, walked quickly past the agitated man in the chair, who by now had calmed down a little. She experienced a sudden flash of memory racing through her brain. The more she thought, the more the unattractive face remained with her, making it almost impossible to forget his whining in both German and Norwegian.

For a few minutes, she focused on the two-page letter from Rebekka. The content was unexpected and totally out of context with their life right now, here in Aalesund. Only some two years ago they had lived almost identical lives, shielded by strong and positive parents and good friends. They day-dreamed about happy and productive futures where their choice of education and professions seemed theirs for the asking. And now?

She could almost hear Rebekka's voice emerging from her miniscule handwriting. Ingrid wondered if Rebekka purposely had chosen to write in small letters as she had so much to include.

Dear Harald, Tante Leyla and Ingrid:

Here comes a letter from Sweden! We are in Stockholm. I had hoped to write to you several days ago but so much is going on.

We arrived at the very end of November and Far had arrived about a month earlier. Mor, Ruth, Miriam and I left later. My cousin Frank came with us. This is a long and complicated story but fortunately for all of us, his mother was waiting right there on the Swedish side when we arrived. Oh, Harald, I have so much to tell you and I wish all of you were here with us!

We are now living in an apartment in central Stockholm which is tiny compared to our old place, but it's all right. Mimi, Ruth and I are sharing a bedroom. Ruth has taken some small jobs with different people to make pocket money because Far is not making as much money as he did before. He has a job at the Jewish Congregation in Stockholm where he is in charge of seeing who among the Jews have made it to Sweden and who have not. Every day he looks for your names hoping you will show up. There are still many Jews and non-Jews crossing the border. The first thing we ask him every day when he returns home is whether he has seen your names, or if he has heard from you.

I have started school and it's okay. The Swedish language is not that different from Norwegian. I can understand when people speak to me slowly but sometimes they speak too fast and I just stand there and look at them like a fool. Do you know the word for sugar in Swedish means socks in Norwegian? So how can you know if you are talking about something sweet in your coffee or something warm to put on your toes? Ha ha!

It's strange to be in a neutral country where people can walk, drive or shop, or do anything they want. And everything is lit up. The stores are full of new clothes, and you can buy all kinds of food, including candy—everywhere. The first thing my mother bought me was a pair of new boots as the old ones, which I inherited from Frank's mother, were much too small. No wonder they no longer fit me. She is tiny. Now she has to bend over backwards to speak to me. So good-bye to her boots!

Last night I dreamt about all of you and the last time when we all had dinner together with Bestemor. I know she had a hard time that day worrying about Uncle Leonard. Now she worries about all of you because you haven't arrived here yet. I hope we will see each other soon so we can enjoy being a family again with aunts, uncles and cousins. Much love from Rebekka.

Ingrid reached the lobby on the main floor and exited through the front door. The cold air hit her in the face once more, and she buttoned her coat and grabbed her scarf to shield herself against the mid-December wind. The shiver, however, persisted despite the warm coat. As she ran towards the waiting bus, her memory overcame her. She felt as if she had been hit by lightning. The man in the corridor was Mr. Gyldendahl. She remembered his voice, which brought her back to the horror of the early morning hours a few weeks earlier. She no longer visualized an angry fat man sitting in an easy chair complaining. Now she remembered an angry, brutal and menacing high-ranking Nazi trying to intimidate her mother, expressing rage outside the entrance door to their apartment. It was he, the uncle. The half uncle. The nemesis. It was Thomas Gyldendahl, the head of the Nazi Department who was waiting for her brother to get well enough so he could be arrested! She suddenly felt faint.

Chapter Thirty-Four

Time Is Running Out

AALESUND, DECEMBER 16, 1942

The next few days passed slowly for Harald. The better he felt physically, the worse he felt mentally. It was a waiting game for everyone involved. They didn't talk about it. Why? Because as usual there was nothing to say.

Sleeping continued to be a major problem. All the terrifying thoughts raced through his mind. An occasional siren would interrupt the silence. When most of the patients slept, Harald would lie in his bed, ruminating. Some days he would turn night into day, and be asleep when his mother and sister arrived. If he were awake, he felt almost obligated to cover his face, because their concern for him was obvious when they looked at him.

Dr. Fjellstrand came by as often as possible, as did Dr. Mathiesen. However, their visits served no purpose because it was clear they had nothing positive to report. So Harald didn't even ask.

On one occasion, Harald had the courage to ask Fjellstrand if there was any news, but Fjellstrand just shook his head.

"Harald, I wish I could tell you something positive, but I can't. We are at a dead end. Every time someone has a suggestion, someone explains why it won't work. I am thinking about this day and night. I am sure that we will come up with something. By the way, Gyldendahl has announced that he will be away from December 23 until the 28th, so I feel that we are safe until then."

Harald looked at him, smiling sadly.

"How can a man that evil even think about celebrating a religious holiday? Where is God and where are his laws that govern decent behavior and kindness to your next of kin? Where is the definition of good and bad? I have always wondered what it would be like to be lost in a labyrinth. Now I understand."

Fjellstrand had no answer and turned his gaze away from Harald, pretending he hadn't seen the tears beginning to accumulate in the young man's eyes.

Around December 19, when Dr. Fjellstrand reappeared, Harald knew from his face that he had bad news.

"Harald, I have received an official letter from Gyldendahl today. The Gestapo in Oslo has made a decision about you and your medical situation. It seems that time has run out. You can stay at the hospital until December 27, but then you will be discharged. They insist that you move back home with your mother and sister in what they refer to as house arrest, until further notice. According to this order, you have no choice. You should consider yourselves prisoners of the powers in charge of Norway. You and the other two members of your family will have to report to the police each morning. You will be monitored and followed by the police staff whenever you leave the apartment."

For a moment, Nikolas Fjellstrand hid his face in his hands. He couldn't bear looking directly at Harald. A few seconds later, he gave Harald a quick look to see how he handled the news. Harald was staring back at him with an apparent indifference. Shrugging his shoulders, he mumbled in a barely audible voice, "That's what I have expected for a very long time, but now it's here. Have you told my mother and sister?"

Dr. Fjellstrand nodded.

"Is there anything I can get you or do for you, Harald?"

The young man looked at him, and answered quietly, "No, not that I can think of. I believe you have done everything within your power already. Thank you.

"No, wait—there *is* something you can do for me."

And this time his voice had an infinitesimal trace of energy.

Harald slipped his hand into the lining of his backpack under his bed and pulled out a pad of paper. He tore off a number of pages, which he folded neatly.

"This is a letter for my cousin Rebekka Davidson from Oslo. Her father's name is Martin Davidson. She is very important to me. Here is her address in Sweden."

He stopped, swallowed and said in a low voice, "Of course she may never know it, but writing this letter has probably sustained me."

He turned away from Dr. Fjellstrand, and looked out the window. The physician took the sheets of paper. Harald remained in the same position and didn't turn around.

For a short time, Harald allowed himself to reminisce about the past. It seemed to pour over him. He thought of his father with his smile and constant optimistic attitude that no one could challenge. He thought of Uncle Leonard who always was calm and willing to answer questions. He thought of Rebekka next to him at the family dinner in Oslo at the beginning of the war, just when Leonard had been arrested. He remembered being allowed to look at her sketchbook which was her escape when she wanted to be alone or when she wanted to make sure she would remember an event or a person. For the most part no one was allowed to look at her sketchbooks. At that time they were all oblivious to the evil that was waiting for them. It was just too horrible for the Norwegian Jews to understand it. It had felt cathartic to be able to put all the anxiety, fear and sadness into writing the letter.

Harald turned away from the window and shook Dr. Fjellstrand's hand. Why exactly, he didn't know.

Dr. Fjellstrand didn't answer his request for assistance. He didn't have to. Harald trusted him and knew everything within his power would be done to get the letter to Rebekka. Somehow. Somewhere.

Christmas was just around the corner. This holiday was normally celebrated by all Norwegians on Christmas Eve as a family day, despite its religious significance. Relatives would gather to enjoy each other's company with focus on the children. Santa Claus, also known as Julenissen, would make an appearance in each house dressed in red, with a white beard and a big smile, while handing out the presents.

Whenever possible the patients would be discharged in time for Christmas. The staff was reduced, allowing as many as possible to take a few days off to be with their families.

On December 24, Mor and Ingrid arrived around midafternoon to keep Harald company. All of their close friends were Christians and observed their own traditions.

They had been invited to attend the holiday meal with Harald at the hospital. Naturally, they gladly accepted. Sofie had invited them to join her sister and the sister's family, but their decision was to remain with Harald.

"Mor, did you get the message that Gyldendahl received from the Gestapo in Oslo?"

Harald brought it up gently, needing to know how much they knew. Mor and Ingrid responded that they had heard.

"Yes, Dr. Fjellstrand told us. There is nothing we can do about it today. We will deal with it after the holidays. For today, let's celebrate being together in a peaceful environment. It's not our holiday, but let's try to take a message from the Christians, and hope for peace on earth."

Mor had a very specific tone in her voice, unusual for her. Normally a mild-mannered person, she was uncomfortable making major decisions and avoided telling others what to do. On this occasion she acted more forcefully. They started walking around the corridors smiling and nodding to the other visiting relatives.

Harald thought how nice it would be to hear Ingrid play the piano. As he turned towards her, a young woman dressed in a navy winter coat with a heavy scarf passed them in the corridor. Long, shiny blond hair floated on her shoulders, and she was carrying a small overnight bag. She tapped Harald lightly on his shoulder, saying, "I am leaving for the rest of the month and I want to say goodbye to you."

Harald was confused. Who was she? Then the warmth in her smile and her bright, cheery voice made him recognize her. He had never seen Agnes out of uniform. She whispered, "May I?" and she put her arms around him without even waiting for an answer.

"I'll never stop praying for you. It has been a privilege getting to know you." She whispered into his ear, "I am sure you don't understand how proud I was to be appointed your primary nurse. I have always admired you and your sister, and I know much more about you than you realize. Maybe one day we will be able to sit down somewhere, laugh and discuss our secrets. For now, I want you to know that I am Dr. Fjellstrand's niece even though he asked me not to tell you. He felt that it might be easier for you not to keep any more secrets. I pray that you will be gone from here when I return, and that you and your relatives will welcome the new year in safety and security."

Mor and Ingrid looked at them in an inquisitive manner as Agnes tore herself away quickly and entered an elevator and waved. Harald chose not to comment on the unexpected display of warmth and kept on walking.

Passing the auditorium, they found it already half-full of people. One or two of the nurses were approaching the piano at the small stage joking to the audience about their lack of skills. Another approached the loudspeaker, asking for help.

Harald heard himself turning to his sister.

"Ingrid, the piano! Any chance that you would offer to play? They need you and it would mean a lot to them. And to us. We could all use some music, especially today."

He couldn't believe he had suggested that Ingrid play Christmas music, but it felt good. The thoughts came from somewhere deep inside. The sound of his sister's talent at the piano must be imbedded in his mind and memory. He suddenly had a strong need to hear and see her play.

Ingrid's face lit up. Harald knew the importance of music in her life. It felt like an extension of her mind and body, he thought to himself.

Slowly but steadily she approached the grand piano on the podium, still appearing a little shy, questioning if it was okay. She turned to one of the nurses, asking permission to play.

"Ingrid, we have been talking about you all day, hoping you would play for us. We were afraid that you would be uncomfortable if we asked you, since it's not your holiday. Please, please do play. Anything you want."

The nurse's voice carried through the primitive speaker and was heard by everyone. They burst into loud applause. It was obvious that Ingrid's talent was known throughout the city.

The atmosphere in the auditorium changed. Ingrid didn't waste time. She threw herself into the music as the melodies had already begun to circulate in her head. Even though some of the Christmas songs had already been sung by the patients and their relatives, there was a different tone and emotion emanating from the audience when their voices were mixed and led by Ingrid's incredible talent and projection. One of the elderly women whispered to the man next to her, which for some reason was heard through the speaker, "It feels like the music is coming from the angels." Maybe it was.

Within one minute after Ingrid had started playing, a very different group poured into the auditorium, occupying the last few rows in the room. They were all men, wearing either Norwegian or German Nazi uniforms.

An almost inaudible mumble arose among the audience. Heads turned toward the new arrivals, and heads turned away. Questions were asked by the patients and passed on to the visitors. It was clear that the presence of these uninvited men was not because they wanted to observe the holiday gospel or hear the Christmas songs—at least not initially. Their task was to supervise the three Jewish citizens present.

When the agitation subsided, Ingrid started playing again. Tranquility fell over the large room, as each individual person allowed his or her mind and heart to react in whatever mood appealed to them

To Harald's surprise he noticed that not only one, but several of the unannounced late arrivals surrendered to the holiday music and melodies, participating in the singing. Such surprising behavior was most likely stirred up by memories of days gone by and awakened thoughts about relatives and dear ones, either near or far away. For a brief moment, Harald experienced something which might be called empathy, even sympathy, for these young faces, not much older than himself. The sentiment passed quickly, leaving Harald with a flushed face. When he became aware of his own emotional response, he quickly dismissed it as an unwarranted and unreal interpretation of human emotions. He thought of his father and his two uncles who he knew had been arrested. Thereafter he concentrated on hearing his sister play.

After a while, Ingrid got up, feeling she had played enough. The patients and relatives were enthusiastic in their applause, calling for more.

Harald was amazed at the audience's reaction. It seemed that every person present had transferred all their feelings to his sister and her music— fears and worries, sentimentality and sadness, concern for sick relatives, worries about the war. They appeared to look at Ingrid and her music as if they were stranded in the desert and were offered an unexpected drink of water.

Ingrid sat down at the piano again, looking serious but calm. Without hesitating, she chose a piece which wasn't necessarily known to the audience, but which held them spellbound regardless. The music was melodic, soft and strong. Ingrid's emotional efforts were exceptional, and it was clear this music meant much to her, but perhaps never as much as at this particular moment. When she finally got up to face the audience, her exhaustion, both from playing as well as her mere presence on that day, had drained her. Ingrid waited until the applause had subsided, and spoke gently.

"I thank you for your enthusiasm and participation in these memorable and appreciated songs from many, many years of history. This last piece was a theme by Beethoven, called *Pathetique*, which is French and means something similar to the word Sadness.

"I wish a speedy recovery to those of you who are still patients in this hospital and best wishes to your relatives who stand by waiting for you to heal. May you have a meaningful and memorable family holiday, and may all of us present here today stand on the threshold of a happy future in the New Year, together with those close to us, as well as for all the citizens of the country of Norway."

Tears ran down her face.

The audience broke into applause again and didn't stop. It was obvious that the Jewish girl's words were more than a standard message. Her brother sat quietly, thinking of her few sentences. His face was burning.

He remained immobile during the improvised concert and subsequent speech, thinking to himself. I wonder what exactly prompted her in that particular manner? Was she speaking to the audience or perhaps to her own family? The patients are sick and full of fear and sadness, while our family is on the verge of experiencing sadness of a different kind. Perhaps with the worst yet to come.

Chapter Thirty-Five

The Journey with No Return

AALESUND, JANUARY 23, 1943

Darkness and heavy clouds hung over the town in the late afternoon.

A crowd had gathered by the docks. The people wanting to see them off arrived one by one; occasionally two at a time. Silence prevailed. Some were dressed in heavy winter coats and work attire. Some were dressed totally in black like attendees at a funeral. Both types of attire were appropriate. Their faces conveyed their emotions—shock, sadness, anger, inability to understand. How could they speak even if they wanted? They didn't know what to say, even less what to think. Some were crying; some had already cried for a long, long time.

The police cars drove up. Four armed soldiers appeared with guard dogs. Two familiar female figures emerged, walking slowly, encircled by guards. Their faces were expressionless. Right behind them two soldiers carried a combined chair and bed contraption for a third person, a male.

Black cloth covered the prisoners' heads, preventing visual contact. "Why?" the crowd asked themselves, not daring to speak out loud. "We know who they are."

The process lasted less than a minute, but seemed like an eternity. The female prisoners were ordered to board the waiting boat. The young man was carried.

Silence continued. The crowd gazed with disbelief, accompanied by their pounding hearts only.

The almost empty ferry left and disappeared in the fjord. The crowd remained immobile, but gradually started to leave, once again quietly, feeling separated from reality.

245

One person wasn't ready to leave and lingered, staring at the water. She was wearing a black and white raincoat, belonging to someone else. This was the last tangible proof of desperate vain attempts to reverse destiny.

The dark clouds had already obliterated further sight of the ferry. Yet the woman remained.

Eventually she started walking toward the parking lot and the street. The lot was empty. Her car had been left at home, as she had felt a need to walk, absorbing the painful thoughts in her head.

At the very corner of the lot, next to the official building, she noticed a dark Chevrolet. Neither the car nor the license plate was familiar, although in the back of her mind she thought she had seen the car before. The darkness prevented her from seeing if anyone was inside, although the backlight was lit up. She approached the car as if drawn by an unknown force. She was approximately three meters away when she spotted the outline of a man in the driver's seat, leaning forward with his head on the steering wheel.

Her first thought was that the driver might have taken ill and needed assistance. She approached the car door and immediately recognized the person. Sofie opened the door, placing her hand gently on the driver's shoulder, about to inquire if he was unwell.

To her surprise, he lifted his head, turning his face to her. Tears poured down his cheeks and he seemed unable to stop sobbing. With severe agony in his voice he said, "How could this have happened?"

"What else could we have done? What did we miss? We failed and now it's over."

The face and voice belonged to Nikolas Fjellstrand.

Chapter Thirty-Six

When the Lights Went Out

SWEDEN

Two years later, 1945. The liberation is here. Rebekka is waiting for news whether the other part of the family has survived the camps. She is reserved and introverted. Instead of discussing horror and bad news, she sits quietly rendering her thoughts into her sketchbook.

The key in the door; Rebekka's father finally arrives. Silently, he walks into the room. His face looks grey, haggard. He avoids looking at both wife and daughter.

Finally, he faces them, without expression. His eyes are empty. He sits down, leaning forward, his face covered with his hands.

That's when Rebekka knows.

She hears her voice, in a whisper, "You got the final confirmation, didn't you?"

There is silence.

"Did any of them make it?"

He shakes his head.

"They are all gone?"

The silence speaks again.

Rebekka, sketchbook in hand, leaves the room pressing the pages to her chest, like an anchor. But relief doesn't come. Relief, which usually motivates her to draw, isn't there. The white pages remained just that, white pages. No inspiration welcomes her. No thoughts offer her solace. Not this time.

Despite herself, she opens the book slowly, knowing that her usual incentive has failed her. But this time her brain offers another form of motivation. This time it comes from her heart.

She starts to write.

The thoughts and feelings appear out of nowhere. No, not out of nowhere. From a place deep inside her heart where they have incubated for a long time, intentionally ignored by her fear.

Time has come to open the door to her heart and force her to accept reality.

She starts to put her loss into words—for the first time.

When the Lights went out in Norway
We fought, we tried, but we lost
The enemy fought, they brought Evil, they won
We saw them take our friends away
God wept, we wept
Three among eight hundred
Their Angels ran out of time
We saw them disappear into Darkness
We waved good-bye
God wept, we wept
The journey brought them to Evil
God wept, we wept
Yet Evil prevailed and destroyed them
God lost, we lost
Norway's darkest chapter
Among Six million lives extinguished in a bonfire of Evil
God wept and made us pray
We cried, we prayed and looked to the stars
God heard us and we will pray together
For eternity

Afterword

How can a book be described as historical fiction?

This is fact-based fiction, sometimes known as a genre of historical fiction, as it refers to things that really happened. The characters have been expanded with imagination, consistent with the historical events.

In this book, all the major historical episodes pertaining to the Jews in Norway were included as legitimate experiences during World War II. These include the German invasion on April 9, 1942, and the so-called "Panic Days," referring to the following two days, April 10 and 11, when a large number of families left Oslo having been alerted that the capital might be bombed. Fortunately, this did not take place.

In 1940, 2000 Jews lived in Norway. The mass arrest of all male Norwegian Jews, not already in hiding, took place on October 25, 1942. The Norwegian police rounded up the Jews as directed by the Gestapo. The prisoners were held in a variety of primitive and unhealthy facilities prior to being transported to Auschwitz on the ship *The Donau* on November 26, 1942. Women and children were arrested the same day and were included in the horrendous transport.

More than 100 men were detained earlier and had already been sent to Auschwitz. Except for 28 men, none of the hundreds of Norwegian Jews survived. The men who appeared to be strong were forced to carry out slave labor until they perished from exhaustion or disease in the camp and were sent to the waiting gas chambers. It is estimated that 787 Jews living in Norway were murdered. Close to 40% of the Jewish population perished at the hands of the Gestapo. The men who were incapable or too old to work upon arrival, were annihilated immediately together with the women and children.

The fictional Davidson family was based on the story of Marcus and Rosa Levin, my parents. When the war broke out, my parents become acutely aware of the impending danger for the Jews. Two of my father's brothers were arrested early on, prior to the mass roundup. Father and his third brother placed their families in the hands of resistance units willing to help them escape to neutral Sweden. The men were primarily at risk, and for that reason they were brought to safety first, with women and children next. In most instances the success involved in being able to implement this plan, was due to an extensive undercover system. It created the basis for the families' managing to escape to Sweden.

The stories are fictitious. Ruth, the nanny/housekeeper, is probably the most factual character. She escaped with me, my mother, brother and cousin, Frank, when we left on November 25, 1942. This was just hours before the arrest of all women and children, which culminated on the Oslo dock and forced almost 500 Jews to board the ship. Ruth was not Jewish, but was alerted by the resistance units that she would most probably be arrested if she chose not to escape. Ruth remained with my family her entire life. Rebekka Davidson, the teenager, was a total figment of my imagination. However, I wanted somehow to integrate my brother into a fictional character and he was the source of making Rebekka an artist! My brother's exceptional talent at drawing was the inspiration when I "gave" Rebekka the same talent.

The Marcus Levin family.

A little girl called Miriam, who is part of the Davidson's family story, was two when the war broke out. I felt strongly that she had to be part of the story. She spoke often and quickly, loved to visit the ducks in the park and was left handed. I decided to include her because she would represent my childhood memories from the pre-Sweden days. I think of her as the "child star" of the blue tooth chapter in the park. When they were on the train during the escape, she asked in a loud voice when the train would arrive in Hadeland, creating severe anxiety for Ruth as the train was moving in the opposite direction. Miriam was carried in a large rucksack where she fell asleep, while the others walked through the Norwegian woods to reach Sweden. Yes, I will admit it: all this happened to me.

The story of Frank is also real from the moment he left Oslo with his mother. During the journey they were accidentally separated from each other when they reached a train station. Frank entered the wrong train. Within less than a minute, he realized the train was moving and headed back to Oslo. He showed up at our house the same evening. By luck we were scheduled to leave the next morning and he came with us. Frank was eventually able to rejoin his mother, who had been forced to continue the journey without him. When our small group reached the border the next day, the Swedish sheriff asked if we had the boy, and everyone called: yes, yes and yes. Some fictional details were included in the Davidson story to relay this true story of a young boy who went on the wrong train and found himself alone in an occupied country, but managed to escape enemies and reach freedom.

The second part of this book is devoted to the Rosenberg family in Aalesund. Their names are fictional. When I started my research, I chose not to use their proper names. I had never met them because I was just a small child at the beginning of the war, and they lived far away. I heard about them for the first time when we returned after the liberation. The family of four consisted of my father's sister, her husband and two children. The only Jewish family in town, they became victims of the Holocaust. The real story and the fictional version tell about three years of their life, beginning with the invasion and ending with their deportation in January 1943 when they were annihilated in Auschwitz.

When I started research on my first book *"We Are Going to Pick Potatoes" Norway and the Holocaust, the Untold Story* in 2007 in Norwegian, I was compelled to learn more about the family, which had totally disappeared. I placed an ad in the local newspaper hoping to connect with someone who had known them. Within three days, I received nine letters. Each letter expressed emotion, love and sadness. Some wrote about close friendships and school days; another about their mother having been the family's housekeeper; and another who had been in jail with the father. One person had taken violin classes with "Harald," and was eager to hear from me.

My cousins, the real-life models for Ingrid and Harald.

I felt like another chapter of my life opened and perhaps I would get part of the unfamiliar memories, after all. Gradually I contacted each person, mostly by telephone and I actually met some two years later in Aalesund! It felt as if they needed me as much as I needed them. Little by little, I put my "puzzle" together. I asked, they answered. They cried and I cried. They had hoped for someone in our family to get in touch with, even now sixty years later!

One woman had traveled to Auschwitz in their honor. I learned about the family's personalities. I heard that Harald was introverted and loved to read. Ingrid was highly musical and outgoing. Their friends told me of parties and school musicals. One of her close friends recollected when she and Ingrid had gone to school on the very day the war broke out. Another friend shared a story that made us both cry. She and Ingrid had been out walking one evening in early 1942 when Ingrid confided in her that deep down she was afraid Hitler would eventually come to Aalesund and arrest them. Her friend had laughed it off hoping to lessen her anxiety.

But I was still the outsider, trying to learn from them. Consequently, I chose to approach these recollections as fiction only, and include a few true events, which I told as closely as I could—the piano audition in Oslo; the story of our mutual grandparents; and yes, the wonderful story of Ingrid standing on the balcony waiting for her father.

Several people told me that Harald had his appendix removed in the hospital by brave and kind Norwegians trying to save him. Sadly enough this strategy did not succeed.

I was also told that Tante Sofie was Leyla's best friend. I therefore included her in a chapter where she arranged a graduation party at her home. I was told that this story was real. I heard repeatedly that she did everything possible within her power to help save them during the dangerous time.

During my research so many years later, I learned from the Norwegian national archives that my father, together with "Aunt Sofie," went to great lengths to find details about the family's tragic and heartbreaking short stay in Auschwitz. Both mother and daughter were sent to the gas chamber immediately upon arrival. Harald, who had been both sick from surgery and depressed, was brought into the camp and put to work digging stones. He collapsed and was shot to death on the second day.

Obviously, my parents were not alive when I wrote this book. This resulted in interviews with various other survivors who I had known as a small child. Father never knew of my intense interest in the "Rosenberg" family and my independent research for both books. However, when I started this phase of my life and my father had been dead for fifty years, I had a very strong feeling that his hand was resting on my shoulder throughout.

About the Author

Irene Berman was born, raised and educated in Norway, after which she moved to the US as a young bride. The first recollection of life back to 1942 was how as a child she had to escape with her family to Sweden, a neutral country. Germany had invaded Norway and the persecution of the 2,000 Norwegian Jews had started; 771 persons were deported and annihilated by the Germans, including seven members of her father's family.

Irene's first book, *"We are going to pick potatoes," Norway and the Holocaust, the Untold Story,* is a narrative of that journey back in time. The book was suggested and supported by The Norwegian Resistance Museum. Irene examines the label of being a Holocaust survivor with the subsequent resulting introspection. Irene's strong dual identity as a Norwegian and a Jew forces her to explore all the open doors previously closed.

The book was well received in Norway, then she translated the book into English; it found a "home" immediately. Irene found large groups of readers who were totally uninformed about the Holocaust in Norway. She had the pleasure of traveling around the country speaking to people of many different nationalities, in particular among Norwegian Americans.

Norway wasn't too small offers a totally different content. goal is to reach as many young readers readers and adults as possible. We are coming to the end of the Holocaust generation and Irene, like millions of other Americans, is trying to immortalize the importance of keeping this horrendous story alive for those that come behind us.As the story unfolds, the fate of two Jewish families during the Holocaust in Norway is in jeopardy. Young Rebekka Davidson lives in Oslo; her cousins, Harald and Ingrid Rosenberg, belong to the sole Jewish family in Aalesund, a small commercial city in Northwest Norway. The two families both struggle bravely to survive. However, only one succeeds by escaping to neutral Sweden, while the other, despite fierce effort, eventually is consumed by their German oppressors.